Aug/25-1977

To Leonard

from

Cousins Annetta Vecellio
and
Erma V. Brogan

The VENETIAN

The

VENETIAN

A NOVEL

by David Weiss

WILLIAM MORROW AND COMPANY, INC.

New York 1976

Printed in the United States of America.

1   2   3   4   5   6   7   8   9   10

Library of Congress Cataloging in Publication Data

Weiss, David.
    The Venetian.

    1. Tiziano Vecelli, 1477–1576—Fiction.   I. Title.
PZ4.W429Ve   [PS 3573.E415]   813'.5'4   76-18940
ISBN 0-688-03098-X

BOOK DESIGN   CARL WEISS

TO STYMEAN KARLEN

The
VENETIAN

WHAT DO I REMEMBER

WHAT DO I REMEMBER

I tried to conquer my own heart
That was love affair enough

I tried to conquer my own mind
That was conquest indeed

While most spent all of life
loving only other things

Stymean Karlen

WHAT DOES one remember?

What do I remember?

Today, despite my extreme age, I can still recall that I am known as Titian, The Venetian, The Most Triumphant Eye of The Most Serene Republic, and a world figure, confidant, favorite, and painter of popes and emperors and a multitude of other eminent personages. This is common knowledge and I have experienced such excellence for many years. But the older I become the less I seem to remember. I am confused. I am afflicted with doubts. I, who so many have considered disciplined, serene, purposeful, certain of my direction.

Is it that too much has crowded in on me? That I am too tired?

Or is it that there are things that I do not want to remember?

I must put down what I do recall of my existence before it is too late. Not to preserve an image for posterity, my work should accomplish that, but to see more clearly. It is to see more clearly that I painted. Soft colors as much as rich colors, nudes as much as madonnas. My paintings are no miracle, but stubbornness, pride, skill, and an eye.

So much to remember and letters and notes to read.

Yet as I stand in the great studio of my mansion in the Biri Grande quarter of Venice and stare at the easel and the painting on it that I have been unable to finish, I am very weary. And sorrowful.

Is my gift being taken away from me? My hands feel bound.

I am surrounded with a wealth and elegance that is the envy of many, and suddenly it is a burden. I think of the simplicity of the tiny mountain village of Pieve di Cadore, seventy miles north of Venice, where I was born and baptized Tiziano Vecellio after the town's patron saint. But then I could do anything with my hands I wished. I remembered everything that happened to me: I was young, avid to learn. Cadore is clear in my memory. Although I came to Venice when I was a boy, I have returned often to this clump of houses among the soaring peaks of the Dolomites and loved it dearly.

I recall being told that my family had lived in Cadore for centuries, that I was the first Vecellio to become a true Venetian and painter, but I do not know when I was informed of this. But I believe that Venice is where I belong. It is one of the few things of which I am still certain.

How dangerous is memory!

My age is still a matter that causes me to wonder. Now it is 1576, and it is said that I was born in 1477, almost a hundred years ago, and so I must be ninety-nine, but there is no proof. There are no written records in Cadore. Yet I encourage this view, for it adds to the respect with which I am regarded. My fellow Venetians are proud of that, as if there is an excellence in such longevity which bestows an excellence upon them, and so it may be. It is useful for even a triumphant eye to have outlived all other painters, particularly Michelangelo Buonarroti, who is a Florentine, and who has died at a mere eighty-nine, as if, in achieving this, I have performed an impossible feat. So I accept that I am ninety-nine, although privately I believe that I was born between 1487 and 1490, for my first memories do not come until 1492.

At this moment I feel so old the years are beyond counting. My name is inscribed on the painting at the easel but this is all that I have been able to accomplish this afternoon. My body hurts when I stand, yet I hate to sit when I paint, and my hands are numb and my vision seems blurred. Yet I have blamed my failure to work on the poor quality of the paint and I have sent my two sons in search of better oils.

Now I am anxious for they have been gone several hours and Venice has been cursed with the plague for a year. I turn away from my easel to stare out the window in search of them. I lean on the sill and the sight before me is a familiar one, but there is no sign of

my fifty-four-year-old Pomponio, whom I cannot trust to do anything although I have indulged him, or my fifty-three-year-old Orazio,
who has studied painting with me and who is as devoted as his older
brother is faithless.

There are fleets of black gondolas carrying numerous corpses from
the plague-ridden city to be buried at sea, I see everywhere dark
smoke from the pyres of infected clothing and furniture, yet I hear
also the inhabitants' need for pleasure. There is laughter just below
my window and for an instant I think it is Pomponio. I know his
love for the flesh; it is one of the few traits he has inherited from
me. But I do not recognize the magnificently dressed courtesans
with their yellow handkerchiefs to indicate their profession. They
are courted by a group of patricians and are rowed by two gondoliers
in a rich livery.

I realize that summer has come to Venice once again, for the air
is mild and full of a natural beauty. It is alive, transparent, and yet
phantasmal. I can still see the mountains to the north, the lagoons
that surround my quarters, the island of Murano nearby, and below
me, my greatly admired garden which has entertained many distinguished visitors.

But I, born Tiziano Vecellio, who have adored these sights of
Venice, find them dross now. Nothing matters but the unfinished
painting in my studio. Weary as I am of so much in the world, I
know I am not wrong to have to finish this *Pietà*. I feel that I stand
just one minute before eternity. Whatever my age, I have a premonition that my end is near.

The Franciscan brothers of the Frari church have agreed to bury
me in their chapel in return for this *Pietà*. It is a bargain I suggested. Accomplished, I will not fear to stand alone before Him.

The warmth of the sun has eased the numbness of my fingers and
now there is some feeling in them and in the brighter light I can
see more clearly. I know in this instant that it is not my craft that
is at fault but my conception. The old man kneeling at the body of
the recumbent Christ is an image of myself but there is nothing extraordinary in his devotion and grief and there should be. The
figure of the Mary Magdalen must be more vital, passionate, and
tragic. This is a reckoning, as the *Pietà* is for me. I look back at the
self-portrait that dominates the entrance to the studio in the hope
that it will stimulate my eye. But while it was painted when I was
considered an old man, when I was seventy, it seems so long ago.

In this self-portrait my hands are robust and firm, my face, although it is aged, is still assured and powerful. I wear the golden

chain of knighthood which the Emperor Charles V had given me and this portrait has none of the tone of mourning which I desire today. Instead, despite my age, I have painted myself as a handsome figure—as I have done with so many others. But I do not wish to please now. I must prepare for the grave and what follows.

"Twenty years ago . . ."

The voice sounds like my own, and then I realize that it is Pomponio. He has entered without my hearing him—is my hearing failing, too? Or is it that I have been so absorbed? He is gazing at the self-portrait, too.

Orazio, who is slighter than his tall, burly older brother, whispers, "Pomponio, you will disturb Papa."

"He will not hear me. He never does when he is painting."

But I do hear you, I want to shout. Instead, I say, "Sons, the *Pietà* is not being painted for material favor."

"Are you listening?" I add with annoyance. Pomponio walks away and Orazio looks distracted. I wonder if they desire to dissociate themselves from my reverence for Jesus, as do many Venetians.

Orazio says, "I could not buy any of the oils you requested, Papa."

Pomponio says, "Not even for a Titian."

I feel that he is sneering but I do not like to scold him.

My older son continues, "Too many are dying of the plague for there to be any concern for a painter. Even in this city of painters. Everyone is afraid of death, especially when their bodies burn worse than fire."

I think that a son does not appreciate the sufferings of old age until he has experienced it and then it is too late to admonish him.

Yet Orazio must have observed that I am agitated and upset, for he says with a vehemence that is unusual for him, "Papa, why do you not paint the *Pietà* as you usually create your other pictures? Do it over. Begin it again with a mass of color which will serve as a bed or foundation for what you wish to express. With a few strokes you are capable of suggesting a magnificent figure. And after you apply the important foundation, you could turn the picture to the wall and leave it there, without looking at it for months. Then return to it. As you usually do."

My younger son has learned his lessons accurately, I think, but now I do not have that much time.

"Papa, with this reflection, you can bring the figures to the highest degree of perfection. You have done this many times."

"Besides," I hear Pomponio saying, "there is no need for you, dear Papa, to rush toward the Sacraments of the Church. You say you feel no illness. Even if you have withdrawn from public affairs and prepare for the end."

My elder son is taunting me, I feel, but then I have spoiled him.

He continues, encouraged by my silence, "Papa, you must live up to your reputation as an indomitable old man. A few months ago, in your ninety-ninth year, you proclaimed that you were strong and healthy, that you could see the smallest object without glasses, and that your digestion was so sound that you could eat anything, even cucumbers and lemons."

And you have been waiting a long time for me to die, I reflect, so you can sell my paintings and possessions. But it has been a trying day and I have no desire to make it worse and so I remain silent.

Pomponio goes on, "Do not take it too hard if you do not finish this *Pietà*. One of the painters in your workshop, you still have six at your service, can fill in the details. As they have done often."

"No, No!" I shout. I know the rumors that I can no longer see what I am doing, that my hand trembles so much that I cannot finish anything, but have to leave that to my assistants. But when I do this it is because I am no longer interested in preciseness and smoothness but in passion and purpose. "I will finish this *Pietà*! Even if I cannot hold a brush!"

Orazio agrees, stating, "Papa, you can do that with your fingers. With them you can apply a spot of black in one corner or heighten with a dab of red, like a drop of blood, the liveliness of the surface."

I nod, although at this moment I feel that Pomponio hates me, for he declares, "You should allow Veronese or Tintoretto to finish this canvas. You respect them. And they know your style, for they studied with you."

If I possessed the strength, I would push Pomponio out of my studio. But I remember that my older child has been spiteful from birth.

"Or allow Orazio to finish it, Papa. He is a Vecellio, too."

And commit suicide, I think bitterly, and I shake my head violently in dissent. It makes me dizzy and I have to lean on the easel to keep from falling. I wonder if Pomponio's words are my last wound. Then he is gone and I say to Orazio, whose slender, pointed, delicate features remind me of his mother, "Do you believe that this *Pietà* is more than I have bargained for? Too difficult for me to complete?"

"You have always said nothing was too difficult for you to finish."

"That was last year. This is 1576."

"You drive yourself hard, Papa."

"You do not answer my question, Orazio."

"So often you have declared that it is a matter of energy."

"I must do it. I must do it." I am really trying to convince myself.

"Papa, if you paint with your fingers instead of with the brush I believe you will finish the *Pietà* the way you wish."

I thank him for his advice and return to the canvas. But the colors are poor, insufficient, and I pause. I realize that it is not a touch I need or even oils but a point of view. What about myself? What has brought me, Titian, The Venetian, supposedly the most successful and worldly of painters, to the feet of Jesus Christ?

I sense that Orazio does not like the despair on my face, that he feels that I am lost, but if this is true I am the only one who can find my way. Therefore I say, "Orazio, I am grateful that you care about me, but I must finish this *Pietà* by myself. I will see you at dinner."

Orazio leaves obediently and then I do miss him.

I sit down at my desk, which holds communications from many of the great of the world, and pick up what Pietro Aretino has written about me. Friends have called him "The Divine Aretino," but enemies have named him a monster. Neither is true, I think, as I read his words.

"Titian Vecellio is the most versatile and productive painter of his day. Even more than such masters as Michelangelo Buonarroti, Leonardo da Vinci, and Raphael Sanzio. He is idolized by the common folk and the mighty princes of the state and the church. He stands at the very top of his profession, excelled by none as a portraitist, or as a painter of landscapes and religious scenes. Yet for all of his fame he remains a Venetian. He will last as long as Our Most Serene Republic does."

Pietro Aretino was my best friend, I remind myself, and so, not wholly to be trusted. Others say that I have betrayed Venice by favoring my Florentine friends and by serving the Pope and foreign emperors. Most of my work has been taken elsewhere by the rapacious. I recall that Michelangelo said, "I think highly of Titian's color and style, but it is a pity that the Venetian has not first learned to draw."

Even Vasari, whom I have befriended, has written, "Titian has created works which deserve much praise; if he had possessed good draughtsmanship he would have been put alongside of Michelangelo and Raphael."

I stop remembering what others have said. All that matters, I assure myself, is what I believe. Yet part of me cares about what others think.

Day is departing and in the growing darkness I gaze at Venice, for it has been the best witness to my life. Time turn backward, I cry to myself, give me back my youth and my fond memories of it. Venice, allow me to gaze at you once again as you were when I fell in love with you. When everything was new and triumphant and I possessed a fresh eye and could see all there was to see and you were the center of the civilized world. But perhaps memory is a delusion, perhaps I am too old, for my eyes blur and I see nothing and for the moment I cannot even remember.

I return to my *Pietà*. I desire to express my love of God, but I doubt that He loves me. My hand fails me. Has He deserted me?

This is almost too much to endure. I wonder if the plague is in my house and bones, too. Am I dead already? Am I unable to paint any more?

I have worked all my life to learn how. I cannot halt as long as there is breath in me. Is it that I cannot finish my *Pietà* because I have forgotten how to draw? Or never truly knew how? As the Florentines say.

Yet I always wanted to be a painter. Ever since I can remember.

THE WONDER OF ARRIVAL

THE WONDER OF ARRIVAL
of whatever it is

The wonder of departure
of whatever it was

The wonder of being in-between
these great wonders

Stymean Karlen

I THINK I was ten the first time I saw Venice.

I am not sure; I have never been sure about my age. Yet I still remember vividly my first view of *La Serenissima*.

It was in the winter of 1500, for it was wet and cold, although some say that it was an earlier time, but I saw Leonardo that same year and it was 1500 when he came to Venice. And it was the sight of the city that gave me the hope that I might become a painter.

The start for me was when my papa agreed that I could be an apprentice in the workshop of Zuccato, a painter and mosaicist and officer of the Venetian Guild of Painters. I knew he was unhappy that I did not want to be a soldier like himself, or a lawyer like my grandfather. Drawing seemed to be the only thing I was fit to do. So he gave his reluctant consent and I was prepared for the arduous trip to Venice.

The day I was to leave Cadore was clear and the mountains that circled our home stood out with a startling clarity. While my mama dressed me, I observed them so I could imprint their splendid contours on my mind.

We stood in the bedroom I shared with my brother, Francesco, and Mama wrapped a warm cloth around my throat. She was small, frail, with black hair and dark, deep-set eyes, and she worried con-

stantly about my health, although I was strong, for her side of the
family had suffered four early deaths from exposure. Only when she
was satisfied that I was properly prepared did she lead me into the
front room for Papa's inspection and approval.

He was a heavyset mountaineer, proud that his robust legs could
climb any peak in our Alps and that his eyes were as keen as an
eagle's.

"Do not disgrace me," he warned. "Remember, you are the son of
Gregorio Vecellio, who is the son of Conte Vecellio, a councillor of
Cadore."

Mama added, "And you are the descendant of many Vecellios."

"That is important, Lucia. We are one of the oldest families here.
Never forget that, Tiziano. Allow no one to take advantage of you."

Mama said, "You will have to dress yourself now."

I said confidently, "Mama, I am a big boy." I felt grown-up for
my age. I was taller and stronger than any of the other ten-year-olds
in the village. I could even wrestle my brother, Francesco, to the
ground and he was two years older. But it was also time to leave
and suddenly I was homesick and I had to gulp to hold back the
tears.

Papa said sternly, "No tears, boy. A good soldier is brave."

He was joined by his brother, my uncle Antonio, who was a
merchant in Venice and who had arrived to take me there by cart
and donkey. I knew that my stocky, swarthy uncle had no faith in
this venture, for he had no regard for objects that did not possess
an assured value, and the only thing that made a painting worth
anything was the reputation of the artist. Antonio was doing this as
a favor for my father, and for two scudi.

Papa must have sensed his brother's disapproval, for he explained
suddenly, which was not like him, "Antonio, I am not pleased that
Tiziano does not want to be a soldier like myself, but all he seems
able to do is draw. I put him in the mines with the other boys and
he hid a piece of coal on his person and scratched my face on a
whitewashed wall. And when I scolded him for drawing on such a
wall, which cost money to be cleaned, he said the whiteness would
help form a clear impression. It was insane."

"Gregorio, did he clean it off as you commanded?"

"Only when I said that he could go to Venice and be an apprentice.
I was so angry I could have disowned him. He is as stubborn as a
mule."

"He acquired that trait from you."

"He was not taught to read and write to become an improvident artist. It was to prepare Tiziano to be a lawyer like his grandfather."

Yet I recalled that after he had forced me to erase the drawing, I overheard him tell Mama with gratification, "The face had a likeness to me."

"So, Antonio, take him to the workshop of Zuccato and I will find out if he is worth anything. Which I doubt. He will be back here soon."

I did not utter what I was feeling, that I could not be content if I could not put down what I saw. I said, "Papa, I must try, I must."

"I have given my word. You will have your chance. But if you fail, do not expect another. I will leave it to Zuccato to judge."

That troubled me. Suppose the master did not like me, or worse, I did not like him. But if I mentioned this, I would never reach Venice. I said, "I will do whatever he asks. I am strong and tall. Like you, Papa."

This thought appeared to please him, for he stated approvingly, "You have my looks, which could help you. You are fortunate that you resemble me. You have my long, straight nose, my sharp jaw, my firm mouth, brown eyes, and your hair has many reddish tints, like mine. And when you are not slouching over a drawing, you have an erect, strongly proportioned frame. Use it and it will make matters easier for you."

I had no comprehension what he meant by that—who would care what a boy of ten looked like?—but I nodded so he would be satisfied with me. But I wished I was grown-up, for then I could do what I wanted, I thought.

It was time to say good-bye and my sisters, Orsa and Caternia, who were younger, whom I considered children, were brought in and so was Francesco. They kissed me, as they were told, and then Mama's wet face pressed against mine. My skin was as smooth as hers and I wished I had a beard like my father, but while I had rubbed my face with oil as the older boys had told me to do, no hair had grown. I grasped my uncle's hand to go with him. I felt his callouses and I feared his grip would crush my fingers—I had stopped biting my nails so that I could draw better—but no one had noticed and I wondered why grown-ups did not see more.

Then Papa said, "Tiziano, no matter what happens, even if you are facing the Doge himself, hold your head high, stand straight, and do not look afraid even if you are. God will not deny you if you are brave."

The journey to Venice was hard and my uncle was greatly relieved when the city came into view. Until then, I sensed, he had not been certain that we would arrive safely. He was pleased with my excitement at the sight of Venice. He acted as if this conferred a distinction on him. He left the horse and cart on the mainland side of the lagoon and arranged for a gondola to take us to the Piazza San Marco, where he felt the space and grandeur were breathtaking. As he hoped, I was astounded. Venice was like a floating city and I was fascinated by its shape. I was convinced that it was one of the great sights of the world and I said so.

"Yes," he replied, "here Satan himself would admire God's triumph."

Venetian ambassadors returning from some far-off land—"Barbarian England," I heard someone whisper—were being ferried across the lagoon and I gloried in the brilliance of their velvets, silks, and jewels.

At the same time a religious procession marched by at the other end of the piazza. I was attracted by the many colors. This was more like a festive pageant than the somber rituals I saw at home and I was surprised.

My uncle muttered, "They are celebrating a miracle of the True Cross."

I said, "I was told there are many sacred relics in Venice."

"Miracles are all very fine," he advised me, "but a Venetian must get on with the business of making a living. I will show you the Rialto."

But I paused, for the great piazza was so huge that several other events were occurring there also.

An immense throng of people crowded around a column of smoke and when I tried to press closer my uncle stopped me abruptly and said angrily, "A Franciscan friar is being burned to death for getting two noble nuns with child. There are devils even in cassocks."

I remembered that my mother had warned me to be careful, to trust no one; Venice, she had said, was a wicked city, where even boys were slain.

My uncle added piously, "Child, you must realize that by exorcising this evil priest, we are also exorcising the plague that has afflicted us."

Ever since I could remember, I had heard about the plagues of Venice. However, I was too intoxicated with the city to be afraid of what I could not see. Then suddenly I shuddered. I saw a dead body, richly dressed, swinging by one leg between two columns. I was not prepared for such an ugly, horrible sight and I wanted to flee.

My uncle said, "He was executed for treason. Publicly humiliated."

Possibly Venice was not so fine after all, I thought. But as the sky cleared my fear vanished, for now I saw enchanting colors. I let go of my uncle's hand and ignored his admonition that the plague was still about and I ran to the edge of the Grand Canal to see better.

He followed me and for an instant I expected him to punish me. Then his pride in being a Venetian overcame his anger and he informed me, "The Grand Canal is crooked. It is constructed in the form of a Roman S. It divides Venice in the middle and it is in length a thousand and three paces and in breadth at least forty, in some places more."

"Uncle, are the colors always so vivid?"

"More so, usually. Wait until you see them in spring and summer."

The palaces in the sun were brown and yellow and red. There were sharp shadows and blue waves. The dome of San Marco took on a lavish pink and golden glow. I felt bathed in an intoxicating light. My imagination was stirred. Then as the sun began to set I saw a red that was a miracle. I felt conquered, yet triumphant. I murmured, "It is a Venetian red."

"What is that, child?"

Even now, so many years later, I wonder if I should have answered him, for when I did not he dragged me away from my vision. But I was afraid he would not understand what I was feeling and so I was silent.

We were almost at the Rialto when I asked, "Are all the sunsets so lovely?"

"Some more," he grumbled, "some less."

"Why?"

"Child, you are full of whys. Too many." But when I did not move, he added, "Tiziano Vecellio, it depends on where you stand."

Then I knew that he liked my admiration for his city, although he held my hand tighter than before and I was forced to move with him now. He said, "We could travel by gondola on the Grand Canal and land at the Rialto but it is shorter to walk and it costs less. But stay close to me," he insisted. "Thieves frequent these streets for there is so much wealth in these shops and porticos that there is much to be stolen."

Even as I was fascinated by the lively streets, the animation of the people, the multitude of scents and colors, my uncle was so self-important that I could not resist asking, "Is it truly such a remarkable place?"

"Truly," he said. He regarded me with scorn as if nothing better could be expected from a provincial child from Cadore. At the foot of the wooden humpbacked bridge he stated, "The Rialto is in the middle of the Grand Canal, for it marks the center of the commerce of the Republic."

But I noticed that while the ancient bridge was in a bend of the canal where it was most conspicuous it was rickety. The abundance of goods did not impress me as it did my uncle, but I was intrigued by the Turks, Germans, Egyptians, English, French, Flemish, and Florentines who stood as if they were the greatest of the foreign lords of the world.

As if they assumed they would be painted, my mind ran on.

I have painted many of them since. Even now I have Vasari's words in front of me: "There is hardly a noble of high rank, scarcely a prince or a lady of great name whose portrait has not been painted by Titian."

I am told this is one of the distinctions of my time. But I wonder if my sitters ever see themselves as I do. Or are their portraits their vanity of vanities? Or a record of my time? Perhaps I have painted too many portraits, but I could not have painted as I desired without patrons.

Even Michelangelo realized this necessity and toiled for them.

My uncle informed me, as if this were essential to know and might yet alter my wish to be an artist, "The Rialto is the greatest market in the world. Anything a man wants can be bought and sold here, but our main commerce is luxuries. They command the best price, thus they are the most profitable. Silver, glass, spice, jewels, cargoes that are small in size but large in value. In return for these that we convey from the East, we offer the finest cloth from Flanders, strong tin from England, copper and steel from Germany, and sacred relics for the pilgrims who come here as devotedly as they go to Rome. Everything in Venice is for sale."

"Including love," a resonant voice broke in. "We have more courtesans here than anywhere else in the world. And we are proud of them."

My uncle turned on the intruder and he was scornful as he retorted, "Palma Vecchio, you do not belong here. You have nothing to sell."

"I do, Antonio," said a tall, dark, attractive young man. He held a painting in one hand and with the other a girl about my age. "Is this lad another apprentice for your shop? He looks too alert for that."

I was rarely praised, it was thought unseemly, and I was pleased.

"No. He is destined tomorrow for your master's studio."

"He will learn nothing of consequence there."

"He is my nephew. He will learn how to earn a living. That is of the greatest consequence. But you do not appreciate Zuccato, although he has given you a great opportunity by allowing you to assist him."

"That is of no importance."

"What blasphemy have you put on canvas this time?"

Palma Vecchio displayed his painting to my uncle.

It was a portrait of Jesus in a pastoral setting and my uncle stated contemptuously, "The figure is neither manly nor grand and you have made the study of nature paramount rather than the figure of Our Lord. No one will want to buy it. You waste your time at the Rialto. Even barbarians like the Germans and the English have better taste than to desire this."

The painter replied, "This is the first painting that is truly my own."

"It is not decorative enough. It will not do."

"It owes nothing to anyone else's influence."

I wondered if all artists were so intense, especially Zuccato, for Palma Vecchio had spoken with such passion.

"I would hope that it is only your expression," said my uncle. "And it should not be in oil. You have done it too heavily to please."

This was the first painter I had met and I viewed his painting carefully. I liked the way the warm light was modulated into brown tints and I thought that he had blended them cleverly. Then as I saw the girl better I was distracted. She possessed the beauty for which I yearned. I decided that she was older than I was, for she was taller. Her skin was fair, her eyes were blue. Just to gaze at her did wonders for my heart.

Palma Vecchio must have noted my interest in the girl, for he said suddenly, "This is my niece, Violante. Child, what is your name?"

"Tiziano. But I am not a child, I am going to study painting."

"With Zuccato? You will not learn much. How old are you?"

Older people were always asking my age, so they could decide how to treat me, and I resented that. But I saw the girl regarding me with interest, as if, for the first time, I might matter to her. I stated, although my parents had told me that I was ten, "I am fourteen."

"You do not look it. You are tall and have large shoulders for a child, but you are beardless and you blush when you speak."

Only when I was in love, I thought, and Violante was the prettiest girl I had seen and she fitted my image of romance. So I could not afford to be younger than she was and I stood on tiptoe to be as tall. I expected my uncle to chide me for lying, but he said, "My nephew is what he says he is."

"Zuccato takes no one under twelve. He says they are too weak. Come, Violante, I have wasted enough time with this merchant, Antonio."

After they were gone, with her beauty still lingering in my mind like a vision of a girlish Venus, my uncle whispered to me, "He pretends she is his niece but I am convinced that she is his daughter."

"He looks too young to have a daughter," I replied.

"Vecchio hides his age for he is still an assistant and not a master. He is closer to thirty than to twenty but he is ashamed to admit it."

"Where is his wife, Uncle?"

"He has no wife, child." Before I could ask any more questions, my uncle took me to his home, which was a short walk from the Rialto.

He was proud of his rooms but they bore no resemblance to the Venice I had just seen. They were away from the water and the shops and the devil himself could not have had privacy. My aunt, Daria, regarded me with hostility, as if my presence was taking bread from the mouth of her son.

After I was put to bed the shutters were closed so my five-year-old cousin, Toma Tito, could not climb out. Daria was a heavy woman, whose stoutness made her appear older than she was, but she was proud of her bulging breasts and her Roman ancestry. My cousin uttered funny noises as he dreamed but I was too agitated to fall asleep. And I was confused. I felt in love with Venice and Violante and they seemed far out of my reach. I grew so homesick I could have cried only I was afraid that my relatives would hear me. Then I was shaken by loud voices.

My aunt shouted, "Antonio, you must take him to Zuccato tomorrow. Did you see how much he ate? Everything I put on the table. Even the melon."

"It was a long journey from Cadore and he had a very active day."

"It was a mistake to bring him here. Your brother must be insane. He will never be an artist. Did you see how clumsy he was? He dropped his meat on the table and spilled the melon into his lap."

"He was nervous. He felt you disapproved of him."

"I did. But that was no excuse. He did not know it."

I wondered why she was a mother only to her own child. My papa had told me that Daria Vecellio was renowned for her piety. Yet the rags I lay on were worse than the straw we used at home. To comfort myself, I thought of my grandfather, Conte Vecellio, and that he was a member of the governing council of Cadore, and that my papa, Gregorio, had been a captain of the local militia. Yet I seldom saw him. Most of the time he was away on military business for the Republic, while my mama, Lucia, was always busy with my younger sisters, Orsa and Caternia, since I was considered able to take care of myself. Yet I felt they loved me.

I did not remember when I fell asleep, but when I awoke the shutters were open, the sun was streaming in, and as I felt it on my body I was revived. It was as if I must build my own Venice if necessary, beyond the reach of time and the eroding tides. I dressed expectantly, properly.

Downstairs, as I prepared to accompany my uncle to the workshop of Zuccato, I ignored my aunt's scowls and my cousin's tears—Toma Tito had cramps from overeating—for the bright winter sun gleamed with a new whiteness. My uncle examined my appearance to be sure that I would not embarrass the name of Vecellio. Then we walked toward the workshop of the painter and mosaicist. I felt changed already. I was determined to keep up with my uncle's longer stride but to see Venice with my own eyes.

I was bursting with anticipation and eager to be intoxicated.

YOU KEEPERS OF ART AND WISDOM

> YOU KEEPERS OF ART AND WISDOM
> although not the originators
> But soon to be
>
> give back something
> to the originators for their gift
> if only in an effort
>
> Their hungers are as starved
> as yours
> give back something
>
> *Stymean Karlen*

WE WAITED a long time for Zuccato to appear and this upset my uncle. But he hid his anger and bowed politely to the artist, and ignored Palma Vecchio, who escorted the master into the studio. Zuccato sat behind a desk, which was on a raised platform where he could see all of his large bottega, for it was filled with toiling apprentices, and examined me.

I thought that the master was not much to paint. Even while Zuccato was in a position of superiority, he remained a little bow-legged figure with an ugly nose, florid cheeks, a fat stomach, and small dark eyes that regarded me suspiciously, and his voice grated as he addressed my uncle.

"Antonio, he is an unsightly boy. He is dressed like a peasant."

"Sebastian, he has just arrived from Cadore."

Zuccato grumbled, "I do not know of any artist who has come from there. Ferrara, yes, and even Vicenza and Verona, but Cadore? It is absurd!"

"We can trace our ancestry in Cadore for hundreds of years."

Zuccato addressed me. "Boy, what are you called?"

"Tiziano Vecellio, son of Gregorio, a captain of the highest valor."

"How old are you?"

I hesitated. I was afraid and Palma Vecchio, who stood behind Zuccato, acted as if he had never seen me before. And the master looked so severe.

He said sternly, "I take no one under twelve. They are too weak."

"I am fourteen, sir."

"You are small for that age."

"But about right for twelve," said Palma Vecchio.

I could not tell whether he was being sarcastic or helpful. My uncle added hurriedly, "Tiziano is strong. And he is willing to work hard."

Zuccato surveyed me critically and stated, "If he enters my bottega he must obey me completely and possess strong hands for my mosaics."

I asked, "Maestro, will there be any face painting?" Ever since I could remember the human face was the most important thing to paint.

"No! God comes before everything. We work only to express His glory. Face painting is forbidden in my bottega. It is impious and impractical."

"Then it is settled," said my uncle, anxious to end this transaction.

"What about my fee? My apprentices pay for their instruction and keep."

"You said this is not necessary. I send you much business."

"I will watch how the boy develops. But remember, any money his work earns will go to his instruction and keep. Agreed, Antonio!"

My uncle nodded.

"I will have the contract drawn up. He will be bound to me as an apprentice for seven years and as a journeyman for five more."

At the idea of the long bondage I winced, but my uncle was pleased.

Zuccato added, "Antonio, I am doing you a great favor. I never take an apprentice without a fee. My studio flourishes. Today I met with an envoy of the Council of Ten, who selected me to replace the mosaics of San Marco. That was where I was most of this day."

While my uncle congratulated the master, his assistant, Palma Vecchio, reminded me, "Boy, you will be beaten if you do any face painting here."

Zuccato said, "But if you obey, I will teach you how to earn a living."

* * *

I was put in the charge of Zuccato's oldest son, Francesco, who was fifteen. I felt that he resented my size, for I was as big as he was. This wiry, brown-haired, square-featured boy, who was indulged by his father, was devoted to exercising his family's authority. He supervised the ten apprentices who ground colors, cleaned palettes, washed brushes, and prepared the mosaics, which were the main activity in the studio.

Then Francesco, as was the custom, forced me to bathe, to make sure I did not carry any vermin. I stood in an old wooden bucket while he had me doused by two other boys. One threw hot water on me, the other cold, while I was not sure whether I was going to be scalded or frozen.

I was ashamed of my nakedness, for no one except my parents had seen me that way, and when the apprentices saw that I lacked pubic hair, they made fun of me and shouted that my penis was just a child's toy.

Francesco was proud of his—he claimed it was the largest in the bottega—and it made him feel superior to me. The clothes my mother had dressed me in so carefully were confiscated and I was given a coarse garb to wear, a heavy brown tunic that itched and hung loosely on me.

My long reddish-brown hair of which I was proud was cropped close to indicate my low station in the workshop and the bed I was given—which I hated—was a few slats of wood. It was in the attic above the studio and I was crowded in with the other apprentices, except for Francesco, who shared a room with his younger brother, Valerio. There was no privacy—we were herded in like pigs in a sty—and the other apprentices made fun of my accent. They sneered that I sounded like a mountain goat. And when I bent over to undress I was butted in the back by the biggest boy in the workshop, Leo. I did not reply, for he was sixteen and he towered over me.

But the second night, when Leo knocked me about without cause, I realized this could happen often unless I fought back. Then he grabbed my hands and wrenched them and I was afraid that he would damage them. I had to prevent such a disaster and I rushed at him.

He was surprised by my resistance—he had not expected me to fight back—and I kicked him in the shin. He grabbed it with a howl of pain and then I hit him in the groin, where it would hurt the most. Leo cried out that I was a low-bred fellow, but while I was frightened my anger was stronger. I made a face of rage and ran at him as if to attack him again and he cringed and sobbed, "I will never be able to have a girl again!"

I assured him that he could when his pain went away, although I did not know whether this was true, since I had never known a girl.

As Leo's pain diminished, he whimpered, "They said you were not fourteen, but you fight as if you are."

The other apprentices regarded me with astonishment and crowded around me and felt the muscles of my arms. They admired my bulges and I thought, My penis might not be as large as theirs yet, but my arms and hands, thanks to my constant drawing, were as strong as anyone's in this attic.

Even now, so long afterward, my physical strength has been a source of pride. So much of my work grows from my fingers and my fists. And then, for the first time in my life, despite my lack of pubic hair, I felt grown-up.

No one taunted me any more, although I was given the dirtiest work, for I was the newest apprentice. Vecchio, as the master's assistant, directed the labor in the workshop and he continued to ignore me as an individual.

I expected to practice drawing and painting, but neither was allowed. My entire time was spent on mosaics and this labor made me miserable. I felt I would never become an artist. When I washed my hands to prepare for the fish, fruit, bread, and wine we were given to eat, I felt they were betraying me, that I would be only a workman for the rest of my life.

I sought to make my labor more palatable by assuring myself that I was performing a worthy service in preparing these mosaics for San Marco. But when I mentioned this to Leo, who was teaching me, he laughed. Leo was friendly now that I had stood up to him and he replied, "Tiziano, it is a lie. The best that Zuccato can do is fit only for a parish church. But he likes to pretend that he is the pope of mosaicists."

The thought that I was not even working for something that mattered was infuriating but I felt trapped. Art in the Republic was controlled by the Venetian Guild of Painters and it was impossible to be a painter without a certificate from them. Zuccato possessed the authority to bar any of his apprentices for life. So I tried to be obedient. What was even worse was that we were forbidden to leave the workshop. When the shutters were open to let in the sun and air, I could smell the multitude of scents and hear the varied sounds of life that attracted me to Venice. But we were warned that the city streets were dangerous, that last year an apprentice had been found dead in an alley after a brawl with a bravo, and that anyone caught outside the studio would be dismissed. Yet when Leo told me that Leonardo the Florentine was in Venice and at the invitation of the Senate would be at San Marco to fortify Venice against the Turks and that he intended to see the artist, I begged to go with him.

However, I asked also, "What about Zuccato? Could we be caught?"

"The master and Palma Vecchio are part of the delegation from the Venetian Guild of Painters who are welcoming the Florentine. No one will be on watch here. Others will slip out, also. Yet it could be risky."

The next day I stood with Leo at San Marco. We hid behind a pillar where I had seen a body hang and I tried to observe Leonardo. Everyone said that the Florentine was a man different from all other men.

Leonardo was surveying the Doge's Palace but instead of speaking about art as I had expected, he said to the Venetian Senate, which was assembled around him, but loud enough for the large crowd in the rear to hear, "Your Excellencies, I have devised war machines and a nautical apparatus which can be used by this Republic for both offense and defense."

My resolution was to see him in addition to hearing him, and so I left Leo, who was afraid to move any closer for fear of being detected, and eased my way forward through the cracks in the crowd. No one appeared to notice me as I was able to edge close to Leonardo.

I had heard that the Florentine possessed a beauty of person and an effortless grace and elegance, and I was surprised at how old he looked. I knew he was almost fifty, which was ancient to me, but I expected such a famous person to be tall and broad, and without age. Instead, although his hair was carefully curled, his hands perfumed, and his silk-sheathed figure was perfectly groomed, he was of moderate height, and stooped, as if the years weighed heavily upon him. And his face was wrinkled.

It was the youth whom Leonardo called Andrea that was appealing to look at. This boyish attendant was as attractive as any of the lovely ladies of Venice, yet I felt that his appearance distracted and disturbed the Florentine. Then, with obvious effort, the artist focused on his audience. He said to the Venetian Senate, "Your

Excellencies, if my devices do not defeat the Turks, you must inundate your countryside."

"What about our people and their crops?" a Senator asked in dismay.

"You will have been another Noah and nothing will remain, not a single enemy soldier." Leonardo's eyes glowed and he looked pleased.

I had assumed that he would discuss painting and the splendid shapes and colors of *La Serenissima* and I was disappointed. I wondered if all the great men I encountered would afflict me with this feeling. But I inched closer, for the venerable Gentile Bellini, the most renowned artist in Venice, addressed Leonardo. "Maestro, does our city please you?"

He was ignored. Was this what the Florentine thought about Venetian art? As I asked myself this question, I possessed a burning desire to speak to him. But what could I, a mere boy, say to such a great artist!

I saw Palma Vecchio next to Gentile Bellini, apparently to console this aged and honored master for the Florentine's snub, and I knew that Zuccato must be nearby—the assistant always remained close to his master. I retreated behind a pillar and heard Leonardo say to the Senators, "If you do not approve of my military devices, I will present them to Cesare Borgia. This great soldier has need of my skill. Venice may be, as it is reported, the most beautiful city in the world but I do not care for it."

Nothing happened the next two years that was worth remembering. By then, while I was only twelve, I considered myself fifteen, for I could do anything that Leo and Francesco did. But I was allowed only to perform the menial tasks of a mosaicist's assistant. Leonardo had left Venice soon after I had seen him and the Republic's interest had turned to other things. I doubted that I could still draw, I had not done so for such a long time, and I felt like an onion in a stew. I was very unhappy.

Then an extraordinary event stimulated me. It was a summer day and the shutters were wide open in the workshop, for otherwise the heat would have been unbearable, and the other apprentices were around a long wooden table admiring a mosaic. It was the first one that Francesco had done by himself and he expected our approval. But I was bored. I was setting *tesserae*, which Zuccato called "painting without paint," when I saw a pretty girl undressing in the window across the alley. I pretended to clean the windowsill so I could observe her better and so that no one would be suspicious. I was excited by her thick black hair, her olive skin, and her soft round features. She was the first naked female I had seen and I wondered how old she was. She looked about my own age but I could not tell whether she had any pubic hair, for suddenly she turned her back, as if to defy me and yet to tempt me. As I was still seeking to recall what she looked like, she turned toward the window, where I could see the upper half of her body. Her breasts were full and ripe like melons. Then I was afraid that she was too old for me, yet my yearnings for her increased and I felt my penis swell. Just as I thought her presence was an invitation she closed her shutters with a bang.

From that moment I longed to paint the female body. Her figure so delighted me that I felt prepared to give up much to win her and sketch her. I wondered if the girl I had met with Palma Vecchio was so fully shaped. Since I had entered Zuccato's studio, he had not mentioned Violante, but I had heard rumors that he was attached to a young girl.

When no one was watching I examined myself in a small wall mirror to see if I were old enough to court her. Now I saw the beginnings of my pubic hair but I felt that there was not enough to satisfy her that I possessed sufficient masculinity to please. My only consolation was that my features were more attractive than the other apprentices', long and sharp and regularly formed, and that my brown hair had a vivid reddish tint that was brighter than anybody else's in the studio.

The next morning, before anyone was awake, I arose and tiptoed in to the bottega and took paper and crayon from Zuccato's desk. And after dinner that night I climbed up on the roof, saying that it was cooler there, and sought to construct the girl's face and figure as I recalled them. Once I began to draw her I forgot everything that had upset me. This became a labor of love, the act as absorbing as the subject.

My fingers were stiff at first, but gradually my hand grew stronger. Then I was dissatisfied; I wanted a model, to be sure I was accurate.

Several days later while Zuccato sat in his elevated chair and lectured us on the traditions of mosaics—that he was constructing them exactly as they had been done for centuries—I drew him. There was nothing else I could focus on. His paintings were on the wall behind him, but they depressed me. His figures were forced, the expression on the faces was vapid, and his color was devoid of feeling. So I sketched his features. I was in the rear of the studio where no one should detect what I was doing. And by now I had done several drawings without being discovered and I drew Zuccato carefully and slowly, as it were, from nature.

I was finishing off his black hair with charcoal, so intent on obtaining the correct shading I had forgotten my circumstances, when I heard an irate voice and someone snatched the drawing from me. It was Zuccato himself, furious that I had portrayed him as he was: short, fat, bandy-legged, with a bulbous nose and thick lips.

He summoned Palma Vecchio to his side and cried out, "How could you permit such disobedience. This is a slander!"

I was glad that I had hidden my other work, for after he showed his assistant my drawing he tore it to shreds. He declared that I must be dismissed from his studio, as an object lesson to the other apprentices.

My papa came to take me home. I could tell that he felt disgraced, while my uncle, who accompanied him, assumed that I had failed, as he had predicted. I heard them consulting with Zuccato, who stated that I was hopeless, that I would never amount to anything in art. I saw Palma Vecchio standing within hearing, but saying nothing.

Suddenly, as Papa boxed my ears for disobeying the master, I pulled loose from his grasp—he was about to take me back to Cadore —and I shouted desperately, "Papa, I will not leave Venice!"

I expected him to strike me to the ground for such unheard-of defiance, but something in my manner must have appealed to him, and halted him, for he merely said, "I can pay nothing for you."

My uncle added, "I told you that he should not have been apprenticed. If Tiziano continues in this way, he will disgrace the name of Vecellio."

Gregorio said, "I should have beaten him when he mentioned painting."

"Papa, that is just it!" I exclaimed. "I am not painting here!"

"What are you doing?"

"Only mosaics."

Zuccato stated, "He was learning how to construct them. So that he could earn a living. But no longer. I am finished with him."

"Papa, you promised me that I could learn how to be a painter."

Zuccato sneered, "No one will have him after I dismiss him."

I cried out, "I have not practiced any painting here! Or drawing! I had to do that secretly or I would never have done any!"

I saw that Papa pondered what I revealed. His dark, bushy eyebrows rose and there were wrinkles on his wide forehead. Yet I realized that he could not give in to me in Zuccato's presence. He replied, "I will decide my son's future." He pushed me out of the studio.

It was too late to return to Cadore, so our relatives had to put us up in their rooms. That night, after a meal of sausages and eggs, which Papa supplied to stop my aunt's complaints, Palma Vecchio visited us and asked if he could speak to me privately. Papa's impulse was to say no, but there must have been something in the assistant's expression that appealed to him, for he consented and left me alone with the artist.

I expected Palma Vecchio to chide me, for Zuccato had scolded him for what I had done. Instead, he laughed.

That upset me. I cried out, "Do you think my drawing that ridiculous?"

He answered, "Tiziano, do you have any other drawings?"

It was the first time he had addressed me by name and I was surprised and pleased. But I was also suspicious and I did not reply.

"You must have. That sketch of Zuccato was too finished to have been your first. Show me the others. I will not destroy them."

I was still afraid that he would betray me, but I had to trust someone, for the thought of leaving Venice was something I could not accept. So I handed him drawings of the girl and of himself.

I assumed that he would lose his temper when he saw that I had drawn him, but I was curious what he would think of it.

He asked, "Who is the girl?"

"Not your niece!" I exclaimed, and then I wanted to bite my tongue.

He said quietly, "I know that."

"It is a girl I saw across the alley from Zuccato's bottega."

"And you desired to reach out for her?"

"I had to sketch her face and figure."

"Your use of chalk suggests whiteness and you have given her flesh an appropriate fullness. But you flatter me. You must be more accurate."

Palma Vecchio, with his fine features and bright eyes, had delighted me. I asked, "What is wrong with this drawing? I sketched you as I saw you."

"You could spend the rest of your life drawing and always have something wrong. I will speak to your father. It is as I thought."

He was so mysterious I did not know what he intended.

He said, "Gregorio Vecellio, Zuccato was right. Your son does not belong in his bottega." I was stricken. I felt I should burn all my drawings and I started to throw them into the fireplace.

Palma Vecchio asked me, "Tiziano, is that why you did them?"

"No, but you said. . ."

"Boy, I am saying that you are wasted in the studio of a mosaicist."

Papa asked, "Signore, what are you suggesting?"

"Your son has strong hands. He should study in the studio of a painter."

Papa shrugged, as if that idea were impossible.

"I would like your permission to speak to Gentile Bellini."

"He is very old!" I announced. But now I did not destroy my drawings.

Papa wavered, and then I wished I had not been so impulsive. But Palma Vecchio said softly, yet with a persistence that was persuasive, "Gregorio Vecellio, Gentile Bellini is still one of the best in painting."

"He is a great master, Palma Vecchio. I have no money to pay him."

"Neither of us has," insisted my uncle. "He is the first painter in Venice. Perhaps in the world. He will not consider Tiziano. The boy has already failed a lesser artist. How could he please a Bellini?"

Palma Vecchio sighed as he said, "Nothing is certain in this world. But I have worked for Bellini and I believe I can persuade him to view the boy's work. He can always use a promising draughtsman. They are scarce in Venice. If he sees these drawings, he may be willing to accept him as an apprentice. But I cannot promise that this will happen."

Papa mumbled, "All that I do for the boy, I do for the Vecellio name. Even in Cadore, Gentile and Giovanni Bellini are well known."

"Then I can stay in Venice, Papa?"

"I thought you had decided that long ago."

"With your permission and blessing."

"Wait until Gentile Bellini agrees to have you as an apprentice.

If that unlikely event should occur, I will decide then. Palma Vecchio, it is more likely that my son will be rejected?"

"Yes. The master takes very few apprentices into his studios these days. But I would like your permission to try."

"Granted."

It was agreed that I would remain with my uncle while Palma Vecchio spoke to Gentile Bellini. But only for a short time, my uncle insisted, declaring that he could not afford to feed another growing boy. I was hopeful, yet apprehensive. I felt I might be one step closer to being a painter, but just one step. Then, as a week passed before the master would see me, I was positive that his door would be closed to me also, and I was sick at the prospect of returning to Cadore.

ALLEGIANCE MUST GROW

ALLEGIANCE MUST GROW
Like an order from Nature
Not from a Master

Stymean Karlen

THE STUDIO of the Bellini brothers was on the Grand Canal just before it reached the Rialto, where the city teemed with vitality and color. Palma Vecchio led me into their establishment with an ease that indicated his familiarity with these painters. They possessed an old palazzo that had belonged to a patrician, and I was intrigued by the Byzantine facade and spires, the numerous spacious rooms, and the inlaid marble floors. I felt a divinity in this elaborate and handsome palazzo and I followed Vecchio eagerly.

He paused at the entrance to Gentile Bellini's bottega and announced, "Here, Venice is the jewel casket and the master of the world."

He seemed to be speaking to me as an artist and I was excited. Were my drawings that skillful, I wondered, or was he angry at Zuccato?

"And where the business of the world is transacted. In art, also."

I listened attentively as he desired and he added, "The brothers have converted the Palazzo Bellini into a series of studios. The largest is on the ground floor where no steps have to be climbed and is Gentile Bellini's. He is the head of the bottega by virtue of his age and seniority."

"Signore, what about the other brother?"

"Giovanni Bellini is a partner, too. But out of deference to Gentile's legitimacy—Giovanni is a love child—he uses the floor above. Then there are studios on the top floor for assistants like myself."

Surprised, I asked, "Signore, have you left Zuccato, too?"

He smiled as if the comparing of my person with him was amusing, but he said, "I have been working with the Bellinis for some time. This is the finest studio in Venice, but I needed the money Zuccato paid me."

I could believe his praise of this workshop. It was much larger and attractive than the one I had come from and it contained genuine work. The walls were crowded with Gentile Bellini's paintings but one dominated: his vast *The Procession of the True Cross in the Piazza di San Marco*. The detail was astonishing and it reminded me of the pageant I had seen the day I had arrived in Venice. Everything was as I had observed it; the spectacle and the multitude were exact to the tiniest stroke of the painter's brush.

A dozen apprentices labored in various parts of this bottega while I was brought before Bellini, who sat in front of a large painting on an easel. He was resting but when he saw Vecchio he ordered him to speak.

Vecchio asked, "Maestro, have you observed the boy's drawings?"

"Zuccato designs honorable mosaics. If he was dissatisfied with his work, what place is there for him in my studio?"

Vecchio paused, as if to find a way to answer this challenge, and I observed Bellini, so I could learn how to address him. His face was full and strong, with a firm jaw, tight, thin lips, deep brown eyes, and gray hair carefully combed to his shoulders. He wore a skull cap and his monkish robe matched the color of his hair. He did not look as aged as he had by the side of Leonardo the Florentine, but his expression was severe. I felt he regarded me critically even before he knew me.

"Maestro," I ventured, "what did you think of my drawings?"

Bellini ignored me, looking very tired, and went to dismiss Vecchio.

This moved him to declare, "Maestro, you are the greatest painter and draughtsman in Venice, possibly the whole world."

"My brother, Giovanni, is my equal." But now Bellini was listening.

"Because he is a Bellini, Maestro. That is why I brought the boy here."

"He is too young."

I thought angrily, Am I to be punished eternally for my youth?

Vecchio stated, "Maestro, Tiziano is fourteen and a hard worker."

"All my apprentices work hard."

"Maestro, no one can teach this worthy pupil more about painting and drawing than you can. You possess an exactitude of line and detail that is unmatched. Even by the Florentines. Even by Leonardo da Vinci."

Bellini remained stern but he agreed to accept me on a trial basis.

I entered his studio as one of many apprentices. I had no idea whether he had examined my drawings or what he thought about them. He assigned me to the care of Vecchio, who was his new assistant, and ordered him to instruct me in drawing and painting in the manner he practiced. Then he ignored me. I felt like just an object to him.

The year that followed was devoted to learning the routine of Gentile Bellini's bottega. Much of the time was spent grinding colors, cleaning palettes, washing brushes, stacking cartoons, arranging implements, and sweeping the floor. I was permitted to practice drawing—that was Gentile's passion—and occasionally I was allowed to prepare the surface for the master's paint. But Bellini did not permit me to put in any of the background figures or fill in landscape details as several of the older, more experienced apprentices did. I resented this and I was disappointed in the dullness of his color. What little painting I managed to do, I did secretly. Then Bellini's manner of work distressed me. It was marked by hesitancy and timidity. Often he took an entire day to finish what even my inexperienced hands could have done in an hour and I felt that he approached each picture he painted as if it were to be his last.

Bellini was preoccupied most of the time, concerned only with himself. He was past seventy and I felt he was preparing for his end. Childless, he kept making his will. There were three in quick succession. When I cleaned out his basket, I found the torn scraps. I could read and write, unlike most of his apprentices, and so I became aware of his melancholy.

This troubled me; I doubted I could advance in his studio.

But he was dedicated to drawing. Even, I felt, for its own sake.

My difficulty was, I differed with his style. He preferred pen and ink, usually brown ink. He said it was exact. And when Bellini desired coloring in his drawing, or an expression, he used black chalk. I liked his precise modeling, but I favored charcoal. It was more sensuous. So while I did many pen-and-ink drawings, generally with brown ink, then with black chalk, I wished I could have done them with charcoal.

I disliked his routine; there was no striving or adventure in it.

And as my second year in Bellini's bottega began it remained unchanged. I was tempted to flee. But there was no other place to go.
So I sought to hold my head erect as my father had advised and not
to appear afraid.

And to observe. Always observe.

Just as I prayed that I would never have to copy another Gentile
Bellini cartoon or painting again, I found them pompous and dry,
I was ordered to assist Vecchio in the studio of Giovanni Bellini.
I had been upstairs only to do errands—I had kept to myself ever
since I had left Zuccato's workshop—and I missed Leo, and even
Francesco, and I was lonely, bored, and unhappy. But this could be
exciting, I thought. Giovanni Bellini was younger and had a reputation for being interested in new ideas, unlike his brother. And I was
ready to be grown-up. I approached fourteen and while I wished my
pubic hair would increase faster and that my masculinity would be
more pronounced, I was almost as tall and large as any of the apprentices in the Palazzo Bellini.

Today, such a long time afterward, I still recall this first impression vividly. It is one of the most vital of my life, and fortunate.

Much has been said and written about the circumstances of my
learning. That I was dismissed by Gentile, taught by Giovanni, and
influenced by Giorgione. That I would have amounted to nothing
without Big George.

This is stupid. These assertions still infuriate me. I am no one's
disciple. Except, possibly, God's. No one else has dominated me.
Nature is my master and has been always. I recall my beginnings
differently.

"No, no, do not argue with me!"

I say these words to myself, for there is no one in my sumptuous
studio at the Biri Grande. I stand up, tired of writing—it is almost
as arduous as painting—and I hobble to the window. Now I am
sorry that I dismissed my sons. I am afraid that they will never find
the oils I need to finish my *Pietà*. Or that my memories will restore
my strength.

Water is the primal matter of Venice, I feel, and yet my mind is
not absorbed with the Grand Canal or the great lagoon, but the
studios where I truly started to believe that I could become a genuine
painter.

Patches of blue skies and crimson sunsets and pink flesh. A gondolier giving a smooth swerve to avoid a rival. The girl passing by with a red-colored shawl that is enchanting. And I am living a life I have chosen.

The jangle of keys reminds me where I am. Now I dress much as Gentile: in monkish black. I carry always a ring of keys through a belt loop. They are precious to me; they are for the closets in my halls where my paintings are stored. No one has access to them but myself. I do not trust my work to other hands any more. Yet I realize it is foolish to carry these heavy keys. I know that after I am gone the paintings that remain in my possession will be disposed of without regard for my wishes.

But these days I wish I had my other pictures back. Instead, they are scattered all over Europe. I miss them dreadfully. Now they are my best friends; sometimes, I think, they are my only friends. I cannot bring myself to throw away these keys. It would be as if I gave away a large part of myself, the best part, the unique part. I fondle the keys, fascinated by their differences.

What do I remember?

Giorgione is one of the few I may have truly loved.

Upstairs, in Giovanni Bellini's studio, the present Doge of The Most Serene Republic, Leonardo Loredano, was sitting for his portrait. The previous one the painter had done was so satisfactory the Doge desired a duplicate. Two of Giovanni Bellini's apprentices were ill and I was needed to help mix the oils. This was supervised by Vecchio and I sensed that he had asked for me because he had detected my misery in the older brother's studio. Vecchio did not scold me when I was not sure what to do, but told me to watch his colleague, Giorgione, and then imitate him.

This painter—I could tell that he was one by the deference with which Vecchio treated him—did not regard me as a child but acted as if I were his equal, although he was quite grown-up, about ten years older than I. While Giovanni Bellini concentrated on this portrait with a passionate single-mindedness, and his subject, the Doge, sat in the painter's arrangement so that it gave him a quiet strength and authority, as befitted such a benign ruler, I realized that for the painting of this picture we were outside of their world.

I felt the Doge's face was that of a typical Venetian patrician: long, narrow features, a sharp chin, a resolute nose, a face bred to command and to ceremonial. But I was captivated by the painter's appearance.

Giovanni Bellini was only a year younger than Gentile, but his

skin was smooth, without wrinkles, and his round, plump countenance gave him a sweetness and sensitivity that his brother lacked.
His hair was gray and worn down to his shoulders. His eyes were
hazel and reflective. He was heavier than his brother, but his gray
garb, which was handsomely brocaded with touches of white, gave
him, I thought, presence and distinction.

I remember this as if it were yesterday.

Giorgione patiently showed me what to do and treated the oils
with love. Gentile Bellini preferred tempera but when I saw the
luminosity and richness of Giovanni's colors, I felt as if a new light
flowed through the high Venetian windows. And suited this studio.
Gentile's bottega was formal, cold, but Giovanni's was symmetrical,
warm, with many mirrors and musical instruments, which the artist
obviously cherished, for they were hung with great care. Yellow was
the dominant color and I was not certain I agreed with the way
Giovanni used it on his walls. But the paintings I saw, especially his
madonnas, were human and gentle, and possessed deep feeling. My
mind teemed with impressions.

Giorgione noticed my absorption in the oils and he was pleased.
I did a wrong thing and he remedied it without criticizing me.

Gradually, as the morning passed, I grew more skillful. By the
time the Doge and Bellini paused to have lunch, I was avoiding
mistakes.

They were served in the painter's private quarters, while Vecchio
ordered another apprentice to bring us cheese, fruit, and wine.

He said, "We must not eat heavily while working, but moderately."

Giorgione poured my wine without reserve, as if I were old enough
to know how much to drink. He said, "It is not too sweet, not too
heavy."

"And it has a lovely red color, Signore," I added.

Vecchio said, "Tiziano is from Cadore, but draws with a firm
hand."

Giorgione said, "I am from Castelfranco. Giorgio Barbarelli,
friend. But we are all Venetians now. It is a great virtue in painting."

Vecchio said, "Tiziano, he is infatuated with oils. That is why he
prefers Venice. He believes we are more disposed to new effects."

"Where else could men like the Bellinis, of humble origin, rise
high? It is why I have come here. We owe it to our work."

It was the first time I was being treated as a man and I felt exalted.
"You have the capacity to learn. You took to the oils swiftly."
"Signor Giorgio . . . "
"Giorgione," he interrupted me.
Vecchio added, "He prefers that. He sees himself as Big George."
"But he is!" I exclaimed, then blushed, as if I had revealed too much of my feelings. However, Giorgione only said, "Thank you, Tiziano," while Vecchio merely smiled indulgently, and I thought, Beauty has come together in Giorgione. He was tall, lean, finely built. His nose was straight, his lips red and full, his cheekbones high and sharp, his eyes a dark, rich brown, and his brow wide. No wonder he smiled so easily, I felt, nature favored him and he could afford to be generous.

I said, to change the subject and because I was interested, "Signore, do you prefer oil to tempera?"
"Infinitely. It is the way of the grand. And of the future."
Vecchio asked, "Is that why you are influenced by Giovanni?"
"I am influenced by everyone and no one. Tiziano, you agree?"
I nodded. Then I frowned.
"But now you are bored with Gentile's dry and labored manner."
I hesitated, but I had to trust someone. "Yes, that is true."
"Tiziano should study with Giovanni. You should have brought him here."
"I had to approach the older Bellini first. He is the chief painter of the state, the Republic's official artist."
"Tiziano, have you ever worked with oils?"
"No," I said sadly, for the colors that Giovanni was using were the richest I had seen. I yearned to know this substance as intimately as I could. I could see that it completely altered the character of painting, but I added, "Gentile Bellini prefers tempera. He claims it is more exact."
"Exact! Exact! I would rather be free when I paint. Behold and believe! But Gentile Bellini must always be sensible and shrewd."
Vecchio said, "He believes only what he sees, and in God. But you, Giorgione, are carried away by your imagination and intuition."
"I do not like it that everything must be identified. It is absurd. There is much that simply should be observed. And blessed with color."
There was silence as Giovanni Bellini resumed the portrait while we attended his wants. I reflected that perhaps Giorgione was not always discreet, but there was something wonderful in his passion for oils and colors. I felt this was an artist who thought with his heart,

for he was more interested in protecting me than in punishing me, as was the custom.

Did he need love, I asked myself, as I did?

I doubted that Giovanni Bellini knew that I existed.

I was returned to Gentile Bellini's bottega that night and the next day the absent apprentices were back and I was not needed. Oil painting was forbidden by the older brother and anyone caught doing it was dismissed from his workshop. Yet I felt that there were splendid pleasures in this new style and that I must learn to work in it with skill and taste.

When Vecchio entered the older brother's studio a few days later, I begged him to take me upstairs again and he replied, "Gentile will resent your preference for Giovanni's manner." Yet there must have been something in my plea that appealed to Vecchio, for soon after he found an excuse to use me in the younger Bellini's studio.

This painter was finishing his portrait of Loredano; he was giving the elderly Doge a wise but wrinkled look. There was no need for me to help, yet Vecchio and Giorgione pretended that my services were valuable.

I observed that where the older brother stressed drawing, the younger used just a few strokes of his pen. He did not prepare his pictures elaborately with many sketches as his brother did. He said to Vecchio, "I draw only in my moment of hesitation, when I must. I prefer to paint, to trust to my hand and to my invention." Giovanni Bellini was emphatic.

Stimulated, I persuaded Vecchio to take me to the top floor where he and Giorgione painted. My desire to see their work, especially Big George's, was overwhelming. I felt that they could introduce me to an even greater freedom and daring. My passion was to work in oils.

Vecchio assured me that it was safe to be absent. Gentile Bellini was writing a new will, while his brother was at the Doge's palace to touch up the first portrait to conform to the second, Loredano liked that one so much.

The top floor was as spacious as the other floors, but it was divided into two separate rooms by gold and black drapes. Then, as Vecchio led me into his studio, I was uneasy. His oils were done with skill and they were in the style of Giovanni Bellini, but they lacked the latter's feeling.

What could I say? I wanted help from Giorgione, but he had

wandered over to the high window which looked out on Venice and he seemed to be far away. I heard the splash of a gondola, laughing voices.

Vecchio said abruptly, "Tiziano, you do not like my manner!"

"I do, Signore. It is just that. . ." I paused, unable to finish.

"You expected a step beyond Giovanni Bellini."

"Signore, it is not for me to judge. I am just an apprentice."

"You are not always so humble. And you do have grown-up eyes."

"I do not understand."

"Why do you think I grant you special favors? Take you out of Zuccato's bottega? Soon I may need a young, strong, gifted helper."

"You honor me, Signore. It will be a great privilege."

"If you are uneasy with my style, we should make other plans."

"No, Signore!" With Vecchio I could be my own master. "Your work has much delicacy and your textures are that of a virtuoso. I could learn much from you. As I hope to learn from Giovanni Bellini and Big George."

"Good. I will show you Giorgione's work now."

Big George's studio was so disorderly I was afraid to look at his paintings. Everything had been dropped and discarded where it had been used. Dust, paint, debris, and female clothing covered every inch of his floor. Yet I had to examine his paintings; it was as if my life depended on it.

Vecchio had hung a dozen of his oils but Giorgione displayed only two. Breathing deeply, I stared at them as if paralyzed. Yet I grew calm. His paintings were immaculate. The two oils expressed an idyllic harmony between man and landscape and his graceful colors were the unifying element. They were the richest and most exciting I had seen.

I thought passionately, *Gentile is good, Giovanni is better, but Giorgione is the best.* I knew I must work with him. But the doing, I feared, was too difficult. No apprentice was supposed to choose his own master.

Many days I used oil in Gentile Bellini's bottega despite it being forbidden. Most of the time I worked early in the morning or at night, when the light was bad or there was none. This did not trouble me as much as I expected, for I copied Giorgione's style from memory. Gradually I felt that my painting improved, stimulated by my sense of color. I was possessed with an intense eagerness to learn and to discover more.

Since I preferred the grace and beauty of the female form, I painted a Venus. I used sweeping proportions so she would be wide-hipped, large-breasted, and sensuous. It was vital that I gratify my growing desires.

Oils had altered my way of seeing and feeling.

I became so absorbed in what I was painting as the Venus took final shape that one morning, even after our class in drawing began, I felt compelled to continue. Four of the most advanced apprentices sat behind small tables while Vecchio instructed us in the master's technique with crayons, while the master waited to judge our efforts. But this could go on all day, I felt unhappily, and I could not wait so long. I substituted my brush and began to tint the flesh of my Venus. She was the same size as my supposed cartoon and I believed that no one would notice what I was doing.

I was so involved in coloring her soft skin, I did not notice Bellini approaching me. When he saw what I was doing, he shouted, "No wonder Zuccato dismissed him! He is a disobedient rogue!"

Vecchio hurried to his side and I expected to be beaten.

Bellini declared, "There is no draughtsmanship in his work! He paints too boldly and rapidly. He will never amount to anything. I do not endure dissatisfied apprentices. Release him from my studio."

But when Vecchio saw me looking desolate—I had risked ruin for a few strokes of oil—he said, "Maestro, your brother likes his work."

"Then let him suffer his indulgences. I will not."

"You will not be offended?"

"No more than I have been. This apprentice is of no consequence. Without the ability to draw, his painting is worthless."

I yearned to retort that I had a fine susceptibility to emotion and a great need to be free, with luck I might become a master, too, but I was afraid. Gentile Bellini possessed the power to bar me for life.

Vecchio said, "Maestro, I will take the boy upstairs at once."

Bellini, when he saw my relief, declared angrily, "Do not rejoice, boy. I will warn my brother about your inability to draw and your disobedient ways. He will not find you acceptable either."

Shaken by his vindictiveness, I hesitated to go upstairs. I felt his brother would reject me, too, but Vecchio insisted that I see him. When I was brought before Giovanni Bellini, he had Gentile Bellini's words before him and if he recognized my previous visits to his studio, he did not show it. He stared at me blankly and coldly and stated, "My esteemed brother writes that you stole oils. How can I trust you?"

"Maestro, I could not afford to buy them. I am just an apprentice."

"That is no excuse."

"Maestro, I had to paint in your manner."

Bellini prompted sarcastically, "Because you adore oils?"

"No, Signore," I replied, "it is more than that."

Bellini smiled cynically and waited impatiently for my final excuse.

"Maestro, your palette is different from any I have seen. When I experience your colors, I long to caress them. I am full of new sensations, I feel as well as see. Maestro, I am sorry if I bore you, but your palette is marvelous and I yearn to study it. Please, Maestro, forgive me."

Bellini grew thoughtful and then exclaimed, "I do remember you!"

"Maestro, I was in your studio when you said, '*I draw only in my moment of hesitation, when I must. I prefer to paint, to trust to my hand and to my invention.*' That was why I favored your oils over crayons."

"Even though my brother could punish you drastically? Bar you from every studio in Venice? Exile you from painting completely?"

A black cloud seemed to envelop me, but I had to defend myself, and I knew only one way. I cried out, "Maestro, would you ban me from painting because I favor oils?"

Bellini shrugged, then said, "Vecchio, he is a shrewd one."

"He draws skillfully, Maestro."

"Even though my brother differs?"

Vecchio hesitated and I was afraid he would not support me. I blurted out, "Maestro, your brother was upset by my preference for your style."

I thought he was going to dismiss me even more severely than his brother had, for I had criticized a Bellini. But when he frowned, Vecchio said, "Maestro, what Tiziano expresses, perhaps awkwardly, is so. Your brother has chided me, too, for following your manner instead of his."

"Yet painters, however they prefer oils, must still know how to draw."

"I do, Maestro," I declared. "I have done hundreds of drawings."

"You will have to do far more. Over and over."

"Signore, will you teach me?"

"It depends." He examined my small Venus and said, "You must have painted her on a hot day. Your pigments are not firm and give the impression that she is perspiring. But there is some honesty in it."

"Maestro, may I study with you?"

"I am very busy. But since Vecchio recommends you, you may work as his assistant. As you have done already, on several occasions. Then I will decide whether you will be useful. If you behave yourself."

I could not fall asleep that night. Every sound, every impression stirred me intensely. I sat on my new bed, sketching another foundation for the Venus I intended to paint as soon as I learned the true consistency of oil. Several apprentices snored nearby, and although I hated this noise usually, I pretended that it was noble music. I heard a lute and a soft voice singing above my head and I glanced out the window in the hope that it was Giorgione, but all I could see was a large palazzo with triumphal arches across the canal. Now, however, I felt it was within my reach, if I trusted myself.

I WOULD RATHER TRUST MYSELF

WHAT MAKES a man?

My memories of my youth force me to ask. Once again, in my old age, I am haunted with this question. I ask it often about my older son.

I have done all that is in my power to help him; I have even risked humiliation; yet his childish follies still upset me. To escape this pain I put aside my memories for the moment. I become engrossed in my *Pietà*, recalling how I learned from Giorgione to trust myself, when I hear a commotion on the floor below. I halt; my hand is stricken with despair.

My steward is shouting, "Pomponio, the master must not be disturbed!"

Then I hear my middle-aged son, loud and assertive, defying my steward's declaration. Before I can decide whether to allow this interruption, Pomponio hurries in with two companions and introduces them before I can say that I am too busy to see him.

I observe that Luigi Gerro is a balding, hard-faced, elderly courtier, who dresses as if he were an envoy from an important prince. I think that the female, Bella Ricci, is far too young for my son; she looks no more than sixteen. And while she has a voluptuous body— and I am an expert on such matters—I dislike her bold, coarse expression, although she has a pretty face and sensual black hair. I wonder where he has found her; there are many more attractive courtesans in Venice, as I know well.

I feel angrily that she regards me as in the grave already, even though the courtier views me with deference in spite of the reflection of gold florins I see in his narrow gray eyes. I am surprised that my son, wanting to impress his friends with my wealth, has brought them to my studio instead of to my reception room, which is more elegant and fashionable.

But perhaps, I decide, he needs to prove that he is truly the son of Tiziano Vecellio and that he has my paintings at his disposal.

As I prepare to dismiss them, Gerro bows and says flatteringly, "Maestro, your son was kind enough to invite us to view your famous original paintings that hang in your studio."

I retort curtly, "So that you can judge their worth."

"Maestro, they are beyond such measurements."

"Let us not praise indecently. My son desires to find out how much you can obtain for them when I am gone. That is obvious."

The girl smirks, amused by my frankness, but Gerro replies, "Maestro, Giorgione's Venuses may be pure spirits, idyllic creatures in a dream landscape, but your goddesses are far more alluring and real."

I like his taste even though I still do not trust his praise.

"Maestro, I first saw your paintings when I was a child and ever since they are my favorite work. I had many quarrels in my native Florence with those who prefer the Florentine manner. Once I was thrown out of Michelangelo Buonarroti's studio for pointing out that your colors contain a celestial brightness that no one else has equaled."

That might be true, I think, but he is using this for his own advantage.

Pomponio blurts out, "It is such beauty that makes me want to inherit them. But while you have taken in Orazio as a partner and given him your profitable broker's patent, you have given me nothing."

"I moved heaven and earth to obtain a high position in the church for you. I appealed to popes and emperors and many princely patrons on your behalf, and now there is no one left to appeal to."

"Not even yourself, Papa?"

I am silent. I do not want to reject him, but I cannot give the custody of my work to someone I do not trust.

"Papa, may I show my friends the paintings in the closets?"

I fondle the keys in my belt, tempted to heed his request, but I ask also, "So they can determine the value of my estate?"

Gerro says, "Maestro, I have negotiated art for many lords. Your estimable son merely desires that I report to you on their present value."

"Then why is this young woman's presence required?"

"Papa, her body has great natural gifts. She could entertain you."

I had thought it impossible to be shocked any more but what my son implies shakes me. I wonder, Is Pomponio that greedy for gold?

"You adorned wherever we lived with many beautiful women. Even before my mother died. Even before you wed her. And after she was gone, our quarters were always filled with young, pretty females. Your behavior was the talk of Venice. It was common knowledge. But if you are too old now?"

We do not understand each other and never have, I reflect sadly. But I still crave his regard and respect, and I ask, "Pomponio, if I make you heir to all my paintings, will you establish them in a museum?"

"Whatever I say, you will not believe me." He turns to his friends and adds, "Behold, Luigi, my father may paint like an angel, as you say, but he acts like a devil. And you, Bella, are not good enough for him. But when it suited his pleasure, he was willing enough to conceive me."

Before I can defend myself my other son interrupts me, which is unusual, and screams at him, "How can you bring strangers here when the plague rages outside! How do you know they are free of it! The girl especially. It spreads swiftly among courtesans."

Pomponio grows pale at what he has risked—or is it a desire to end my life, I ask myself with horror—and he replies, "We will go now."

The courtier nods, as if he knows time is on his side, and he takes the courtesan by the arm and leads her out. Pomponio follows, at a distance.

Orazio gives me the oils I need, says, "You can finish the *Pietà*."

"I hope so." I am so upset by Pomponio's behavior I am in no mood to paint, but I always seek to be strong and so I try to go on.

Orazio says fiercely, "Father, do not ask how I obtained them!"

"Was it that difficult?"

"Do not reproach me. The plague grows worse in Venice. Father, you work too hard. Would you like me to finish the *Pietà* for you?"

"No!" Yet I recall that I did such work for Giovanni Bellini and even for Giorgione. "Do you think Pomponio's irresponsibility is my fault?"

"Father, you must not question yourself. It will make you ill."

"Sometimes, I think he is still a child."

"Your gifts obscure his own career. He can never achieve what you have and so he is always in rebellion against what you are."

But there is sadness in Orazio and I feel he is talking about himself, too, and I wish I could help him become a better painter. Yet, with all of my instruction and encouragement, we both know that he will always remain mediocre. This time he suggests that I work alone.

When he is gone, I think, Children, at best, are never quite as you are or wish them to be. And so, as I rock back and forth in my loneliness and misgivings, the question rises again to haunt me.

How does one become a man?

Giovanni Bellini, who was childless, treated those he favored as if they were his children. When I developed a facility with oils, he made me feel like a son. In a few months I learned to render landscapes and draperies so that they resembled the actual thing. Then he allowed me to paint in some of his backgrounds. He was having so much difficulty keeping up with the demand for his work that he assigned this to those in his studio he trusted. I became one of his preferred pupils.

But I was not content. I desired to follow Giorgione's manner. His colors continued to stimulate my imagination and I craved a companion.

When Big George invited me to paint with him and set up an easel for me in his studio, I was excited. Then I was confused. His model was naked. As she lay on the couch in front of us, her flesh distracted me. It was soft and sensuous and her dark hair heightened the whiteness of her skin and her breasts were round and full. She was the first naked model in my experience and I felt a mixture of shame and desire. Yet I was proud that I was fifteen and that in the entire bottega, only Big George was taller than I now. There was the start of a beard on my ruddy face and my pubic hair was thick enough to satisfy me.

If Giorgione noticed my agitation, he did not show it. He began to paint and he acted as if I should do the same.

By the next sitting I felt more at ease and when the nude was finished a week later, I saw her only as a subject for my Venus, although my desire for a young, pretty girl increased. I wondered if that was why Big George had worn fine velvet when he had painted her, listened to music, and drank wine to refresh himself. He treated me like a friend and I sipped wine with him, at his invitation. But I did not put velvet on my back. I did not own any. I enjoyed the music, but I was afraid that he did not like my Venus.

He sensed my anxiety and he said, "It has excellence." He paused. "But . . ." I felt a criticism in him.

"You are too real for my taste. I prefer my Venuses more spiritual."

"Even in bed?" I blurted out, suddenly unable to contain myself.

He regarded me wryly for a moment, and then burst out laughing. I turned away, my face aflame, but he halted me at the door.

"Tiziano, would you like me to introduce you to the genuine thing?"

I nodded passionately, and then was sorry I had revealed this much.

He merely shrugged and said, "I will arrange it. Bellini will not mind if you go out with me. I know two charming ladies."

Several nights later he took me out of the studio by a back door. He wore black velvet that set off vividly his dark hair and white skin. He had lent me a gray doublet and a cape, for I had nothing to fit this occasion, and while they were large on me, they made me look older and I liked my appearance. He put on a sword and fastened a dagger to his side, and when he saw my alarm, he said, "There is no need to be apprehensive, my friend, but it is wise to be cautious. We have far fewer murders here than in Florence, but we still have our share. If it is evident that we are armed, it is less likely that we will be attacked."

"Exactly!" I declared, sounding more confident than I felt.

Once we were on the street I was more at ease, for he walked with a familiarity and confidence that was reassuring. I hurried to keep up with his longer stride, and I was grateful that he regarded me as a friend and not as a pupil. At the humpbacked bridge we were accosted by a young woman. She wore red satin trimmed with yellow lace, black silk stockings, and foot-high chopines. I thought her a brazen, tawdry sight, but I noticed that she possessed an excitingly voluptuous body and I was tempted to accept her inviting gestures.

She ignored me and addressed Big George in a heavily slurred Venetian accent, "Most magnificent Signore, I can show you many pleasures."

"It is a common thought," he replied. "Only I am occupied else-where."

"I am a daughter of the Republic. I know all of love's practices."

"So do many. But we are interested in simpler things."

He disregarded her efforts to stop us, and said, as we paused be-fore a large, pleasant house, "It is no great trick to find courtesans. Their names and addresses are published and this book is the most popular reading in Venice. But my ladies are old friends and they are content with company, not crowns. That street whore could disgust you and repel you forever from the pleasures of the human body."

The residence was on the water; there was a second-floor terrace, and I liked the arched doorway with the finely carved lion's head.

I knew many courtesans possessed learning and when we were greeted politely by two well-dressed women, who looked like middle-aged matrons, I feared it was going to be merely a conversational evening. Big George introduced me to Clarabella and Isabella Montoni as a friend who had joined him in Giovanni Bellini's bottega, which elicited immediate approval and the difference in our ages was ignored. I was surprised that they were brown-haired, which was not the fashion, and that they were plump rather than pretty. But they wore gowns that were cut low and I saw bulging breasts which filled me with passion. They served us a soothing wine and Isabella sang a sweet Venetian love song while her sister accompanied her on the lute, and this enticed my senses further.

After Giorgione disappeared with Clarabella, Isabella led me into her bedroom. Everything in it was designed for sensuality: the thick Turkish carpets, the red Levantine drapes, the pink bedspread, the soft lights, the fragrant perfume, and the bed shaped like a gondola.

When she was naked I realized why my friend favored the sisters. Isabella's hips were inviting and as she pulled me down upon her, they undulated and yet were yielding. She guided me so skillfully that I hardly realized that she was the teacher and I was the pupil. I felt submerged in her flesh and her spacious bed was even more like a gondola as in our lovemaking it seemed to rock back and forth. Our consummation seemed to occur together and was easier than I expected, but one thing did trouble me. I was so quick. But she assured me this was my virility, and that the second time would be longer and even more satisfying.

She demonstrated her skill again and now while I lay quiescent,

yet gratified, I wondered if Isabella Montoni had posed for Giorgione, for she resembled a nude I had seen in his paintings.

We left them after Clarabella kissed Giorgione farewell and
Isabella suggested that I return soon.

He was silent until we reached his studio. Then he said, "They
are rather plain, but they are daughters of Eve. Fine for a start."

The next few months I visited Isabella when I had a scudo to
spare. Giorgione always made sure that I had a coin to give her,
although she never asked. She gave me the feeling she preferred my
young virility to the older men who supported her. I came to believe
she would have granted me her favors without a fee, that she truly
enjoyed my youthful exuberance, which gave me the greatest gratification of all. But when I assured Big George that I would repay
him, he laughed and said, "It is my pleasure. I like to see my friends
content. But do not take her seriously. She is skillful, pleasant, but
there are others more desirable."

One day I was assisting Giorgione in his studio when Vecchio
asked me to help him lift a canvas, which he said was too heavy for
one man. By now I was allowed the freedom of the palazzo except
for Gentile's studio, and I went to aid him reluctantly, for I was
absorbed in the nude I was painting with Giorgione. I was seeking
to create another Venus, but neither the plump model nor Isabella
Montoni fitted my conception.

Then I almost dropped Vecchio's canvas in my distraction. He was
painting a portrait of the girl I had met years ago, whom he had
introduced as his niece, and whose attractive appearance I had never
forgotten.

Her beauty put me in such an exciting mood. Violante's long
red hair streamed down her back, her eyes were a bright blue, and
her face possessed a delicacy I thought delightful and fascinating.
And perhaps it was my need to fall in love with someone my own
age, with someone romantic, but her living flesh seemed to reveal
itself through the shapely young head rising from the long throat,
the dainty little nose, and the round chin and full, soft cheeks and
the firm, red lips. I felt as one possessed.

Vecchio said, "Violante, Tiziano is a big boy now. He paints with
excellence. Especially with oils. Which he prefers, thanks to me."

I resented his paternal tone but I sought to be the courtier as I
replied, "I would be honored to paint such a charming model."

Neither of them replied. I was about to return to Giorgione's side, disappointed that I was ignored, when Vecchio caught his hand on a nail. The bleeding did not stop until he wrapped the wound with a cloth, and then he could not paint because of the pain. He did not want this sitting to be wasted—he was almost finished with the portrait—and he asked me to finish the sleeves.

She wore gold brocade that was lined with violet and her fashionable low-cut gown stimulated my desire. I tried to concentrate on her sleeves and to give the fabric the right tone, although that was not easy. I preferred to paint her face and her flesh. I was confused; I felt awkward and when I came to her hands Vecchio halted me.

"Tiziano, I am better with the flesh. I will do that."

I felt I had surpassed him already in my skin tones but I was still an apprentice and I obeyed him. Violante had not said a word.

I bowed before her as if she were a great lady and said, "I trust the signorina does not object to my humble efforts to express her beauty."

She smiled and said in a voice that surprised me with its resonance, "I understand that you are the most skillful pupil in the bottega."

Vecchio interrupted impatiently, "When he heeds me. Violante, that is enough for today. Tiziano, I will call you if I need you again."

I assumed this was the end of such a sitting, for Vecchio's dismissal was emphatic. But several days later he requested my presence again. He sat in his studio, his hand bandaged, and he told me disconsolately, "My fingers have swollen and I am unable to hold a brush. Yet this work is promised to one of the Council of Ten and I cannot put him off any longer, or I will lose my fee. He wants a portrait that will please him, of an authentic Venetian beauty, and so I chose my niece. Models are expensive and she is suitable, if a little young. Her complexion and hair are becoming the fashion and I am gifted at illuminating them."

Most suitable, I thought, but I said, "Am I worthy to assist you?"

"Enough to brighten her hands, hair, and complexion."

It was unlike Vecchio to be in an evil humor and I realized this portrait mattered much to him. So I sought to give it a finish that would please all of us. But gradually, I saw that while she possessed purity, she also reflected sensuality. And that this was different from Vecchio's view.

The next few days he watched me anxiously while I expressed my own taste more and more. Violante sat silently, a typical model in her patience, and I sensed that she had modeled before, perhaps frequently.

There was a horrible stillness when I finished. I felt Vecchio was dissatisfied, for he complained about the pain in his hand, and then he did something I did not expect. He asked Violante her opinion.

She said, "I must be going home now. The sun will be setting."

"You could stay here. You have done so in the past."

"But that worries you. Even though I am your relative."

"Violante, you cannot tell me the truth either?"

"I am expected. My mother will be upset."

"It is a short walk, not miles." But when he saw that she looked unhappy, on the verge of tears, he put his hand caressingly on her arm, with an emotion I felt was excessive for an uncle speaking to his niece, and declared, "I want the best for you. So that your portrait will be like a cool morning and attract a worthy husband. But he has painted you like a hot, passionate day. It is too sensuous and too risky."

She flushed and said, "You promised I would not wed against my will."

I was embarrassed, although I did not want to alter one stroke of my brush—in my view she was the Venus I desired, and it did not matter that she was dressed—and I started to leave, but Vecchio halted me.

He said, "Tiziano, I am not ungrateful for your assistance."

"Then why are you so distressed, Signore?"

"Violante is a nice Venetian girl, but here she is like a courtesan."

"Or a Venus," I retorted quickly. "Of the most honorable lineage."

He blushed, as if I had touched a vulnerable spot.

She asked, "Will you sign it?"

"Why not! He is my student, too. He filled in for me, as he has for Giovanni Bellini and Giorgione. It is the common practice."

"But his strokes are more individual."

I felt a sudden joy. She sounded as if she were defending me.

"We are all individuals in this bottega. But that does not mean that Signor Labia will accept this work. If he does not, I lose much money."

I told Giorgione about this and he said, "Vecchio has a smaller gift than some of us and he needs your aid to enlarge his own. Your palette already contains a vivacity and a strength that his lacks."

"Is Violante truly his niece?"

"It is hard to know. There are rumors that she is his daughter, but that he does not admit it for fear it will lessen her. Tiziano, I would move carefully there. She is probably a virgin, which is difficult, and he expects anyone who fancies her to wed her. But he desires a prosperous husband for her, not a painter. And she has no dowry."

A week later Vecchio ordered me to paint another portrait of Violante. He said his hand was not healed, but there was a demand for a second painting from his brush and he could not afford to wait. Since it was the usual practice for an apprentice to do much of the preliminary work for a master, I did not question Vecchio. But I did not trust his excuse, and I asked Giorgione—as a friend—his opinion.

He said, "Alberto Labia is so pleased with the first portrait—he says this girl is like a dream come to life, the most beautiful thing he has seen in years—he wants another rendition for his personal pleasure."

"Why does Vecchio need me? He did most of the first portrait."

"You gave her skin and hair a vividness that his delicate touch lacks."

"Big George, I do not care for this situation."

"Tiziano, you have nothing to lose. If Alberto Labia does not like the painting, which is unlikely, Vecchio will be blamed. If he does, and he is inclined already, our friend will use you again."

"My name will not be on it! Although it is my work!"

"I have done work that others claim. Even I cannot measure how much of Giovanni Bellini's painting contains my brush. But it is the work that matters. To the rest, I am indifferent. My signature is of little consequence. An intelligent eye will recognize my manner whoever puts his name to it."

But I was eager for recognition, especially in Violante's eyes.

The second portrait was different. Instead of posing Violante in a formal and ornamental brocade gown, Vecchio arranged her in a flowing yellow robe, which hung loosely and enticingly, to suggest sensuality.

Vecchio muttered, "Labia desires her flesh to glow, her hair to burn like a flame. The patrician is fascinated by red tints."

But I told myself that Violante was still a girl, still closer to my age, and not to Labia's, not to Vecchio's, not even to Giorgione's.

I tried to remember the best of what I had learned. I did not begin this picture elaborately, as in the old manner, but trusted to my mood and invention. I used dark shadows in the background to heighten the lighter tones of her person. Since Raphael of Urbino and Michelangelo Buonarroti had painted finished work by the age of fifteen, I felt I could, too. Giovanni Bellini had instructed me in the control of natural light and color to endow the figure and the flesh with a reality that was palpable. But these were only details, I thought, as I followed the design of his madonnas. I saw Violante's robe as a veil covering her flesh and I felt that the richness of my colors bestowed upon her portrait her natural elegance.

As I struggled to finish this work so that it seemed to be composed of living flesh rather than of paint, I felt that Vecchio was upset by it and I was worried that he would interfere.

One day he called in Giorgione to observe what I was doing. Neither of them said anything to me, but the next morning Vecchio was absent.

When Violante saw my anxiety, she assured me, "It is not on your account."

"Do you think that Big George spoke on my behalf?"

"It is possible. He likes your vitality. But Palma has to work below. The duke of Ferrara is angry that Giovanni Bellini has failed to produce the work he commissioned years ago, and Palma and Big George have been ordered to prepare something that the master can present to His Highness as the work in progress. My uncle informed me that you should continue without him, and accompany me home afterward, but before dark. Signor Labia waits impatiently for this second portrait."

I painted exuberantly, elated by this approval.

Violante lived nearby and the day was magnificent. Spring was in the air and as I escorted her home, I offered to take her in a gondola, but she said that was not necessary, that it was an extravagance.

She did not return the next day, although the portrait needed more work, and I was disconsolate. Just as I feared I would not see her again, she appeared a week later, accompanied by Vecchio, who said, "I cannot remain here, Bellini still requires my presence. Tiziano, you must finish today. The patrician refuses to wait any longer."

When I finished later that day, reluctantly, I asked, "Violante, will I see you again?" and she shrugged and said, "It is not likely."

As she saw the pain on my face, she added hurriedly, "You paint me like a goddess. It is unusual."

"You are what is unusual. You are . . ."

She interrupted, "Do not swear. It is too Venetian."

"I thought you were."

"We come from Bergamo. Palma brought me here at an early age."

"May I visit you?"

"It is not allowed."

I felt she was afraid of the consequences, yet eager to continue.

For she said suddenly, "I will come again to sit for him. I will find an excuse. And although he is noted for his glowing colors and delicacy, he knows these portraits are praised for your passion and brightness."

"You are very kind. Thank you, Violante."

"Big George told Vecchio this and that he could trust you. And that while you painted me as a Venus, you painted me also as a madonna."

The second portrait, which Vecchio signed, was lauded so widely there were more requests for such paintings. This was the first time that his work had received popular approval and that he had earned money for his signature, and he felt compelled to fulfill these commissions. But he was so busy assisting Giovanni in what had become the most vital work in the entire bottega that I became essential to him as his substitute.

I realized that Vecchio had to trust me as he commanded me to portray Violante in various poses suitable for visual pleasure.

Then the plague settled on much of Venice, but when our side of the Canal remained free of the pestilence Vecchio moved Violante into his studio to reside there for the duration of the affliction. He had his own personal quarters and now he could make even better use of her.

Giorgione was amused that I did not want to leave the palazzo now. He asked me why I had not visited Isabella lately; he pointed out that she was in the safe quarter of Venice and that she esteemed my virility.

I mumbled that I was too busy for such frivolity and he replied, "Isabella says that you have natural gifts," but when I refused to pursue this matter, he added, "I will tell her that you fear the plague. You may still desire her skill when your infatuation flounders on the rock of virginity. Do not be too reverent in your new-found devotion."

I was startled by his recklessness. The plague struck terror in everyone, but not Big George. I wondered, Does he think himself immune? Or is this part of the same indifference he displays to recognition?

While Giovanni Bellini labored on a mythological bacchanal for the duke of Ferrara, and Giorgione and Vecchio assisted him, I was alone with Violante. Gradually I came to feel that she desired me as much as I did her. When I took her hand to arrange it across her breast, so that she would appear wistful, I felt that her heart leaped at my touch.

Plague-ridden Venice was remote. I scented myself and noticed that her brilliant red hair was carefully combed for each sitting. I called her my madonna and viewed her as my Venus and desired her passionately.

One night I worked until the moon had risen. The plague had subsided and Vecchio, who always came upstairs at the end of the day to see that Violante was attended properly when she went to bed, did not appear. I learned that he had been sent to Ferrara—against his wishes—to inform the duke that the painting was ready to be viewed, so that Bellini could find out whether the conception was as his patron wished, and I was jubilant, for I knew that no one would interrupt us.

I took her to the door of the room that Vecchio had converted into a bedroom for her. As she stared at me, I sensed that her wish was the same as mine. Our first kiss developed into a fervent embrace. Then she drew back, but I could not restrain myself any longer. I saw the canopied bed, the madonna in blue over it, and a drawing I had done of her, and I hear her cry out, "Tiziano, this is folly!" but when I put my arms around her, I realized that I could do anything I pleased.

I was glad that Isabella had taught me some of the arts of love, for Violante was, as I hoped and yet feared, a virgin. But my entrance was easy and we fitted each other and she was soft and yielding. And I was glad I had the presence of mind to use the devices that Isabella had given me to prevent conception. Afterward, I assured her, "I love you, Violante, I do. You believe me, beloved, you do?"

"What am I to believe, Tiziano? Will you marry me now?"

"I am a painter. I have my life ahead of me."

"You have the divine gift. You have made me beautiful."

"You are beautiful."

She fondled my hand as we lay side by side and she whispered, "This is the best part of you. But you must go now, before Vecchio returns."

"He is in Ferrara. Violante, you are the glory of my world."

"And some day our love will lie in ashes. Do not swear, Tiziano."

"That will never be! How could I abuse what I adore?"

Violante pushed me out of her bed and I stole back to my quarters.

When Vecchio returned several days later he was preoccupied. Bellini's painting, which he had titled *The Feast of the Gods,* displeased the duke of Ferrara, who said the women were too cold, unreal.

Vecchio took this as a personal slight, for he had painted most of them, and he told me that Alfonso d'Este was insolent, a barbarian.

He was relieved that no one in the Palazzo Bellini had caught the plague, and pleased that I had finished another portrait that he could sign and sell, and he was hopeful that it would increase his reputation.

I was grateful that he suspected nothing. The next time we were in his studio so he could decide on a subject for another portrait, he told Violante that she could return home, for the plague had ended.

She nodded and averted her eyes from me.

He said, "Tiziano, I will do the next portrait of Violante myself."

"Signore, I thought you were pleased with my humble efforts."

"Your brush was competent, but you are too young to give the portraits the warmth they require."

"I am eighteen," I declared valiantly.

"You may pretend that you are, but I know better." However, when Vecchio saw my unhappiness at being reduced in age, especially before a pretty young woman, he added, "You must not take my admonitions unkindly, Tiziano. After all, remember, I am almost old enough to be your father."

A new interference drives me back to my old age. I am luxuriating in my memory of my first love, one of my fondest, when a friar hurries into my main studio. It is impossible to ignore him, for he is by my side like a gray shadow. He has come unannounced, too, as if to avoid being turned away and introduces himself as Fra Angelico.

The young friar is deathly pale, with an angular face that refuses to smile, his lips are thin and bloodless, and he informs me,

"My parents named me after that accomplished and devout artist. They desired me to follow him, but I preferred to serve only Jesus."

"What is your present resolution?"

"I am a Franciscan brother in the Frari church."

Then I realize that he is staring at my *Pietà* and that when he sees it is unfinished, there is no sympathy in his eyes but disapproval. I ask, "Is this an official visit?"

"I am instructed to inquire when the *Pietà* will be completed."

"Because the plague prevails and I am very old?"

"Maestro, what happens if God should take you before it is done?"

I reply angrily, "It will be finished, one way or another."

"Our agreement reads that this *Pietà* must be by your own hand."

"What will happen if circumstances should halt me?"

"I cannot say. But the plague has slain a quarter of our population and at your advanced age, Maestro, you are certainly vulnerable."

After he is gone I wonder if anyone else can finish my *Pietà*, should that be necessary. I cannot ask Orazio, he lacks the touch. None of my assistants please me, as I pleased Giorgione and Vecchio.

TELL THE TRUTH

ARGUMENTS OVER THE QUESTION of who painted the final oil of *The Feast of the Gods* have upset me for many years. Legend and Giorgio Vasari state that Giovanni Bellini did this allegorical bacchanal, with some aid from me, when he became too old and feeble to complete this large work. But I, caught between *what is* and *what was* and *what might have been,* remember that many hands, even Giorgione's, labored on this sumptuous painting.

This started shortly after I expressed my love for Violante, when the master began a new conception of his commission for the duke of Ferrara.

Vecchio told me, "Giovanni wants you to do some of the underpainting. He likes the way I have taught you to render landscapes."

Giorgione added later, "And because the old man is dissatisfied with how Palma performed on the previous request of Alfonso d'Este."

I was dissatisfied, too. I wished I had been assigned to paint the figures. Yet I also felt flattered that Giovanni desired my brush. I knew it was dangerous to outdo an older, established painter like

Vecchio, and I wanted his favor so that I could court Violante, but my portraits of her had increased my ambition. And I was eager to secure the duke of Ferrara's attention and esteem. The d'Este family was illustrious and wealthy and renowned throughout Italy for their patronage of artists.

As I entered Giovanni's studio now, I felt that the foothills had been traversed, today the true climb was ahead of me. I hoped that Violante would be able to accompany me, if she did not hinder me. I had begun a self-portrait and I was painting myself as a handsome man, with a trim red beard worthy of a patrician and eyes and lips that burned like fire.

I was surprised that the master was devoting most of his energy to his preparatory drawings. This indicated to me that he was hesitant about his conception and planned to paint without his usual freedom. But I labored patiently to create the landscape as he sketched it, even as I yearned to paint the nudes that fascinated me. I felt that Bellini idealized his nudes as he did his madonnas and that this was wrong. They reminded me of the Botticelli Venuses I had viewed, which were too slender and virginal for my taste.

Vecchio supervised my brush, while the master corrected it, usually ordering me to be more meticulous in my details, while Giorgione was employed to give the painting his softness and elegance.

The next few weeks I saw Violante briefly and never intimately. She was always in the company of Vecchio, but I felt that now she desired me even more, as I did her, for each time she was in my presence she became beautiful. I feared that Vecchio would detect our feelings, but he was so occupied with *The Feast of the Gods* he did not seem to notice them.

At the same time Bellini surrounded himself with luxury and friends. His studio had become the center of art and he was holding court. He stored his oils in a Venetian lacquered cabinet whose finish glowed and he regarded them as if they were precious jewels. I was grateful I no longer had to mix oils; this was left to lesser apprentices; I had improved enough to graduate from this chore. Giorgione, Vecchio, and I did most of the painting while Bellini sat at a fine Venetian table, struggled with his preparatory drawings, and held forth on the virtues of his oil painting. He was proud of the thick rug at his feet, which the Turkish Sultan had given his brother as a present for two portraits.

The studio filled with painters and advanced apprentices, as if the painting of *The Feast of the Gods* was the event most worth viewing in *La Serenissima*. I was surprised that even Gentile, who had aged, came in to see how the work progressed and to exchange opinions with Giovanni. He looked past me as if I were not there. Then, one day, he was joined by the middle-aged Vittore Carpaccio, once his favorite pupil, but now regarded as the strongest rival of the brothers in the Republic. I was also surprised by the Bellini politeness to this slight, wrinkled, dark-complexioned artist. His lush panoramas of Venice pleased the city, but I did not share the popular view. These pageants of Carpaccio were too much like illustrations for me and I did not care for them.

I had some feeling for Sebastiano del Piombo, who was only a few years older than I. Like myself, he was a pupil of Giovanni's but he preferred Giorgione's manner. Sometimes I felt he resented that I was advancing faster than he was, but when I mentioned this, he denied it hotly. His pale, small face lit up and his sad, heavy-lidded eyes glowed and he said that his friendship with me was dear to him, that I used color better than any other apprentice and perhaps we could be partners some day. But the only painter I could think of joining was Giorgione, and even there, I was not certain that that was what I finally desired.

Bonifazio Pitati was closer to me in age, but I doubted I could trust him. This wiry, agile youth, black-haired and dark-eyed, called even Palma Vecchio "Your Magnificence," and I felt he had three hands. One for Vecchio's manner, one for Giovanni Bellini's, and one for his own.

Giovanni Antonio da Pordenone was a little past twenty, and he insisted that the younger apprentices call him by his full name. I felt that this tall, intense artist desired to rival Giorgione, and while he was no longer an apprentice, he continued to frequent Bellini's bottega, as if that would bring him the best commissions.

I ignored Paris Bordone, for this fat, stocky brown-haired boy was no older than I and looked much younger, although he trailed me about the studio and imitated me every chance he got. In turn, I was ignored by Lorenzo Lotto, who was the same age as Giorgione. He, too, was an acknowledged artist and I liked what paintings of his that I had seen. But he wore monkish robes although he was not a member of any religious order, and he seemed in such fear of God that it was wearisome.

Then two courtiers entered the studio and brought a new excitement. Ercole Strozzi and Pietro Bembo, who were friends, were poet-emissaries from powerful patrons for whom Giovanni was working. Yet neither of these noblemen, who had inherited their position and wealth, seemed concerned whether Bellini satisfied their lords. They appeared to be more interested in impressing us with their humanism.

Giorgione said to me cynically, "They pretend that the greatest excellence is in man, but they waste their breath. And our time."

I was not sure I agreed. Strozzi was heir to a famous name; he came from the Ferrarese branch of a noted Florentine family. But he had been born lame and he had to walk with a crutch, and his square face, while strong, possessed a coldness that his elegant manner could not hide. And while his master, the new duke of Ferrara, was reputed to loathe him, Strozzi was such a connoisseur of art that Alfonso d'Este had chosen him to negotiate the present commission with Bellini. His presence encouraged me and I felt that Bembo could be of benefit to me, also.

This Venetian patrician was younger than his companion and properly formed, tall and slim, and his features fascinated me. Pietro Bembo had one of the most paintable faces I had seen. His head was very long, with an aquiline nose that was almost as long and dominant, and vivid gray eyes that seemed to see much, and a sharp, high jaw. Moreover, he was an envoy from Alfonso's sister, Isabella Gonzaga, who ruled the small but influential duchy of Mantua, and was one of the best of patrons.

I longed to paint these courtiers, but they ignored me. Yet I saw that when I painted Bembo watched me. I wondered why.

One day as I painted a tree while Bellini sketched a figure and every one was about him, although he had not used any color on *The Feast of the Gods,* Strozzi said suddenly, "I hear that Leonardo has lost still another commission because he has failed to finish it on time."

I felt he was goading the master, who had become dilatory. And now, I observed, everybody was attending Strozzi, as the courtier desired.

Bembo replied, "That is not unusual. I hear that our Holiness is uttering the same complaint about Buonarroti."

Bellini said, "We must not be restricted. It cramps our hand."

Strozzi said, "My lord desires to know when you will be done."

"When it is done. I cannot be hurried. It will show in my work."

"My lord's patience is not eternal."

"Neither is my hand. I will not take unjust liberties with it."

Bembo interrupted. "Unlike my good friend from Ferrara, my

mistress will allow you to pick your own theme, provided it comes from the antique."

" 'And has a fine meaning,' she says. 'And must be something allegorical.' She is as demanding as her brother. If she wants a Bellini, she must be patient. Besides," I heard him mutter, "how can I believe her?"

"You can believe Her Highness. I give you my word."

"I am a painter of religious works. I have no feeling for paganism."

"Signor Giovanni, what will satisfy you?"

Bembo was so insistent that I thought, Isabella must want to outdo her brother very much, for Giovanni had not even begun her commission.

"My lord, write her that the treatment of the theme will be dictated by the imagination of the man who is painting the picture, and that I do not like to have my style cramped. I am used to taking my own time in painting. Only God can tell me how swiftly to pursue my gifts."

Bembo nodded to indicate that he agreed with every word and sat down to write this letter, quite pleased with himself.

Vecchio, Piombo, and Lotto crowded close to Giovanni to express their approval, while Giorgione left, looking bored and indifferent.

Strozzi glowered, angry that his friend had outwitted him, and said abruptly, "Signor Bellini, you must finish your work for Alfonso before you paint anything else. Otherwise, this commission will be revoked."

"My lord, that is not necessary. There are always other works that occupy me. Even now the Senate of Venice awaits my pleasure."

Believing that this discussion would continue endlessly in spite of the agreement, for I felt that the master did not truly wish to paint for Isabella, whatever he professed—she was too demanding and insistent for his nature—I turned back to *The Feast of the Gods.* It looked neglected and I had a desperate need to do something that would make me feel better. I was tired of painting trees; it was a month since Violante and I had known each other—spring was in the air and I missed her painfully; I had even been unable to finish my self-portrait. So I began to paint a nude over the figure that Bellini had sketched into the lower right corner. He had used a pedant's knowledge of anatomy—like an old man, I thought—and I felt that I could express sensuality better. To show my emotion, to create the luminous tone of female flesh, I sought to depict a robust and palpable Venus in the image of Violante.

I was starting to feel in command of my brush as the nude developed a natural fullness when Bembo exclaimed, "What an enchanting signorina!"

Everyone stared at me and suddenly Giovanni Bellini shouted, "I am not averse to nude women, but they must be in their proper place. No nude is intended here and must not be allowed."

Bembo said, "You must not be harsh. His painting evokes pleasure."

"When his signature goes on a picture, then he may do as he wishes. But when my name is on it, it is my responsibility. And his brush is not up to the standard of the Bellini bottega. His colors are disorderly."

But when Bembo preferred the Venus as I had painted her, Bellini did not scratch out the nude as he had intended to do, although he was still very angry at me.

Then Bembo asked to see some of my work.

I had none. Whatever I had done bore someone else's name.

Bembo asked, "Young man, are you afraid to allow it to be viewed?"

"No, my lord, but as an apprentice I am not allowed to sign my name."

"You are a gifted one. You will challenge all of these men some day. Your brush is more like a caress than a stroke. You must work on."

This consoled me until Bellini informed me that my services were no longer required on *The Feast of the Gods*. Piombo replaced me and I was ordered to clean the studio, which took up almost all my time.

I offered to assist Vecchio and he snarled like a suspicious father, "You have abused my friendship. There was much of Violante in that nude you put in that bacchanal. I will not allow you to indulge in such liberties from now on. She will not model for you any more."

Giorgione was absent—he had gone to his native Castelfranco—and I was too disheartened to lift a brush. I hovered around the edges of the commission for Alfonso and hoped that Bembo and Strozzi would return. Both poet-emissaries had gone back to their courts and the excitement that had pervaded the studio had left with them. Giovanni painted the figures himself and ignored me, while I was placed in the charge of Lorenzo Lotto, who had become one of his assistants.

The short, heavy, homely Lotto, who had tried to auction twenty of his pictures and had sold only two, and then for a pittance, was in a vile humor. He ordered me to paint a harpsichord cover.

It was a strange thing to me and I asked him how to do it.

"With your hands," he sneered. "You are such an accomplished artist."

I recalled that Botticelli had painted banners and *cassoni*, and so, while I was unhappy, I did my best. But when I spoiled the cover, I was punished. I was made to paint furniture, a task I despised. I could not look at *The Feast of the Gods* now. That hurt too much.

ALTHOUGH I KNOW

ALTHOUGH I KNOW

I cannot see in the half-dark

I know I will be able to see
in the remaining half-light

Or what are measurements for
If not to serve us

Stymean Karlen

I FELT completely ignored by Giovanni Bellini, and it was as if I did not exist. It was a harsh situation and I could not endure such a painful condition. I decided to flee to Florence, although I did not know anyone there and I had no money. It was a heartrending decision, for I was in love with Venice.

One morning, soon after I was put in the charge of the dour Lorenzo Lotto, when he descended into the cellar to relieve himself I deserted the cupboard I was decorating and tiptoed up to Giorgione's studio. He was still away in Castelfranco, and I needed the canvas bag in which he stored his brushes. He used it also to pack possessions, but I had none. As an apprentice I did not even own the clothes on my back and the brushes I used were the property of the bottega. But I could not exist without them, and so I took the bag, and I added crayon, charcoal, and chalk, for the Florentines preferred skillful draughtsmen. I borrowed a cape of Giorgione's, too, for while it was big on me, the velvet lining was warm and the nights were cool even though summer was approaching.

Then as I started toward the door I paused. I was frightened. My uncle Antonio, who resided nearby, would beat me if he caught me, and so would my father, and my mother would weep, but I could not return to Cadore; there was no painting in my birthplace. I would rather starve. And I probably would on the road to Florence, I reflected bitterly, if I survived. It was dangerous to travel there without an armed guard.

Yet not to paint was to die. A great anger rose within me and I could not submit any more. I started out. I held one of Giorgione's lutes in my hand—it must be worth something, I felt, for he owned the best musical instruments, and I needed money to buy food—and I had the bag in my other hand and was at the door when Lotto blocked my way.

He went to hit me, for I could not protect myself, then someone caught his arm. It was Big George, who had hurried in after him. Since he towered over the diminutive Lotto, my grim custodian desisted but he did snarl, "This boy is stealing. He must be flogged."

Giorgione replied, "He is not stealing. I ordered him to deliver my brushes to a courtier who was to bring them to me in Castelfranco. But I had to return unexpectedly. Tiziano is in my service, too."

"Bellini will view this circumstance differently. This apprentice was leaving without his permission. I must report it to the master."

"And shall I remind him that you touched up one of his madonnas and sold it as your own? Bellini will be much offended."

"Giorgio Barbarelli, you have no proof."

"Your patron approached me first. He turned to you only when I refused him. Now he boasts he has a genuine Bellini, even with your name on it."

"What can I tell the master about this apprentice? Vecellio was put into my custody."

"Tell him nothing."

"He might ask me about this boy's whereabouts and I cannot afford to lose my position with him. As it is I am impoverished."

"Your concern with your financial situation is tedious."

"You are a difficult man, and irresponsible. You will end badly."

"Blame me. No one believes the truth. And God will forgive you."

When Lotto was gone I felt like weeping but it was not manly. I pretended that the moisture in my eyes was sweat and I began to explain, to apologize, and Giorgione cut me short, "Never apologize, never explain."

"I want to express my gratitude."

"It is not necessary."

"You are not angry about the lute? Or the cape?"

"I have others. Although you did take the best lute." He glanced into the bag and said, laughingly, "I would have taken better brushes."

Offended, for I felt he was making fun of me, I retorted, "Giorgione, I took what I used. I prefer thick brushes."

"You will prefer many before you are satisfied. Now let us not be so hasty." He sat down, still out of breath from having rushed up the high, winding stone stairway, looking heavier than usual, as if he had eaten too much in Castelfranco. He added, irritably and impatiently for him, "Tiziano, you can sit down, too. You are not my servant."

I did hesitantly, not quite sure what I was.

I have forgotten much of what has happened—my life has been long, I have been in the center of a multitude of enterprises, I have painted more pictures than I can remember—but what followed is one of the most significant and vivid memories of my existence.

Giorgione stared at me, his large, dark-brown eyes thoughtful and penetrating, as if to observe all of me, while I waited anxiously for his judgment. I heard my blood beat deafeningly in my ears. I was even more frightened than before, but my anguish was mixed with excitement and yearning.

He declared, "You cannot remain with Giovanni Bellini any longer."

"That is why I . . ."

He ignored what I was saying. "Yet Florence would be a grievous error. Wherever you were born, at heart you are a Venetian."

I longed to embrace him, but I did not want to be embarrassed.

"You are gifted enough to venture on your own."

"You are kind."

"I am not kind," he said sharply. "I am never kind when it comes to painting. That is for fools and mediocrities. But you are not old enough to set up your own workshop. It would not be allowed."

I was so overwhelmed with his praise I did not know what to say.

He sighed, then said abruptly, "There is only one solution!"

"What is that?" Was he going to get rid of me after all?

"You will assist me." He must have seen the doubt in my eyes, for he added, "I will not rule you. You can paint in any manner you please."

I did not wholly believe him and I was not certain I desired to be totally free. I asked, "You mean I will be your apprentice now?"

"No!" He was angry and impatient with me. "I did not say you will be my assistant. I said that 'You will assist me! As an equal.'"

My blood cried in my ears, "Yes! Yes!" but I had to remind him, he looked so self-satisfied suddenly, "What about the Venetian Guild of Painters? I have not completed my seven years of apprenticeship to a master. They will not allow me to work under these circumstances." Before he could interrupt me, I added, "You know very well the lives of the painters are regulated by the Guild and the Republic and both are very strict."

"I am head of this bottega. That will suffice."

Despite his assurance, I still was not certain he was right, but he looked so pleased with his decision and I was so infatuated with his manner and person that I nodded in agreement. But I was still anxious, for if the Guild, which controlled painting in Venice, found out that I had left the studio of Giovanni Bellini without his consent, I could be banned for life in Venice and possibly everywhere else, even in Florence and Rome.

I started to say, "Giorgione, I . . ." and he interrupted me instantly, "I told you, 'Never apologize, never explain.' If anyone questions you, ignore them. Now we have to decide what to do with your person."

"What is wrong with my person?" I asked indignantly.

"Your surroundings, clothes, and person must match your brush."

"All that costs money."

"We will manage. I was paid finally for the Enthroned Madonna I did as an altarpiece for Castelfranco, since they desire another work."

He placed me by his high Venetian windows, where the light was good.

Then he said, "You could have a fine figure if it were dressed attractively. Now you must have your own quarters."

I was tired of sleeping in the same crowded cellar with nine other apprentices, a prisoner to their snores, belches, farts, and stench, but his proposal was a blessing too rare to believe. Besides, his own quarters were so untidy. And what about Palma Vecchio, who shared the top floor? Surely he would object, too.

Giorgione moved the gold and black drapes which divided the spacious top floor so that they formed two rooms. I was even more positive that Palma Vecchio would refuse to permit this compression of his own studio, but when I mentioned that Big George shrugged. He cleaned the space he gave me, put the couch he used for models by the window so that I could sleep on it, and returned to what he considered a more vital matter, my appearance and person.

He informed me, "A painter is not considered a gentleman unless he dresses like one. I must get you out of that apprentice's tunic at once."

I disliked my appearance, too; I looked like every other apprentice in Venice with my gray, humble, ugly garb. But what he was suggesting was impossible and I told him so.

He replied, "You must be clean in appearance and free from offensive odors or no nobleman will sit for you. Come, we will attend to this now."

He took me by the hand to lead me out of the Palazzo Bellini. I held back, saying, "I am not allowed to leave without permisssion."

"I will assume the responsibility."

Giorgione's hand was soft, like a caress, and I could not resist him. We saw no one on the stairway, although I heard Giovanni Bellini's voice as we passed his studio, and his brother's was closed, for he was ill.

When we reached the street I wanted to sing. There was such a prodigious flow of life and color about me that I felt transformed.

At the top of the humpbacked bridge which spanned the Grand Canal at the Rialto, he paused and pointed to a building on the west bank and said, "I intend to live there. As soon as I am paid for my new work."

I agreed with his enthusiasm. I felt that the Grand Canal was the most beautiful passage in the world. There were boats everywhere, and many of them were so rich and elegant they dazzled my eyes. I knew this was no ordinary water. Even though it was muddied by the seepage from the shore, it had an earthy redness and vivid green and blue tints, and other colors, too, as if they had been mixed together by a painter's palette. I was filled with physical pleasure. The sun was at its highest and I swam in light. The sky poured it down, the water colored it, the reflections multiplied it, and it stirred my imagination intensely and I realized that whatever happened, I must be a Venetian.

I followed Giorgione down the wooden bridge steps to the shops on the other bank. I tried not to see the beggars and view only those dressed in silk and velvet. The fruit markets were amply stocked with grapes, pears, plums, and musk melons, which I had never tasted.

He saw me eye them hungrily, for he said, "We will get them

later. They must be eaten carefully. Their sweetness is immoderate and can sicken one."

I smelled much fish and saw an abundance of fowl and I wondered why anyone should have to beg with such plenty in the Republic.

Giorgione halted before a building which contained the most elaborate clothing imaginable and warned me, "We must refrain from appearing eager."

I asked, "What should I do?"

"Follow me. Whatever they ask, it will be double what they expect."

"Why?"

"Because they know I will offer half of what they want."

"Is that necessary?"

He regarded me as if I were childish, but he said, "Whatever happens, do not interrupt me. I do not worry about the cost, but I will not allow anyone to take advantage of me. The Venetians are the sharpest traders in the world. They are difficult to outwit."

But when we entered the shop no one attended us, and only when Giorgione started out and motioned me to follow him, did someone approach him. The middle-aged man wore a black satin doublet and fine hose, as if he were displaying his own wares, and he stopped Giorgione at the door.

They agreed on what suited me, but they did not agree on anything else. The brown breeches, the dark blue doublet, and the fine gray hose gave me a distinction I had not felt before. But when the merchant stated his price, Giorgione ordered me to disrobe. I did so unhappily, for I had become attached to these clothes, and he chided me for being slow. By the time I had discarded the elegant doublet the price dropped, and as I struggled out of the fine breeches the cost came down a third.

The merchant seemed on the verge of apoplexy as he shouted, "I will perish if I sell my merchandise for any less," and Giorgione told me to leave. I started out reluctantly, feeling that we were losing a bargain, but Giorgione did not waver. He marched to the door, with me lagging behind, and the merchant grabbed his arm and blocked his way.

"How much?" Giorgione asked sternly.

"The young man is well grown. My clothes give him stature."

"How much?" repeated Giorgione, even more sternly.

The more the merchant became apologetic, the more Giorgione showed indifference. When we left the Rialto with the clothes

bought at half the price we had been asked, Giorgione was triumphant, as if he had painted a masterpiece, but I thought it was too
strenuous a business. At the studio he gave me the cape I had borrowed and a gown to paint in, and then I felt it had been a profitable
expedition after all.

I passed Giovanni Bellini on the stairs a few days later and he did
not recognize me in my new garb. I heard that he was concerned
about his brother's illness, and thus, preoccupied. Nonetheless, I
was proud of my new appearance, but hurt that no one appeared to
be aware of my departure from the Bellini bottega. Palma Vecchio
was in Ferrara and Giorgione was alone in his studio, except for
me, while Lorenzo Lotto remained below.

Giorgione was pleased with the solitude on the top floor. "Now,"
he informed me, "I can finish my own work."

I was more involved with how I could assist him. I had spent the
past week preparing the oils and I feared that I would paint only
when he needed someone to fill in. Then he asked me to model for
him.

I objected. "You said I could paint in any manner I pleased."

"When you have a subject. Do you have one?"

I felt eager but my mind was blank.

"When you have one I will pose for you. Stand here. Hold this
staff. Bend your legs so you look at ease. Gaze into the distance."

Before I realized what was happening, I was posing as he ordered.
I heard a shouting match on the street outside. He had his windows
open; he preferred to paint while the air was fresh and fit to breathe.

I said, "I am surprised. I did not expect such noise from
Venetians."

He replied cynically, "I am not surprised. It is their main form
of entertainment. What else is there to please them except an occasional carnival, hanging, courtesan, or religious service? Shut the
window."

As I did I wondered if I had eluded one bondage to be trapped
by another. But I was fascinated by the way he was working. Instead
of his canvas being gargantuan, as was favored, it was a small, intimate easel picture with a new treatment of figures in a landscape.
More remarkable, he was applying the oil directly to the surface.
This was the first time I had seen anyone paint without any preliminary drawings. Even Giovanni Bellini used a few. Then abruptly
he frowned and stopped.

"What is the trouble?" I cried. "Am I standing wrong?"

"I must change my dress. It is too drab. It gives me a dull mood."

He put a fresh canvas by the side of the one he was painting for me to use while he was gone, but I was so absorbed in the way he was working that I could not pick up my brush. This was unusual, to paint was my greatest pleasure, but I had to learn more about his manner. It was different from any other I had seen; it was even different from any other painting of *his* that I had seen. I waited eagerly for him to return.

He did quickly, dressed in velvet of the finest quality, looking more like a courtier than an artist. He said, "I must avoid a morose and difficult disposition if I am to paint beauty as my fancy dictates."

By now I felt he loved ambiguity as well as beauty. As this work became a landscape with a storm in the background, which he painted first, then a young man—for which I modeled—and a naked nursing mother, I expected it to become theatrical, a dramatic tale of sensuality. Instead, although it was hardly more than a miniature, it grew into a beautiful, glorious evocation of mood. But what was he saying? I had no idea. Yet the more I looked at it, the more I was moved.

I lean back in my chair reflectively. My hands, once able to use a brush for countless hours, feel exhausted from using the pen. But I halt for other reasons. I am still not certain, even so many years later, why Giorgione's work excited me so intensely, but it did. Veronese, Tintoretto, and El Greco studied with me and I know their work and respect it. I have seen much of the work of Raphael, Michelangelo, and what remains of Leonardo's, and the efforts of many other artists of quality, and despite the malice of gossiping tongues, I have praised when I felt that praise was due. Yet Giorgione remains one of the most profound experiences of my life. I am still trying to learn why.

When Giorgione finished his new painting, I asked, "What does it mean?"

He shrugged and did not reply.

"It must mean something," I insisted.

"It is a painting," he replied. "It does not have to possess a meaning. It is enough that it exists. That I enjoy it."

"What do you call it?"

"It has no name."

"Then how do you identify it?"

"That is not necessary. It is the way I feel. I did it for my pleasure." He halted, annoyed at himself for having explained anything, and turned to the portrait he was painting of our old cleaning woman.

Giorgione did not even ask me if I liked the oil that fascinated me, but I continued to return to it, to seek to comprehend how he had achieved such marvelous effects and feeling. I called it *The Tempest;* it was the only thing in the picture I could identify. Yet in spite of the storm in it, the fork of lightning in the rear of the painting, the turbulent look of the clouds, there was a pervasive mood of quiet, almost of melancholy, and in the youth and the nursing mother, intense feeling.

He worked on the portrait of our old cleaning woman with the same devotion. At first I thought there was no beauty in this old crone with her frowsy gray hair, her decrepit body, her toothless mouth, her dirty shift, but again, the more I viewed his work, the more it appealed to me.

I longed to achieve the same effect, but how?

Now Giorgione offered to model for me.

I did not know which way to turn. I still desired to follow his style, but it did not seem suitable for the subject I had in my mind.

He said, "Paint anything you want."

The nude in *The Tempest* sat without any consciousness of her nakedness, but the one I imagined was aware of her opulent sensuality. I decided to do a Magdalen. But when I finished this oil she was more the courtesan than the madonna she was supposed to have been converted to.

I expected Giorgione to be offended. Instead, he was amused and he said, "At least you pleased yourself."

I did not agree with him, but I did not explain. The nude did not resemble Violante as was my wish—I was afraid to reveal my yearning for her—and this work annoyed me, and thus depressed me. I had followed his example by applying the oil directly without any preparatory sketches and I thought my colors blurred and heavy. I wondered if I had been wise to be influenced by Big George, no matter how much I admired his painting.

He was doing a pastoral scene and when he saw my depression he asked me to assist him with the landscape. The composition seemed simple but I found it difficult to blend with his style. He was lyrical, romantic, mysterious, while I felt more animated, vigorous, realistic. Yet he asked me to continue, even as he sensed that I was upset.

"Not to imitate me, as you are trying to do now, but express yourself. Spontaneously. As we paint, we invent. Others have worked together."

Although I knew that I should be pleased to share his easel, it was such a struggle to work in his manner. And as I painted in some of the landscape I wanted more blue than he did. To indicate there was some clearness in the sky, but how much was permitted?

He said encouragingly, "Tiziano, you are doing splendidly."

That did not answer the questions that plagued me now.

I SAW A RAINDROP BREAK

I SAW A RAINDROP BREAK
and fall into twenty sections

each complete
and a perfectly formed
raindrop

No vanity was shown
by any of them

Stymean Karlen

WHILE I SEARCHED for a style that suited me, Giorgione asked me to depict two men sitting on the grass. He had painted two lovely nudes, one standing and one reclining, but they were idyllic and detached.

Before I could say that I doubted my manner fitted his, he donned a red cape, took a lute, and sat in the pose he wanted painted. Then he played on his lute, and the music was sweet, at times melancholy, as he accompanied himself in a fine tenor voice. His attractive, long black hair, his handsome features were appealing, but what did he feel?

He saw me hesitate and he stated, "Owe nothing to anyone."

Yet I felt I owed much to him. But I was not his twin.

I still wavered and he reminded me, "I can abide disagreement."

"In the same composition?" I asked unbelievingly.

"It is possible, although not easy."

I wondered, Has he snatched me away from Giovanni Bellini to spite the master? Or to blend into his rich, warm, soothing colors until my manner was no different from his? I was suspicious now, and wary.

When I did not respond to his urging I thought he would castigate me. Instead, he looked so disappointed I could not endure it and I started to paint him as his pose suggested. Then suddenly, I lost my capacity to feel. It was as if I placed his face on mine. I felt overwhelmed by his palette. I lost my nerve and I dropped my brush.

A knock on the door interrupts my reverie.

"Who is it?" I cry out. I cannot be in the grave already, I think, yet this voice sounds as if it comes from a tomb. I have lived so long that all my contemporaries are dead. I feel desolate. "What is wrong?"

I hear Orazio say, "Papa, are you all right?"

I am pleased with his solicitude but I am annoyed that he is worried, as if it were a slander, and I pretend a vigor I do not feel. "I am fine."

"Papa, you did not come to dinner. I was worried."

"Is Pomponio concerned, too?"

"He would be if he were here. But he had to leave with his friends. Can I bring you something? Fruit? Wine? A bit of the roast?"

I am famished but I do not wish to relinquish my memories. At this time in my life they are the best part of it. I shout, "Have the steward prepare the roast. Bring it in an hour. Now go away. I am working."

These are sacred words in my studio, so while I doubt that my son believes me, he says, "I will be back in an hour. Please be careful."

When I am positive he is gone, I recall another time I dropped my brush.

It was about thirty years after I painted *The Country Feast* with Giorgione, and I was starting one of the most important commissions of my life. I was painting the official court portrait of Charles V, the Holy Roman Emperor, ruler of most of my world, and the most powerful patron in Europe. It was a difficult task, for even the emperor knew that he was a homely man. When I began, he said to me, "Since I am ugly by nature, I am always painted uglier than I am. Yet I like the truth."

How much truth, I wondered. His posture was awkward, his legs were thin, he had the thick Hapsburg mouth, a low forehead, and narrow eyes. But as I painted him this collection of irregular pieces became a harmonious whole, for his presence suggested a compelling majesty.

This did not solve all of my difficulties. One afternoon, while I was finishing his mouth, I grew nervous. The mouth was vital in my portraits and his lips overlapped and were ugly. I sensed, too, that the courtiers waiting to approach him on state business resented the time he was giving to my sittings and were critical of me. The emperor stirred restlessly and I feared that my truth was not his truth. I dropped my brush in my nervousness but before I could apologize to him and retrieve it, he picked it up. The courtiers were shocked and he retorted, "I can create as many lords as I wish, but only God can create a Titian."

Someone said, "Your Majesty, he represents you darkly."

Charles V replied, "He has given my melancholy a dignity I respect."

I had learned, focusing on his feelings, that he felt he was a martyr to his imperial responsibilities and he used an air of melancholy to express this. He assumed this attitude as others wore a cloak.

He added, "Now that I have been painted by Titian, I will never allow myself to be painted by any other artist."

I felt he had given me marching orders and I resumed his portrait. My hand was steady now and I modified his mouth so that it expressed his strength, which I believed was the emperor's essential self.

He viewed it and declared, "If this is not true, it should be."

And he kept his word. From then on, no one else painted him. I became the emperor's painter. Portrait painter of my world.

Most faces have blurred in my memory but Giorgione's remains clear in my mind. Have I painted too much? I have become the most sought-after portrait painter of my time, but all I want to do now is my *Pietà*. Have I been too greedy for money? I desire it only for my children. Many physicians have read the stars and given me pills and ointments to ease the aches of old age but nothing ends the anguish of my daughter's death.

Lavinia is my most private grief and I realize that I have refused to think about her up to now because it hurts too much. At this moment I long to join her in the grave, then I try to shake off my melancholy.

I recall one of my assistants asking me yesterday, "Maestro, do you wish you were young again?" and I pretended indifference and replied, "Of course not! I do not fear death! It is only my work that I will miss!"

Today I possess a hundred opportunities and I struggle to finish one.

Suddenly, unable to endure these reflections, I take one of my prized possessions from my locked closet. It is a *Madonna and Child* by Giovanni Bellini and I stare at it intently. The blue madonna is perfect, as perfect as Violante was when I met her. And the lovely child could have been my daughter Lavinia in her infancy. I smile to myself. Bellini himself, near the end of his long life, gave me this painting.

"Tiziano, for work you did for me. Despite our differences."

Afraid, however, that I am sentimental, I put this painting back into the closet. But it reminds me that Bellini did it when he was old. I flex my fingers but I cannot make them supple. They hurt and pain runs the length of my arm. I pick up my brush but I cannot hold it and this essential extension of myself drops lifelessly to the floor. I wonder if this is why Bellini worked so slowly, erratically, and finally not at all on *The Feast of the Gods*. The pain mounts to my shoulder and it requires both my hands to pick up the section of the *Pietà* I am striving to finish and to place it in the closet next to the Bellini. Then I lock the closet so that no one else can finish my work.

Giorgione picked up my brush and presented it to me and said, "Tiziano, you should continue, you are going in the right direction."

It was a moment I have remembered always, yet I blurted out, "Whose name will be on the picture?" even as I felt presumptuous.

"None, perhaps. Does that matter?"

Giorgione did not wait for a reply, adding, "My friend, I wanted you to learn by doing. All the talk in the world is not worth one stroke of your brush. But if you do not wish to share it, that is your privilege."

He stood up to end this situation and now I was sorry I had created such a scene and I hurried to say, "My wits were unsettled. I am honored to be your assistant. I will follow your manner."

"You will not do so for long. You have too much temperament for that. It is why I do not fear that I will corrupt you."

"You corrupt me? Dear George, that is impossible."

He smiled enigmatically and returned to his pose on the grass.

The next few days I painted the substance of the two men while he finished the landscape, the nudes, and completed the composition. As my style melted into his it seemed natural to me and I felt I was achieving a new skill with oils. We were painting for the joy of painting, gently and naturally. As if we lived in this *Country Feast* and I felt bliss, tenderness, and I realized this was a kind of lovemaking. The process of putting oil to canvas and evoking feeling through color and design gave me a pervasive sense of well-being and enjoyment.

One morning I moved back from this painting while Giorgione examined it to see if it were finished and Pietro Bembo entered. He moved with gusto, obviously pleased with his mission. He said, "Giorgione, my mistress, the duchess of Mantua, desires a *poesia* from your hand."

"Because she cannot have one from Bellini?"

"His hand is cramped with the infirmities of old age. As I have told her, your *poesias* are more newly designed and better finished."

"I do not find the master's pictures insufficient."

"They were the finest of his time. But his time is gone. Is this painting you have just finished for sale? It will please the duchess."

"It is not finished."

"Is it for sale?"

"No."

Bembo frowned and stated, "You have great natural gifts. I hope you do not waste them. The duchess will not be happy with your attitude."

Giorgione addressed me, "Tiziano, the landscape needs more foundation."

I thought the painting was finished but I obeyed him.

Bembo ignored me and said, "Big George, your work gives pleasure. You could become one of the most sought-after painters of our time. Otherwise, you will remain in financial difficulties."

"I do not need her benefices. My needs are simple."

"With your passion for fine clothes? For the best lutes? For oils of the highest quality? My friend, you are not logical."

I was not sure he would give in, but we had been eating less extravagantly the last few days and he had done no work since his return from Castelfranco except for his own pleasure.

He said softly, as if ashamed, "My lord, what do you propose?"

"She will forgive you if you paint a pagan fantasy with a Venus."

"Suppose it does not suit my brush?"

"She commissions you as she did Perugino and Mantegna. Even Leonardo worked for her and you know how difficult he is."

Giorgione was not impressed as Bembo expected, but he did say, "I will paint a Venus. If she pleases me, she may please the duchess."

"Please her first. The rest will follow."

Giorgione motioned for me to stop painting *The Country Feast.*

I was depicting the hills in the landscape more like my native mountains at Cadore and I felt he was annoyed, although his voice remained soft.

Now that Bembo thought that his mission was accomplished, he was able to notice me. He said, "By the way, what is young Tiziano doing here? I have not heard that Giovanni released him."

"He is my assistant," said Giorgione, as if that sufficed.

I feared that Bembo would report my departure, but Giorgione did not think that mattered. I was irritated that the poet-emissary had not praised me as he had done in the Bellini bottega. Am I that obscure? I asked myself, but I did not dare to speak of this to Big George.

He turned *The Country Feast* against the wall and said, "We will look at it next year. Perhaps then we will be able to finish it."

He employed a model for the Venus, a local courtesan.

I do not remember her name but I still remember her body.

It was sensual and enticing, but Giorgione prized her patience. As she lay on the couch that I used for sleeping, he suggested that I paint her, too. Since I had done this with him before, he assumed that I would see her only as a model. But when she stirred, I yearned to feel her warm mouth, to caress her full breasts, to enter her. He ignored her sensuality while he created a heavenly innocent, lying on the grass, asleep and modest despite her nudity. I painted my Venus on the couch where she was actually. Her eyes were open, inviting, and her flesh was suggestive. Where his Venus was virginal, mine was voluptuous.

Just as I thought his nude was finished, he turned her against the wall and said he would return to her later. So while I felt that my Venus was done, I did the same with my picture.

Soon afterward Palma Vecchio came back from his travels and when he saw that I was living in their studio, he shouted at Giorgione, "I cannot permit this! I do not have enough space as it is! And Giovanni Bellini will not allow such a move without his consent. He will never forgive us if we go against his judgment. The boy must leave."

Giorgione replied, "So matters went badly in Ferrara."

"I accomplished nothing," Vecchio grumbled. "The duke of Ferrara was not interested in my work and when I went to Florence it was even worse. The Florentines insist that Venetians cannot draw, that we do not comprehend the antique, that we infect our work with Venetian license."

"Would no one employ you?"

"Not a soul indicated interest in my work. Yet they envy our power, wealth, and stability so much that Florence has organized a republic modeled on ours. They admit that we are the best-governed people in Italy. But they regard us as inferior artists. It is offensive."

Giorgione listened attentively but I was uncomfortable, for Vecchio glared at me as he spoke. I was hurt; I had valued his friendship.

He stated that Bellini would expel us from the palazzo when he found out that I had taken the law into my own hands, and Giorgione lost his temper, which was rare, and retorted irately, "I am my own master! I will do what I please. Now desist, before we are no longer friends."

Vecchio retreated into his part of the top floor without another word and yet I felt he was dissatisfied, for he still regarded me critically.

A few days later we were visited by Nicolo Foscari, the chief inspector of the Venetian Guild of Painters. Everyone in the Republic knew his family, it was one of the most notable in Venice. He was in the premier grade of the nobility, *The Apostolic,* and he was a member of the Council of Ten. He was dressed in elegantly embroidered silk and velvet to demonstrate his position and he entered the studio with the stride of a man conscious of his power. Yet Nicolo Foscari, who was about the same age and size as Giorgione, was one of the ugliest men I had seen. His lips were thick and heavy, his eyes bulged, his nose curved like the beak of a crow, and his oily skin was pockmarked. Despite the heavy scent he wore, I smelled an unpleasant body odor. But his voice was commanding.

He addressed my friend. "Giorgio Barbarelli, I am here on behalf of the Republic and the Guild of Painters to investigate a complaint against you. It is reported that you are using the services of an apprentice bound to Giovanni Bellini, which is contrary to the rules."

Vecchio was absent and I felt it was because he had informed on me.

Giorgione asked, "Who is the source of this complaint?"

"It is nameless. The watchful eyes of the Republic are everywhere."

"Was it through the Lions' Mouths?"

"We are not permitted to reveal where our information comes from."

* * *

I pause in my reflections. Even in my old age, and in spite of all my trials, I cannot think about this dreaded accusation without revulsion.

The Lions' Mouths are familiar to the citizens of Venice. They are the boxes built into the loggia walls of the Doge's Palace to receive secret charges. They are so named because each is adorned with the sculptured head of a lion and the openings, the slots where the charges are received, are in the shape of a lion's mouth. It is a method of spying on the citizens of Venice that I detest. In my own life it has brought me before the all-powerful Council of Ten to answer serious charges, most of them anonymous. The fact that there is an accusation, even if it is unfounded, causes most people to assume that it is true.

Once, I recall, when brought before the Ten on the charge that I was perverting a commission of the Republic by placing a nude in my *Magdalen*, I cried out, "Allow me a little Christian compassion!" and I was ordered to clothe her or lose the commission. Despite the many assignments I received from the Republic, they did not come easy.

Giorgione was indignant as he told Foscari, "Whatever the charges, they are unfounded. Tiziano Vecellio is in my service. As my assistant."

He sounded positive but I was apprehensive.

Foscari replied, "No apprentice can leave a Bellini without their permission. This boy is not old enough to be anything else."

Giorgione said, "He is tall. He is almost as tall as I am."

"He has no beard. His skin is soft like a girl's." The patrician was contemptuous and at the door he announced arrogantly, "If Giovanni Bellini supports this complaint, the only remedy will be to bring the accused before the Council to be judged and punished."

"That is not fair. He has done nothing against the Republic."

"He has flouted our authority. An example must be set. Without public order, we are nothing. He could be confined in the Torresella."

Even Giorgione was shaken by this threat—the Torresella was the most dreaded prison in the Doge's Palace—and his voice was uncertain for the first time as he said, "Signore, my assistant is not a heretic."

"If he violates the laws of the Republic he is."

Giorgione's fear was momentary. The instant Foscari was gone he threw open the windows. "To remove the stench," he said, and added, "Only political persons are thrown into the Torresella. He wants to impress us with his importance. He considers himself a man of action as well as a philosopher. While his ancestry is patrician, he is proud that he has degrees from the universities of Padua and Bologna in astrology and philosophy. He makes many speeches on those subjects."

"Would I be safer in Florence?"

"It is doubtful. I will speak to Giovanni Bellini."

"What good will that do?"

Giorgione gave me a look intended to wither me with scorn. It was so unlike him that I was shocked. Then I realized he had to prove that he was strong, ever prepared to attack, saying, "I will think of something."

He left the studio after dinner and when he did not return that night my anxiety increased. I could not sleep. Left alone with my thoughts, they grew more pessimistic with each passing hour. By the second morning of such solitude, I could not wait any longer. I hated waiting, it was like hell on earth, and so I decided to take my fate into my own hands. Thus, although I felt I needed a miracle to save me from prison, I entered Bellini's studio determined to submit to him with the proper reverence, to kneel at his feet as a repentant sinner and to beg for his mercy and forgiveness. But I did not expect what I saw.

Giorgione was at the master's easel and Palma Vecchio was working with him. I was stricken with jealousy and then my curiosity about what they were painting overcame my· indignation and I edged behind them. It was a study from the antique and Giorgione was painting the landscape while Vecchio was doing the nude. I was resentful; I felt that my nudes were better than his. Several apprentices noticed me and whispered about my unexpected appearance and Giorgione and Vecchio heard the commotion.

Giorgione asked irritably, "Tiziano, what are you doing here?"

"I came to beg for mercy, to accept my punishment as necessary."

"It is not necessary." He turned back to the canvas.

I was not to be put off. I could be brave, too, I told myself, and I was angry at him for working with Vecchio, who, I believed, had informed on me, and I retorted, "I came to see Giovanni Bellini."

"He is attending his ill brother. Finish your Venus."

"It is finished."

"No painting is truly finished. You must not stay here."

"Why not?" I asked defiantly. Did he fear our association, too?

"Because I say so. Or am I not trusted either?"

I was not sure. My nerves demanded an explanation, and yet I

sensed that Giorgione's patience was wearing thin. His eyes were
tired and he seemed in a rush, which was unusual—he seldom worked
that way in his own studio—he was the most leisurely painter I
knew.

When I did not reply, he said, "If the Venus is done, try a portrait."

"What do I tell the inspector if he returns?"

"He knows where to find me. Now go, before you distract me so
much that I ruin what little I have accomplished."

I still did not know which way to turn but when I saw Vecchio
regarding me critically, as if my concern were childish, I obeyed
Giorgione.

Now I was grateful that there was no one else in his studio. There
was an ample stock of oils but browns and greens—which Giorgione
preferred—were most in abundance. So while I favored blues and
reds, I filled my palette with his colors. Then I decided to do a portrait in the manner of one I admired, Bellini's meticulous view of
Doge Leonardo Loredano.

But this was only a start. I lacked a subject. After much pondering, I decided to paint a self-portrait, yet many doubts remained in
my mind.

I knew my outside clearly enough but I was not certain about my
inside. I decided to create my own reality. I lost track of the time as
I explored the mystery of myself. My hand was conveying information: the sitter's nose was straight and long, the mouth was well
formed, the eyes were large, the hair and the perfectly trimmed short
beard were a reddish, earthy brown. I felt there was life in my hands
but there were other problems.

I was painting myself as I would like to be, not as I was. And I
longed to use blue, but my eyes were hazel and my complexion reddish. Then I felt that the blues and reds I had borrowed were insufficient.

I was pondering this when Bembo entered. He surveyed me so
critically that I became self-conscious; my hands grew cold, and I
expected him to disparage my work.

Instead, he asked, "Young man, where is Giorgione?"

That was worse, for he was ignoring my portrait. I answered
curtly, "In Bellini's studio, Signore. With those who informed on
me."

He shrugged, as if that was a matter of complete unimportance.

Even more annoyed, I said, "Unless you did, my lord."

"Why would I do that? I have no need of your services."

"It must have been Vecchio, Signore. He resents my place here."

"So does Piombo, who is eager to work with Giorgione, and even Lotto, or any one of a dozen apprentices. There are many who would give much to be in your position. Big George is blessed with a fine future."

"Signore, I cannot suspect the world."

"Some artists do. Michelangelo does. He trusts no one. Giorgione must be painting the *poesia* that the duchess requested from Giovanni."

"Why?"

Bembo stared at me as if I should know but he did not explain.

"My lord, will she not be able to tell the difference in manner?"

"I doubt it. Giorgione can suggest Bellini's style when it is needed. After all, he was the old man's pupil before he became his own master."

He wanted to see Giorgione's *Venus* and I showed him where it was.

He turned it around, regarded it approvingly, and said, mostly to himself, "The duchess will like it. I must tell Giorgione."

Now I could not paint, even when I was alone. He had not made a single reference to my work and that indifference paralyzed me.

Bembo was back soon, accompanied by Giorgione, who insisted that his *poesia* for the duchess was not finished and thus could not be delivered.

When Bembo disagreed with him, he suggested an alternative. "She will have Bellini's *poesia* which should satisfy her."

"Not with your landscape and Vecchio's nude."

"It contains Bellini's concept and design. It will have his name on it. That should suffice. Many works that come from his studio with his signature have been done by several hands. It is the custom."

Bembo said angrily, "Big George, if you do not deliver your *poesia* on time to the duchess she will lose patience with you. And she is one of the most influential of patrons and has much influence elsewhere. A word from her can give you commissions or end your chances at court."

I waited for Giorgione to submit, but he replied, "I will not deliver a painting of mine until I am satisfied with it."

Bembo left, swearing that he would never approach him again with a commission, and Giorgione regarded that statement with indifference.

I asked him why he painted a *poesia* for the duchess in Giovanni Bellini's name when he refused to give her his own and he would not explain.

He said, "May I see your portrait?"

"Did you find out who informed on me?"

"No. Tiziano, we must not pursue this matter, it will lead only to unpleasantness. It is enough that the master has agreed to release you."

"Are you sure?"

"The master has given me his word."

I thought, I am the price of the painting he did with Vecchio. But I had to ask, "How did you persuade Vecchio to help you?"

He replied, "Vecchio is not your enemy."

"Is that why he desires me out of this studio?"

"He resents your interest in Violante. Whether she is his niece or his daughter, she is precious to him, a flower in his garden."

"Will the inspector be satisfied with my presence here?"

"Foscari will heed Bellini. No Venetian, not even the Doge, will dispute the most eminent artist in the Republic. He will think that you are foolish to prefer my studio, but do not be concerned any longer."

"So you did paint in Bellini's name to rescue me."

"Tiziano, you are boring. We have much work ahead of us. May I see your portrait? Unless you are ashamed to have me view it."

This was a challenge I could not resist. I showed it to him.

He said, "There is much energy in your browns. The colors are strong."

"Do you mind that I am painting myself as I might be?"

"I have been doing that ever since I could hold a brush."

"I have not seen any of your self-portraits."

"Tiziano, I am the model for much of what I have done."

"What do you find wrong in the portrait?" I waited anxiously.

"It is a good start. You will do remarkable things."

Then I longed to embrace him but I was afraid that it was not manly. So I turned away so that Giorgione would not see the tears in my eyes.

What I remember most afterward is the approval with which he treated me, deeper than anything he said. That and the lack of fault-finding.

There is another knock on my studio door and I hear Orazio saying, "Papa, here is your roast. I have brought it myself."

I admit my son, sensing that he desires to talk to me. As he serves my dinner there is excitement in him and, I fear, anxiety.

Yet I satisfy my hunger before I ask him, "What is troubling you?"

"Papa, when did you first believe that you could become a master?"

"It was a long time ago."

"Was it when you met Giorgione? You still speak much about him."

So Orazio yearns to assert himself, I think, after all his years of allegiance to me. Only he lacks the gift and nothing I say or do will alter this harsh fact. Yet I want to protect him from pain. I point out, "I have transferred my broker's license to you. It is an honor."

"Papa, I am doing a self-portrait. Will you look at it?"

I do not expect to see anything unusual and I am very tired, but I walk wearily downstairs to his workshop to examine what he has done. It is stiff and ordinary, but I manage to mumble, "It is interesting."

Then he pulls a paper from his pocket and says, "Ever since Dolce wrote this about you, I have remembered it."

He reads: " 'Titian's portraits are of such great excellence that there is no more life in the life itself.' "

"Do you remember this, Papa?"

"I certainly do. It is one of the comments about my work I value."

"I value it, too. I may not be a Tiziano, but I am a Vecellio."

Heaven knows, I need emotion that I can trust. I embrace him fervently. I wish I could touch up his portrait and give it more life, but that will offend him and so I say, "I treasure your affection, too."

"When did you first think that you could have your own studio?"

My son's tone is so earnest I seek to give him an answer that will satisfy him. I say, "I believe it came when the Fondaco dei Tedeschi, the warehouse of the Germans, burned down. It changed the tempo and structure of my life and it gave me more control of my own palette."

SOMETIMES WISDOM IS

SOMETIMES WISDOM IS

right

but I would rather have the quality
that knows
when wisdom is
wrong

Stymean Karlen

THE DAY the German warehouse burned I was painting a portrait of Big George. It was our third sitting and by now I felt that he had asked me to paint him as a way of expressing his faith in me. He wore his best clothes, a yellow velvet shirt, a green doublet, and brown breeches, colors that he favored in his own work, and a gray cape. This, I felt, was because he wanted me to practice the painting of fabrics, for he believed that they were important in a portrait. Yet he did not hold a sword like a courtier, although he was dressed as a gentleman, or pose with a palette in the manner of a painter; he preferred to carry a lute.

I ignored the cold, although I had to exercise my hands to keep warm, while he sat close to the fireplace. I knew he desired me to paint him against a landscape, but I used a dark background to strengthen his features. He saw his sitters obliquely; I saw them dramatically.

As he strummed on his lute, I thought, Each painter must live with his own music and mine is the oils I love. I was learning that they contained a consistency that gave my colors a brilliance without the necessity of varnish. Just as I finished his high cheekbones, wishing next to show his dynamic fingers poised on his lute, and not to be ambiguous, as he was often, I smelled acrid, irritating smoke.

I paused, fearing it came from our fireplace. Then I saw the flames reflected on our Venetian windows. Both of us ran to them, afraid that the humpbacked bridge—the only link to the other side of Venice—was on fire, for it was all wood. But the blaze was beyond it.

Giorgione exclaimed, "It is the Fondaco dei Tedeschi! Come! It will be a great sight!" He did not sound stricken or surprised.

I followed him down the winding stone stairway and along the Grand Canal. The warehouse was on the same side as the Bellini bottega and just above the Rialto bridge where the Grand Canal curved abruptly to the left. Giorgione forced his way through the mob watching the fire with excitement and delight, as if this were another entertainment furnished by the authorities for their pleasure, and we joined the line of citizens passing buckets of water in an effort to quench the flames.

Vecchio was next to me and Lotto and Piombo, and most of the apprentices, but it was evident that we were too late. Some of the copper, spices, cloaks, swords, and silver stored in the Fondaco were saved, but the paintings were singed and the books charred. The fire burned too fast to be stopped and the authorities ordered us to douse the wooden bridge with water to save it from destruction. Several times I was deluged with carelessly thrown buckets—once, I thought, deliberately by Lotto—but I could not complain. Now we were serving the Republic and disobedience could be punished by death. I tried not to shiver, although my soaked body was frozen from the cold, for with the sun down the air was icy. We did not halt until the Rialto bridge was pronounced safe by the authorities. But the Fondaco dei Tedeschi was a gutted ruin.

I realized that no one knew how the blaze had begun, although I heard whispers: "An informer reported that the Germans were stealing from us. So it was set on fire as a punishment. That is fitting."

"We cannot trust the Germans. They cheat us constantly."

Yet when the German etcher and painter from Nuremberg, Albrecht Dürer, visited Venice the following year many of the artists in the Republic were invited to meet him by his host, Giovanni Bellini.

I had finished my view of Big George to his satisfaction, but not to my own; now I was painting a group portrait of a concert with him.

He halted when he received his invitation. Even Giorgione, usually indifferent to the work of others, was interested in seeing Dürer's. I had not been in the master's studio since my release and

I felt I should refuse Giorgione's request that I join him. But he regarded my fears as foolish and stated that we might learn from Dürer, that I liked his engravings, and so I decided to risk disapproval and, possibly, scorn. I was curious, too, as to what would happen when the German artist met painters whom he had accused of stealing his work.

As Giorgione said, "Dürer claims that woodcuts and engravings brought to Venice by German merchants have been sold without his permission. He says his designs have been copied by Venetian artists. I understand that the main reason he came to Venice was to halt these practices."

"And to study our colors," I added. I was beginning to feel assertive, for Giorgione listened to me more and more. "His are drab and flat."

My friend looked enigmatic and he did not comment.

The day of the reception I brushed my wisp of a reddish beard so that it would look larger and suggest the manhood I desired. Then I put on my finest clothes, those that Giorgione had bought for me, so, at least, my appearance would not be ridiculed, and we walked downstairs. I was very nervous.

No one noticed me. Everyone's eyes were on Dürer, who sat between the Bellinis to show that he was the guest of honor. And to celebrate this occasion the older brother displayed his prized marbles from the antique, while the younger exhibited his precious musical instruments, and all the splendid furnishings from the entire bottega were in use.

Dürer exclaimed in astonishment, "It is incredible! Every window is paned with glass! Giovanni, does it truly keep the chill out?"

"With great efficiency. Even our poor enjoy glass windows instead of those covered with paper and waxed cloth that are the custom elsewhere."

I longed to examine Dürer's work—Giovanni had given it the most conspicuous place—but I was eager also to observe who was present. I expected to see Vecchio, Lotto, Piombo, Pitati, Pordenone, and Bordone, for Giovanni Bellini had made this a notable occasion, but I was surprised to see Carpaccio, he worked so differently from the German.

Dürer was most attentive to Bembo and Strozzi, who sat close to him.

Three new gentlemen attracted Giorgione, who identified them to me as: "Giorgio Spavento, the city architect, who will be in charge of the Fondaco if it is rebuilt, Girolamo Tedesco, a German who may design the building, and Anton Kolb, a friend of Dürer's and an influential merchant."

I still wished to see Dürer's work but Giorgione added, "I hear that if the warehouse is rebuilt, the outer face will be frescoed."

This was so unlike Giorgione that I regarded him with surprise.

"Never mind my reasons. I want this commission. It will help you, too. Now let us see what Dürer has brought us to praise."

"Suppose we do not like what he has done?"

Giorgione sighed and said softly, "He will say that we are jealous, spiteful, not to be trusted. But his engravings are skillful."

We joined the others who were viewing the six paintings and a dozen woodcuts and engravings by Dürer. I was disappointed that most of his work was religious, although my attention was attracted momentarily by two separate nudes: *Adam* and *Eve*. I thought that his drawing was exceptional but I was disappointed by the gloom of his colors.

Then I was driven toward his self-portrait. This painting was so alive it seemed to approach me, to speak to me. But the sitter was handsome, while Dürer in person was not. The portrait depicted an Apollo but the painter's features were lined, his thick brown hair was tinged with gray, his long face was leaner and older than the sitter's and careworn. His self-portrait, I reflected, was an expression of love of himself. But I still liked his deep feeling, individuality, and passion for detail.

My thoughts were interrupted by Foscari, who declared as he strode in, so everybody would hear him, "Signor Dürer, your complaints have been brought to my attention. They are erroneous."

"Artists in Venice are selling my work without my authorization."

Foscari retorted abruptly, "You impugn our honor."

"My lord, a Marc Antonio Raidmondi, a native of Venice, bought a series of my woodcuts of the *Passion* from the merchants of Germany, and has sold them on the Piazza San Marco as his own, without my monogram."

Giovanni Bellini said, "Signor Foscari, you must investigate this matter."

The inspector was more polite as he replied, "As you wish, Maestro."

I noticed this did not relieve Dürer's anxiety or agitation. I felt that he was searching for a personal vision with such passion that he had to work incessantly and was so nervous he rarely stood still.

He stated, "I am grateful for Maestro Giovanni's aid, but distressed by the unfriendliness I have met among other painters in Venice."

This charge even upset Giorgione, while most of the artists were angry and Giovanni Bellini flushed and Gentile was uncomfortable.

Foscari said indignantly, "I do not understand your allegation."

"In the brief time I have been in Venice, I have been summoned before the magistrates three times to establish my right to paint here, and I have had to pay four florins to the Venetian Guild. It is outrageous."

Giovanni Bellini said, "My friend, this is the custom for all of us."

"And I still pay it," said his brother, "after sixty years."

I was shocked to see how frail he had become and I realized that it must have taken an enormous effort of his will for him to be here.

Giovanni Bellini said, "Signore, it is necessary if you intend to reside here."

"I am not certain. I may stay only a few weeks."

"That would be unfortunate. Venice is the crossroads of the world. It is too bad that the Florentines and Romans do not realize this truth. There is a unique advantage to being a Venetian, especially for a painter. The air and light here are of irreplaceable value."

However, Dürer remained sulky and critical until Giovanni Bellini admired his work.

Giovanni asked, "Will you be so kind as to gratify a friend?"

Dürer replied, "I will do anything you ask if it is within my power."

"I want to understand the mystery of your fineness of touch. Would you make me a present of one of the brushes with which you draw hairs?"

Dürer produced several brushes and offered them to him.

He said, surprised, "But these are the kind that I use."

"They are what I used for the beards of the Pharisees you admired."

"I do not mean these brushes, but the ones with which you draw several hairs with one stroke."

"I use no others than these and to prove it you may watch me."

When everyone gathered around him, he took one of the brushes that he had given Giovanni Bellini, and drew very long wavy hair with marvelous detail.

Gentile mumbled, "It is a miracle."

Giovanni turned to the noblemen in attendance and said, "My lords, you should commission Signor Dürer. His hand is remarkable."

Foscari did not reply, but Bembo said, "I would be privileged, but the duchess prefers the Italian style, while Strozzi stated, "The duke waits for your *poesia*, Maestro Giovanni, then he will consider others."

This was ignored by Giovanni Bellini, who turned to Dürer and asked him, "Friend, would you do something for me? I will pay you well."

Dürer seemed to grow in stature and he nodded happily. I expected Giorgione to introduce me to him now. Instead he approached Spavento, Tedesco, and Kolb, who were speaking to Foscari, and I followed, for I did not have the courage to approach Dürer, and the four men greeted Giorgione and ignored me.

He said, "I trust you will consider me for the German warehouse."

Foscari reminded him, "There will be other artists in competition for the exterior. If it is rebuilt. That is not yet decided."

Tedesco added, "Some of the German merchants recommend Dürer."

Giorgione said, "He cannot do frescoes. His gifts are elsewhere."

"Possibly," said Spavento. "But what qualifies you?"

"I have done many frescoes. And they are of the highest quality."

I was surprised by his ambition; he had ridiculed that until now. Kolb said, "We have an obligation to consider Dürer."

Giorgione said, "He does not qualify. He is not a Venetian."

"It is fitting that a German warehouse be painted by a German artist."

"In Venice?" Giorgione was skeptical as he added, "I doubt the Guild of Painters will allow an outsider to do a building under their control."

The Germans were worried while I was attracted by Giorgione's passion.

Foscari was noncommittal when my friend asked, "The Guild will not permit a German, will they?" but he did say, "Giovanni Bellini holds the broker's patent. He will decide who paints the frescoes. He may do it himself."

"He is too old. And I have had more experience with frescoes."

Foscari asked, "Who would assist you, Giorgione?"

"Tiziano Vecellio."

"He is not qualified. He is not even a member of the Guild."

My heart sank. Then I was sure Giorgione would defend me. Instead he asked, "Would Palma Vecchio qualify? Or Sebastiano del Piombo?"

"It is possible. If they are members of the Guild."

"They are. My lord, I have confirmed that."

I felt betrayed. After all the work I had done for him and with him, and the constant devotion I had given him, it was as if he cast me aside. I could have wept, but I was too proud to show how much this mattered to me and so I stood rigidly although I longed to flee.

My son interrupts. "I thought Giorgione and you were close friends."

"We were."

"And you told me that he received much assistance from you."

"That is true. As I received from him."

"And since you gave me your broker's patent, Papa, you must think I have a gift for painting. Or you would not have arranged it."

There is so much entreaty in his voice that I nod, although I had done this for other reasons.

This gives Orazio the courage to say what must have been on his mind a long time, for while I sit wearily in the royal armchair that Charles V had given me for one of my paintings, lost in my memories, Orazio blurts out, "Papa, why not allow me to finish your *Pietà?*

I am wide awake suddenly. I am horror stricken. He should know that such an achievement is out of his reach. I feel torn in half. Much as I love him, much as I want the best for him, he would ruin it. Commissions for the Republic which the broker's patent gives him are not vital and can be touched up, but the *Pietà* is myself, is my redemption.

"No one will know the difference, Papa."

Everyone will know, I want to shout back, or at least, *I* will. But I do not wish to hurt him and so I say, "Let me think about it."

"May I look at it? See what has to be done?"

That seems like a natural request and I stand up to return upstairs. However, the climb is such a harsh effort that I realize how Gentile Bellini must have felt when he got out of bed to greet Dürer. I think, Time has encrusted me with barnacles that are as heavy as chains. To unlock my closet and to allow Orazio to take my *Pietà* out and to examine it gives me more pain, for

I fear that he will find it faulty, and his regard for my work still matters deeply to me.

As Orazio lights a brace of candles so that he can observe the work properly, starts a blaze in the fireplace so I will not catch cold, for the Venetian nights, even in summer, are cool, and puts the parts of the altarpiece against the wall, I feel his respect for my painting. Then my critical instinct overrides my sentiment and I wonder if I have made this *Pietà* too large. Especially in view of my ebbing strength. So much of my art has been energy, will, and faith. The *Pietà* is about twelve feet high and fifteen feet wide, and yet that should not trouble me, I decide, I have painted some of the largest and best known altarpieces in the world. Many of them are in churches within walking distance of my studio. I have a sudden impulse to view them.

Orazio says reflectively, "This *Pietà* is very dark."

As dark as death, I think, but he is too discreet to suggest that. He waits for me to explain and I cannot tell him that I paint my entrance into my own tomb; that I even seek to paint without color—I, Titian, who has been praised most for his colors.

My son lights more candles to examine it better, then shakes his head, and states, "You have made the figure at the foot of Jesus so old."

It is myself, but that is something only I must know, and I reply, "Joseph of Arimathea was old. What else concerns you?"

"The figure of Mary Magdalen is so dark, too. I could lighten her."

"This is precisely what I must not do. She is not a Venus at this time in her history, but a person of sorrow, mourning Jesus."

"I will do whatever you suggest. Please, may I assist you?"

This is one of the most difficult decisions I have faced in my life, and so I avoid a direct answer. "I will consider your brush, but first I must put it away, not look at it for a few months. Then I will know what to do."

"Do you dare risk such a delay?"

"My son, you think that I will not live that long?"

"I pray that you will live many years, but the plague grows worse. It infects more people than even the contagion of 1570. Papa, I do not feel safe. I am afraid to open our windows, although it is getting warm, for the wet, windy weather spreads the contagion."

I shrug. I have lived through many plagues. Perhaps I will survive one more. Neither of us speaks while we return the *Pietà* to the closet. When I lock it, I say, "This is not directed against you, but others."

"You should trust Pomponio more. Then he might trust you more."

I cannot tell him of all the times I have trusted him, only to regret it.

Before I can retire to my bed, which I yearn for now, he asks, "You have experienced much history. What has affected you most?"

"I am not sure. I was born in a century when Constantinople was lost to the Turks, when Columbus discovered a new world, although no one knew that at the time, when Vasco da Gama found a route to India around the Cape of Good Hope, and ended Venetian supremacy in trade. But we were not aware of what was happening to us. Fistfuls of wealth were coming to the Rialto from many countries. Nobody listened to the warnings of possible disaster, we were indifferent to history. Now, however, on our islands that are shaped like fish hooks, as if they were designed to extract wealth from the seas, we look on the past as a succession of great moments, although that is an illusion."

"Nonetheless, you have lived in a great time for painters."

"Yes, yes, I have been fortunate in that respect."

"Did Albrecht Dürer influence you or Giorgione? Or was he the one who was influenced? I have heard many conflicting reports."

"It is foolish for an artist to be forever defending himself. He wastes time that is better used for his work. But my friend, Aretino, defined it best for me. I have always treasured his words."

"What did he write, Papa?"

I went to my desk where I stored my favorite communications and read:

" 'Titian's horizon was not limited to Venice or Northern Italy. He learned from the antique, but also from Michelangelo, Raphael, and Dürer. All these influences nourished his originality. No other artist appropriated so much while making so few concessions, no other artist was more pliable while remaining so utterly himself.' "

Orazio says, "I agree with Aretino. He was shrewd."

"However, I dislike the stress on who influences who. Influence is a detail. What matters is the total."

"Do you think that Dürer felt the same way?"

"I possess a letter he wrote to the patron who paid his way to Venice. I used the same scribe as Dürer, and he copied the letters he considered important and sold them later. Dürer desired to save his hands for his work, so he hired a scribe to write his letters, as I did, too."

We examine Dürer's letter together. It is dated February 1506.

"Would that you were in Venice, my honorable and wise friend, there are so many pleasant men among the Italians who seek to associate with me, which is pleasing to me—reasonable, learned men, good lute players and pipers, judges of honest virtues, and they show me much friendship and honor. On the other hand, there are also most false, lying, thievish rascals, such as I would not have believed were among the living. If one did not know, one would think them the nicest men alive. I cannot help laughing to myself when they talk to me. I have many good friends among the Italians, who warn me not to eat and drink with their painters. Many of them are my enemies, and they copy my work in their churches wherever they can find it. Then they revile it and say it is not antique in style and thus not good. But Giovanni Bellini has highly praised me before many nobles. He wanted to have something of mine, and asked me to paint him something and said that he would pay me well for it. Men tell me what an upright man he is, so I am favorably disposed toward him. He is very old, but he is still the best painter of them all. But I have not seen anything among the younger painters that moves me."

Instead of this quieting Orazio, it gives him the impetus to ask, "Papa, how did you meet my mother? Did she model for your nudes, too?"

I do not wish to talk about this and I reply, "If you are so concerned about my health, you must allow me to rest."

After my son helps me into bed, he departs without another word. But I cannot fall asleep. My restless spirit is still not assuaged.

When Giorgione finished his argument he left without any further view of Dürer's work or an explanation of his apparent preference for Piombo or Vecchio as his assistant. If anyone had noticed my presence, it was unknown to me. Yet I did not leave his studio, as I was tempted to do, for I had no other place to go.

The next few weeks he resumed work on his painting of a concert and he assumed that I would continue to assist him. He acted as if nothing had altered between us, and I was too proud to plead my own cause. Once, I did suggest that I apply for admission to the Guild of Venetian Painters and he replied, "It is too soon," but he would not tell me why.

I was gratified that he was painting a background for the three figures in *The Concert* that was as dark as I had done in the portrait of him. Finally, I felt, I was influencing him. But I was uneasy when he invited Vecchio to assist him in the preparation of the drawings that he was submitting to the Senate in the hope of obtaining the commission to paint the Fondaco. The Senate had decided to allow the Germans to rebuild their warehouse, for they did not want to lose their business to Florence or Genoa. I felt even more displaced in my role as assistant, although Giorgione asked me to finish the faces in *The Concert*.

I was annoyed that he assumed that I would agree, and yet I did what he asked. I told myself that it was because I had fallen in love with the group portrait, but I decided to take advantage of Vecchio's presence.

They were drawing the heads of the Apostles in the manner of *The Last Supper* by Leonardo, which had become the talk of Venice, with the intention of submitting them to the Senate as possible figures for the frescoes. So one day, when the sun was bright on our faces and spring was in the air, which put everyone in a good mood, I halted my own work.

The Concert was almost completed, although Giorgione had neglected his portion of it lately, and I gazed at an Apostle as if fascinated. It was the head of St. Bartholomew, which I knew to be Vecchio's, but I pretended that it was Giorgione's and I said it was amazing.

Giorgione corrected me, believing that I had made an honest mistake, and Vecchio beamed, and for the first time since he had chided me about Violante, he spoke to me. He said that my taste was improving and he offered to show me how he achieved such excellent effects.

Giorgione, who was finishing a head of Jesus, motioned for me to heed Vecchio, as eager to end this quarrel as I was. So Vecchio instructed me in the art of fresco painting and I listened attentively. When he felt that I was sincere, he grew animated, and I realized that he had been jealous of my devotion to Giorgione.

By the time their work was submitted to the Senate we were friends again, although I still resented my exclusion from the Fondaco project.

As soon as it was announced that the warehouse was to be rebuilt by Spavento and designed by Tedesco, with murals on the exterior, Giorgione ignored everything else in his efforts to secure this commission.

Giovanni Bellini, as holder of the broker's patent for the Republic, was offered the work, but Giorgione persuaded him that it would be bad for his health since he would be exposed constantly to the vagaries of Venetian weather, uncertain even at the best of times. Then Gentile Bellini died from a chest congestion brought on by exposure and old age and that convinced his brother that Big George was right.

Next he warned Foscari, who represented the Senate in this matter, that Dürer, who wanted this commission, lacked the proper experience and, as a German, could not be trusted. Since suspicion was a natural part of Venetian life and no foreigner was ever trusted—the Republic did not allow the Germans to live or work anywhere but in the Fondaco, and then kept them under constant surveillance with the many spies who worked there—Giorgione's contention prevailed without an argument.

More difficult were the other painters who desired this commission who were Venetians. Vecchio and Piombo did not compete, for they expected to assist Giorgione, but Carpaccio offered his services and so did Lotto and others. Foscari liked Carpaccio's work, he felt it illustrated Venetian life at its noblest, but when Giorgione offered to do a life-sized portrait of the inspector in the official manner usually reserved for the Doge, Foscari was flattered. Sittings occurred regularly and the inspector's portrait developed a romantic dimension that gave him a grandeur that overcame his natural ugliness.

When Giorgione was given the commission to decorate the new Fondaco I was not surprised. In addition, he was allowed two assistants. I expected him to ask Vecchio and Piombo to assist him. I was stunned when he requested my services.

We were eating a late dinner under a starlit sky near the bridge. It had been sunny all day and the stone still contained some of the heat, although the night air was cool. For an instant I felt joyous, then I was suspicious. He could be devious and I was not sure I trusted him. Yet when he saw me staring at the rising wall of the Fondaco with a fixed, dazed, absorbed expression, he burst into laughter.

I was furious, but before I could convey my anger, he took my arm and together we walked along the Canal and to the Fondaco. The torches that lit our way cast shadows but he seemed to see clearly as he pointed to the facade and said, "I will do the front and you will do the side."

"But you told Foscari that Vecchio and Piombo would assist you!"

"I did not want to destroy him as an ally. The agreement does not specify any conditions concerning my assistants."

"I am not a member of the Guild. They will not allow it."

"This work will make you a member. It will prove your worthiness."

"What about Vecchio and Piombo? Surely they will be offended."

"Sometimes you are impractical. They will take care of my studio. There will be many requests for my work now that I have the Fondaco."

He kissed me on the cheek to demonstrate that my doubts and suspicions of him were forgiven.

THE PEARL SKY
WITH DARK AMBER

THE PEARL SKY WITH DARK AMBER

thoughts
saw the little wood people
from the Island
stand tightly in one corner
staring
at the giant torso
that had not seen anything
since the day the sculptor
decided
not to give it a head

the pearl sky with dark amber
thoughts
disapproved
it shook its pearly quality
regrouped itself and made sure
it had all of its own limbs
and a mouth
to rumble rumble from
in a proper face

Stymean Karlen

AFTER GIORGIONE signed an agreement with the Senate to paint frescoes on the exterior of the rebuilt Fondaco, he received an advance of thirty ducats, and it was understood that he would be given a total fee of ninety ducats if his finished work was satisfactory. The moment he had the money in his pocket he moved out of the Bellini bottega and rented a three-story palazzo on the other side of the Grand Canal, directly across from the warehouse, and furnished it lavishly with blue draperies, medieval armor, musical instruments, and books by Dante, Petrarch, and Boccaccio. He was proud that he had his own gondola now, which he tied to the striped yellow mooring poles in front of his palazzo, and that his new home had two stories of loggias in the facade overlooking the water.

He told me that these loggias with their slender columns and elegant sculptures reflected the beauty and splendor of Venetian life.

Then he offered me the second floor for my own use, saying that the first floor would suffice for domestic purposes while the third floor would be his studio and sleeping quarters. As I hesitated, greatly tempted and yet worried that I would be seeing images only in his colors and not in my own, a growing concern of mine, he handed me ten ducats.

This was the most money I had known and I was moved by his generosity. But I also feared that he would demand too much for this.

When I continued to hesitate, he asked me, "Is this fair?"

"More than fair," I replied, "since you obtained the commission."

"So why are you doubtful now?"

I mumbled, "I do not like to feel obligated."

"It is for your services on the Fondaco." His voice grew irritable. "Unless you do not think they are worth that much."

He had attacked me where I was weakest and he knew it.

He added, as if I had to give in, "Besides, we need this money so that we can buy the best materials and not be beholden to anyone."

Embarrassed, I muttered, "Big George, you are a good friend."

"Not unless your work is of a high quality. Our frescoes will face the challenge of Leonardo's *Last Supper* and far more people will see our heads for we paint at the Rialto of Venice, which is the crossroads of the world."

He had assumed that I would accept his offer and the second floor as a studio-residence and he started to pack my belongings and I halted him.

"What is wrong now?" he asked angrily.

"Are Vecchio and Piombo going to share your quarters, too?"

"Tiziano, you are a jealous painter."

"That is no answer."

"Palma prefers to remain close to Bellini. As the master grows older and feebler, he hopes to do more of his work and to eventually inherit his broker's patent. There are no Bellini children to leave that to."

"I thought Piombo had his eye on the state license?"

"Possibly he has. That is probably why he remains with Bellini, too. They will struggle for his broker's patent, each being excessively polite to the other, when in reality they wish the other ill. And in the end someone else will most likely inherit the master's position. That is usually the way. If you desire something very much, you rarely get it."

"Who do you think it will be?" I wondered if he wanted the license.

"Not Albrecht Dürer, that is certain. The artist will have to be a Venetian. The Guild is inflexible about this. As it is, the artist is handicapped if he is not born here, even if he has spent his entire career in *La Serenissima*. Venetians are provincial in such matters."

"Then this will be out of my reach should my time come."

"Why?" Giorgione was puzzled.

"Even my friends refer to me as Titian of Cadore."

"It is not a slur. But now we waste time. I have to prepare for the party I am giving to celebrate the acquisition of my own studio."

A week later artists whom Giorgione considered his contemporaries were invited to enjoy his good fortune. I doubted that any of them were truly pleased that he was surpassing them, or that he believed they were, for behind the facade of his good nature was not a naïveté but the subtle wit of the most crafty Venetian. But as he met his guests at the door, everyone greeted him warmly, even Dürer, who proudly wore the French cape and Italian coat that had been purchased in Venice.

Tables were filled with appetizing meats, wines, and sweets, yet Dürer regarded this feast as an appeal to his sinful nature. He was upset when Giorgione offered him his best white wine. For a moment, I felt that Dürer was afraid that he would be poisoned, for he took the wine only after I did. But several goblets of the sparkling vintage eased his pain and suspicion. When he had entered his expression was one of suffering.

I saw Vecchio, Piombo, Lotto, and Pordenone, but not Giovanni Bellini, and I heard Giorgione tell Dürer, "The master is too old, he would not approve," and a minute later I understood what my friend meant.

Some young women arrived at the studio and I could not tell whether they were courtesans, housemaids, or casual friends, but they were young and attractive. Giorgione played his lute and several of the painters danced with the prettier girls. I envied Dürer when he asked one of them to dance with him. But he moved like a piece of wood and I thought that he was grappling with his partner as if she were a creature of the devil, instead of enjoying the warmth of her presence.

Afterward, Dürer grumbled to Giorgione, "I took dancing lessons in a school, so I could enjoy myself in Venice, but I gave it up. To learn dancing I should have had to pay away all that I have earned, and at the end I should have known nothing about it."

Piombo joined us, but he did not desire to discuss painting either. Giorgione introduced us to Beatrice and Felicia, two pretty young women who had approached him, and Piombo's small, pale face glowed as he bowed flatteringly to Felicia, for it was evident that Beatrice was attached to our host. I was unhappy, for I wanted to know Felicia, too. I was fascinated by her flaming auburn hair and her delicate oval face.

Then she was attentive to me, ignoring Piombo's courtship, saying, "Tiziano, Signor Giorgione told me that you have a fine brush."

I felt Piombo, who was inches shorter than I was, although a few years older, grow tense and try to blow himself up in size.

Giorgione, who eyed Beatrice affectionately, and I could see why, for she was beautiful and voluptuous, declared, "Felicia, you should model for Tiziano. He will make you look divine."

I blurted out, "It will be enough to create her in her own image."

She smiled and said, "I would be honored."

Piombo cut in, "Felicia, the light in this studio is not good enough for your fair complexion."

I believed that my purpose was stronger than his and I took her hand, and when her fingers tightened around mine, I felt triumphant, and I stated, "I will show you where the light is best for you." When I felt that she was acquiescent, I led her to the loggia where we could observe the sun setting over the Grand Canal. I tried to ignore the stench of rotting fruit and fish and other refuse that came from the markets behind us, for I was enchanted by the fragrance of her perfume. And the light gave her skin a delicate rosebud tint.

I exclaimed, "Felicia, the colors here are fresh and spontaneous!"

She did not reply and I was not sure that she was listening, but I sensed that she was interested in my person, for she leaned closer to me as we bent over the loggia facade, and her breasts pushed against my body, and they were firm and yet yielding. I put my arm around her waist and when she did not resist I felt potent. I wondered if she were a courtesan, or the daughter of one, for she seemed amorously inclined.

I asked suddenly, "Do you know of any other city like Venice with such beauty and excitement and color? There is no other!"

She nodded and her smile was that of a temptress. My excitement grew and I suggested that we go to my studio.

Felicia appeared to expect such an invitation. After I enjoyed her voluptuous body, I realized that she was very skillful in spite of her youth. At the instant of consummation I felt that our passionate delight had come to a passionate end.

Yet when I kissed her to express my approval of her response, she said, "You are not thinking about me, but about someone else."

I had been comparing her to Violante. Felicia was far more experienced, but Violante had given her body with a greater passion.

To change the subject, I stood up to close the windows, for with the setting of the sun the night air had grown chilly. And as I saw her lying with a natural sensuality, I suggested that I paint her.

"Perhaps," she replied. "If someone wants a portrait of me."

We lay for a long time with our arms around each other. Then I asked Felicia if she would share my lodgings.

"It is not sensible," she whispered. "You cannot afford it."

"I have ten ducats. And there will be more."

"And I am obligated to reside elsewhere."

"I think Beatrice is going to live with Giorgione."

"That is different." But when she saw my disappointment, she added, "However, I will see you again. If that is what you desire."

The next few weeks Felicia visited me occasionally while Beatrice moved in with Giorgione and became his mistress. I hoped that Felicia would follow the same course, but while she permitted me to make love to her, she never stayed overnight and she always came during the day when it was least suspicious. I wondered if she was living with another man, but when I asked where she went, she replied, "It is too complicated to explain," and was annoyed by my question.

I inquired about her background to Giorgione and he said, "Some say she is the illegitimate daughter of a patrician, or of a painter, for she seems to fancy artists, while Beatrice thinks her father is a sea captain who is away trading with the Turks. But one thing I know, she does not have to be taught the arts of love. Be grateful for that, and the future will take care of itself."

I resented his cynicism. Each time we met, she gave me a new sensual delight. Felicia was proud of her ability to excel amorously. I trimmed my reddish-brown hair, used an enticing scent that she fancied, and did my best to satisfy even her most outrageous sexual demands.

Then it was time to start work on the Fondaco. Giorgione arranged for Vecchio and Piombo to meet in his new studio for consultation, although it was evident from the instant they entered that he was more interested in their approval than in their advice. Instead of asking their opinion, he told them what he was going to do.

I was surprised that he had no intention of using the heads of the Apostles that he had sketched with Vecchio. I questioned this, saying that a religious subject was the proper one for the Fondaco, and he retorted, "Venetians are the most irreligious people in Italy. They prefer a painting that will express their craving for excitement. I will give them an allegory of war and peace. I have convinced Foscari, who has the greatest influence, that this is most pleasing."

Vecchio said, "Your choice of a subject is wise, but I do not trust outdoor painting. It seldom lasts."

Piombo added, "Especially with Venetian weather. Frescoes should be done in the open only when the climate is free of moisture, and Venice is always damp. Even in spring and summer it is usually wet, and you will be working over the Canal where the weather is worse."

Giorgione said, "I have done many frescoes. I know what I am doing."

"But you have never done any over a canal," Piombo reminded him.

"And you will have other problems," Vecchio said. "Materials, labor, and the cost will exceed your fee. Ninety ducats is not enough."

"So I will increase my fee."

I asked, "How will you do that? The agreement is signed already."

"Do not worry. I will manage that. And the other objections are wrong. My work will not scale off. Time will not mutilate it."

I awake, drenched in sweat. I have been dreaming that I am hanging over the roof of the three-story Fondaco with my head down and I am terrified, for Piombo and Vecchio shout in my ears, "Paint! You are so sure of yourself, Titian of Cadore!" And I cannot fight back. My hands are tied and I have no brush and my oil has turned to water.

I wonder if my nightmare is because I do not like to think about what has happened to these frescoes, even in my own lifetime. Seventy years is not a long time in the existence of a painting, but the elements have been harsh. It does not improve my spirits to know that Leonardo's *Last Supper* has been shedding paint like our allegory of *War and Peace*.

Piombo asked, "Giorgione, do you truly believe that the duchess of Mantua will be satisfied with the *poesia* I am painting in your name?"

"Yes. And for the time being she will stop pestering me. Palma, you, too, should paint for Isabella instead of for Bellini."

"I do not agree. She is too difficult, but the duke of Ferrara will accept my work if it bears Bellini's name and is in his style. Since his brother's death, he has aged. Now he allows me to finish many of his commissions and if I continue to assist him, and no one damages me, I could inherit his studio. He admires the delicacy of my brush."

Their behavior troubled me and I wondered if Piombo was right when he said, "Dürer may be wiser than any of us, obtaining the contract for the altarpiece for the German colony's church, San Bartolomeo."

Their objections only increased Giorgione's determination to paint frescoes that would be the talk of the world. When the roof of the Fondaco was in place, we began work. It was May 1507, and bright sunshine shone on the walls and yet I was still not sure that I knew his purpose. He had not even drawn cartoons in the Florentine fashion.

I asked him about his design and he replied, "Improvise. Use your imagination. Do fanciful figures which express war and peace. From your reminiscences of the classic as displayed in antique sculpture."

He worked on the principal facade on the Grand Canal, while he gave me the side looking over the small street that led into the Fondaco.

By summer there were many male and female figures on his walls, some of them nude; there were also cupids, a lion's head, several angels.

I felt he was expressing the richness of his imagination and I sought to work in harmony with him, but as I painted an Eve above the entrance to the building I was confused. Generally in summer Venice glowed with a multitude of colors. The city began then "to compose." But when I followed his palette, my compositions were too bland for me.

His frescoes were becoming too static, too idyllic for my taste. I wanted mine to be more energetic, dramatic, to be distinguished from his. I still admired his brush, but I was no longer flattered when I was told that our styles were the same. I yearned to be master of my own house.

One day, unable to paint because of my uncertainty, I strode along the Rialto where Venetians boasted that *"the business of the world is transacted,"* but the tumult and the crowds blurred the vision I sought. I walked up the bridge to the top where I could see Giorgione's work most clearly but my perplexity grew. His figures were charming but I could no longer imitate him; I was no longer satisfied to be second best.

I did not paint the next day either, for Felicia was visiting me. I had not seen her for a month and I was afraid that I was losing her. So I was grateful when she appeared on time and gave copiously of herself.

Afterward, while she prepared to depart, I blurted out my doubts about the wisdom of following Giorgione's manner.

She replied, "He adores his mythological figures and you should, too. They are pretty and as long as your work and his are consistent no one will question them."

She left quickly, for the street torches were being lit, and she said she had to be home before night fell, although I knew no more about her situation than before. I wondered if she would stay if I offered to wed her, but I felt too young for such an accommodation, even though the wedding feast could be rich with sensuality; I craved more experiences.

By now no one seemed capable of helping me and so I sought refuge in San Giacomo di Rialto. This church was on the other side of the Rialto from the Fondaco and the oldest one in Venice, an oasis in the middle of the marketplace. Coming out of the blinding sunlight and into the gentle flow of the interior gave me some tranquillity. I was alone, and I liked that, the quiet, the peace and simplicity that reigned. Here, at least, I had the illusion of beatitude that had evaded me on the Rialto. And as I sat there I prayed for clarity.

Now I was able to give my frescoes a different accent, but I still did not trust my fancy. My figures remained vague and too much in his style.

Several months later Dürer exhibited the altarpiece he had done for San Bartolomeo. It was an occasion of occasions, for I saw in his studio Doge Loredano and the cardinal of San Marco's, Domenico Grimani. They were the leading connoisseurs in a city of connoisseurs and they were joined by patricians, German worthies, and painters. But all eyes were on the altarpiece and the Doge, who was about to utter his verdict.

"I have never seen a nobler or more charming picture."

The cardinal added, "The madonna is worthy of Giovanni Bellini."

I separated the painting from those around it. Dürer's depiction of the madonna placing a rose wreath upon Maximilian, ruler of the Holy Roman Empire, while the Christ Child rewarded Pope Julius II with a similar garland, was perfect in detail. I thought that *The Feast of the Rose Garlands* was not a painting to compare with any others, that Dürer's eyes had given the madonna theme a unique treatment.

This realization enticed me into a passionate study of the other work he had done in Venice and which he had hung proudly. There was a painting of a young girl that revealed his mastery of line, yet the portrait of a woman that was next to it was in the manner of Giorgione, with soft modeling and subdued, delicate colors. Then, in a work he called *Christ Among the Doctors,* I observed that his brush was grotesque, even macabre, but he had applied his paint with great freedom, like Giorgione.

Foscari drew him aside and I heard the inspector offer him an annual pension of two hundred ducats to become a permanent resident of Venice.

Dürer turned to Giovanni Bellini and said, "Maestro, should I accept? Here, at least, I am a gentleman. At home I am a nobody."

Bellini replied, "I doubt that the last is true."

I ventured to say, "Signor Dürer, your work is much admired here."

If he heard me, he did not show it. I felt that as far as he was concerned, I did not exist. Yet I liked his work very much and I longed to tell him so. I wondered if that would matter to him.

He said to Foscari, "I do not think Italian painters would like my presence here. So far, I have earned much praise but little profit. I still have not been paid for the work of mine which was stolen."

Foscari said apologetically, "Signore, that cannot be proven."

Bellini said, "My friend, you must not look back, but ahead."

"I do not wish to leave you. How I shall freeze after this sun!"

"Have you ever considered settling in Venice?"

"Yes, at the outset, but I cannot, dear friend. My wife and family in Nuremberg need me. But I have silenced those who said that I was good as an engraver but did not know how to handle the colors in painting."

Dürer stood like an evangelical prophet. His ceremonial clothes, his narrow features, fervent yet severe, his long brown beard, his imposing presence all seemed to speak with the voice of God. And yet, I reflected, even in his own flesh he had to idealize himself, if not his fellow painters. Still I would have liked Dürer to pay attention to me.

I learned years later that he was suffering continually from depression and torturing nightmares. But so have I suffered, I think sadly, in my old age.

Many Venetians still say that his work is ugly, barbaric, and harsh in its appraisal of humanity, but I differ. I find it unique.

As I dress myself, to prove that I am not yet in my dotage, I recall something else that Dürer said that I have inscribed on my mind: "What beauty is I do not know. Nobody knows it except God."

Now I sought to work in my own manner without violating Giorgione's concept, vague though it was. By the time we halted for the winter, I had changed my style so that my figures became more forceful than his, grander in stature, and more concerned with color than with fancy.

I felt better and I was free of melancholy. I became single-minded about the human body. This was so strong in me that my nudes dominated my frescoes and I thought, Every artist has favorite things he prefers to paint and mine are the expressions of the flesh.

When we resumed work on the Fondaco the following spring I was more confident. I no longer cared whether others said that I painted in the manner of Giovanni Bellini or had assumed the style of Giorgione. I did my figures naturally. We were approaching completion and he seemed satisfied with what I was doing. His figures were more plentiful than mine, but I was content, for I felt that mine were stronger.

I was particularly pleased with my figure of Judith. Although she was seated, I felt that I gave her majesty. She held the head of a giant while she wielded the sword which she had used to dismember him, and I colored his blood a vivid red on the sunny surface of the wall.

I was almost finished when I was informed that Francesco Barbarigo wished to speak to me. This was not a request to ignore; he belonged to the highest aristocracy; his father had been the Doge when I had arrived in Venice; his family was one of the most influential in the Republic.

So I descended my scaffold nervously. Several servants stood behind the elegantly clad personage, but he wished to speak to me alone.

He was younger than I expected, short and stocky, with brown hair that fell to his neck, hazel eyes, and a commanding presence. I was surprised when he told me that he wanted a portrait of himself from my brush.

As I bowed and mumbled, "I am honored, my lord," he added, "In the fashion of your Judith. She attracts attention immediately. She has presence. My steward will arrange the details." With that, he strode off.

Tommaso Carita, who had served his father, the Doge, was experienced in such matters. The elderly steward, whose features resembled a hawk's, with his pointed chin and curved beak of a nose, stated that his lord, Francesco Barbarigo, would be at my studio a week from today, and that I should be prepared to paint him in oil in the manner of my Judith, and if it were satisfactory I would receive fifty ducats. He was gone before I could inform him that I was not a member of the Guild of Painters, and so, ineligible to do this portrait. There was only one possible remedy.

I climbed up Giorgione's scaffold, although this was forbidden while he was working, and interrupted him. He was angry—he was painting a tranquil nude to represent Peace—and for an instant I felt he would push me off the raised platform. It was swaying dangerously, for it was not meant to hold both of us and a wind had sprung up, but I had to speak.

"Giorgione, you promised to ask the Guild to admit me."

"You scramble up here, risk our lives, for that? You are childish!"

I clutched a rope to keep from falling. Hanging over the Grand Canal seemed more dangerous to me than dangling over the street, and his anger was strong, yet I had to go on. "Barbarigo has asked me to paint him."

"He can wait."

"He will not wait. Please!" I reached out to implore his mercy and I knocked his paints into the water.

For a desperate moment I thought he was going to hurl me after them.

I cried out, "You did promise to speak to the Guild on my behalf!"

"I do not remember. Moreover, it is not necessary."

"Giorgione, I need the ducats."

"I gave you ten."

"You swore that you would ask for more. But we are almost done, and so far, you have not uttered a word. Perhaps that is why you do not approach the Guild on my account. Because you are afraid."

For another instant I thought he was going to strike me. Fear was one challenge that he could not abide. Then he regained his self-control and said, "Such a comment is unworthy, but I will speak to the Guild."

The following week, and the day before I was expected to meet Barbarigo at my studio, I was ordered to appear before the governing tribunal of the Guild of Venetian Painters in their office next to the Doge's Palace.

I expected Foscari to be one of the judges, but I was surprised to see that Giovanni Bellini was going to examine me, too, and dismayed that Zuccato, as president of the Guild, was the third judge.

Giorgione was by my side, but I felt that Zuccato and I were irreconcilable. I doubted that Bellini would support me either, and I was not even certain about Foscari, although he was friendly to Big George. I wore my quietest clothes and a sedate gray cape to show my respect for their authority, yet I felt equal to them in painting. I was as tall as any of them now, my hands were a man's hands, and very strong.

Zuccato growled, "Vecellio could not even execute my mosaics! How can he be expected to do the fine arts! I do not recommend him!"

Bellini said, "And he is not notable for his obedience."

Giorgione said, "Maestro, he was very young when he came to your bottega. But he has learned much since then."

Zuccato snarled, "Under your tutelage?"

"Under all of us. You and the master taught him much."

This did not appease the mosaicist and I still thought he was the ugliest man I knew, with the possible exception of Foscari.

"And he has served the required seven years."

Foscari asked, "Are you sure, Giorgione?"

"Positive. And no one has questioned his work on the Fondaco."

"I do," Zuccato said harshly, "since he is not qualified."

"The excellence of his frescoes qualifies him."

Bellini said, "I can see his side from my studio. I look at them often. His use of perspective would have pleased Dürer."

I blurted out, "Which I have learned from you, Maestro!"

"Young man, what other qualifications do you have?"

"I learned about oils from you. I execute my colors in your manner."

I saw an expression in Bellini's eyes which said: What should I do?

But Zuccato stated, "He failed his apprenticeship with me. I do not need anybody else's opinions. I do not support his admission."

While the other two judges wavered, I said, "I have learned how to work at all the branches that pertain to our profession. And I honor what I learned in the Bellini bottega. I will always be grateful that I was allowed to partake of its wisdom. And that I am a Venetian."

Bellini said, "Giorgione, perhaps you are right that this young man has matured and gained some wisdom. Foscari, do you agree?"

"If Giorgione will vouch for him. And guarantee he pays his fees."

My friend did so and I was admitted to the Venetian Guild of Painters by a vote of two to one. Zuccato ran out after he shouted, "No!"

Giorgione gave me permission to be absent from the Fondaco the next day so that I could start the portrait of the patrician. Barbarigo was attended by his steward and he wanted me to paint him quickly, for he said that he had to be in Rome soon on government business. But I refused to be hurried and I spent the first afternoon arranging how he should sit.

Meanwhile, as he strode around my studio and viewed my self-portrait and the one I had done of Giorgione, his impatience vanished. I sensed that in his own way he was as nervous as I was, that he felt he was taking a risk in asking an obscure artist like myself to paint his likeness.

Now he was willing to allow his sittings to fit in with my work on the Fondaco. He put off his journey to Rome.

Then, although at the best Barbarigo was just a pleasant-looking man of about thirty, and not beautiful, the developing portrait became beautiful to look at. While I painted him as he was I gave his person an importance and presence that demanded the viewer's immediate attention.

Barbarigo was so pleased that his steward presented me with two gold-embroidered shirts in addition to my fee of fifty ducats, and asked me to do a portrait of his unwed sister, Elisabetta Barbarigo.

I consented enthusiastically but when she appeared at my studio with his steward I was distressed. She was fat, homely, and middle aged. I could not do with her what I had done with her brother. But if I refused this new commission, there would be no other from this rich and influential family. So I bowed before her and said, "I am privileged."

Since I could not portray her as a beauty, I sought to give her strength. Finally, with the use of color, I painted a person who possessed warmth and dignity.

I wanted to turn both portraits to the wall, then return to them in a few months to improve them, but Barbarigo said that was unnecessary.

But when he saw my distress, he seemed to consider my feelings for the first time. He consoled me, declaring, "Vecellio, I do not expect them to last a lifetime. It is enough that my family has these portraits to identify our place in the new palazzo I am building."

I did not agree with him, but the fifty ducats I received for his sister's portrait silenced my questions. Even so, I was not totally satisfied with these paintings, although I hoped that they would obtain me other commissions. And I was grateful for the Barbarigo patronage.

For the first time, I was able to sign my own work. Before I delivered the portraits, I put at the bottom of each picture two strong and distinct initials: "T V."

I WAS WRONG YET RIGHT

I WAS WRONG YET RIGHT

You were right yet wrong
It will not happen again
Not until it does
And then
We will both see
        as clearly again

Stymean Karlen

JUST AS I FELT that the completion of the frescoes was within our reach, Giorgione climbed up my scaffold and ordered me to stop work.

When he saw that I did not want to, he declared, "I have informed the Senate that we have run out of money for materials and that we cannot continue unless another fee is forthcoming."

I said, "That is not true. We could manage with what we have."

"That is a decision I must make. The agreement is in my name."

I was still unhappy with his decision and I stated, "This is the first clear day we have had this week, although it is August, and by September there will be much rain, and we cannot work after October. We take a great risk. They will ask other artists to finish our frescoes."

"On the contrary, it is the best time to stop. Too much is done for anyone, even the most skillful copyist, to finish in our manner. Moreover, the Fondaco is scheduled to open this autumn and they will not delay it for a few hundred ducats. Do not argue. Come down."

"You will not get that much money."

"Yes, I will. The monthly expenditures on the building alone

are six hundred ducats. They can spare half of that. Dürer received a hundred ducats for *The Feast of the Rose Garden* and
he took only five months."

A week passed without word from anybody. No one worked on
the frescoes while we waited for a decision. I walked by my side
of the Fondaco every day. The weather had become consistently
sunny and I felt that if I saw someone else finishing my figures,
it would be unbearable, I would pull the painter down, although
that could be punished by death.

Giorgione, however, insisted on remaining in his studio. He told
me, "I can see my frescoes clearly from my window. The pause
will refresh us. It will give us the time and opportunity to refine
our work."

I refused the wine he offered me and stared out the window
which was closest to my figures. I had done them with such loving
care, it had given me great pleasure, but now I felt deprived. I
was willing to finish them for nothing, if necessary. I wondered
if I should work alone from now on.

Giorgione said, "I hear that some of the members of the Senate
are bitter about what they call my 'unpatriotic behavior,' but they
cannot find a painter who can guarantee to finish the frescoes in
our manner. And the German merchants are very impatient about
the delay. If the opening is postponed any longer, they will lose
much money."

"So that is why you halted when you did!"

"Of course. I considered all these things."

The next few days, to ease my anxiety, I walked around Venice as
if my life depended on it. I had to find a new dimension in my work,
but I could not establish where. Altarpieces of the scope of Dürer's
were out of my reach; no one would take such a risk with me. Yet
there were churches in abundance in Venice, even on the most
insignificant squares and off tiny alleys, fragments of life, struc-
tures of piety, many of them barren inside.

I had expected, too, to hear from Barbarigo, he had seemed
pleased with my portraits, but after a week without a word from
him, I doubted that I could create any interest in my brush.

About two weeks after we had halted work on the frescoes,
Giorgione ran excitedly into the studio and exclaimed, "I told
you not to be afraid! As I expected, the Germans agreed to contribute to our fee!"

He handed me a hundred ducats. It was the largest single amount

I had received for my work, and yet I was not satisfied. I asked him intensely and suspiciously, "How much did they give you?"

He replied just as suspiciously, "Why do you ask?"

"I wondered if you obtained what you wanted."

"Exactly what I demanded. Three hundred ducats. As my assistant you are entitled to a third. Or do you think that you deserve more?" I felt like his equal now but I did not wish to quarrel with him. So I shrugged even as I thought of opening my own studio.

Instead, after we finished the frescoes a month later, I decided to visit my uncle to show him that he had been wrong when he had predicted that I would never amount to anything. I knew he did not approve of Big George, or the way I lived, and so I clothed myself in a gold-embroidered shirt, my most ceremonial hose, a velvet doublet, and a fashionable cape in my determination to impress my uncle with my affluence. He resided near the Rialto and as I strode purposefully toward his shop in a back alley of Venice, I sought to appear successful and mature.

The neighborhood walls pressed in on his quarters and they were so high and narrow they shut out the sky, and there was the nauseating stench of garbage and constant dampness, ugly and oppressing. But as I stepped into his shop my heart beat violently. He was putting his gilt madonnas in the front where they would attract the most attention and behind them his glass trinkets, painting materials, and art objects. His thirteen-year-old son was dusting a small glass lion—a replica of those in front of San Marco—and he saw me first. In his surprise he dropped the glass and cried out, "Papa, it is Tiziano! And he is dressed like a gentleman!"

Antonio stiffened, then shouted, "Tell your mama that he is here!"

Toma Tito yelled that news into the kitchen and my aunt screamed back, "Has he come for dinner? I only have enough for three!"

I said, "Not for dinner, Uncle. Just to see how you are feeling."

"I am feeling. You neglect us for your painter friends."

My aunt emerged from her kitchen, wiping her greasy hands on a dirty apron, and shouted, "You never visit us unless you are in trouble!"

I doubted that anyone in my uncle's family spoke quietly or calmly and I felt like fleeing, but I longed to feel close to someone and at this moment there did not seem to be anybody else. I missed my parents very much and Antonio was my father's brother. At this thought I said with vigor, "Uncle, I came to celebrate my good fortune with you."

"Have you finally obtained a permanent position?"

"I have finished my frescoes. I would like to show them to you."

"I will see them when I pass them. Is that why you wear somebody else's clothes? Or have you put all your money on your back?"

"The shirt is a gift from Barbarigo for painting him and his sister."

"Is that all he gave you?"

"I also received a fee from him, as I did for the frescoes."

"How much?"

"If you are too busy to see my frescoes, I can come back later."

My aunt blocked the door—she had grown so fat she filled every inch of it—and asked, "Did you truly paint a Barbarigo?"

"Yes. Why do you ask?

"You attended him in his palazzo?" Her tone became respectful.

"Barbarigo is building a new one. He sat in my studio."

"Antonio, we should look at his frescoes. It can do no harm. Barbarigo is a great Venetian patrician and a man of large influence."

My uncle grumbled that I was selfish but he donned a cloak while my aunt changed her clothes and then I led them to the Fondaco.

Antonio glared at the frescoes, exclaimed, "What is your argument?"

"Uncle, judge them from the way they look."

"But there is no recognizable story. Your figures should express our greatness, but I do not understand them. And your friend's side is even stranger. No wonder there has been so much criticism of them."

I was shocked. I asked angrily, "Who told you that?"

"Many people say the frescoes are not worth looking at, most ignore them, and the few who do observe them wonder what they are about."

My aunt interrupted, "Antonio, he did paint Barbarigo."

He sneered, "It must have been before he did the frescoes. If the nobleman saw these, he would never have given him such a commission."

"Uncle, he asked me to paint him because he admired my figures. But you think that I am mad."

"You have a long memory. It is a question of taste, I suppose. We have the best artisans in the world. If you followed my trade there would not be such uncertainty in your life. With what you learned in the Bellini bottega, you could sell oils, crayons, pens, inks, and you could become an expert on the proper uses of canvas."

It began to rain on my frescoes and for a moment I had a sinking feeling that the moisture would diminish them. But after the shower passed, they looked as they had when I had finished them. I yearned fervently to stand at the peak of the bridge and shout to the world that the street side was mine! mine! But who would listen?

I asked, "Have you heard from my parents?"

My aunt said, "Your mother wrote me recently. She asked me how you were. I think she still misses the little boy who left Cadore."

"Does she still doubt that her baby can walk? I cannot stay a child all my life. What did you tell her?"

"That we see you rarely but that you seem free of contagion, in good health, and that you are growing up. I am not sure she likes that."

"Thank you for coming with me. I will visit you more often."

My uncle said, "You should see your mama first."

"Has she been ill?" I was alarmed and suddenly stricken with guilt.

"No more than is usual in these evil times. But she is frail."

I escorted them back to their home, while I thought, No one is going to force me to give up my dream. Yet I decided also to return to Cadore to see my parents as soon as I was free from other obligations.

Giorgione said we must celebrate the completion of the frescoes by inviting Beatrice and Felicia to spend the night with us in the studio.

I told him that Felicia was never free at night and he replied that he would arrange it, and as he planned, a week later she and Beatrice joined Giorgione and myself at his studio. He supplied a sumptuous feast and yet she ate nervously, glancing over her shoulder repeatedly, as if she expected to be followed, although there was no sign of anyone outside.

And when she walked I was startled. She wore the lofty chopines that were the fashion among many of the Venetian women and they raised her in height above me. I did not like that she was taller than I now and I was angry. Moreover, I thought these elevated stiltlike shoes were dangerous; I had heard of women who had fallen and broken their ankles. I begged her to remove them. But she refused. I tried to dance with her but she teetered so precariously on the chopines that it was impossible.

Beatrice, to ease my irritation, suggested that we view the frescoes. Felicia minced to the windows on her high wooden clogs and I thought, She moves as if she were on stilts; this fashion is ugly and stupid.

Torches were lit with the coming of nightfall but I saw women still sitting on their terraces where they had spent the afternoon in the sun so that they could bleach their hair. I did not like that fashion either; I preferred hair that was a natural red, brown, or black.

As we stared at the frescoes Giorgione was reflective and suddenly he asked Beatrice, "Are you sure you can tell mine from Tiziano's?"

She replied diplomatically, "Both are admirable in their own way."

"I seek to arrest time," he said, "while he dramatizes it."

Felicia said nothing. She was preoccupied with her chopines.

Two gondolas passed the frescoes and I heard laughter and I feared they were ridiculing our work. This added to my irritation and when I asked her to spend the night with me in my studio—a pleasure I had craved since it had been denied me—she looked like a stork as she crossed the floor, then fell and lay helplessly and could not get up. I refused to assist her despite her pleas and in her rage she threw her chopines at me. I responded by using them as fuel for our fireplace.

I had never seen her so upset, so irate. She sobbed, "They were a gift. I will be flogged if I return without them." But by the time she retrieved the chopines they were too charred to wear. She screamed, "Tiziano, I wore my best things for you! I will never forgive you!"

I said, "I will buy you another pair on the Rialto tomorrow morning."

Giorgione and Beatrice assumed that we were engaged in just another lovers' quarrel and they retired to their bedroom and I suggested that we follow their example. She seemed appeased by my promise and she followed me to my quarters in her bare feet. She looked lovely and natural, her figure slender and enticing, but she was distracted. It was the most disappointing time we had spent in bed. Her sexual response was reluctant, more from habit than from desire.

The next morning I bought her a pair of regular-heeled shoes but she was not pleased. As she left, she told me, "Without my chopines,

I will not be able to see you again. Their destruction has betrayed us."

I thought she was exaggerating out of spite but Beatrice warned me to be careful. However, she would not explain and I did not know what she was talking about.

Felicia did not return. After several weeks I realized that I would probably not see her again. Then Giorgione drove her out of my mind.

We were discussing the possibility of applying for a commission to paint decorations for the Doge's Palace when he said somberly, "That may be a mistake. I doubt that you will be satisfied with what I pay you. Perhaps you should seek this work yourself."

Bewildered, hurt, I said, "You do not like my art?"

"That is not the question. If you bargain for yourself, you will be more satisfied with your fees." He was gone before I could comment.

I sit in my royal armchair, a gift of the emperor, waiting for my steward to bring my breakfast, and I turn this memory over and over, and still, so many years later, I wonder where I might have erred.

I know I have been charged with an inordinate affection for money, but if I have been preoccupied with my fees it is because my patrons paid me so slowly, often not for years, while my expenses accumulated. Then there has been my need to provide for my children. Once they were born that became my mission in life. Yet it has given me much pain.

I think bitterly, A father who loves his children is not quite sane.

I have painted so much in order to provide for them.

Pomponio, my elder, has been destined for the church from birth. There, I believe, he will be secure for life. I have even dared to believe I can provide for him as the Medicis have for their own, and the Borgias. But despite the benefices I have bought for him, he has lost them with his dissipations, although they have cost me a fortune.

Orazio has become my partner and that, too, has been expensive, for the only works he can sell are those paintings which bear my name.

Just to think of my daughter cracks my heart. Beloved Lavinia, the image of her charming mother, has been an overwhelming passion in my life. Since her mother had suffered so because I had not married her until after the children were born, one of the great purposes of my life was to marry off my daughter favorably and honorably. When the family of the noble Cornelio Sarcinello, one of the most patrician in Venice, was willing to allow their son to wed Lavinia in return for a dowry of fourteen hundred ducats, although this was another fortune to me, I did everything in my power to furnish it. But this marriage had to be postponed because my patrons paid me slower than they had agreed by contract. It took me several years to raise the necessary fourteen hundred ducats. Often, in my effort to raise this dowry, I felt I was pledging my soul to the devil.

And now Lavinia is dead and I am afraid that Pomponio hates me and that Orazio merely tolerates me for what I can do for him.

My steward's knock ends my reverie.

Soon after Giorgione implied that we should part a boy came to my studio while I was carving a woodcut. I was seeking a religious motif and I was following the manner of Dürer. The interruption annoyed me until the boy informed me that his lord, Francesco Barbarigo, desired to see me at his new palazzo. I was surprised by the suddenness of this request but patricians had a reputation for being impulsive, and I decided that he liked my portraits so much that he desired another one.

I hastily put on my best clothes but by the time I reached the street the messenger was gone. I turned in the direction of the new Barbarigo palazzo, which was on the Grand Canal close to the Doge's Palace, and wished I possessed a gondola like Giorgione; I was uneasy in the darkness and the winding, narrow streets and alleys. Then, just off the entrance to the studio, a young, burly soldier stepped out of the shadows and attacked me. For a terrifying instant I thought he was going to run me through with his sword. Instead, as he neared me, I saw that he held a cudgel. I recoiled, feeling trapped, and as he swung the cudgel at my head I instinctively threw up my arm to protect myself and so that my hands would not be damaged. My arm took the main force of his blow and as he prepared to attack me again I heard people approaching.

The bravo vanished and a moment later Giorgione appeared, accompanied by Piombo and Vecchio.

I told them what had happened and Giorgione replied sharply, "You may be becoming too good a painter. Some of them fear you."

"I doubt it was a fellow artist. I think it was because of Felicia. The bravo seemed more interested in punishing me than in killing me."

"He could be in the employ of her master, a Turkish sea captain."

"Giorgione, I thought he was her father."

"That is a story she spreads to protect herself. She does not like others to know that she is the mistress of a man twice her age. It was your youth that caused her to favor you. I did not warn you about him because I did not wish to spoil your pleasure."

"Then you think the story that Barbarigo wants to see me is a ruse?"

Piombo cut in knowingly, "That nobleman is in Rome."

"Are you certain?"

"He desires a commission from me, too. You are not the only portrait painter in the Republic."

I was envious and I wondered what Barbarigo could want from Piombo.

"As it is, Tiziano Vecellio, you are overpraised."

His tone was mocking and I disliked it. Yet, although I sensed danger ahead, I felt compelled to ask, "What are you referring to now?"

"A number of noblemen told me that Giorgione did better work on the facade over the street than on the wall over the Grand Canal."

I saw Giorgione stiffen and stare at me suspiciously and I said hurriedly, "They were joking. They knew that I did those frescoes."

"Why should they? Did you sign them?"

"I was not supposed to. I was the assistant. But my manner is different from Giorgione's."

"That was what they preferred. They said the street side was more dramatic, pictorial, that they did not understand the Canal side."

Giorgione asked me sternly, "Is that true?"

I said, "I do not like my work being attributed to someone else."

Piombo added, "Yet you cannot deny what I say. You were there with the noblemen and when they praised your work as Giorgione's, you did not utter a word. You allowed them to make this grievous error."

"I wanted to find out if their praise was sincere. If they knew it was my work, I could not have trusted their words."

Giorgione said caustically, "That is a weak explanation."

I stammered, "I am sorry, I . . ."

He interrupted me curtly, "Do not be sorry. You have given me much evidence lately that you no longer wish to work with me."

"But I do. I would rather work with you than any artist in Venice."

"As an assistant?"

I hesitated. I did feel there were new possibilities in my life.

"I doubt that. Piombo, what else did these noblemen say?"

"They must have thought the frescoes over the Canal were Vecellio's for they were critical of the figures, they said they contained no plot, or anything representing the deeds of a particular person. They claimed that they were too fanciful to please Venetian taste."

Giorgione turned to Vecchio, asked, "Have you heard similar views?"

I felt he was determined to flagellate himself, and me. He halted my effort to explain and urged Vecchio to speak.

Vecchio said, "You are already a renowned artist but Tiziano still has to establish a reputation. It is natural for him to use you."

I cried out, "To equal you, Big George, but not to excel you!"

Even as I expressed that, I realized that was the wrong thing to say, for he flushed irately and declared, "Others have warned me that you are utilizing your position with me to your own advantage and stabbing me in the back. But I hesitated to believe that until now."

"Who spread such false reports about me?"

"It does not matter. It is enough that it is true."

I turned back to Piombo and Vecchio and implored them to tell Big George that this was not true. Vecchio did not commit himself, but Piombo said, "Vecellio, it distresses me to bring this affair to our friend's attention, but I would betray my obligations to him if I did not tell him the truth. When I heard that you painted Barbarigo, it was clear to me that you were not content to remain an assistant."

"Should I have refused this commission? Would you have done so?"

"I would not have allowed the patricians to think that your work was Giorgione's and thus seek to gain their esteem at his expense."

"I did not ask for the comparison. I do not like such situations."

"Nonetheless," Giorgione stated positively, "you encouraged that to my detriment. I have thought for some time that it is foolish for us to work together. It will be better for both of us if we separate. I need your quarters. I will appreciate it if you vacate the second-floor studio by tomorrow." He rushed upstairs to express his determination.

I was shattered. Piombo followed Giorgione, but Vecchio lingered and said, "I have my own workshop now, too. It is not as fine as Big George's, the rooms are not on the Grand Canal, but they are suitable for painting, and you are welcome to use them until you find your own bottega."

Bewildered, distraught, I asked, "You did not speak to me for a long time. Why do you desire my presence now?"

"I was hurt and offended because you preferred Giorgione's manner, although I was the one who got you into the Bellini bottega. You are the only apprentice I recommended to them. Do you wonder I was troubled?"

"Palma, I thought it was because of your niece."

"She is precious to me. I will kill anyone who harms her. But if the intention is honorable there is nothing to fear."

Despite my grief over Giorgione's rejection of me, I realized that each of the three painters was confirming—in his own way—that I had matured enough to become a serious rival and so was an artist to fear, to destroy, or to use. I said, "I respect your niece very much."

"Good!" Vecchio said decisively, as if that were settled, at least for now. "We can be useful to each other until you are settled."

I went upstairs to say good-bye to Giorgione but his door was locked. Yet I knew he was in, for I heard him speaking with Piombo.

Many times I have wondered what would have happened if I had knocked.

But I was proud, too, as proud as he was, and so I decided to move my belongings into Vecchio's quarters without another word. The following morning Vecchio helped me carry the only possessions that truly mattered to me, my paintings, along the cramped alleys until we reached his rooms. They were a few minutes away from the Rialto, smaller than Giorgione's, but intimate and more private.

I thanked Palma for his hospitality and aid and told him that I was going to visit my parents in Cadore. He looked disturbed, as if I were using his rooms just to store my things, although he had suggested that himself, and I added, "I will be back. I cannot do without the air of Venice. I must pick our many colors out of the air and put them on my brush. But I must see my family. I have neglected them too long."

Vecchio nodded approvingly. He even looked solicitous.

But after he left to visit Bellini's bottega—he had to finish a painting of the master's—I could no longer control myself. Ever since I had seen Giorgione's locked door I had been afflicted with a cold numbness. I knew that if I lived to be a hundred I would never forget the pain of this moment. I retreated into my private misery and wept until I thought the tears would never end.

* * *

Now I turn away from the fruit and wine my steward has brought me and read what Vasari wrote about Giorgione:

". . . the pain of Giorgione's loss was made tolerable because of the accomplished pupils he left behind. Piombo the Venetian and Titian of Cadore, whose work far surpassed let alone equaled what was done by him."

I differ with Vasari. He has listened to the roar of the mob, but I place as high a value on Giorgione's work as any I have known.

Even now, so many years later, I ask myself: What could have gone wrong? When there was so much that was right between us.

I find no answers and so I do what I have done most of the days of my life. I start to paint, this time on a self-portrait where I hope to find what is missing in the *Pietà*. But when I think of Giorgione there are still tears in my eyes. And a great stillness as if we are the only two creatures on earth.

WIND

WIND

stop blowing through my window
those beautiful
perfectly sculpted dead leaves
Especially the tiny baby ones
just born

I do not know if they cry
or I
as they lie on my floor
by the window
waiting for me to bury them

Or do you blow them to me
in sympathy
Knowing finally only I
would do that for them

Then do not stop blowing
all your dead beauties
through my window
But do not tear them
from their homes
until they stop breathing
inside their sculpture

Stymean Karlen

I RETURNED to Cadore just before the autumn colors faded.

It was late October and it was an arduous journey in spite of the fine weather. The winding road was dusty, then rocky and uphill, and finally mountainous as it approached Cadore through wild gorges and past towering cliffs. I sat in a wooden wagon next to

Filippo Forni, who whipped his horse while he talked about the trade he expected to establish with the iron mines that sustained the life of Cadore. He left me off at the Piazza dell' Arsenale, the heart of the village. My home was near the square and I walked toward it eagerly. No one was about—it was in the middle of the afternoon—and I realized that the siesta prevailed even more in Cadore than it did in bustling Venice.

I had traveled while the weather was good and at a time when I recalled Cadore fondly, and yet so I could give myself an excuse to return to Venice before the snows came and made the road impassable.

Bright sunshine dominated the day and the scenery was etched with a clarity that delighted me. The gray peaks of the Dolomites pierced the blue skies, the horizon was vast and heavenly, and the colors of the landscape were vivid and beautiful. There was a grove of trees in front of my home and the colors of their leaves fascinated me. At the center were reds of many shades, yellows that I yearned to paint, and browns that gave me great pleasure. The wind blew a cluster of leaves onto the doorstep of my home and I saw the sapling at the door, still not fully grown, and I longed to bend it— as I had done as a child to prove to myself that I was growing stronger—but I did not, feeling that would be childish. There was a stone lion in front of the house that my papa had put there to show he was a faithful citizen of the Republic.

The rest of the two-story house was as I remembered it. The solid stone walls that had been carved out of the surrounding Alps were as sturdy as ever, and I liked that the low-pitched tile roof extended beyond the wall so that it sheltered the balcony. The windows behind the wooden shutters still were without glass and I resolved that when I earned more ducats I would rectify that lack in the Venetian fashion.

Then I was afraid. I had dressed carefully, but I had not told anyone that I was coming. I desired the advantage of surprise and I was not sure that my family would approve of the way I had changed. Yet this time I knocked vigorously on the door. It was opened at once and I was glad that it was my mama, for I trusted her feeling for me.

She was so startled to see me that for an instant I thought she would faint. Then her incredulity became wonder and joy and she cried out, "Francesco, Orsa, Caternia, come quickly! Tiziano is home!"

Although she was a small woman, I felt she would smother me

with her embrace. Yet even as she warmed me, I was chilled by her frailness.

My brother and two sisters ran in and kissed me. Now I was taller than Francesco, although he was older, but he was heavier and darker, while both of my sisters had developed into attractive young women.

Mama exclaimed, "Child, I did not know that you were coming!"

I started to say—I am not a child any longer—but she was so happy to see me that I said instead, "I wanted to surprise you."

"If I had known I would have cooked a plump hen for dinner, you like white meat so. But with the war coming our fowl have become scrawny."

"How is Papa?"

"He is meeting with the other town councillors this afternoon to decide who is to command the militia against the invading Germans. But he will be glad to see you. He misses you and talks about it often."

"Mama, is the threat of war serious?"

"All the men in Cadore are arming. Is this not so in Venice?"

"No. Everything goes on in *La Serenissima* as usual."

"Venetians expect us to fight their battles. But this is too festive an occasion to spoil with such concerns." She eyed me closely. "Your nose and chin are the same and so are your eyes and coloring. But my little one, you have grown so. You have become the tallest Vecellio."

While we waited that afternoon for Papa to return—Mama yearned to tell him that I was home, but Francesco warned her that he had left word that he was not to be disturbed under any circumstances, the town council's business was vital—she wanted to know how I lived, what I ate, but her main concern was my health, while I felt uneasy. I doubted that Papa would agree with the course I planned to follow, and although Mama did not ask about my work, my brother did.

"Tiziano, what opportunities exist for an artist in Venice?"

"It is uncertain. It varies from artist to artist."

"Are you not favored by your association with the Bellini bottega?"

"That studio's value and reputation are exaggerated. Many artists in Venice suffer from oppressive influences. Francesco, why do you ask?"

My brother shrugged and changed the subject. My sisters were silent, as was the custom, but they did admire my fine clothes with their eyes.

I heard the clank of metal and Papa strode in clad in heavy armor. He bore an ornately carved pike as a symbol of authority and he announced proudly, so excited he did not notice me, "Lucia, I have been appointed captain of the Cadore militia again. To lead our soldiers in the war."

"Gregorio, it is a great honor, and Tiziano has joined us to celebrate it. Our little one is back."

I yearned to embrace Papa, but I did not, for he was very angry. He shouted furiously, "Francesco should have notified me!"

Francesco said, "Papa, you said I must not. I simply obeyed you."

"Obey! Obey! Have you no judgment of your own! Tiziano, let me view you properly. What have you learned? Are you strong?"

He grasped my hand to test my grip. I responded firmly and he nodded approvingly and examined the rest of me with great care.

Then he stated, "Sometimes these past years I have thought that you were trying to avoid us. Does it take so long to learn how to paint?"

"It takes a lifetime."

"That is no excuse not to come home."

I possessed my own passions and energies, but I did not wish to define myself, to explain, and so I replied, "I had my memories."

"Memories, what are they but illusions? But you look well. You still have my strong jaw, my straight nose, my splendid posture."

I thought that Orsa resembled me the most now but I was quiet.

"And now you return just when I must leave."

"Papa, I came just to visit. I have work to finish in Venice."

"Antonio wrote me about your frescoes. He said there is much talk about them, some good, some bad, and that they are difficult to comprehend."

"Everything cannot be explained, should not be explained."

Orsa asked, "Tiziano, have you painted beautiful things?"

Mama stated, "We can talk about that later. Now we must eat."

We sat down around the kitchen table, which was the heart of the house, and as Papa discarded his armor I asked, "May I paint you in this battle dress? It should be a portrait worthy of a captain of militia."

"How do I know that you will represent me properly?"

"Papa, I have painted Barbarigo and his sister."

"Did they pay you?"

"Fifty ducats for each portrait."

He hesitated, then declared, "I will consider it."

"Papa, I do not have much time. I have to return to Venice soon."

Mama cried in alarm, "My little one, you will not be punished for painting for the Germans?" When I looked puzzled, she added, "The Fondaco is a German warehouse. And they have become our enemies."

"We were commissioned by the Venetian Senate, not the German merchants."

Papa asked, "Are you still Giorgione's assistant?"

"We have separated. I intend to open my own studio."

"That is a mistake. You are too young and not yet well known."

"I must make the attempt. And Barbarigo does like my work."

"You cannot trust a patrician. They change with the wind. And the time is difficult and dangerous. You could not choose a worse moment to open your own studio. Europe has united to ravage the Republic. Venice has grown so rich that the poorer countries have decided to divide our lands among themselves. We face the combined might of the Holy Roman Emperor Maximilian, Louis XII of France, and Pope Julius II. They say he is going to excommunicate Venice. The days ahead will be harsh."

"Yet you prepare to fight despite the overwhelming odds."

"I am a soldier. My father was also a soldier."

"What do you want from me?"

"Stay home. Take care of the family. A man is needed in the house. You could paint here. The light is good and the landscape is strong."

"I thought that Francesco would supply that need."

"Your brother has been ordered to accompany me."

"Is that what he desires, Papa?"

"Are you insane, questioning me? Is this the heresy they have taught you in Venice? No wonder you were expelled by Bellini."

"I left of my own choice. And Bellini was one of those who voted for me to be admitted into the Venetian Guild of Painters." But my heart ached as I remembered how Giorgione had struggled on my behalf.

"Nonetheless, your battle has not ended but just begun."

"That may be, but I think Francesco wants to assist me in Venice."

He said, "I have done some painting lately. But soldiers are needed more than artists now, Tiziano. I must serve Papa and Cadore."

Papa asked me eagerly, "Then you will stay here after all?"

"I cannot. If I remain away from Venice now, I will lose whatever opportunities I have established for myself."

"Then why did you return here?" Papa exclaimed angrily.

"To see you. To see all of you." I longed to add, Because I love you, Papa, but the words stuck in my throat. "I did miss you. Very much."

"Is that why you dress like a patrician? They will never accept you whatever you wear. Has Barbarigo invited you to dinner?"

"No. It is not considered fitting."

"And it never will be. If you were Giovanni Bellini's assistant, I could see a reason for your remaining in Venice. Since he has no kin, you might inherit his workshop. But instead of cultivating him, you try to outdo him, and thus you offend him. It is more madness."

I was so annoyed I started to leave the table, but his hand, still strong, pushed me down as he growled, "Eat! Or Mama will worry!"

Disturbed, I was unable to savor Mama's cooking. Papa grumbled that I had become too educated for his table, but I did not consider myself a learned man. I had not read Petrarch and my fancy for Boccaccio was only for his salacious tales, and I was still studying how to play the lute, and I preferred the feel of velvet and female flesh to country fare and hardy living, and yet I was proud of my affection for my family.

Papa stated sadly, "Tiziano, some day when you have children, you may understand how I feel. A man needs a son to carry on his name and to comfort him in old age. It is a necessity of nature and God's wish."

He looked so appealing, so emotional I wanted him to sit for me. I pleaded, "Papa, please, allow me to paint you in your armor?"

"With what? Mud? Rocks? Dust? You have no materials here."

Francesco said softly, "I have some oils, canvases, brushes, and a palette that Tiziano can use if he desires. You look well in armor."

"I will decide later. If there is any time left before I depart for the wars. And if I can be spared from my duties as a captain of the militia. Francesco should be a soldier. It is the nobler calling."

THE SONS OF TITIAN WHEN

THE SONS OF TITIAN WHEN
genius looked at them—they
like mirrors—felt they had to
reflect the genius of their father

This their instinct for survival
was stronger than necessity
yet pain was never intended
by the father   He loved them

But they did not want to die alone
as mortals
but be immortal with the father
and only as genius could they be with him

immortal then eternal

Stymean Karlen

I AM thinking happily of that first visit home to Cadore and of my need to paint constantly when I was young, even difficult subjects such as Papa—having paused on my new self-portrait, for I do not like the way I look in my mirror—when there is another loud knock on my studio door. It infuriates me, for it destroys my concentration, which is so essential to me when I am painting, and it is very loud, as if I were deaf. Yet its urgency forces me to ask, "What is wrong?"

My steward shouts through the thick oaken door, "Maestro, Paolo Cagliari, the Veronese, desires to speak to you! He says it is vital!"

So while I prefer to be alone with my memories, I open the door, for Paolo Veronese is not an artist who creates emergencies. My former pupil, who has won a large reputation with his brush, is as amiable as his work.

He bows respectfully before me and exclaims, "Maestro, it is as if a hundred years have passed since I had the joy of seeing you."

"I have been busy. Painting, as usual." I dismiss my steward, the slight, elderly Stefano Ballo, and ask, "Is your news so grave?"

It does not show on his face. Veronese is almost fifty, but he looks youthful. He wears the sumptuous silks and velvets of a gentleman in search of constant pleasure. His brown hair and beard are combed carefully and his high, receding forehead and long, pointed nose give him an attractive appearance. He seems free of shadows, but suddenly his tone becomes as gloomy as Tintoretto's as he says, "Pomponio is in serious trouble. He is charged with signing your name to someone else's work."

"My son is accused of forging my name?" I ask incredulously.

"That is the charge. He sold a Venus to Leonardo Donato, the Venetian envoy to Madrid, as a genuine Titian, but the ambassador, who has seen much of your original work at the court of Spain, became suspicious when he found that the surface had been extensively repainted."

"I do all my work over and over."

"Donato insists that this Venus lacks your spirit and color."

I feel stricken but I cannot accept such a bitter situation even as I fear that Pomponio is guilty. "Paolo, the envoy must be mistaken."

"Your son denies the charge. But he has been brought before the Holy Office of the Inquisition. If he is found guilty, he will be punished severely. He is to be tried today. Only your word can save him."

"Why was I not informed sooner?"

"Donato is determined to convict him. He is furious at Pomponio. He feels he has been made to look foolish, that this is a disgrace. I heard about this only through the Guild and I rushed here at once."

"Will they allow me to testify?"

"I doubt they dare to ignore the most eminent artist in Venice."

"How much time do we have?"

"A few hours. Maestro, are you painting anything new?"

I cover my just-begun self-portrait for I have not even reached the flesh and say, "Only a *Pietà*. It is not quite done." He appears so interested, I cannot resist asking, "Would you like to see it?"

"I would be honored. I am sure I will be richly rewarded."

I am not so certain but there is a new urgency in Veronese. Nervously I unlock my closet and he helps me remove the *Pietà* and place it where the light is best. While he examines it minutely,

I put on my darkest, most sedate garb and a black cape that is pious, but at the last moment I add the golden chain of knighthood that Charles V had given me and I decide to confront the Inquisitors boldly. Yet despite my experience and my reputation I am anxious when I ask him his view of the *Pietà*.

"It is very different from your usual manner."

"Does that trouble you?"

"Your painting grows darker while mine grows lighter."

"Perhaps the light is poor. The day is becoming cloudy."

"No, no, it is not that. After years of admiring your palette because of your glorious colors, it is as if you paint without color. Yet there is great power in the Magdalen. Her face is superb."

"I have painted many faces, but few are worth remembering."

"Maestro, your brush makes them worth remembering."

"Paolo, there is never just one way to look at anything."

"But you seem disheartened? Does your health trouble you?"

I stare at him, wondering whether I can trust him. My former student, who came to me as soon as he arrived in Venice from Verona at the age of twenty-five, has been a favorite of mine from the beginning. For while his present colors have become so rich they surfeit me, his earlier palette was delightfully shimmering and silvery. Yet in spite of his success he has remained a pleasant fellow, always willing to praise other painters, a most unusual trait in Venice and Florence. Then there is a need in me to confess that is almost overwhelming.

"I know a worthy physician, Maestro. He would be happy to examine you."

"No! I am not ill. It is old age that exhausts me."

"When you paint a *Pietà* with such power? I do not believe you."

"But it takes me so long these days. When I was your age I was able to paint four pictures at the same time and to feel exhilarated. Now I labor on one and I am exhausted. I awake each morning not knowing if my fingers will even be nimble enough to apply paint. My hands are numb often. They ache when it rains and it rains frequently in Venice and I cannot hold a brush then. Even on sunny days my hands tremble and grow weary quickly. Blurred vision forces me to question myself. Yet last year I worked with ease. This is the first time it is difficult for me."

"Maestro, it is no wonder you tire, you have painted so much."

"That does not console me. Without my work I am nothing."

"Allow Orazio to finish it. He is an official painter now."

"My son does not possess my manner."

"Then entrust it to Palma Giovane. He lacks your passion and color but he knows your manner better than anybody else. My brother, Bendetto, aids me, as Tintoretto's son aids him. It is the custom. I broke my finger last year in the middle of a vital commission and I felt blessed that my brother could paint in my style and complete my work."

No one understands my condition, I think, and I suggest that we go.

Veronese has come in his gondola and I order my steward to tell Orazio that I am going to the Doge's Palace on state business and that he should join me there. Then I ask Veronese to travel through the small canals which will lead us past the Fondaco. I am eager to see my frescoes, although I am not sure it is wise, for they are beginning to erode.

We float by the frescoes and I am grateful that almost seventy years later they are still recognizable, although lines have blurred, colors have faded, and I cannot identify some of the figures that Giorgione did. Time has served me better, I think, because the street side is less exposed to wind, dampness, and bad weather than the Canal walls.

Veronese asks, "Maestro, did you think of Giorgione when you chose me, just a year after I arrived in Venice, to paint frescoes by your side?"

"I chose you, as I hope he chose me, because you were qualified."

"These frescoes must have been magnificent when you painted them."

"I am not sure. I have never been sure. Not everyone admired them. Vasari, when he saw them about thirty years after they were finished, wrote: 'I have never been able to understand Giorgione's figures.' "

"He was prejudiced. He favored the Florentine manner."

"That may be. I do believe that if I had been dead when he saw them, as Giorgione was, I would have been damned, too."

Veronese orders his gondolier to pause so he can look more carefully.

I ask, "What do you think of them now?"

"They are weatherbeaten. But some of the figures could be cleaned."

"You do not answer my question!" I am annoyed and my tone shows it.

"Maestro, despite the erosion, they are still the finest frescoes in Venice." He orders his gondolier to move on to end a possible quarrel.

We approach the Doge's Palace from the lagoon and wherever I am—and I have seen Florence and Rome and many other highly praised sights—I am reminded that this remarkable building pleases me as much as anything I have ever seen. As we land at the foot of it, although I have observed it countless times, I continue to marvel at the miracle of its order and symmetry. The great oblong structure sparkles in the bright sunlight and as I absorb its luminous facade and the admirable balcony I am grateful that I can still clearly see this work of art. I know the orders of the Doge's Palace from memory: eighteen arches and thirty-eight pillars. I infinitely prefer its beauty to the clutter of styles that is San Marco. This beautiful, beautiful palace has such a harmony.

Veronese is silent until we reach the great staircase that leads into the ducal apartments, and then, as he offers me his arm to ease my climb up the thirty-one steps—I know each one of them intimately—he says passionately, "I will always be grateful for the way you supported me at my own trial. No other artist was willing to testify for me then."

It was a few years ago, I recall the time vividly, for I was astonished to hear that the Holy Office had summoned Veronese to *"explain"* his canvas, *The Feast in the House of Simon.* He had painted this immense Biblical banquet scene for the Dominicans but the Inquisition was critical of many of the details of this painting.

They ordered him to appear in the Hall of the Council of Ten so that they could examine him. This was where important political and criminal matters were judged, particularly those concerned with espionage and treason and public morality and other affairs that involved the security of the state. When he asked me to attend him there to testify in his behalf, I realized that the charge against him was serious.

I was warned that to support him was dangerous in spite of my position and I hesitated to appear. But when I learned that he was to be questioned about the quality of his work, I was offended. He was my pupil, he was a follower of mine, although our styles differed in many ways, and so I felt that I could not evade this situation, but my uneasiness remained.

So I joined him in the Room of the Council of Ten—one of the largest and most feared chambers in the Doge's Palace—and I was startled to see that no other artist was present. I expected Tintoretto to be there—he was supposed to be Veronese's friend—but possibly his absence was because he shared the Inquisition's views. His piety was fanatical.

I tried to find a comfortable seat along the side wall of this great and spacious hall, but the only good chairs were the three on the large curved dais at the head of the gallery and they were for the three Inquisitors. And while everyone was respectful to me, they were surprised to see me there. Several of the paintings on the wall had been done by me and Veronese and their pigments glistened in my eyes, yet I was uneasy.

The tribunal marched in escorted by armed guards and I realized that this was a trial of importance. The three monks were in black and I knew the leader, Father Alfonso Contarini, whose uncle was a cardinal.

This squat, scrawny, middle-aged priest had inquiring dark eyes, a sly expression, a thin, tight mouth and bloodless lips. He saw himself as an authority on art, which displeased me, for I found him lacking in emotion and imagination. He advocated that all painting must be devoted to holy themes and regarded those who portrayed worldly affairs with a malicious envy, as if it were sinful to indulge in pleasure.

He was the spokesman as he ordered Veronese to stand before the tribunal and he stated, "How dare you paint such offensive details? It is especially reprehensible in a work commissioned by our Holy Church."

Veronese replied, "My lord, what details? Whatever I did was artistic."

"Is that why you painted two German soldiers with halberds and an Apostle picking his teeth and other vulgarities offensive to Rome?"

"I paint as I see and as skillfully as my talent permits me."

"We have grave doubts that this is all you consider. Were you commissioned by any person to paint Germans and buffoons in this work?"

"No, my lord. The conception is my own. Besides, these figures are outside the banqueting room."

"That is not relevant. Do you know that in Germany and in other places infected with the Lutheran heresy it is customary to corrupt with pictures full of scurrilousness and similar inventions to mock, vituperate, and scorn the Holy Catholic Church in order to teach their vile Lutheran doctrines to foolish and ignorant people? And you further this depravity."

"My lord, I had much space to fill and I filled it."

"Is that why you had an Apostle use a fork as a toothpick?"

"I intended no irreverence but the fork is incorrect."

"And you placed a large dog in the forefront of the painting."

"My lord, what would you find more suitable?"

"Mary Magdalen. In her most pious mien."

"My lord, she does not fit the subject of a banquet scene."

"You are not contrite. It is a grave offense."

"I am devoted to our Holy Church. But I was asked to paint a feast."

"Veronese, I have not seen German figures introduced into any other painter's work. In times like these, it is most suspicious."

I sought to defend my friend and I was hushed until Contarini saw who it was, and then he allowed me to speak.

"But not to testify," he added. "We have all the testimony we need."

I stated, "My lord, my good friend intended no irreverence or heresy, but was concerned with the beauty of his pictorial art and the animation of his scene, and thus he should not be censured."

I was disregarded. After I finished speaking, the tribunal ordered Veronese to change the contents of the painting within three months or suffer the just punishment of the Holy Office.

But when other matters occupied the Inquisitors, he did not alter the work, but changed the title. And soon afterward *The Feast in the House of Levi* was accepted by the Dominicans but now Veronese justified his theme.

He wrote: "It is a banquet attended, according to the Gospel of St. Mark, by tax collectors and other sinners."

Other artists, however, took heed of this warning, and no more Germans appeared in anything that was painted in the Republic.

I console myself with the memory that, at least, Veronese had not been jailed, as I prepare for my son's trial. It is in the same Council Hall, the Interrogators are unchanged, as if they have become a permanent part of the Venetian landscape, and their expression is very grave. I am given a more comfortable chair this time but I can hardly sit when my son is led in by armed guards and the painting in question is produced.

I know the ambassador, a tall, attractive young man, whose greatest virtues are his appealing looks, the wealth of his family, and their trade with the Orient. And as he castigates Pomponio, I sense that his worst complaint is that his purchase is not a work of magnitude.

Donato declares, "This painting is not worthy of a Titian."

Pomponio, who is allowed to defend himself, I note with relief, retorts, "Then why did you buy it, my lord?"

"You are his son. I desired a genuine Titian. They are much prized at the court of Spain. But this work has been retouched several times. After I studied it, I realized it could not have been done by the master."

This time the Interrogators, even Father Contarini, are allowing Donato to try my son as an officer of the Republic, while they wait silently to pass their judgment. It is a situation that terrifies me.

As the argument continues, my mind wanders. I wonder where I have gone wrong. I must have failed, I think, for Pomponio has failed.

Veronese, who sits beside me, whispers, "Be compassionate, Maestro. To be the son of Titian is very difficult. It is a constant challenge, yet most of the time your sons feel like dust, and so they are forced to compete with you, even if they do not want to. You are a thing that they are forced to live up to. As even I have to sometimes."

I do not have time to reply for I am called to testify. I examine the full-length Venus that stands enticingly but obviously against a Grecian urn in the style of several of my earlier nudes while I desperately search for the best thing to say. I know at once that this work is not from my brush. I have painted so much, often a painting a month, that I do not remember everything that I have done, but I do know my manner. This work is too rough, too smeared. It may be from my workshop but that is all. Yet Pomponio regards me defiantly, with a smile that is almost a sneer, as if to say, Go ahead, Papa, condemn me, you always do.

But Veronese has said, "Be compassionate . . ."

Contarini states suddenly, "Vecellio, you were not so reluctant to speak in defense of Veronese a few years ago."

To admit this is my work is to confess to an incompetence that I hate.

Contarini adds, "The charge is simple. Your son signed your name."

"My lord, my name is his name."

"His brush is not. The envoy bought this painting because your son told him that you painted it. If this is not true, he forged your name, and he will be punished harshly. This is decided already."

I examine the signature on the painting. It is cleverly done but again, it is not mine. I look around the great room for I see no mercy on any of the Inquisitors' faces, while Donato glares fiercely at Pomponio, whose swagger is a mixture of arrogance and indifference, although I can tell from the way his mouth curls and trembles that he is afraid. Then I see Orazio standing in the doorway and his agitation adds to my uneasiness.

Contarini says, "Silence will be assumed to be guilt."

Veronese replies, "But, my lord, no man will know the truth until the master chooses to speak."

I think, To deny my son is to deny myself. And what is pride and honor next to the death of a child's love! Perhaps I have lasted too long. But I cannot be a bent old cripple. I straighten up, as erectly as I can, and I say, "My Lord Ambassador, you were clever not to be pleased."

Donato exclaims, "Then I was right! Your son fooled me!"

"I was the one who fooled you, Signore."

Donato is puzzled, Contarini frowns, the other Inquisitors stir restlessly, Pomponio regards me with disgust and even Orazio is angry with me, and I hear Veronese sigh sadly, and I blurt out hurriedly before I lose my courage and change my mind, "Signore, this Venus is an inferior work. I must have been preoccupied with other matters when I painted it."

The hush that follows is oppressive, like the hush before a storm.

I say, "I am not satisfied with it either. But you cannot blame my son for that. He did not know that it was not finished. I must redo it."

Donato grumbles—I feel unwillingly, to save face—"Everyone does a bad painting. Even a Titian. But what about the money I paid your son?"

"I will return it. How much did you pay for the Venus?"

"A thousand ducats."

I shudder. Even now, that is an exorbitant fee. I am tempted to say, You were cheated, but I declare instead, "The money will be in your hands within a few days. Unless you would prefer another painting."

"No. I am not disposed to approve such carelessness."

I turn to the tribunal and address them. "Then the case is closed."

They confer among themselves and after a heated argument, Contarini announces, "Not completely. Pomponio Vecellio is put on probation. There are other complaints about his behavior. If there are any more suspicious circumstances surrounding his person, we will confine him where he cannot indulge his propensity for irresponsibility and irregular transactions."

Orazio embraces me to express his approval but Pomponio, the instant he is released, rushes away without even a "Thank you, Papa."

I am hurt but Veronese says, "Maestro, you were skillful. Pomponio will appreciate what you have done for him when he recovers from his loss of pride and he realizes that he has been saved from humiliation."

I do not answer. I am very tired.

At the dock of my home an hour later—Orazio has gone ahead to prepare my couch, for I am in desperate need of rest—Veronese suggests, "Maestro, why not retire to your villa at Cortina? The air there is cool and clean and free of contagion. And you have brushes and canvases there, too."

"My children, my painting need me here."

"What more could you desire from your painting? You have achieved everything a mortal man could want."

But my *Pietà* is more than a painting. It is a cry to God.

Veronese adds strongly, "Maestro, you must leave Venice soon. Otherwise, no one can guarantee your safety. The plague grows worse daily and is always at its peak in the heat of the summer."

I recall something my mama had said when I left for Venice after visiting her and I reply, "I will ask for God's guidance."

Then I hear loud voices upstairs. Orazio is begging Pomponio to make his peace with me, and I hear him shout back, "I cannot! I am not Tiziano Vecellio but there is much of him in me!"

Veronese is embarrassed and he excuses himself. I hardly notice his departure. I am reminding myself that even when Pomponio was a baby he was not content to lie in my arms quietly like Orazio but squirmed and kicked and bawled until I put him back in his cradle.

It is a relief to recall my second departure from Cadore.

That was an exciting time for me—my first stay in Venice had been to plant the seed—but now I was on my own, and while the time was difficult and many were skeptical about my future, I was young and healthy and I felt that everything I attempted was within my reach.

Is it, I wonder, that the further the past is from us, the more attractive it becomes?

I lie on my couch and try not to yearn for my sons' affection. Perhaps, I meditate, I was not much more considerate when I was in their situation. Then the forged Venus catches my eye and I am unable to sleep. I am furious that anyone could have painted such an appealing subject so poorly, and that Leonardo Donato, supposedly a connoisseur, could have thought that such an inferior nude was a Titian.

NONE ARE SILENT

NONE ARE SILENT
Who were here
And were heard

The dead
Make me believe this

Stymean Karlen

PAPA POSED for me reluctantly and so many sittings were interrupted by his military duties that I painted much of his full-length portrait from memory. But one day, although his presence was requested by the town council, he ignored their summons in favor of continuing the sitting.

I expected him to praise my color as I focused on his ruddy complexion, but he stated irritably, "You neglect the most vital part of my portrait."

I halted. Criticism was even more distracting than his interruptions.

He stood proudly in his armor, dominating the living room I was using as a studio, and declared, "No detail of my metal is unimportant. It is of the best quality. My breastplate was forged in Milan for a Sforza."

I felt that his suit of armor was ornamental rather than protective and I was more interested in his countenance and I did not answer.

"Tiziano, this work has no monetary worth, but the town council, out of deference to my military services, may hang this painting in the town hall. They must be able to recognize me and where I stand."

What was needed, I decided, was a better background. The rugged hill country of the landscape became a Dolomite peak, a lofty castle, a clear mountain stream, and a vibrantly blue sky, all features of Cadore.

Papa still felt that I neglected his metal, but after a long argument we reached a compromise. I painted him holding a battle shield with his name on it and a defeated soldier lying under it, while he discarded his helmet and allowed me to paint his features as I saw them. I was grateful that this kept him quiet and that I had his presence for an entire afternoon. I painted more hurriedly than I liked but at the end of this sitting he was excited by the strength of his armor, while I found his face striking. Since I preferred the vigor of his jaw and the poignant vividness of his eyes, I stressed them instead of his posture and his armor as he had demanded. Yet when I finished he seemed pleased.

He said, "This likeness is good enough to hang in the town hall."

I knew he intended this as a compliment although he sounded stern.

"Will you stay now?" he asked suddenly.

"I cannot." I packed my materials to show that I meant what I said.

"You are selfish," he said morosely. "Most children are. Especially sons. Until it is too late. And then they are sorry."

"I am sorry, too, Papa, but I must go."

He walked away from me abruptly, furious with me.

It was our last sitting. But now Papa was not commonplace.

Just before I was to depart for Venice, he was ordered to lead his militia north of Cadore to oppose the invading Germans. Francesco was assigned to be his aide and once again he stated that I should remain with our family; he stressed that a man was needed in the house. But I knew that if I had not come back to Cadore, he would have left with my brother anyway, and I felt compelled to return to Venice; Venice was my work. Nonetheless, I was relieved that as we parted he embraced me.

I wonder in the intervening years what would have happened if I had not denied my parents' wishes but I never regret this decision.

When it was time to leave with Forni—the merchant was going back to the city, too—Mama put on her best black dress to indicate that she was in mourning. We said good-bye at the door and she cried out amid her tears, "At least you are healthy and strong and that is a blessing."

I asked, "Mama, you are not worried about Papa and Francesco?"

She shrugged fatalistically and said, "I will ask for God's guidance. It is in His hands. If He wills it, they will return safely. They serve Him faithfully and I do not think that He will desert them now."

I nodded, kissed my tearful sisters farewell, and ran out to Forni's waiting wagon before I became as distraught as they were.

All the way down the winding, harsh road that led to the lagoons the merchant complained about Cadore's preoccupation with the war. But I was more interested in visualizing Mama as I had last seen her. I inscribed on my memory her massed black hair, her olive skin, her small, lined face so that I could paint her as soon as I possessed my own studio.

Venice was quieter than usual when I arrived at the Rialto. I was surprised to see that many of the busiest streets were empty. I hurried to Vecchio's rooms and I was glad that he was in. He should be able to answer my questions and to ease my growing apprehensions.

I asked him, "Are we to be invaded, too?" He looked so somber.

He replied sadly, "No one knows. But the news is bad. The French king has seized Brescia, Bergamo, Cremona, and nearby Padua. Papal armies have annexed Ravenna, Faenza, and Rimini. We are being defeated everywhere."

"Have you heard anything about the German army north of Cadore?"

"They have beaten us and they have occupied Cadore. You were wise to leave it. You are safer here. Our navy is still strong and the natural barrier of the sea may save us from invasion. Why are you worried now?"

"My father and brother may be victims of the conquering Germans."

"It is possible. There are many casualties north of Cadore. You must console yourself with your work. It cures all ailments." He discarded his melancholy then and informed me triumphantly, "While there are no commissions in Venice because of these difficult times, Bembo is approaching me with a vital *poesia*. I expect him in a few days."

"Why do you need me?"

He replied impatiently, "I have more work than I can do myself."

I felt there was another reason, he was so eager to change the subject, and I persisted. I asked, "Will work for Bembo jeopardize your situation with Bellini? The master may resent that you compete with him."

"Tiziano, if you ask any more questions I will not use you."

When I did not appear impressed with his threat, he became angry.

He added sarcastically, "You cannot see Giorgione, he has closed his studio to you. And Bellini rejected you years ago. However, if you prefer not to work with me the door is open and you are free to leave."

I gave in, even as I vowed there must come a day when I would not have to submit to anyone else's orders. Yet I could not resist asking, "Is Bembo's commission so important?"

Vecchio was excited. "Fool, with Strozzi assassinated, Bembo's influence has doubled."

"Was he involved?" I was shocked. "Strozzi was his dear friend."

"It is hard to say. Murder is so common it is impossible to tell who is responsible. But it is the fashion and be careful. You are headstrong and your independent ways offend many. Think before you act impulsively."

I knew this warning was not to be regarded lightly. Poison and the dagger were used often and it was wise to be suspicious. My tone softened as I said, "I am grateful for your advice and that you can use me."

He grumbled, "Pray that Bembo shares my view. He is particular who he recommends, especially today. Now that Strozzi is dead he represents Ferrara's interests in Venice, in addition to those of Mantua, and he has become close to the Medici cardinal, who may become the next Pope."

"But if Venice loses, he loses, too. He is a Venetian and a patrician."

Vecchio smiled cynically and said, "You are naïve. His family take no risks. Two of his relatives support Venice while the other two support the emperor. If the emperor wins, those two will save the family fortune; if Venice wins, the other two will. They are not about to lose anything." He became reflective as he added, "I hope the work he wants is something that becomes my manner. I am tired of painting in the style of Bellini."

Bembo entered Vecchio's studio a week later with a flourish. Two servants attended him and announced his appearance as if he were a great connoisseur. He did not apologize for being late, or explain

why, although Vecchio had waited for him anxiously and then unhappily. He did acknowledge my presence and he seemed to expect
me to be here.

He addressed Vecchio eloquently, "The duke of Ferrara desires
a *poesia* similar to your two nymphs, which resembled Giorgione's
manner. He is tired of waiting for Bellini to execute his commission. The old man is too feeble these days and is weary even before
he begins. It is said that he can no longer hold a brush because of
his age, yet he does not submit to the will of his betters, even when
he should. And Giorgione is irresponsible. He refuses the noble
commission, then does a *poesia* for a miserable fee to show that he
is a free man. He is impossible."

Vecchio asked suspiciously, "What does your lord require?"

"The duke liked your niece's face that was painted on the nude
Venus in *The Feast of the Gods.* He desires another of such excellence."

I painted that, I thought angrily, and it had led to my dismissal
from the Bellini bottega, but Vecchio was assuming it was his work
now.

He said, "I am delighted that my efforts pleased the duke."

I recalled, too, that it was Bembo who had praised the way I had
done this nude and had stopped Bellini from scratching it out. I
wondered why he had to attribute this work to Vecchio and my
doubts about him grew.

"Frankly," Bembo continued, "my lord also prefers that this *poesia*
have the polish of a Bellini, and you, Vecchio, know his manner
better than anybody else. I know I can depend on you to give it his
touch."

"How am I to sign it? I am not a forger."

"At the proper time I will tell him that it is from your brush."

"When will that be?"

"I will decide when the painting is finished. No one is asking you
to do anything unworthy. But I must move carefully. Compared to
Bellini, you are still an unknown master. However, if you use your
niece as the model and paint her as enticingly as before, you could
improve your situation with the duke. Her lovely figure and face
remind him of his mistress. And this could lead to more commissions
from Ferrara."

Vecchio agreed to follow these instructions, although, I felt, unwillingly.

"Give Tiziano the reds. His Barbarigo portraits have excellence."

Vecchio protested, "It is my responsibility to decide what part of the *poesia* to assign him. If my name is on it, as you say it will be."

"Your greatest responsibility is to please my lord, the duke."

"Then why do you come to me when it is his brush you want?"

"Ferrara likes the skill with which you express Bellini's manner, your exquisite craft, your gloss, but he also desires voluptuous colors and robust energy and that is why Tiziano Vecellio should help you."

What he really desired, I sensed, was flesh. Flesh that was like no other substance on earth. But I asked, "Signor Bembo, what brought me to your attention? Most of the time you do not seem to notice me."

"Your likeness of Barbarigo is powerful yet pleasing. The hair is so distinctly painted that each one can be counted, as if done by a Dürer. And the coloring is so cleverly tinted that I would have taken it for a picture by Giorgione if you had not written your initials in the corner."

I realized that I was here because he had ordered Vecchio to use me, although neither of them, for their own reasons, would admit that.

Bembo said, "Vecchio, I trust you will execute this *poesia* promptly."

"As you wish, Signore. I am ever at your service."

"Good. I am tired of old men who never finish what they start."

But I am not Bellini, I think angrily, as I turn backward.

Two days have passed since I lied to save Pomponio from prison, but he has continued to avoid me and he has not thanked me. So I resume work on my *Pietà*, determined to show that my hand is still steady and that I still possess a triumphant eye. For the first time in months I feel that I am making progress. I am resolved that no one will be able to say about this picture, "Everyone does a bad painting, even a Titian."

The fourth day of my labors Orazio asks, "Are you working too hard?"

"I am working and that suffices. Have you seen Pomponio lately?"

"No, Papa. He has to express his independence in his own way."

And spend the money he has stolen, I fear, but I am too proud to admit my apprehension and I ask, "Has there been any word from Donato?"

"Not so far. Perhaps Pomponio has returned the money."

"I doubt such a miracle. More likely, he is busy spending it."

Orazio does not reply, which indicates that he agrees with me. I see that he is about to ask me again if he can assist me, and I am excited by the tragic expression in his eyes. It suggests a devotion to God that I must capture—I am dedicating this work to Him—and I order my son to pose for me. I explain, "I must put two adorers of the *Pietà* on the votive tablet. They will give more passion to the gravity of the scene."

He stands for hours while I block out his head. He is astounded by the ease with which I work; I have not felt such a grace for a long time.

He wears his beard short in the Venetian fashion and as I paint it and his upturned face, he says, "Papa, I pray that you forgive Pomponio. He does what he has to do. As you do. So single-mindedly."

"I will discuss that later." Must even he distract me? I think irately. I am determined to give this composition such pictorial strength that no one will dare to imagine that any part of the invention is attributable to anybody else. As I mute the colors that are too rich, I have hope that my brush will never falter again, no matter how much longer I live. When I turn this canvas to the wall to dry, I do not lock it in my closet, for I expect to return to it tomorrow. And I want to show my sons that I trust them. But my preoccupation is with the painting. I feel possessed by the substance I am using. The texture of the paint fascinates me. I realize it is better that this *Pietà* have none of the bright definitions of outline that once dominated my brush, or the brilliance of color that obtained for me so many commissions. My palette has become somber grays and browns and greens, and many shadows, like the grave.

I am not certain that Orazio shares my vision. When this sitting is finished, he exclaims, "You have made my features so blurred!"

"No more than my own." I have painted my face beside his on the votive tablet and now we are the two adorers of Christ. I am no longer interested in creating beautiful faces but those that will appeal to God. I am not certain that anyone else, even my son, understands this.

But I can ask what has been in my mind a long time. "Orazio, does your brother have a mistress?" Yet even now, this is not easy to say.

"How should I know, Papa? And does it matter?"

"It could explain why he needed the money."

"He always needs money. That is his way."

Pomponio always needs a mistress, too, I decide. He has always placed his amorous affairs before everything else. But it is Orazio who worries me the most when it comes to women, for I do not know whether he indulges himself or not, he is so secretive. Neither of my sons has married, which is another grievous blow, for I do not have any descendants. Yet no self-respecting Venetian is without an heir that links them to the future. I believe that Orazio frequents the casual courtesans that are common in Venice, but I have no proof. I wonder what to say next; I feel at a loss for words; and Orazio asks if he may have dinner with me.

I take his arm, glad that he wants to attend me. I doubt that anyone would believe that even a Titian is lonely. We go downstairs together.

After Bembo's departure, Vecchio told me that while he esteemed my manner, he would decide what part of the *poesia* I would paint. I was in no position to object, I had only a few ducats left from my work on the Fondaco and the Barbarigo portraits, and I agreed to obey him faithfully.

Violante appeared at his studio as soon as he was ready to sketch the *poesia*. She blushed when she saw me by Vecchio's side, while I thought joyfully that her figure had become classical. Her face was rounder and fuller, and so was her plump, voluptuous body that I recalled fondly, and her vivid red hair was even more brilliant. I had an instant impulse to paint her. But I knew I must not be aggressive.

Vecchio said, "Violante, remember Tiziano? He assisted me a few years ago and he painted you several times. He is working with me again."

I felt aroused to a high emotional pitch as she replied, "I recall him very well. You said that he had a gift for portraits and flesh tones."

"Thank you," I said, "I will be honored to paint you." I was glad that I had trimmed my beard short in the Venetian fashion and had worn my most fashionable doublet and hose, for she appeared to view me approvingly.

Vecchio grumbled that I was dressed too much like a gentleman to paint suitably and I answered that Giorgione said that an artist should wear fine clothes when he painted, and that Leonardo supported this attitude, particularly when the Florentine portrayed beauty. Violante blushed again. Vecchio was still dissatisfied with my garb but he did not insist that I change, for now Violante was beautiful and he was proud of her.

He put the two lovers on the grass and framed them in a lovely landscape and used me to represent the male figure. But he clothed

Violante, while it was the shepherd who was nude. I realized that he could not endure that I see her naked, whatever Bembo had instructed. He told me to paint the landscape and the blue sky and he painted the figures. And after he completed them, he ordered me to paint her dress and added, "This is your opportunity to use your palette as Bembo suggested."

I adorned her in a red I felt was life itself but it irritated him.

He stated, "Her clothes must not attract more attention than her face. This is not a drapery painting and you are not a drapery painter."

I was offended. I knew that the drapery painter painted the clothes of the sitter while the master painter did the face and was known as a "face painter," and was considered the superior artist, but I could tell from her pleasure that she felt that my fabrics were more attractive than her face. I decided that this was as it should be. I did not dare to paint her as the Venus I desired, but I could court her by painting her dress as beautifully as I could and I sensed that she knew what I was doing.

At the last moment Vecchio felt that the *poesia* needed more nudity. He had been uncertain about the conception from the start despite Bembo's instructions, which was rare for him. He blurted out, "Tiziano, do some cupids in the corner to replace the nymph that was commissioned."

I painted three voluptuous cupids that expressed my yearnings. I sought to give them grace and dignity as well as flesh and blood.

The work took a month. He fussed with the details, not satisfied with her hair. Finally, he painted it yellow, for that was the fashion, although I would have colored it a brilliant red, as was Violante's. And his male figure was too delicate for my taste and the girl too pale.

Then a letter arrived from the duke of Ferrara which upset Vecchio. It was delivered by one of Bembo's servants and it was addressed to the patrician and it said, "We instruct you to tell the painter that he must deliver the *poesia* at once or he will incur our great displeasure."

Vecchio decided to bring the work to Ferrara himself in the hope that that would appease the duke. He arranged for Violante to reside in a nearby room and I asked him if I could use her for a Madonna and Child that I wanted to paint. He seemed pleased with the pious devotion that subject suggested and he assented and then hurried off with the *poesia*.

Violante was prompt the next morning and as she sat for me,

dressed demurely, I felt the same joy was in her that was in me. Bellini madonnas were the best known in Venice but I resolved to surpass them.

There were obstacles. I had to use inferior wood, I could not afford canvas, my oils were those left over from the *poesia,* and it was a subject I had done only in the Bellini bottega, and then infrequently. Yet how lovely and loving she looked, I thought, and now it was possible to see her as a madonna. Until now, I had been more excited by her flesh than by her person, but today I saw that she was also kind, gentle, and devoted. She spoke of her life in the strict, church-bound Bergamo where she had been born and spent her early years, of her wish to have her own independent place in the world and a family, and how she still remembered how beautifully I had painted her. And I answered with my brush.

I colored her dress red instead of the blue that Bellini favored—I was tired of hearing about the Bellini blue—and I depicted her holding the Child in her arms. I felt it was more appealing, dramatic, and individual than the Bellini fashion of holding the child upright.

She adored what I was doing and the week it took me to paint my first original *Madonna and Child* was a happy one. When I finished and signed my full name, which was also a first time, I was very excited. She leaned over my shoulder to observe how I had painted her and as I felt the touch of her soft breasts, I thought, Violante is the part of me that yearns to dance and sing, to drink strong draughts of the sun and the wind, and to exult in my youth and energy. I embraced her and she responded as if she had been waiting for me a long time.

She seemed more skillful than I remembered and as I wondered whether there had been any other men in her life, she assured me that I had been the first. She did not say whether there had been any others.

By the time Vecchio returned to the studio we had enjoyed a few days of love and I was determined that nothing must part us now. But it was not easy to speak to him. He carried the *poesia* as if it were a sore and he was in a foul humor. I was glad I had decided to touch up the madonna, for Violante was sitting modestly while I made the reds brighter, and Vecchio growled, "I will never endure the miseries of a court again."

I asked, trying to look innocent, "The duke refused the painting?"

"He said it was too reserved. He craved a more erotic female."

"What about the cupids? They were voluptuous."

"Bembo told me that they should have been the tone of the whole *poesia*. It is a bad time for a delicate subject. The duke is obsessed with the war. He is vain about his skill with cannon, yet he seeks to please both sides, and so no one trusts him. Then he prefers large, lustful women whose sensuality arouses him and he said my work made him feel impotent. No wonder a pious octogenarian like Bellini dissatisfies him. As I did."

Violante said, "We did not waste the time. The madonna is done."

"Then why does he work on it now?"

I said, "I want it to be perfect. As an honor to your niece."

"Nothing is perfect. I have no money to pay you for what you did. I got nothing from the duke. And your madonna is strange, unfamiliar. No one will buy a madonna that is not in the Bellini manner. Violante, you are wrong. You have wasted your time on this subject."

Vecchio's vile mood was growing worse and Violante motioned for me to be careful but I could not wait any longer. I felt very much the man as I towered over him and I said, "I want to talk to you about your niece."

"You wish to present this work to someone. No one will accept it."

"Signore, it is more vital than that."

"You want her to model for you again?"

"Always! For whatever I paint! I beg you, Signore, be merciful!"

Now his gaze was devastating and he snarled, "You have ravished her! I can see it in your eyes! And she cannot hide it either."

I thought she would cry then, but I said, more bravely than I felt, "We love each other and it would be an act of kindness to bless us."

"Do you intend to marry her?"

I had not considered such a step, but to appease him, I nodded.

"I have no dowry to give her and you are penniless. You have no commissions or prospect of any. How will you support her?"

"I will manage, somehow. Perhaps Bellini will take me back."

"No one will take you back. You betray everyone who befriends you. Take your madonna and go. The wood and oil cost a ducat."

I felt he was cheating me but I gave him a ducat. Then as I took my belongings I felt desperate. I was so overloaded with my painting things I could not carry any of my pictures, even my madonna. Then Violante picked up that painting and said, "Palma, I am going with him."

I thought Vecchio would burst with rage and he regarded me as if I were a creature of the devil who had ravaged his home. But when he saw that Violante meant what she had said, he put out his hand to halt her and she evaded his grasp. He looked ready to weep and he regarded her with stupefaction and he exclaimed, "From this moment on I will believe anything that is said of human depravity and betrayal."

"Signore," I said, "I will treat your niece with reverence."

"No man treats his mistress better than she deserves. Go, before I strike you both dead." He grabbed a heavy brush to hit me with it.

I evaded it and asked, "What about my paintings that I cannot carry?"

"I will hold them. Until you wed Violante. No one will want them."

"I will marry her. I promise. When I am able to afford it."

"You will keep her as long as she serves your brush and until a better model appears and then you will desert her." He turned his back on us.

Violante was weeping as I led her down the stairs but she controlled her tears when I reminded her that no one would give quarters to a woman in that condition. I had only a few ducats left but I was able to rent a bedroom and a studio for a ducat a month. It was in a quarter near San Marco, for I wanted to be away from the bitter memories of the Rialto.

Neither of us slept that night. There were loud voices next door, I heard wailing, as if someone had just died of the plague, and I kept turning over in my mind which way to move and found no relief in this.

Yet the next morning, after I brought her wine and fruit for breakfast, I left her while I went in search of employment. Many painters had shops on the approach to San Marco and even by the side of the Basilica where they sold anything that could be painted: furniture, caskets, armor, clocks, mirrors, gondola poles, shields, horse trappings, door curtains, and parchments. I noted despondently that there was an abundance of goods but few customers. Even the usually busy Piazza San Marco, one of the most crowded parts of Venice, was deserted because of the calamities of war and the plague. Yet I knew I had to try to earn a living here.

After I assured an apprehensive Violante that there was nothing to worry about, that soon I would be earning a living, I set up a little stall near San Marco. I tried to locate next to the Basilica but I was pushed away by a painter who claimed he had occupied this space for years.

I displayed my *Madonna and Child* but the few people who looked at it were so indifferent I felt I could not even give it away as a gift.

Then Venice was besieged and it was even harder to earn anything. I stood in the shadow of San Marco day after day and only the pilgrims who entered the church to pray for the Republic's deliverance from the invaders seemed to have a purpose. I was so depressed I did not even desire to paint, which was the worst feeling of all.

Yet Violante did not waver in her devotion. Once she felt assured that I would not desert her, she gave freely of herself. It was as if my declaration of love had released a flow in her. Violante's passion was my one consolation these dreadful weeks of war and poverty.

I had just one customer during that time. A man from Padua had me frame a painting of *The Presentation of the Virgin* which he was giving to San Marco as a memorial for his wife who had died of the plague. It was a second-rate picture, I did not even recognize the name of the artist, but he was proud of it and he gave me ten scudi for my efforts.

No one, however, desired my brush.

I wondered if I would have to find some other calling to support myself and Violante and that thought infected me with despair. I learned that painters were being hired to paint the outer walls of the Doge's Palace and as I struggled to bring myself to apply for such menial work, I heard that in a sudden, surprise attack Cadore had been recaptured from the Germans by a Venetian army. And this had led to a truce between the emperor and Venice. Just as abruptly the siege of the city was lifted and the Pope, not trusting his other ally, the French king, made peace with the Republic. Then Julius and Maximilian turned on France.

Papa wrote me that Francesco was wounded but that he was recovering, and that the breastplate I had objected to in his portrait had saved his own life when Papa had led the attack that had surprised the German garrison occupying Cadore. Now, as a reward for his enterprise and courage, the portrait was to hang in the town hall to commemorate this victory and the triumphant leader. This news raised my spirits and gave me the resolution to approach Vecchio and to ask for my paintings.

When he saw that Violante was with me, instead of looking pleased as I expected, he shouted at me, "You should not be in Venice! The plague grows worse despite the peace. Giorgione is sick and may be dying."

"Is he infected?" I asked, horrified by that possibility.

"His mistress caught the contagion but he refused to leave her, although he was warned to do so. Now he is infected, too."

"Is he still in his studio?"

"He has moved to the Campo San Silvestro and adorned his facade with frescoes. But do not visit him, or you will be corrupted, too. I told you only to warn you and Violante to flee from Venice. I do not want her to die. She is all I have." Tears filled his eyes and he could not go on, and now I was certain that he was her father and not her uncle.

She said she would not flee unless I did, and I asked him why he stayed.

"My work," he mumbled. "If I leave it unattended, it will be stolen. But the plague spreads daily and because of it there is nothing for artists. If it continues Venice will become a dead city."

I insisted, "I must see Big George!"

Violante asked, "What about your paintings, Tiziano?"

The news about Giorgione had shaken me so, I had forgotten them. I said, "They can wait. I will take you back to our rooms, then attend him."

She did not want me to leave her, but I had to see him, even if he still slammed the door in my face. I did not know anyone of whom I was more fond. I did not tell this to Violante, but I sensed she knew. Tears of self-pity wet her soft cheeks and she was sad.

She whimpered, "If you visit him, you will die."

"That is a chance I'll have to take."

After I escorted her to our rooms I rushed away in the hope that I could help Giorgione—he had done so much for me before our separation.

The frescoes on the facade identified his house on the Campo San Silvestro; I would have known his manner anywhere. I paused to admire the work on the window embrasures and under the cornice, and then ran upstairs. Nothing was locked and I heard a moan in the bedroom. Clothes, brushes, lutes, and palettes were scattered over the floor in a vast disorder. The windows were shuttered and the stench of brimstone—the favorite way to treat the plague—was foul. I threw open the shutters to air the room and to allow in light and I saw Giorgione lying on the bed in the corner. At first I thought he was dead. He was motionless; his once full, fine, handsome features gray and gaunt and ravaged. Yet I had heard a moan.

A ray of light fell on his face and he opened his eyes and I sighed with relief. At least he was alive. Then he motioned for me to go away.

I did not move and he whispered, "You do not owe me anything. I will take care of myself. As I always have. Do not worry about me."

Ignoring his protests, I bent over him affectionately instead of backing away from him in horror as most people did and suddenly he smiled.

It was like the sun emerging from behind a bank of clouds and I could have wept with joy. He was glad to see me, whatever he said.

He mumbled, "You should not have come. I am afflicted."

Before I could deny that, I saw the sores on his hands, his beautiful hands, which were a sign of just one thing—the plague.

"It is dangerous. I am infected and it is contagious."

"I must nurse you until I can fetch a physician."

"None will come. They take great pains to protect themselves."

"Giorgio, when did you fall ill?"

"My mistress, Beatrice, caught the contagion a few days ago. And I was warned not to attend her, that I would be infected too, but I could not desert her, she was dying. But now I do not even know where they have buried her. The death boat came last night and now she lies in a common, unmarked grave. You will make sure I am buried in consecrated ground?"

I had never heard fear in him before and it had a terrible sound. I assured him, "I will do whatever you wish but you have many days ahead."

"No," he said positively, "I am fatally ill."

"How can you be so sure?"

"I have the symptoms. The sores are all over my body and the purple spots grow larger and much of the time I feel that I am on fire. Tiziano, you will finish my work? You know my manner best."

"Talk about that later. Now I must get you a physician."

"You will not find any who will come. They are the last to be seen when one has the contagion. When Beatrice was stricken, I called a doctor and the moment he saw her condition he retired to the other side of the room where he prescribed brimstone to disinfect her, cordials for her nausea, purslane for her fever, and an amulet to keep away evil spirits. When she grew worse and I fell ill and I requested his services again, he sent an apothecary to inquire about our condition. His first need was to preserve himself from danger, it was a sure sign that I was infected."

"Where are your friends? You have a wide circle of acquaintances."

"No one comes near me now. You are the first visitor I have had in days. Please, you will finish my paintings in my manner?"

"What about Piombo? He has worked in your manner, too."

"No!"

"Vecchio?"

"No!"

"Vecchio has a gentle style that sometimes resembles yours."

"He is jealous of your attachment to my style and he is still angry at me because you favored me. Then his manner does not honor me. And Piombo will damage my tone with his sentiment. You know how to blend your style with mine. You know my intentions better than anybody else."

"You taught me much but I have my own manner now."

"Do not argue. I have very little strength and my mind is made up."

I saw his eyes wander to a small portrait on the wall behind me and I realized that he desired my opinion of this work. I was surprised; this was not like him; he must be very ill.

I asked, "Is it a recent painting?"

"My last," he said sorrowfully. "A self-portrait. I painted it when I had a premonition that my end was near. Do you like it?"

"That is not the way I would describe this portrait."

"Do you feel it at all?"

I paused before answering. It was unusual for Giorgione to be uncertain. He was a painter who had been indifferent to the opinion of others. Yet now he was eager for my view. He rose to a sitting position with a painful effort so that he could see better and waited for me to speak.

I carefully examined this work. The resemblance to himself was unmistakable and yet there were subtle differences in the style. The cheeks were full, the nose large, the eyes brown, the hair black, but tinged with gray where it fell over his shoulders, although he was only a few years past thirty. Clearly, he had done this portrait just for himself. He had limited himself virtually to the face to give the self-portrait an immediate, intimate, and penetrating effect.

He said softly, "I shut myself up alone in my studio to paint this."

"It is almost melancholy, yet movingly human and poignant."

"This is my last stand before I vanish in smoke. But I finished it."

"Giorgione, does that trouble you?" Most of the time, I thought, he did not seem to want to finish his paintings.

"No. For soon I will be unable to possess it."

I realized that he had not finished most of his paintings so that he could keep them.

He fell back on the bed from his effort to sit up and for an instant I feared that he was lapsing into unconsciousness. But he managed to retain control of his senses and he muttered, "You will have the responsibility of deciding what needs to be done to my unfinished work."

I knew he did not wish to give names to his paintings but I wanted him to know the future. I said, *"The Sleeping Venus* is done and any work would spoil her. And whatever I did on *The Tempest* would only lessen it. These works and the self-portrait must be entirely by your own hand."

A faint smile appeared on his lips and he nodded feebly.

"But what is not done I will try to complete in your manner."

"Good. You are my executor. Give me a paper and I will write it. I have no will and it is too late to obtain a notary."

I found pen and paper but he did not have the strength to write and I had to put down his wishes; then he could sign only when I held his hand and guided his pen. He was so frail I wanted to weep, but I forced myself to appear calm, for I knew he hated tears or pity.

He whispered, "Take my books, too. Ovid's *Metamorphoses,* Boccaccio's *Genealogy of the Gods,* and my *Life of Alexander the Great* will help your work. They will suggest many mythological subjects from the antique."

"You taught me better than anybody else."

"I did not teach you. You learned to paint in your mother's womb."

He seemed to fall into a stupor, but as I started out, still anxious to find a doctor, he cried out, "Tiziano, stay with me, please!"

"You need a doctor."

"It is too late. I have only a few hours left and I do not want to die alone."

Giorgione sank into silence and I lost track of the time as I sat by his side while I waited for God to summon him. Just as I thought he was already in His arms and I was praying for his soul, he stirred and he grumbled, "Did you know that Carpaccio and Bellini were called in to judge my frescoes on the Fondaco and to determine their value?"

"I did not know. Did they approve?"

"Fetch my self-portrait. I desire to view it one more time."

I held it before him, but he could not see it. He asked to touch it and as he did, he murmured, "The paint feels good. How do we see into men's hearts? I did not want to quarrel with you. God, forgive that sin!"

I assured him, "It was not a sin," but he did not hear me.

He repeated, "Tiziano, remember, bury me in consecrated ground. And do not allow anyone else to finish my paintings. Promise? Please?"

Even as I promised I doubted that he was aware of it. This time when his mouth opened he did not speak. Terrified that I had lost him, I clasped his hand, although it added to the risk of contagion, and I thought unhappily, If only Giorgione were not so cold! A prayer seemed to form on his lips, he shook convulsively, he gasped for breath, and then as I saw his eyes staring starkly I realized that he was dead.

I felt numb and to restore life to my limbs I walked to the window and looked out on the Venice that he had loved. The moon was as distinct as I had ever seen it. I smelled the tang of autumn leaves and they reminded me that it was October and I wanted to kick them away. Instead, I turned to his side, covered the sores on his hands and closed his eyes.

His beautiful eyes. They have haunted me as long as I have lived, and how helpless he was, the worst humiliation of all.

I locked the door so that his paintings would not be burned as infected on the pyres that dominated the city, and so that he would not be taken away by the death boat and thrown into a common trench with the other plague victims. Then, after I hurried to my rooms early the next morning to assure Violante that I was in good health and that I would return to her as soon as I had arranged Giorgione's burial, I went in search of consecrated ground. But every priest I saw that day gave me the same litany: "The law forbids the burial of a victim of the contagion in any of the churches of the city." I was also informed that the deceased should be put in a *lazzaretto* with the other victims of the pestilence.

It took a week before I could find a priest who would bury him. Father Daniele Giovio was the pastor of a small church on the island of Murano. I was aware, too, that he often wore layman's clothes, hunted, carried a dagger, and took money for ringing the bells and saying the office of the dead. I gave him five ducats, most of what I had left from my work on the Fondaco and the Barbarigo portraits. And as the short, ruddy priest performed the holy sacraments, and Violante, Vecchio, and Piombo stood by my side as Big George was lowered into the grave close to the sea, I could hear the thump of the water against the quay and I thought, He would like that.

Just then, to my surprise, Bembo appeared to honor our dead friend and I realized that there were very few secrets in the Republic.

When the grave was closed and the church bells rang, I prayed that Big George had been called by God's purpose.

Bembo whispered, "I must discuss his paintings with you when a decent interval has passed. So now it will not be pictures by Giorgione or Titian, but by Giorgione and Titian. A splendid mixture."

He was pleased with that idea but I was thinking of something Big George had said to me when we had worked on the Fondaco. We had fallen into an argument over why we painted, for I had grown weary of the frescoes and I was sick of looking at them. Yet when I complained about our calling, he had said, "You should not. You chose your own life."

I had not answered, for I had not known what to say. Now, however, I knew exactly what I desired to tell him. I walked away from the other mourners and as I stood over his grave I whispered to him, "No, no, no, Giorgione, my life chose me. As it did you."

SO IMPREGNABLE IS HIS SEED

SO IMPREGNABLE IS HIS SEED

The final destruction
Will birth new blossoms
So impregnable is his seed

Stymean Karlen

THE SENATE put Bembo in charge of Giorgione's work despite his wishes and I could not dispute their authority. He stated that I was the right man to finish the pictures, that I knew Big George's manner better than anyone else and that my reds and flesh tones were the best in Venice.

This pleased me, but it created a difficulty. If I gave Giorgione's paintings the time they needed, I had no money to support myself.

It was not easy to express this to Bembo, who always had enough money for whatever he required, but when he arrived at the studio a week after the funeral and saw me standing before the unfinished *Concert* without having made a single brushstroke he seemed to sense what was wrong.

He said, "You need oil and brushes."

"Signore, they are expensive. I cannot afford to continue this work."

"I have the remedy. I will pay you from my own funds to complete this painting. I commissioned it from Giorgione and it is my favorite."

He gave me two ducats. Then he advised me to be patient—my frown indicated my discontent—that if *The Concert* pleased him, there would be more work from the Republic and the patrons of Giorgione. I knew I should not continue without a contract, this was the rule of the Venetian Guild of Painters, but I was so eager to finish this picture before another hand intervened that I accepted his payment without further question.

The next month I devoted myself to finishing Giorgione's work. When I integrated his nudes into the landscape of *The Country Feast,* I used Violante as the model, but much of the time she was alone in our rooms. She chided me for not asking for more money, she said that I was underpaid, but I had enough to subsist on and while I worked on the unfinished pictures I felt fulfilled and it made his death easier to bear. And I was helping to perpetuate his memory. So I ignored her criticism and that added to her unhappiness. Yet she did not leave me.

The work was hard. My brush had become precise and animated where his had been ambiguous and languid and I wanted to explore color strongly while he had used it to soothe. But as I worked on *The Concert* and gave the fingers poised over the keyboard of the harpsichord my vitality, I felt I heard him singing sweetly. I glanced at his self-portrait and the blurring of the contours of his black hair, the darkness of the background reminded me of his final manner. Now I believed I was finishing the essence of his intention. However, this did not end my doubts.

One day Bembo noticed my hesitation and asked me why I was worried.

He had come to speak to me about another matter, which he said was important, and he was surprised by my uncertainty.

I replied, "I cannot echo Giorgione's palette and yet I must not do anything to alter the original and essential nature of his work. So it is difficult to achieve his exact intention. I hope he will forgive me."

Bembo said, "It is his own fault. Most of these unfinished pictures were started years ago, and sold, but he avoided completing them so that he could avoid giving them up. But now the patrons who purchased these pictures insist on possessing them. How much longer will it take you to have these paintings ready for their transfer to their rightful owners?"

"To have them done properly it would be wise to turn them to the wall and to return to them later. In about a year or two."

"That is impossible! As it is, I have waited for my painting three years. And the patience of the other patrons is exhausted."

"Then I am not sure that I will hit the mark in these matters."

"You have been useful. Now the Senate desires you to paint frescoes for the Scuola del Santo of the Basilica of St. Anthony in Padua."

"I do not trust frescoes. They do not last."

"Tiziano, if you refuse this commission there may be no others."

"Why was I selected?" In a way, I felt, I was being punished.

"With Giorgione gone, your frescoes on the Fondaco are the most notable in the Republic. You must prepare to depart for Padua. The Senate wants these frescoes done at once."

"What about the work I am doing?"

"I will take care of it. Or you will procrastinate as much as Big George did. These pictures are as finished as they ever will be."

"Please do not rush them. We owe it to Giorgione. Put them away until I return and then I can complete them. I will be refreshed. I will be . . ."

"No! Enough time has been spent on this work. If your frescoes in Padua are satisfactory, you may have more commissions of your own."

I realized I had my first state commission. I was no longer an assistant or even a partner. I packed my brushes to begin a new life.

Padua was a short day's journey from Venice, but despite its closeness to *La Serenissima* it was a very different world. It was a land city of cobblestones and roads that curved in a constant profusion. I knew it was an ancient place, that when Livy had been born there in 59 B.C., it had existed for centuries. And it was proud that it had been the home of Petrarch, St. Anthony, Mantegna, and that Giotto and Donatello had left their mark in Padua with their work.

This pleased me, but as I met at the great church of St. Anthony with Brother Marco, the theologian, Nicola da Stra, who spoke for the state, and Alvise Cornora, the connoisseur of art, I had an uneasy feeling. We sat in the quiet cloister next to the Basilica and even as they discussed the high purpose of the frescoes I sensed that they were intriguing for different purposes. Cornora was middle aged and I thought he must have been handsome in his youth and vain about his looks, but now he was stout, although his face had retained charm. Stra was a thin, stern, elderly soldier who had never been attractive, but who was proud of his ability to accomplish things. Brother Marco was the youngest of the trio, with a round, chubby face, a large stomach, and an assured air.

Stra insisted that the frescoes should reflect Padua's escape from enemy hands; Cornora wanted them to celebrate the city's renown as an intellectual center; Marco said they must reflect the miracles of St. Anthony. I felt no stimulation from any of these points of view. I had formed the resolution, while I had traveled to Padua with Violante, who was waiting for me in rooms I had rented nearby on the Via Vignali, to ignore any tongues that would trick me into painting what had no magic for me. Yet the three of them were waiting for me to speak.

I said, "I am grateful for the advice of such accomplished gentlemen."

Stra barked, "You must not ignore Padua's glorious history!"

Cornora added, "Giotto's frescoes are a worthy target to emulate."

But he had painted them two hundred years ago, I longed to remind this Maecenas. Instead, I said, "I will observe them carefully."

"What about St. Anthony?" the monk asked. "This is his shrine. Where he preached and died and it is his life that we must commemorate."

I said, "I will do the best I can but there may be difficulties."

"What difficulties? You are very young for such an important work."

Stra asked, "Vecellio, how old are you?"

I was not sure and I could not say twenty, which was my own estimate, even if Michelangelo and Raphael had done accomplished work by that age, and so I muttered, "I have had considerable experience. In the bottega of Giorgione and Bellini and I have not been an apprentice for years."

"I know. That is why we employed you. But you lack years."

Cornora said, "Stra, I saw the Fondaco and his work is estimable."

Marco added, "And Bembo did recommend him. Yet . . . ? Vecellio, does the subject of St. Anthony trouble you? Is that your difficulty?"

"No. I will address myself to him with devotion. But I have not been informed as to the practical circumstances of this commission."

"Young man, you will receive ten gold ducats now so that you can be supplied with materials, then ten more when we are satisfied that your intention is correct and ten more upon completion."

"Reverend Father, what about my assistant?"

"Do not overpay him. Or he will become content and do poor work. One hundred and fifty lire a fresco should be enough for him."

My assistant was brought in. Domenico Campagnola was a short, squat, black-haired thirty, with a square face and thick hands, who testified that he would be true to the miraculous spirit of St. Anthony.

I told him, "We will begin after I survey the space we are to fresco and I decide how it is to be treated."

Everyone then, even Campagnola, offered to advise me until I

grew curt and said that I was tired, it had been a long day and I had
to rest.

I did not tell Violante about my depressed feelings, although she
sensed that I was unhappy. She sought to ease my discontent by
being amorously agreeable but I was distracted and the pleasures
of her body did not end my misery. I wondered if now that I possessed her, she was no longer so desirable. Or if my desire for
female flesh had tricked me. I was grateful she did not regard my
distraction as a personal affront.

The next day was sunny and mild and as I left our rooms on the
Via Vignali to walk to the Scuola del Santo my mood improved.
As I strode on the Via del Santo and under its arched, roofed way
I liked that it shut out the sun when it was too hot and the rain
when it was too cold. I arrived at the great piazza before the Basilica
and I could not find the Scuola. No one seemed to know where it
was, even two priests directed me wrongly. But finally a pilgrim
who had come to Padua to worship at the shrine of St. Anthony
knew its location; he had studied in it.

The pilgrim left me after he led me to the chamber and as I
stared at what I was supposed to fresco I was shocked. The Scuola
was a bare room the size of a small chapel, with long wooden
benches on three sides of the chamber. Everything stressed austerity
and penance; I thought, This is a hair-shirt room.

I walked outside to breathe fresh air and to restore my disordered
feelings and I observed that the Scuola was compressed between
two larger buildings. I felt that a more insignificant setting could
not be found in all of Italy, especially by contrast with the grandeur
of the Basilica across the huge piazza. I took another look at the
chamber in the hope my first impression was wrong, but on this
second viewing it was even more depressing, a square block of a
room, yet longer than it was wide, dark, poorly lit, without any
adornments worth remembering. Even the madonna at the head of
the room was unworthy, nothing compared to a Bellini. I felt that
I was being cheated. I had imagined that I would be painting in the
magnificent Basilica where many would view my work; here, I
reflected bitterly, no one would see it. Or for the few who did, the
frescoes would appear in the worst setting, cramped, pale, framed
in a depressing box.

Yet as I sat on the balcony outside and admired the grace and
grandeur of the arches of the Basilica, I saw no way to turn back.
I needed the money desperately; Bembo had warned me that this

commission was imperative to my career; and there was nothing for me in Venice. So I decided to make the best of it, even as I swore to myself, Never again! From now on, I resolved, I must paint what I could feast on!

Tomorrow, however, was always ahead of me those days and so as I met Campagnola the following morning at the Scuola I was prepared to begin. And since the church celebrated the miracles of St. Anthony, I decided to paint him granting speech to an infant so it could testify to the innocence of its mother—a work, I felt, that could be quite dramatic.

My assistant said that Brother Marco would be pleased and I ordered him to sketch more miracles that St. Anthony had performed. I was not sure how to address Campagnola—he was ten years older—and I could not feel toward him as Big George had felt toward me, he was too sober. Then he showed me some of his sketches and his draughtsmanship was weak and his composition dull, but perhaps, I told myself, he was a good copyist and he could serve me as a mixer of paint.

And by the time I painted my first fresco I felt that in some ways this was my best work. I drew a detailed sketch, which was different from my usual manner, and I painted a robust infant. As I became fond of what I was depicting, I handled my brush with a new freedom and gave the infant flesh that was real and vigorous, and my pleasure with my painting grew.

The three men came to view this fresco. Stra was annoyed that I had gone to such effort to paint an infant. Cornora admired my flesh tones. But Brother Marco, who had the final word, was dismayed that I had not given St. Anthony prominence and he said that this must be rectified.

When he put this panel on the floor where it was poorly seen, I felt I was being punished for using the flesh of life in a sacred subject and for my neglect of the patron saint of Padua and I was dispirited.

After I sketched the design for the second fresco, I ordered my assistant to copy it and to paint it on the panel. Campagnola was pleased and he possessed a gift for imitation; it was his one gift.

I decided that all of the sixteen frescoes in the Scuola must represent the best known miracles in the legend of St. Anthony, and as I planned and sketched them, I thought that they were more interesting theologically than artistically, yet I sought to make them worth looking at. This took many weeks and occasionally one of the trio looked in to see how the work was progressing. Brother Marco was the most frequent visitor and when he saw that I was expressing the proper piety and devotion to St. Anthony he seemed content. I put Stra into one of the panels and when I portrayed him in a heroic manner he was pleased and he approved of the frescoes, too. But I was not sure how Cornora viewed them.

One afternoon while I sat on the balcony of the Scuola and stared at the Basilica across the piazza, where I felt my brush should have been instead of in this small, compressed, ugly chamber, I heard Cornora talking to Marco. They did not know that I was sitting above them.

The art connoisseur said, "Brother, I suspect that Tiziano Vecellio treats us as provincials. We are not honored by his brush but by his assistant's. Perhaps Bembo overpraised him in recommending him."

"Signore," the monk replied, "he is young. That is all that is wrong."

"I still feel his frescoes are oversimplified pieces of moralizing."

"We are grateful for your gift that made these panels possible. But once they are within my order, it is our decision what is to be painted."

"I will summon Bembo. See if he consents to these frescoes."

They walked away while I sat silently so that my presence would not be detected. I thought anxiously, Bembo will recognize Campagnola's style and no more ducats will be forthcoming. When they were out of sight I hurried inside. My assistant was finishing the eleventh panel.

I said abruptly, "Campagnola, I will do the next one."

"What is wrong, Signore?" He cringed as if I had struck him.

"Nothing. I simply wish to express the glory of God, too."

"Do you have the subject, Signore?"

"It will come." I resolved to find a miracle that would convey the strength of my faith as I had expressed the substance of my flesh.

That evening Violante, aware that I was depressed, prepared the dinner in the fashion of Mama. She roasted a plump hen until it was tender and then she gave me abundant white meat which I relished, a good red wine, and ripe fruit. This lifted my drooping spirits and I was gratified with her improvement as a cook and with her excellent taste. She had adorned our rooms with small sculptures from the antique which delighted me.

This encouraged me to confide, "I need a new miracle to sustain me. But I do not know what to paint. They find fault with whatever I do."

"Do not be troubled, Tiziano," she said, kissing me gently. "Your fresco showing St. Anthony giving speech to an infant so that it could clear its mother of the charge of adultery was masterly. Brother Marco was wrong to find fault with the flesh of the child."

"I do not trust him. He says that my flesh tones are sinful."

"They express your emotion and they are an experience to be shared."

"Where did a handsome girl like yourself learn so much about painting?"

"I grew up in the household of a painter. I like the story of *The Gentleman Killing His Innocent Wife*. I have read it often."

"Who taught you to read? It is uncommon among females."

"Palma. As he instructed me about art. We are closely connected."

This gave me the courage to ask, "Violante, is he your father?"

She did not answer, as if that question embarrassed her.

"You could have been a youthful indiscretion. He has never wed and he is old enough to be your father. Certainly he cares for you as if he is."

"If he gave me life, it is his secret and we must not spite it. It is miracle enough that we are together. That is all that matters. If you look within yourself, you will find what to paint for the Scuola."

I felt that I needed a great spirit to guide me. The story that she suggested appealed to me, but I feared that it was too dramatic for Bembo's taste and he had become the person to please. The next day I told my assistant to prepare a new panel for my brush and I took Violante to view Giotto's frescoes. I had stayed away from them, afraid that his pictorial expression would make me unhappy with my own work and hesitant to proceed with my frescoes. Yet I had heard his paintings praised ever since I had entered the Bellini bottega, and so I expected something grand. Instead, I was amazed by the simplicity of his frescoes and their surroundings.

We stood at the doorway of the chapel that had been built by Enrico Scrovegni, who had answered Dante's condemnation of his father's usury with a church by Giotto, and I felt this was a fresco painter's ideal. The narrow brick chapel with its plain exterior seemed erected for just one purpose: the work of Giotto. It was a natural rectangle with a single barrel vault that had a modest simplicity. Nothing distracted from the work of the artist. Yet despite the humble dimensions of the chapel, there were sufficient space and walls to engage the appropriate subject.

I counted forty frescoes that narrated the early life of the Virgin and the life of Jesus but my attention, as I walked around the chapel to observe as carefully as I could, was not in understanding what scene I was viewing but how Giotto had achieved such beauty, clarity, and order. I told myself that it was in his line, color, composition, but I knew it was more than that. I felt his figures' joy and grief, weakness and strength. Giotto was a master of ecclesiastical art.

Violante said, "These are by far the finest things in Padua."

I realized I could not compete with them. They possessed Giotto's reason for being, as my work should, too, I decided.

"Tiziano, *after you look, you must pass on.*"

This was a phrase from Dante's *Inferno* and I was surprised that she knew it. I said, "I am not quite sure I know what you mean."

"You must follow your own inclinations. Giotto painted these frescoes two hundred years ago. It was a different world and you are Titian."

She was handsome in her enthusiasm and I resolved to portray her this way, but nude, for when she was naked I felt that she was one of the most beautiful creatures that God had created.

After I read *The Gentleman Killing His Innocent Wife,* I decided to paint it and I returned to the Scuola the next morning with renewed energy.

When Violante viewed St. Anthony restoring life to the woman killed by her jealous husband, while in the front of the picture the husband held his dagger over the prostrate wife, she said, "It has such vitality."

Despite her praise, I was not sure what legend to express next. I sat in the cloister that adjoined the Basilica and sought to capture a sense of what St. Anthony had been. I was enchanted by its beauty and serenity. It was a rectangle like Giotto's chapel, and the perfectly cut grass, the absence of people, particularly the pilgrims who crowded the great church, were a relief from the world beyond these walls. I swore that I must always have nature close to me, even if it were only in my paintings.

While my next fresco revealed St. Anthony restoring life to a young man who, because he had kicked his mother in a rage, had cut off the offending foot in remorse, I gave nature as much prominence as the miracle. I painted Cadore into the background with its rugged hill country and a Dolomite mountain piercing the sky and used rich colors.

As I waited for Bembo, I ordered Campagnola to finish the four final frescoes from my designs. Yet as no one appeared the next few weeks—I sensed that no decision would be reached until I finished —I was restless.

The last of Campagnola's frescoes contained two cupids and I could not resist their flesh. I formed their bottoms as chubby as Marco's cheeks, yet their contours were delicately wrought. I felt I was following Violante's advice: *"Look and pass on."* These cupids possessed my love.

I told Marco that the frescoes were done and he replied that they would be inspected soon, but he did not give me the second payment of ten ducats, which alarmed me. I had only a few left from the first installment and Campagnola grumbled that I had not paid him for a long time. And I had the feeling that though my cupids were excellently created, they might obtain for me a result quite contrary to my imagination.

It was a gray, bleak winter day when Bembo appeared with the trio to judge the frescoes. I felt that he held their fate in his hands.

Cornora declared, "Signore, this work suggests that Vecellio did not think it worthwhile to paint conscientiously in what he felt was a provincial town. Do you not think a master should have done better?"

Marco said, "These panels depict the miracles of our saint."

Stra was silent, waiting for Bembo's opinion. The patrician said nothing but surveyed all of the panels in the Scuola. He paused longest before the cupids I had painted in the last of Campagnola's frescoes.

Marco said, "Only here, Signore, has he violated our order's intention. These cupids do not stress the work of the Holy Spirit but of the devil."

"On the contrary," said Cornora, "they have the life that is needed. But most of these frescoes lack the divine beauty and order of a Giotto."

I said, "His style is not appropriate to the structure of this room."

Cornora said, "That does not justify indifferent work. Only the panels of St. Anthony, granting speech to the infant and restoring life to the woman killed by her husband, express the vitality of a master."

Bembo said, "Signore, you have chosen the best work."

Marco cut in, "Cornora, you agreed to accept our Venetian friend's view."

Stra grumbled, "No one told me of such an arrangement."

"It was understood," said Cornora. "Bembo recommended him."

Some of my pessimism abated. I thought that Bembo would not contradict his own taste, it was contrary to his nature. I saw that he was pleased with the esteem with which the other men regarded him and he said carefully, "Friends, we must remember that these frescoes were ordered for the purpose of celebrating the miracles of St. Anthony. And they have achieved that worthy purpose. For the vast body of people who cannot read, they will learn about St. Anthony's holy spirit through these frescoes."

"And, I trust, find salvation," Brother Marco added piously.

Cornora said wistfully, "It was too much to expect another Giotto."

I said angrily, "My good signori, I was not employed to be anybody else. I worked in my own manner, not Giotto's. But I am grateful for the approval I received. Although I have not been paid."

Bembo said irritably, "But it was understood . . ."

Marco explained, "My lord, we were waiting for your judgment."

"He should be paid. The work is satisfactory."

The monk handed me ten ducats.

I asked, "What about the rest of the money due me?"

"It will be given you before you depart. If everything is agreeable."

Bembo seconded Marco and asked to speak to me privately. The others withdrew, although the monk regarded him suspiciously and Stra said that too much had been decided without his consent, but Bembo ignored them.

When we were alone he told me, "Hereafter, I would be more careful to whom you assign your work. Even Giorgione was."

"I do not understand."

"Many of these frescoes are second-rate. The sacred order was concerned with piety but not every patron will be so lenient."

"I did my best."

"Not here. Fortunately for you, however, you have done other work. The paintings of Giorgione that you finished have become a sensation in Venice. Either it is because he is dead, and so, no more of his pictures can be acquired, or because your styles blend splendidly. Whatever it is, now there is a great demand for his final manner. Which you completed."

So that was why he had defended me, but I said softly, "I am grateful for what you have done, my lord, and I will do my best to please you."

"I think you will. If you use your own brush and power. The cupids in the last panel could be fruitful and bring forth a harvest.

Their flesh tones are worthy of a master. Many will enjoy such rich colors."

"Then I can pack, Signore." I was very tired of Padua.

"Get your ducats first. Venetians respect a strong bargainer."

That was not easy to achieve. At the last moment Marco said that the last two frescoes had not been finished in a satisfactory manner. He did not give me the final fee until I repainted them and the cupids so that, in his opinion, they became more sacred and less profane. I was angry and upset but I had to obey him, for I needed the money. It took several weeks before I was able to conclude what had become chores.

This added to my impatience and I sighed with relief when I signed the receipt for the last ten ducats and prepared to leave Padua with Violante.

TO MY ENEMY A TRIBUTE

TO MY ENEMY A TRIBUTE

In appreciation

> Part of me is hate
> as well as love
> And I must express it

Thank God
He made you

> And thank God
> He was human enough
> To understand it

Stymean Karlen

I CAME back in the spring to a Venice that I loved. My absence from the city had increased my passion for it and by contrast with somber Padua its gaiety was a blessing. The plague and the war were over and the Republic was restoring the entertainments that pleased my eye.

At the shore of the mainland that was closest to Venice I hired the best gondola that was available to cross the lagoon to the city, although it was the most expensive conveyance. Violante protested against the excessive cost, reminding me that the last ten ducats I had earned had forced me into a labor I detested, but I silenced her objections by telling her how much Venice meant to my palette. Bembo's promise of patronage raised my hopes to a high emotional pitch. I desired the gondola because I had to feel like a Venetian and an artist when I arrived. The black craft with its spacious cabin and velvet cushions greeted me like an old acquaintance and it drove out my bad memories.

We arrived at the quay of the Piazza di San Marco in a blaze of sunlight. The harbor was crowded with little fishing boats from Chioggia and great merchant ships from Constantinople and the huge armed galleys that had made Venice's navy the greatest in the world.

This was my favorite view and I resolved to return always to the city by this approach. Venice was a world of ships, I thought, but it was also a work of art. I felt restored by its profile. My beloved Doge's Palace shimmered in the sun and I was enchanted with the newly built Campanile with its beautiful spire, the lovely clock tower with its marvelous metal giants, also recently completed, and the four handsome bronze horses over the principal portal of San Marco. After St. Anthony's sober piety I preferred the cheerful spirit of Venice's patron saint.

I was so dazzled with what I saw that I stumbled as I started ashore. The gondolier, annoyed that I added only fifty lire to his fee, ignored my outstretched hand as I missed the landing. If not for Violante, who pushed me onto the quay, I would have fallen into the water. Since I could not swim—mountain boys rarely did, for the water around Cadore was too cold—I could have drowned. Violante was upset, but I was relieved that I had not dropped my pouch bag. It held my most precious possessions, my brushes, and for a terrifying moment I had thought that I would lose them in the water. Then a cool, clean, fresh breeze blew in from the lagoon and refreshed me. There was not a cloud in the sky and Violante's vivid blue eyes reflected its bright sheen. Triumphal arches and tapestries filled the great square and it was evident that something of great importance was about to be celebrated and I felt that I had come back just in time. I was prepared to be a conqueror and to paint anything.

I rented rooms on the San Marco side of the Grand Canal. I took the entire top floor of a four-story house, although it was expensive and the climb up the stone stairway was dark and arduous, but it had the best light and plenty of space to store paintings.

The location pleased Violante. She had been depressed when we had left Padua—she preferred the quieter, more private family life on the Via Vignali—but her spirits blossomed as she saw that we had a balcony over a small canal and it contained pretty flower boxes and a place to sit.

As soon as I was settled, I went to see Bembo. He had left his address with me and instructions to call on him when I reached Venice. I knew the neighborhood of the Palazzo Bembo intimately.

It was just below the Rialto and the Fondaco and close to the Palazzo Barbarigo and the Palazzo Foscari, two celebrated citadels of Venetian power. And the Palazzo Bembo's facade was considered the most perfect example of Venetian Gothic architecture, imposing yet classical, and reputed to be remarkable for the splendor of its interior and the beauty of its magnificent art collection.

A liveried footman referred me to Bembo's steward and the thin, aged Poggio Pico curtly told me to wait in a tiny anteroom which was like a cell. After I had sat for several hours I grew tense with anxiety. Just as I felt I should bang on the great wooden door that barred my way to the interior, the steward came back and said, "My master is in Rome."

"When will he be back?" I asked anxiously.

"I am not sure. He attends the Medici cardinal." Pico added with malicious glee, "He may be delayed for months. This business is vital."

"He asked me to attend him."

"He left no word with me about you. What did you say your name was?"

"Tiziano Vecellio, the painter."

"Were you the one who was to restore the furniture in the study?"

"No." I was so angry at the steward I could have run him through, but I had to say, even as I felt humiliated, "Will you tell him that I called?"

"I inform my master of all visitors. Even butchers and barbers, too."

"Did you have to keep me waiting when you knew your master was away?"

"What business is that of yours? I run his household as I ran his father's. If you were a person of consequence, you would know that." Pico ordered an armed footman to show me out.

Violante's news was better. She told me that she had visited Vecchio and that he had agreed to return my paintings. I was surprised that he was willing to do this but I hurried to his studio before he changed his mind.

He greeted me amiably and he gave me my paintings and I was relieved that he had not touched or damaged them. He said, "Violante tells me that Bembo seeks your services directly now."

"It is possible. Although he is reported to be in Rome."

"Yes. Julius is failing and he is eager to attach himself to the new Pope. It is no wonder he likes your manner. You learned much from me."

I did not deny that but bowed my head to acknowledge his good wishes.

"Remember, whatever those patricians offer you, ask for twice as much. They always offer half of what they expect to have to pay."

He sounded paternal and I wondered what Violante had really told him.

"Be the highest paid. Then you are the best. That has lasting value. Never paint for nothing. That is a useless labor. I knew from our first meeting that you were gifted. You have an excellent appearance, you are tall and strongly constructed, and you are almost as handsome as Violante. You are an attractive pair. Avoid quarrels, do not be choleric, and you could advance far. But do not betray her or I will hire a bravo myself to run you through." Then he abruptly ushered me out of his studio.

His words had such a fatherly tone I was troubled and I rushed home and asked Violante, "What did you tell Vecchio? He was so paternal."

She murmured, "You should be pleased. He gave you the paintings. And they are still as you did them. I love your *Madonna and Child.*"

I said sharply, "It is adequate but I will do better. You evade my question." Then as she blushed violently I knew and I cried out, "You told him that we are married. That explains his new attitude and advice."

"It was the only way that I could get your pictures back."

"When he finds out that you lied he will want to kill me."

"Tiziano, I told him it was a secret, that no one knows." She added wistfully, yet hopefully, "And perhaps circumstances will change and you will not have to fear his temper."

Whereupon I lost mine and shouted at her that she was a slut who had betrayed me. She retorted that I had promised Vecchio when she had left him that I would marry her. This aroused me to a fury; I felt that she was absolving herself of guilt by blaming me. I almost struck her then, controlling myself only because I did not want to damage the beauty that caused my brush to flower. Yet as she sank onto our bed and collapsed into tears, I was tempted to throw her out. But she was still the best model I knew, and while I turned over these calculations she disrobed and sobbed, "I will do whatever you command." She was naked, which added to my discomfort. Her hips possessed a perfect curve and reminded me of the pleasures I had derived from her flesh. A moment later, as she lay in a voluptuous anguish before me, she was a nude I yearned to paint. Suddenly I felt that I was acting wrongly; I was losing a grand model, who brought me honor and beauty. To bruise and to blacken her exciting flesh was too stupid to consider, and so I grumbled, "I will marry when I want to marry. But that will not satisfy Vecchio."

"I will tell him that you must keep it a secret. To aid your career."

"He will know when our situation does not alter." However, my rage had subsided, for her posture suggested how she should pose for me, and it was a conception that intrigued me, although it might startle many people.

When she saw that I was not going to expel her, the weeping stopped. She began to cook my supper, as if that would appease me. She also remained naked and that enticed me. After she fed me, she satisfied my other desires, too, and treated them to a sensuality that was new to me. As I lay beside her, I wondered how she had learned such delights. The next morning I attributed it to the tone of *La Serenissima*. I decided that an artist without the right model was at a serious disadvantage.

A few days later the German merchants invited the Senate to witness the mummery of a greased pig pursued by blindfolded men while the church bells rang to disperse the evil spirits who might hinder them. This festivity celebrated the removal of the ban that had prohibited trade between the Germans and the Venetians during the recent hostilities. I attended with Violante but I was annoyed that I had to watch from the courtyard, where the smell was nauseating and the crowd was disgusting, while the dignitaries sat at the windows. The pig was heavy, slow, easily caught, and I noted irritably that no one paid any attention to the frescoes I had done with such care. Some of my enthusiasm for Venice dwindled.

My infatuation was revived by a new and more important ceremony. Doge Loredano led a splendid procession through the triumphal arches and into San Marco to commemorate the recapture of Padua. I was fascinated by the lavish colors, which satisfied even my greedy palette.

In a further tribute to the miracle that had brought peace to Venice and relief from the plague, there was a great regatta down the Grand Canal. This was followed by fireworks, balls lasting until dawn, and these festivities went on for days. I luxuriated in the

many lights and colors, but it was the beautiful and dramatic energy
of the reds that attracted me the most. They were striking in their
scope and splendor.

At the end of this celebration I strode to the western end of the
city and as the sun set like a giant ball of fire, I saw a red stretch
across the sky with a brilliance that caused me to gasp with wonder.
I told myself that this was why I must conceive my colors heroically,
that there was no limit to their warmth, intensity, and variety. I felt
that when I truly captured Heaven's red, I would truly feel ecstasy.

This reminds me that my dear friend, Aretino, has said it best for
me. I pause in my recollections and find the letter he wrote me
about the colors of Venice, for I have treasured it ever since I received it.

We were in middle age and he had written me because he was
lonely and he missed me. I was in Augsburg as the guest of Charles
V, to celebrate his victory at the battle of Mühlberg by painting
him as the conquering hero.

Aretino was a little younger than I, but he appeared older with
his vast bulk and his long gray beard. He was bloated from his
indulgences but he still possessed the powerful presence that had
daunted the most potent popes and princes, and had earned him
the reputation of being "The Scourge of Princes." But what appealed to me most about his appearance was his striking head. It
was massive, like a great rock from the Alps. There was such a love
of life in his lively, animated features that I painted them often. I
had the affection of a brother for him—despite the slander of his
enemies—for he was the most entertaining person I knew, with a wit
and gusto that gave the time with him a special relish. He understood my brush better than anybody else did. His views of my work
were a blessing and a constant simulant.

Once again, I read them.

"Having eaten alone, my dear Titian, which is contrary to my custom, or rather having eaten in the company of a cursed quartan
fever, I rose from the table sated with the same disgust that I sat
down to it. But leaning upon my windowsill, my melancholy vanished as I gazed at the marvelous scene that is the Venice we know.
Never since God created the heavens has it seemed to me so lovely
in its subtle pattern of lights and shades. Anyone who wished to

record the quality of this Venetian atmosphere would have been consumed with envy at not being you.

"The buildings, although of solid stone, seemed phantasmal, made of some ethereal substance. The sky was full of variety—here clear and ardent, there dull and overclouded. What marvelous clouds there were!

"I gazed in astonishment at the various colors they displayed. Those near at hand burned like fiery suns. Those in the distance glowed like half-molten lead. Nature's ingenious brush held the sky behind the palaces, just as in one of your own landscapes. The bluish-green in some places and the greenish-blue in others appeared actually to have been composed by nature with a capricious yet wonderfully skilled hand, lightening or subduing the tones in accordance with a personal choice.

"I who know your brushes to be the soul itself of nature exclaimed three or four times in succession: 'Oh, Titian, where are you?' "

"Only you could have painted this miracle."

I put this letter aside with a mixture of pleasure and sadness. He has been dead twenty years, but perhaps I have given him everlasting life in my portraits of him. I am reminded, too, that he had been the only one that Pomponio has heeded. Perhaps that is because whatever my son has done, Aretino had done it, too. This remembrance suggests a plan of action to me, but first I have to return to my memories of the Venice of my youth. At twenty-two I was bursting with energy and dreams.

The long awaited summons from Bembo ordered me to attend him at his palazzo, where he was entertaining some scholars. This lessened my enthusiasm, but Violante insisted that I avoid any risk of offending him, that I wear my gold-embroidered shirt, my ceremonial hose that showed off my long, shapely legs to advantage, and the velvet doublet which stressed my slimness. I assented reluctantly, and yet once I was dressed I enjoyed the way I looked. I could not match Bembo's silks or jewels, but I was as tall as he was, and in my choice of colors, I felt, more elegant.

The steward did not delay me this time but ushered me into Bembo's presence at once. My previous visit was ignored.

Bembo sat in the center of a spacious drawing room that was larger than the chamber I had painted in Padua. He did not address me; he expected me to approach him. I was wary; I could not walk

easily in the house of a patrician; it was not my world. So I halted
and waited. I was proud that I observed quickly, almost instantly—I
practiced this trait wherever I was—and now I put it to use. I noted
that the luxury of his palazzo had not been exaggerated. His floor
was marble and inlaid with gold mosaics and the draperies were of
the finest texture. All the furniture was carved and of solid oak.
The bronze chandeliers were gilded, the candlesticks were silver.
There were books by his side, two classical busts in the style of the
antique, and behind him a wall containing paintings by Bellini,
Giorgione, and Raphael.

He indicated with some impatience that I come forward, and I
did so slowly, and he introduced me to his guests. I was pleased that
there were no other painters present. I knew Barbarigo and Foscari
and I had heard about Jacopo Pesaro, one of the great names in the
Republic, but Aldus Manutius and Andrea Navagero were new to
me. Then Nicolo Aurelio, the secretary of state, entered and I
realized that this was an occasion.

Barbarigo had aged since I had painted him, although he was still
only in his thirties, and Foscari had become even uglier, if that
were possible, although it had not lessened his sense of importance
as he strutted about the drawing room and examined the pictures
on the wall. I wanted to do so, too, curious about Raphael, but now
Bembo wanted my full attention.

He said to me, "Tell them what you did on my Giorgione."

I blushed. I felt self-conscious and I did not like this situation.

He persisted, "Unless it is a lie that you finished it."

"No!" I blurted out. "I did the hands and the heads." Then I was
ashamed, as if, somehow, I had betrayed Big George.

Pesaro said, "I would not hesitate to admit I did such skillful
work. I commissioned Bellini to paint my portrait but Vecchio did
the drapes and Giorgione the background. It is the accepted practice."

I knew that the Pesari were an influential family and that Jacopo,
as Bishop of Paphos in Cyprus, controlled one of the most lucrative
sinecures in the state, but as he addressed me, I was intrigued by
the beauty of his hands, the animation in his dark eyes, the determination on his round face, and the ruddy tints of his brown hair
and his olive complexion.

The middle-aged nobleman added, "The heads you finished in
The Concert are admirable. It is why I wanted to meet you."

Bembo said, "But we are here, also, as members of the New Academy and as sponsors of the Aldine Press. Tiziano Vecellio, I invited you because you have shown an inclination to antique art. But before we move to such business, I have a new Raphael to exhibit to my friends."

When he led us to the painting, I was even more aware of his presence. I felt that in matters of art he would be listened to first. I knew this tall, handsome patrician was a learned poet, the foremost follower of Petrarch in Italy, and that he had a genius for acquiring influential friends. So I focused on his long, narrow face—one of the most paintable faces I had seen—and I was attracted by his lean, pointed jaw, his high, spacious brow, and his sharp, penetrating eyes.

He said, "It is a self-portrait. Raphael gave it to me to express his esteem for me. He says that I am an intellectual father to him."

I hoped that Raphael had less vanity and I was eager to know his face.

Bembo added, "My friend painted this recently, when he was thirty."

But in this self-portrait Raphael's face was softer and more youthful than I expected. His deep brown eyes matched the color of his hair and his swanlike neck fitted the long contour of his face. Yet I thought that his true eloquence was in his brush. This was his speech. His palette was warm, gentle, and his features were pretty, and yet there was a subtle strength in this composition, that with all its sweetness, was rare.

I asked quietly, "Is this a true likeness of the painter?"

"Yes," stated Bembo, "I visited Raphael while he painted this work."

Navagero said, "It is not as masculine as your portrait of Barbarigo. That is a masterful likeness. I prefer a portrait from your brush."

"Signore, I thought it was the finishing of my friend Giorgione's work that brought me to your attention."

"That reminded me of what you could do. But I prefer your faces."

Manutius asked, "Have you thought about a religious woodcut? Your hand shows a precision that favors this kind of work. Do you know Dürer's?"

"Yes, Signore. I had the honor of meeting him."

Bembo said, "Manutius began our New Academy and the Aldine Press and Navagero is one of our best poets and learned in the study of the antique."

The patrician spoke so proudly I regarded both of these men with a new interest. Manutius was small, slight, with a pert, alert face that seemed to pry into everything. He looked sixty, while Navagero was about thirty, with a commanding posture and height that was impressive and appealing.

Aurelio, one of the most powerful men in the Republic, said, "Vecellio, you will be better off with religious work. It is always in demand."

The secretary of state was of middle height. I could not judge his age; his hair was black, he was very straight, his skin was good, and yet I felt that he was older than he appeared, for his face was taut.

To my surprise, he deferred to Manutius and urged him to continue.

The elderly scholar said, "If you could do a woodcut that revealed the triumph of our faith, I would be happy to print it in our press."

"I would be honored. Signore, when would you like it to be done?"

"As soon as possible."

Then it was as if his enthusiasm evoked the same feeling in the others for my brush. Or were they competing with him, I wondered, and seeking to outdo him? I listened to them with the utmost diligence.

Since Bembo claimed to have discovered me, he took precedence. He said, "I desire your imaginative best, as in your Giorgione manner."

Aurelio said, "I prefer a *poesia* in the style of my *Country Feast*. The nudes you painted in it are charming and classical. And sensuous."

"Signore, Giorgione painted them. I worked chiefly on the men."

"Even so, that painting has the richness I desire."

"My lord, you advised me to paint piously."

"For the Republic, young man. This work is for my private gallery."

Pesaro interrupted, "I am interested in a pious subject. One that will demonstrate how nobly my family has served the state."

Barbarigo declared, "I want a portrait, as before. This time, however, as a Knight of Malta. I, too, have served the state honorably."

I thought that none of them were tempered with humility but I listened.

They waited for Foscari to speak. I could smell his body sweat despite the perfumed scent he wore, and I wondered why he was nervous, unless he was the only one who was going to avoid me. He stated, "Painting is the business of a few great artists and countless mediocrities."

"We know your views," Aurelio said brusquely, "but your taste varies."

"Not truly, My Lord Chancellor. When I first met young Vecellio I felt that Bellini and Giorgione and Vecchio were too much in his eyes, but now he begins to paint with an independent feeling."

I did not like being compared to anybody else, but Foscari was not as stupid as I thought, although I waited for him to find fault with me.

He announced, "I want a madonna or a Magdalen from his hand."

"Signore, what about the differences in their nature?"

"That does not matter as long as my piety is expressed beautifully."

Aurelio asked Bembo what he had found in Rome. Bembo replied that the Pope was ailing and that it was likely there would be a new one soon, and that he hoped it would be the Medici cardinal, who was his friend. Manutius agreed with his choice, saying that Giovanni de Medici was a learned man, as befitted the son of the great Lorenzo, and shared the same fondness for art and letters. Navagero was interested in what would happen to Michelangelo with the passing of Julius, and Bembo replied, "I think he will feel relief. The Pope drives him hard." Pesaro asked if that would affect Raphael's position in Rome and Bembo said, "I doubt it. Unless a new star emerges in the constellation of our art. Someone who is willing to challenge the supremacy of Michelangelo and Raphael."

He gazed at me, but I ignored his implication. I did not wish to leave Venice and I was not interested in challenging anyone but myself. Yet I felt that these noblemen wanted me to fight with my fellow artists as if we were swordsmen dueling for their coveted attention and applause.

While they quarreled over the respective merits of the work of Raphael and Michelangelo, Foscari drew me aside and whispered, "Vecellio, did you know that Giorgione overpaid you for the frescoes?"

"That is not true. He gave me a third. A hundred ducats."

Foscari replied triumphantly, "He only received a hundred and thirty."

"Signore, how can you be sure? I did receive the amount I told you."

He gave me a paper signed with the seal of the Republic and I read:

"Bellini and Carpaccio examined the value of the painting upon the facade of the Fondaco dei Tedeschi made by Giorgio Castelfranco, said master, and declared that said painting merits one hundred and fifty ducats in all. The same day, with the consent of the said master, Giorgio Castelfranco, he was given one hundred and thirty ducats."

Foscari said, "He exaggerated to make himself important in your eyes."

Or to help me to sustain myself and to maintain my dignity. I said, "Where did he get the rest of the money to pay me so much?"

"From other work you did for him."

I realized that Foscari would not attribute a worthy motive to my friend whatever I said and I turned away. I felt exhausted from the emotion I was spending. Upon examining my work, or what they assumed was my work, they were praising me immoderately and I was not grateful. I felt that the only reason my position had improved was the growing incapacity of Bellini, the decline of Carpaccio's powers, and the death of Giorgione, whose place I appeared to be succeeding to now.

Bembo interrupted my reverie. He said, "Your presence is appreciated but now we must turn to the business of the New Academy."

I asked, "Did your steward inform you that I called earlier?"

"No. Did it matter?" He regarded my question as if it were a joke.

"I was surprised. You told me in Padua that you wanted to see me."

"Pico resents youth. But take heart. Soon you will be able to challenge Michelangelo and even Raphael. If you play your cards right."

That was not my objective, but he was so proud of his opinion, I said, "Signore, I am grateful for what you have done on my behalf."

"Appreciation is a virtue. Listen to me and you will go far."

"Did your friends mean what they said?"

"Of course they did. Your work exhibits genuine promise."

The next day Manutius and Navagero visited me and the older man asked me to engrave the woodcut we had discussed, while the latter requested a portrait. Both of them gave me an advance of fifty ducats, a consideration I appreciated. Within a month this was followed by work for Bembo, Pesaro, Barbarigo, and Aurelio, and I felt a renewal of energy.

I had so much to do I had to hire Campagnola to aid me, and I looked for another assistant, but I did not find one. I desired a painter of the quality of Vecchio or a Piombo, but I was afraid that if I asked them it would offend them. I did move to improved quarters. I rented the top floor again, but this time in a former palazzo with a handsome facade, marble floors, and oak-paneled walls. It was between the Rialto and San Marco, on a canal that led to most of Venice, and easily accessible. It was the largest and finest studio I had possessed, with excellent light, and closets spacious enough to store many paintings and ample material. I adorned it with a bust of Plato, other statues from the antique, including a full-length nude Adam and Eve, gold draperies that were imitation but that glowed in the sun, and many large inch-thick candles so I could work properly at night.

My living quarters were spacious, too, and I tried to satisfy Violante with comforts that pleased her. I bought her a fine quilt for our new bed, a mirror for her own use, a cabinet just for her clothes. She had a shady, restful room to give her privacy, and a kitchen she liked; it was on a cheerful court and garden as in Padua. And I decorated it with a pretty vase and furnished it with good silver and solid plates.

She was so grateful that she recompensed me in every way she could.

Once I began my woodcut for Manutius, he came to my studio often. He was the first patrician I knew who worked as passionately as I did. When we agreed on the subject—a triumphal procession with Jesus enthroned in a cart led by Adam and Eve, Noah and Moses, and other Biblical figures—he helped me as much as he could. While we worked together I learned that he set his own type and did whatever else was necessary to publish his books, and that he printed everything from ancient Greek classics to the poetry of Bembo, Navagero, and Petrarch. Gradually, as I was stimulated by his encouragement and my desire to excel, to go beyond anything previously done, even the excellence of Dürer, *The Triumph of Faith* became larger than I intended. Manutius said, "This woodcut is too monumental for a book, it will be better as a wall decoration." So he printed it so that each sheet was nine feet long and fifteen inches high; I, for my part, as they were etched on wood, was determined that they express the vigor and strength of my faith and the grandeur of Jesus.

Navagero, too, became a frequent visitor to my studio. When I rested from my labors on the woodcut, I painted his portrait. His fair skin, smooth complexion, and reddish-brown hair caused me to explore my palette for a rich combination of colors. He was the first patrician to treat me as a friend, and occasionally he confided in me.

I asked him if he thought Foscari, who had a reputation for penury, would ever ask for a work from me, and he replied, "His sincerity is suspect. Manutius informs me that your woodcut is remarkable."

"Signore, he flatters me, as you do."

"It is more likely that you flatter me. You give my countenance a finer effect than it deserves."

"It is as I see you."

"My name my be forgotten but I doubt that your portrait will be. The way you paint me, my presence attracts attention immediately and strongly."

Yet I could not leave his portrait as it was. Navagero thought it was finished after a number of sittings, but I begged his indulgence and said I must turn it to the wall and return to it in a few months, and then perhaps, it might possess the excellence we both desired.

He consented, to my great relief, and he continued to visit me to see how my other commissions were progressing.

Bembo's *poesia* became my view of the subject he had requested from Vecchio, where I had been assigned the draperies. Ever since I had assisted him, I had wanted to do this theme in my own way. I did not alter the content much. I clothed Violante and the shepherd was the nude again, but I thought of this painting as *The Three Ages of Man*. So while I placed the young lovers in the prime of life, I painted three cupids to express infancy, and an elderly monk, holding a skull in his hand and brooding on the vanity of human life, representing old age.

Aurelio's desires suggested a romantic study from the antique and I thought of this mythological painting as beauty adorned and unadorned. I painted two seated women, one nude and one fully dressed, and used Violante as my model and as the opposite sides of the same coin.

While I pushed forward on these two pictures with passion, I portrayed Barbarigo as a Knight of Malta and began to compose a subject that would please Bishop Pesaro. This evolved into an altarpiece in which the kneeling cleric was presented to St. Peter by Pope Alexander VI. I knew that the Borgia pope, now that he was dead, was very unpopular, but he had assigned Pesaro to lead a fleet of Venetian ships against the Turks, and I could not distort that historical fact. But even as this work commemorated Jacopo Pesaro's naval victory, I grew restless.

I recalled Aurelio's advice to focus on religious subjects and so, when I had free time, which was only when I put aside my commissions to contemplate them and to allow them to ripen, I began a baptism of Christ with Magdalen at His feet in the hope it would have a beauty and piety that would satisfy Foscari. This did not quench my thirst for oils and I also started a madonna that possessed the gypsy charm of Violante.

I used her as the model and she said proudly, "You must never work in a studio less grand than this one. You look like a god at the easel."

Even as I was pleased by her compliment, I was annoyed, for she had distracted me. I told her to be quiet so I would not distort her mouth.

I labored on so many pictures it was difficult to remember all of them. I told Campagnola to total the paintings that I was doing and he had just retired to the rear of the studio to do this, when a group of fellow artists entered. It was two months since I had met with the patrons at the Palazzo Bembo and I had not seen any of these painters in the interval.

The burly, hot-tempered Pordenone led, the tight-faced Piombo was behind him, with the dour Lotto and the sluggish Bordone in the rear.

To answer the demands of my patrons and my own needs, I was working on four pictures at the same time. They were on a row of easels, where I could meditate about them at my leisure, and at this moment I was focusing on Aurelio's *poesia*. I felt I was on the verge of painting something unique. The nude stimulated me and suggested a boldness new to me.

Pordenone growled, "As I thought! He takes the bread from our mouths. If we are not careful, there will be nothing left for us."

Piombo said, "I am your friend, but you test my affection these days."

Lotto said, "You always pushed hard. Even when you were an apprentice."

Bordone had grown as fat as a barrel and he grunted his agreement.

I sighed, but I tried to be cordial, despite my irritation at being interrupted. "Gentlemen, may I offer you some wine? Or fruit?"

"No!" Pordenone replied angrily. "We came on business!"

I asked, "From the Venetian Guild of Painters?"

"In a way," he said.

"But not officially," Piombo hurried to add.

Lotto said, "The Guild did not appoint us, but we came to serve our fellow painters. They support our defense of their interests."

Pordenone took command while I recalled that this belligerent, impulsive artist considered himself the best fresco painter in the Republic, and that his restless nature had caused him to wander from church to church in search of work, and had reduced him often to painting aisles and chairs.

No wonder, I reflected, that he did not like me.

Pordenone stated, "Work should be shared, not seized by one man."

Piombo said, "Especially when there are painters who are just as worthy."

Lotto cut in, "For some there is too much, for others too little."

By now I felt that I knew their mission, but I answered, "You talk in riddles. Why are you here? Do you come with Bellini's approval?"

Pordenone said, "He has not spoken but he supports our stand. We do not object to your obtaining one or two commissions, but so many threaten our living."

I wondered who was truly behind them. I doubted that Pordenone was shrewd enough to do this on his own. I asked, "Who else supports you?"

Bordone said, "Carpaccio does."

"Sssh," cautioned Lotto.

"But he does," insisted Bordone. "He told me so. He said that Pesaro gave Vecellio a commission that had been intended for him."

Lotto reminded him, "That was supposed to be his private comment."

I asked, "Are there many who share your views?"

Pordenone declared, "Most of the Venetian painters."

Bordone mumbled, "Outdoing them, you offend them."

Pordenone added brutally, tired of politeness, "You are too popular."

"Does Vecchio share your views?"

"Leave him out of it. Your mistress is his kin. How many commissions do you possess? I see four here. Are all these subscribed to?"

I nodded.

"Any more? I heard that Bembo asked for a *poesia* from your brush and Barbarigo, Navagero, Aurelio, Pesaro, Foscari."

"Not Foscari. I have four commissions at the moment."

Campagnola returned and announced, wanting to show how important he was, "Maestro, I count twelve works in progress."

Pordenone said contemptuously, "Vecellio, you are a liar!"

"The other paintings are for my own benefit and pleasure."

"No one will believe you. Certainly no painter will."

There was such hostility in him that I cried out desperately, "Friends, I told the truth. But I do need an assistant. I would be honored if any of you joined me in my studio. There is work for all of us."

Piombo looked tempted, Bordone seemed eager to say Yes, and even Lotto, despite his dislike of me, appeared interested, but Pordenone said critically, "You are too young to serve. Too immature."

"I am twenty-five!" I shouted, determined not to be outdone in this.

"You are the youngest twenty-five I have seen," he retorted savagely. "But you will not listen and thus, you will suffer. It is inevitable."

I saw that Pordenone wore a sword in his belt and I recalled that he was suspected of having murdered his brother. I must wear a sword, too, I thought anxiously, and I looked around for a weapon to defend myself.

Pordenone said malignantly, "Perugino tried to slay a painter who took work away from him and Mantegna attacked an insolent fellow who stole a commission from him. And even Michelangelo has been assaulted."

The others lined up beside him, although Piombo and Bordone moved slowly, while Campagnola stood between us, not knowing where to turn.

Pordenone added insultingly, "You are a headstrong fool."

"And you are an evil rogue," I replied furiously. "Whatever work I have obtained, I have earned by the grace of God and my own hand."

"And the death of Big George," Piombo muttered sorrowfully.

Lotto remarked, "It is even said that you are glad that he died."

Enraged, I shouted, "Who uttered such a slander?"

"It is a common report. You have profited most from his passing."

I picked up a chair to hit Lotto and they retired in haste, even Pordenone, who grumbled unhappily, "I am on probation. I cannot afford another clash with the law. But you will pay for your insolence."

The next day I told Campagnola not to say a word about these threats to anyone, and especially not to Violante, who would be terrified, and I went to Navagero to ask his advice. When he heard that I was agitated, he saw me at once. The Palazzo Navagero was without the usual glitter and ostentation and his favored ornaments were his paintings by Bellini, Perugino, Mantegna, and Giorgione. There was a space in the middle which, he informed me, was for my work. I was pleased but I was too upset to savor this praise as I would have liked to have done. I told him what had happened and he listened attentively.

Then he said, "Painters often try to intimidate other painters. It is not unusual. Generally, it is more apt to be talk than anything else."

"Signore, painters have been murdered in Venice."

"We have just had such a situation reported to the Council. The painter who was attacked died of his wounds. The other painter is now in prison awaiting trial. It will be brought before the Council soon."

"Would I know them?"

"I doubt it. They had shops near San Marco and they quarreled over the amount of space each was allotted. Then a dagger was used."

"My lord, I did not know that you were a member of the Council of Ten."

"It is an official duty. Essential, but not always pleasant."

"What worries me is that these threats distract me from my work."

Navagero exclaimed, "That would be a disaster!"

"My lord, do you think that there is a conspiracy against me?"

"There is always a conspiracy against someone in Venice."

"Even in painting?"

"More often in painting. Where the challenge is greatest. If they attack you, and I do not think that they will, for it would cause a scandal, it will be at night in a dark alley where the assailant will not be seen. Their intention is to frighten you so you will not accept commissions they covet. But for your peace of mind, you should have protection. I suggest you employ Vittore Mocenigo, who has served me. He is at liberty and he will be happy to attend you if I request it. He is in debt to me."

"Is it an important obligation, Signore?"

"I kept him out of prison. On a charge of murder. Now do not be afraid. Mocenigo kills only in self-defense or on the business of the state."

"My lord, was there not a Doge by his name?"

"Yes. Mocenigo claims to be his bastard but he is not always to be believed. But his sword is trustworthy and he is a clever fellow."

"I cannot call him my bravo. It will frighten my friends and Violante."

"Appoint him your steward. He can tutor you in Latin, it is a useful language to know, and he will take care of many of your other needs. With my recommendation, he will be honored to attend you. Friend, be of good courage. Those fellow painters of yours fear you so much that they have paid you a great compliment."

Vittore Mocenigo was a middle-aged, middle-sized soldier whose room was filled with swords, daggers, armor, and fowling pieces. I thought that he might be an escaped slave or a Moor, he was so dark, but he spoke very well and the books on his table were by Dante, Petrarch, and Boccaccio, and when he saw my astonishment he smiled slyly and he said, "I read Vergil in the original. Signore, what is your business?"

After he heard my tale he replied that it would be an honor to serve a friend of Navagero. He discarded his military garb, although he still wore a sword and a dagger, and I stated that this would arouse suspicion and he pointed out, "What it will do is inform your enemies that you can afford both the best sword and the best steward in the Republic." His hint was plain and I gave him two ducats to seal our bargain and he assured me, "Not even the devil will harm you now and certainly no mortal man."

Campagnola lived on the floor below me and I rented quarters for Mocenigo there, too, and he moved in immediately. I introduced him to Violante and he bowed before her as if she were the Doga-ressa herself and murmured that I was fortunate to possess so beautiful a companion.

She acknowledged his compliment with a gracious smile but that night, when I reached for her passionately she did not respond but complained, "I am not comfortable with such a strange man in our house."

I was annoyed and pretended that I did not know what she meant.

She sat up abruptly and stated, "He is nothing more than a bravo."

"He is many things," I insisted, "and a descendant of a Doge."

"And I am the Madonna," she said derisively. "Are you in trouble? You may call him a steward but you have really hired his sword."

"I do not deny his skill with weapons. He is going to teach me how to use them, as a gentleman, but he is also going to guide me in Latin." I reached for her beautiful breasts which I had just painted with passion and I whispered, "I must do a study of you, just as you are."

"You have," she retorted, but now she was not a disheveled innocent as she responded to my caress, which she could rarely resist.

Vittore taught me how to defend myself with a sword and a dagger. Somewhat reassured, I practiced the lute to soothe myself and studied Latin with him to improve my learning. His breadth of knowledge surprised me and I asked him why he pursued his present calling, and he said it was an exciting and interesting life and changed the subject. While no attacks were made on my person during this time, he accompanied me wherever I went.

Violante asked me why he did so, and I snapped, "Because I like his company." When she persisted, I strode away. I had more vital things on my mind. Bembo, Aurelio, and Pesaro desired their pictures, but I did not feel that any of this work was finished.

Since my *poesias* for Bembo and Aurelio were more to my taste than the pious expression of Pesaro's devotion and nobility, I told Campagnola to paint the figure of St. Peter into the panel and I focused on the other two pictures. It was a joy to work on *The Three Ages of Man* again. In this work I was expressing my own passion for nature and for flesh. The young lovers became an amorous study of myself and Violante, even though she remained fully clothed. I wanted her to pursue me, to entice me.

When Bembo saw this work he cried, "This is what Ferrara ordered from Vecchio. I wanted an original *poesia*. Not what is painted already."

"Is it really, my lord?"

He did not reply.

"Look more closely."

My words were a challenge to his taste and he did so.

"Is it not more alive, more sensual than Vecchio's *poesia?*"

"I will consider it," he said curtly. He commanded his servants to take the painting and he left my presence without another word.

Disappointed that he had not expressed approval of my brush, yet unable to halt my headlong rush to paint as I felt, I returned to the picture I cared most for and used my brush with a feverish activity. Violante, posing for it, called it "sacred and profane love," for she said I was displaying the contrasts of romantic feeling, but I could comprehend how Giorgione had felt. I was not concerned with a name for this *poesia;* it was the work that mattered. I gave each detail the same intensity. I was infatuated with the feel and the motion of my brush. The oil itself had such a sensual pleasure I did not want to stop. The red drapery I painted over Violante's naked arm added to her nudity. I was glad now that I had done draperies and I was delighted with their effect. Yet there were moments when I felt this nude was too refined. Was it my model, I wondered, or my own conception? Violante was still perfectly formed and I still desired to possess her. But would the viewer?

Aurelio arrived with a retinue to claim it. He stared at it sharply and declared, "It is done! My steward will settle the account later."

The next day I received a hundred ducats for this work. I should have felt reassured, it was the most money I had received for a picture—Bembo had not paid me, as if he expected his painting to be the fee for his introducing me to patrons—but I felt lost. Good friends had been taken from me. I had put so much into them. And no one had praised them.

I had to do something to show what I had done. I saw Forni. He had established an iron trade with Cadore through my papa and he visited him to supervise the shipments. I gave the merchant two packets to deliver to my parents. Each contained ten ducats. One was for Mama to put glass in her windows; the other was for Papa to put to my account in Cadore. And to prove to him that I was right to remain in Venice.

Mocenigo accompanied me and as I left Forni's place of business —he had waited outside—he looked somber and he strode with his hand on his sword.

Concerned, his gravity was unusual, I asked, "What disturbs you?"

"The painter charged with murder was found strangled in his cell. To silence him. Yet I heard that another painter was attacked today."

"Was he slain?"

"You do not recover from dagger wounds in the back of the head."

At home Violante waited anxiously for me with a new difficulty. She said, "A message from Pesaro demands that he have his panel by tomorrow."

"That is impossible! It is not finished!"

"Pesaro's envoy insists that his master will not wait any longer."

I told Violante to light our largest candles, for I had a night's work ahead of me. The St. Peter that Campagnola had filled in for me was poorly done and while the figures of the Pope and Pesaro had truth and vitality, I knew they could be better. I gave St. Peter's rose tunic an added richness of texture and color and painted the robes of the Pope more sumptuously. I felt this should please Pesaro as it pleased me. And now this picture possessed the dramatic contrasts that I desired.

When I finished the sun was shining. But I could not go to sleep as Violante urged. I was too passionately involved in what I had done.

By the time Pesaro's steward came to claim the picture the paint was dry and I was nodding sleepily at the window. I wondered why these servants of the patricians were old, wizened, and rude. He said, "My lord has heard reports that this work was done mainly by another hand. If this is true, he will return it, but first he wants to see for himself."

I blurted out, "It is my work. My hands are stained with its paint."

"Is that why it is so brightly colored? That is not fitting for a religious subject. No wonder my master doubts its worth."

For a moment I felt helpless, at the mercy of those whose taste I did not respect. Then my necessity to be myself reasserted itself. Just as the steward was about to wrap this picture, I signed it.

Pesaro might not know who had painted this picture, or approve of it, but everyone else would be aware of who had done *St. Peter Enthroned*.

Yet even after this act of defiance, I could not sleep. I was too exhausted. The more I tossed, the more I was certain that none of my paintings would be acceptable. But I was proud of my signature.

PLANT YOUR OWN SEEDS

PLANT YOUR OWN SEEDS

Weave your own pores

Fling high your own sky
Design your own footprints

Shine your own sun
Before you buy

Any of these
　　　　　from sellers

Stymean Karlen

I AM still reflecting upon my struggles to sustain myself while I was young, and the strange and unexpected turns my life has taken, when Orazio hurries into my study. He does not knock; his need is too urgent for such a formality. Yet his behavior puzzles me. As I turn away from my precious memories, I am not sure whether he is troubled or angry.

"What is wrong?" I ask.

"Pomponio is ill."

I am surprised. My sons have inherited my good health and it is unusual for them to be sick. I ask anxiously, "Is it serious?"

"It is hard to tell. But he has taken to his bed. Which is rare."

"Do you think it is the plague? It still prevails in Venice."

"He does not appear to have the symptoms. But I cannot be sure."

I ask hopefully, "Does he want to see me?"

"No. But you may be able to talk to him now. I believe that he is afraid that he is dying, and so he is almost contrite."

"He must be in pain. Is he very sick?"

"Or very frightened. I doubt you will find a better opportunity to talk to him. Papa, he is so distraught he is in a confessional mood."

"Has he called a priest?"

"Pomponio prefers a Doctor Alberti. One of the reasons I do not think he is critical is that this physician attends him in person."

I put on a blue robe to protect myself from the morning chill and I follow Orazio to Pomponio's quarters in the rear of the house. I have not been in them for a long time and as I enter his bedroom I feel unwanted, but I am too worried to allow that to halt me. Yet his quarters are in an even worse disarray than I expect. The floor is dirty, his clothes litter the furniture, there is a rubbish heap of filthy dishes and broken wine glasses, and a rusty bent sword in a corner. My eyes ache so from the disorder, I yearn to close them. Once again Pomponio has betrayed my worship of beauty. But as I become used to the poor light—the doctor has closed the shutters to keep out the pestilence—I observe that my son lies in a tangle of sheets and that there is blood on his pillow.

When he sees me, instead of denying me as I had anticipated, he moans, "I have a violent fever attended by an extreme chill. I am about to die!"

I turn to the plump, gray-haired Doctor Alberti, who is consulting his astrological charts, and I ask him, "What are Pomponio's symptoms?"

"Maestro Tiziano, I am of a most sanguine and judicious nature."

Pomponio shouts, "I am so ill that I cannot sleep!"

I feel he carries a burden within that has pushed him into his sick bed, but I do not wish to offend him, and so I listen to his doctor.

Alberti declares, "His stars are favorable, but his humors are choleric. Men who go about barefooted are not inflamed by sexual desires."

I ask, "Is he infected with the pox? He has dissipated carelessly."

"Coitus in advanced age is dangerous. And you are quite old."

"Doctor, it is my son who is ill. I do not need your services."

"Maestro, while I am in your presence I am happy to attend you, too. Your son tells me that you suffer many of the infirmities of old age."

I am furious, and Orazio, who stands behind me, says hastily, "Papa, I did not suggest that and I am sure that Pomponio intended no harm."

Pomponio whispers, "Alberti could treat you, as he does me."

Alberti says in a pious tone, "Galen has defined old age as the pathway to death. Maestro Tiziano, it is wise to be prepared."

"Get out! You are a quack! You will kill all of us!" I go to eject him and Orazio steps between us and motions for Alberti to leave.

He does, muttering, "Many old men clasp boys to their bosom to promote body warmth, and Aristotle approves of this practice for giving heat, but painters are not to be trusted. Their work inflames them."

Is Pomponio so eager to hurry me into death? I wonder, but I cannot ignore his agitation. I have had much experience with illness despite my own good health. I compose myself and approach him to examine him. He shrinks from me but I am relieved that there are no symptoms of the plague.

Orazio whispers, "Papa wants to help you."

Pomponio weeps, "No one can help me, I am debilitated and undone."

I reply, "Your skin is good, your flesh is firm. Considering how you indulge yourself, you do not show your age. You still have your mother's attractive appearance and my height. You do not appear ill."

"It does not matter what you say. Did you look like me at this age?"

"Very much so. Examine my self-portraits of thirty years ago."

"The magnificent Titian resembles me! How marvelous!" For an instant I feel that he is sarcastic, yet I am not certain, for he sounds as if this is a fond moment. Then he says somberly, "But no, that is a delirium. Last night an ugly old man came to my bed in the black gondola that takes plague victims away and he tried to force me into it. Papa, he had your large hands, those that painted many pictures. Only his were claws and I escaped through my window and I . . ."

"Pomponio!" I cannot endure such thoughts, even if they are imagined. "You had a nightmare. It is natural when one is frightened."

I wipe off his forehead, although he recoils from my touch, and while he is damp with sweat, he has none of the fire of a fever. I am almost certain that he shakes from fear and not from a chill.

I tell him that and he retorts angrily, "You take me for a fool or for a coward. You think that I am the reverse of your coin."

"I think that you are my son."

Orazio says, "Papa does desire to help you. What troubles you?"

Pomponio regards me suspiciously and sobs, "He forgets nothing."

"Has he chided you now?"

"No. But he will."

"Son, have you taken to bed because of threats against your person?"

"What makes you say that?"

"There is blood on your pillow and at the back of your head."

"Alberti forgot to bandage it. I banged myself on the bed."

"With a dagger cut?" I throw open the shutters so I can see better and as the light enters the room, I focus on him as I would on a picture I must finish. By now I am convinced that he is not dangerously ill. "You were attacked. Where did it take place? How and when?"

When Pomponio is silent, Orazio says, "I was attacked and almost slain. I think it is a family curse. But it is better to expose the assailants."

Pomponio says, "And Papa, two of your servants were murdered. Were these attacks directed against you?"

"Probably. But I was shaken most by the one on Orazio. I sent him on an errand that I should have done and I almost sent him to his death."

"No!" Orazio states severely. "It was my own fault. I trusted a fellow artist when I should have known better. I was a fool."

Pomponio asks, "How did it happen? You never talk about it."

"It troubles me too much. But perhaps my experience will help you."

Orazio's soft features stiffen and grow lined and then, with a passion he displays seldom, he gives us his view of the attempt to murder him.

"Charles had just died and Papa was sad at the loss of an old and good friend. Yet the emperor owed him much money. On Christmas Day, 1558, his son, Philip the Second, ordered the governor of Milan, the duke of Sessa, to pay 'all arrears of the pensions granted to Titian by my father, now in glory.' When Papa was told that the governor was holding this money for him in Milan, waiting for him to collect it, I suggested to him that he was too old for such an arduous trip and I offered to take it for him."

I said, "I was not too old. I was only seventy. But I was tired of traveling. I had gone to Ferrara, Augsburg, Rome, Florence, other cities to fulfill commissions, and I wanted to remain in Venice. I was tired of taking more time away from my painting. But I was wrong."

"You were right to stay at home. You did several fine pictures."

I replied, "And you almost lost your life."

"That could not be foreseen. For me, it was vital that you paint rather than waste your time in laborious travel. By then your eminence as a painter was unchallenged. Leonardo and Raphael had been dead a long time, Michelangelo had not created any pictorial work for years, you had far outdone your contemporaries, and the only younger artists who approached your brush were Tintoretto and Veronese and they had studied with you."

I am astonished by Orazio's vehemence—he is prouder of my situation than I am—but I am pleased by his pride, and Pomponio is listening to him with an attentiveness I have seen in him rarely.

"Papa, when you gave me your consent, you also gave me fourteen of your paintings to submit to the governor for the king's consideration. You were eager for Philip to become as devoted a patron as his father."

I do not correct Orazio—Philip had bought a number of pictures from me before his father's death—but I listen so I will know him better.

"To ensure my safety, Papa entrusted me to the care of his most trusted servant, his steward, Mathio, from Cadore. Like all his stewards, he was a skilled swordsman and trained in the use of small arms.

"In Milan I planned to live in modest rooms at the Falcon Inn. I did not like to waste Papa's money, but I was approached by Leone Leoni, and this sculptor begged me to accept his hospitality. I hesitated. He was reputed to be even more violent-tempered and cunning than Cellini, to have been banished from two cities for murder, but he was related to Papa's best friend, Aretino, and he was an excellent craftsman. So when this tall, dark, middle-aged artist entertained me with droll tales about how other painters shrank in Papa's light, I agreed to reside in his palazzo.

"The governor asked for a portrait from my hand and that occupied me the next month. He was pleased with my work, he said it was worthy of the son of the great Titian. He added that four of Papa's pieces sent to Spain for Philip's approval were acceptable and so his pension would be continued. And that all the monies owing to Papa would be forthcoming in gold, and he asked permission to send the other ten pieces to Philip for his approval.

"Pleased with the success of my mission, I consented. But Mathio was concerned about the large amount of cash I was to receive. After we left the governor's palazzo, he told me that a servant of Leoni's, Bando, a doglike fellow, had been observing us like a hound on a scent, and that he did not trust the master's intentions.

"I decided to move to the inn and I went to Leoni's palazzo to supervise the transfer of Papa's pictures. But while Mathio's attention was diverted to the street, where one of Leoni's servants was helping him to find a cart to convey the paintings to the inn, the two men who were packing me were joined by Leoni. The sculptor glared at me, as if he had to work himself into a rage. Then he drew his dagger and dealt me a back-handed stroke, intending to run me through the back of my head. But my apprehension had alerted me and I turned unexpectedly and lifted my arm to defend myself, and he missed my head and stabbed me on the shoulder. Infuriated that he had failed, Leoni stabbed me several more times on my up-raised arm while his two rogues attacked me with staves. I heard him muttering, 'The money, the money, make sure we do not lose it,' but I evaded their grasp, and although I was bleeding from wounds on my arm and shoulder, I staggered out the door shouting for help. Mathio came to my aid immediately and drove off Leoni with his big two-handed sword while the servants fled.

"The sculptor retreated, swearing, 'Next time I will not miss.'

"A doctor was called, but he refused to attend me. He said that he did not treat wounds, that it was a situation for a barber, and I was afraid that my painting arm was going to be amputated. I might not be a Titian, but the thought of not being able to paint struck terror in my heart.

"Mathio refused to allow the barber to cut off my arm, stating that my wounds could be treated with medicine. As soon as he dressed my wounds—he was more skillful than the crude barber—he removed me to the inn. I had not lost blood copiously and in a week I was able to resume my business.

"When the case was brought before the magistrate, I could not accuse Leoni of robbery, for no money had been in my possession during the attack. So when I was asked the cause of the assault, I said that the sculptor envied my situation with the governor. Yet he was neither hanged nor even sent to the galleys as punishment, but he was simply fined and banished."

I interrupt. "When Orazio wrote me what had happened, I wrote at once to Philip. I informed him that Leoni had tried to murder my son, and that he had been expelled from Spain because he was a Lutheran, and so, a heretic, a condition the king of Spain hated, that Leoni had been condemned to the stake by the duke of Ferrara for counterfeiting, and banished from Rome and Florence because of murders he had committed. I begged that the Inquisition be invoked and that Leoni be tried as a heretic and burned."

Pomponio asks avidly, "What did happen to the sculptor?"

"Philip was angry at me because a work he ordered took longer than he liked. Orazio was paid, but nothing further happened to Leoni."

Orazio says, "That is why I did not discuss it when I returned to Venice. For years I went about in fear of Leoni, who had sworn not to fail the next time. And he was known to live up to his threats."

Pomponio exclaims, "That is why I am ill. Was not Mathio slain later?"

"Yes," I say, "some years after the attempt on Orazio's life."

"And another steward of yours was murdered, too. I was a child when it happened, but I remember that you were upset at the time and worried."

I explain, "Vittore Mocenigo was close to me. When he was murdered in 1528, after serving me for many years, I was shocked. Then, in the public records, he was known as Aloysius de Cypro, which added to the mystery."

"Did you ever find out who was behind these attacks?"

"Pomponio, the men who used the daggers were apprehended but to this day I am not certain why my two stewards were murdered."

"Yet you wonder why I take to my bed. And why I am frightened, too."

Orazio has lapsed into a melancholy silence, as if even now, his memories are painful to endure, while Pomponio looks apprehensive. I say, "So I am right. You are using your bed as a refuge from a dagger."

Pomponio blurts out, "Papa, I did not want to tell you, but you force it from me. At the ferry under the Rialto bridge, the boatman of a gondola I hired to bring me here tried to kill me. His dagger only scratched my neck, but it gave me such a chill I had to take to my bed."

"And you were attacked because of the thousand ducats that you owe?"

He hesitates, then nods slowly, apparently with great reluctance.

"Because it has not been paid back to the ambassador?"

"No. I owe it to someone else. That is why I cannot return it to Donato. I need the money to pay back an earlier debt."

"Continue," I urge, and smile, to hide the anger boiling up within me.

"Anna, a nobleman's niece, enticed me. But when I took her to bed, her uncle insisted that I marry her. Or pay for her damaged honor."

"Who is the nobleman?"

"I have been warned that if I reveal his name my throat will be cut. Or if I do not give him a thousand ducats. That is why I sold the picture."

"Why not marry the girl?"

"I do not love her. And she encouraged me and is just as guilty."

"Have you told that to her uncle?"

"He will not listen."

"Would it not be easier to marry her?"

"Did you marry my mother when I was conceived? Or when she carried Orazio? Or only when you were afraid she would die and you had to?"

I could have struck him in spite of my age. Yet he is right, at least in part, although he does not know all the circumstances.

"How did you meet our mother?"

"In time! In time!" I am thinking that it is not really their business. Unless, perhaps, the proper moment comes.

Pomponio falls back in his bed and whimpers, "If I do not use the money soon to pay the nobleman, they will lay violent hands on me. As they have tried to do already. I am not prepared to die or to go to prison. I am cursed with the family affliction. You have offended many powerful people and the only remedy is to pay them. That is why Orazio was attacked and your two stewards. You are to blame, too."

Even as I am stunned by his accusation, I feel there may be truth to what he says. "You think the attack on you is also directed against me?"

"Without a doubt. Many envy you, some hate you. They know that an attack against your sons or servants will be an attack on you."

"Is this possible?" I ask, yet I have speculated on this possibility.

Orazio says, "It is very possible. No one dares attack you directly, you are Venice's greatest citizen. But Pomponio and I are not so blessed, and thus we are vulnerable, very vulnerable."

Experience has taught me not to trust Pomponio but Orazio is different. I gather my blue robe about me to hide my shivering, which is not from the cold. The sun is high now and it bathes the bedroom in a warm light and Pomponio's large features look closer to mine. I pick up the bent sword as if to examine it, but it is to give myself a moment to think. He has betrayed me often and yet, I ask myself, do I bear some responsibility for this? Has my position put my sons in an intolerable situation? Has it been too heavy, too large a burden to bear?

Orazio says, "Yet you have given us a great heritage."

Pomponio adds, "And a harsh burden. We are not treated as other folk. We are the sons of an incomparable eye, of an indispensable Venetian."

"You exaggerate," I protest. "Some prefer Tintoretto's manner now."

"A few. But no one that matters much. That, however, is not my most grievous sorrow. It is that I am expected to emulate you and I cannot."

I feel I am involved in civil strife and I long to shout: Enough! Enough! Stand on your own feet, make your own life, plant your own seeds! But I do not, afraid that if I give in to this impulse I will lose them forever and destroy what little of them I possess, even if it is only their dependence. So I say, "I will pay Donato the money he is owed."

Orazio sighs with relief, but I am not sure that Pomponio truly appreciates my gesture, for while his health improves immediately, he does not thank me, but remarks, "Papa, how old are you?"

"Why do you want to know?" I am suspicious of him again.

"If you are ninety-nine, you are one of the wonders of the age."

I feel no satisfaction from this as I say, "I do not see why."

"To still be painting. To be free of illness. It is remarkable."

"I am not sure about my age. I have never been sure."

"You did write the king of Spain four years ago, describing yourself as 'the king's servant, now ninety-five years old.' "

I respond uncomfortably, "I was asking for monies owed to me."

"So you made yourself older to get money from Philip." There is almost admiration in Pomponio's voice, as if I have exhibited the kind of cleverness that he respects. "But you are not that old."

"It does not matter," I reply wearily, eager to change the subject, yet anxious not to drive away Pomponio. "Some days I feel a hundred, other days, less. When I can still paint. I prefer to remember that my portrait of Philip won the heart of Mary Tudor, the queen of England. It was used to court her and she found my likeness of the Spanish king so appealing that she agreed to marry him." Pomponio, absorbed in what I am saying—this kind of conversation between us is rare—gets out of bed and pushes the crumbs from his last meal out his window and into the water below. I think that it is no wonder the plague frequents Venice. But here, at least, in Biro Grande, we are close to the open sea where there is less danger of infection. I turn to leave and I see my self-portrait hanging behind his bed. I am surprised and I say so.

Pomponio replies strongly, "It is mine. You gave it to me years ago."

"I forgot. Why did you not sell this when you needed ducats?"

"This is an original."

"Yet you tried to deceive Donato."

Pomponio says contemptuously, "He is a fool. If he had not noticed that the work was retouched, he would never have known the difference. But no one is going to take this picture from me. It proves that I am your son. Look how we resemble each other."

I am too tired to pursue this matter further. And I cannot get down on my knees before him and beg forgiveness for something I have not done.

Orazio adds, "I told you Papa would listen if he knew the truth."

"Thank you, brother. Papa, you will pay Donato, please? Whatever I have received from him has to go to the blackmailing nobleman."

I nod, even as I have doubts about the roots I have planted.

The next day I arrange to raise a thousand ducats. It is hard to obtain the cash, my money is invested in land and in houses, but when it is done I ask Donato's indulgence, pleading old age, and request that he attend me. He does so promptly and he accepts the money apologetically, saying that his father, the Doge, whom I had painted and known well, would have been distressed by the sad affair, that this portrait is one of his most prized possessions. "But," adds the ambassador, "my expenditures are large and a bargain is a bargain." I agree. I am too proud to offer him another painting, a genuine Titian. I have not tried to sell any pictures recently, although I still have to beg some purchasers to pay me. I am relieved that I seem to have resolved my son's difficulties.

Just when I think I have emerged from this tempestuous sea of troubles and that no evil will stop me from painting again, I find that I cannot sleep. It is several weeks later and nothing unpleasant has happened, and yet there are still things about Pomponio's situation that puzzle me. I walk to my window and gaze out on the quiet lagoon, which has given me so much peace, beauty, and serenity, and I hear voices. It is very late and there is no other sound in the air. Then I discern a gondola landing at my dock and Pomponio whispering, "Nothing else worked and so I had to try that. Do you think that Papa will allow Alberti to attend him?"

"It is not necessary," Orazio replies. "His health is still sound."

"I wonder. He is irritable lately. Did he pay Donato?"

"Yes. Were you truly sick when you summoned me?"

"Did you think so?"

"I would not have called Papa if I had doubted you. Although I thought your illness was caused mostly by your fear."

Pomponio laughs. "I was afraid, indeed, that he would not help me."

"You have not answered my question."

"Orazio, I have waited so long for money of my own. At least, Papa gives you a salary. But I have no income of my own."

"Papa arranged a benefice for you when you were six, a second one when you were fourteen, and you would have had others if you had not squandered what you possessed. He was even willing to serve the Pope in your behalf. But you never blame yourself for anything you do."

There is a long silence and then Pomponio mutters, "Get out."

"What about yourself? It is past midnight."

"I am not going to sit around and feel humble. I have a friend who lives near the Frari church for which Papa paints so desperately. She is discreet and she shares my desires. I will come home when it suits me."

How can one start again at my age? Even as I ask myself this, I see only one answer. Since I know that sleep is impossible and I am too troubled and confused to paint, I go into my study and return to the part of my life where, at least, if anyone betrays me, it is not my own son.

MY CRITICS YOU BE GREAT

MY CRITICS YOU BE GREAT

I will be myself

My critics you be great
I will be what I am

My critics it can be
If I do not measure my worth
But trust myself
I will be great despite myself

In the meantime my critics
you be great
I will be myself

Stymean Karlen

WHILE I WAITED to hear from my patrons, I painted with more passion. Each picture renewed my vitality, each one added to my energy and to my experience. I rose with the sun every day so that I could be at my easel as soon and as much as possible. I was saturated with color and light and the urgency to use my brushes and oils in a fresh and vital way.

There were times I worried because I did not know what my patrons felt about their pictures. I hated waiting. I was like a fish on a hook.

None of my paintings was returned—as had been threatened—but only Navagero expressed his approval of my work and paid me in full. After a month I felt I would always have to wait for their approval and this added to my hatred of the situation. I was dismayed by my uncertain earnings, too. The noblemen could pay me when it suited them. They were the only ones who voted, who sat on the councils that ruled; they had most of the money. To question them was to end my prospects in Venice.

One day I sought to forget my anxiety by starting a new *Madonna and Child*. Bellini's were the best I had seen, but I was bored with the sameness of his treatment and I felt I could excel him. I ignored the other pictures that I had not finished. As I sketched the madonna, I wished I could depict her like Mama, only Mama was too thin, and I decided to use the landscape of Cadore to strengthen my own feeling. I was doing this when my brother entered, escorted by Violante, who was ill at ease. We embraced fervently, then observed each other. He had recovered from his wounds, but his face was still softer and rounder than mine, and although he was older, he looked less mature.

I introduced Violante as my housekeeper, unable to say she was my mistress, and he said, "You are as lovely as you are reported to be."

She blushed and retired, saying, "You must have much to talk about."

Francesco said, "She is beautiful. It gives her an unfair advantage."

"Do Mama and Papa know about my irregular arrangement?"

"They know but they do not talk about it. Mama would like you to wed a nice girl from Cadore, while Papa fears that this one will cost you money."

"Did Mama put glass in her windows?"

"She says she has done without for so long, she will do without now. She is saving the money for you. She says you will need it some day."

"Was Papa pleased with the ducats I sent him?"

"He grumbled that you should have saved more, that you are wasteful, but I think he was pleased. He agreed that I should join you."

"As a painter? Are you serious?" I was not sure that *I* agreed.

"I have been painting ever since I came back from the war and I can do a good likeness and clear landscapes. And you do need assistance."

He showed me two of his pictures and they were competent, although not unusual. But perhaps, like the Bellinis, we could work together.

I told Violante that Francesco was going to assist me and to arrange for him to live below with Mocenigo and Campagnola, and I had him meet them. Campagnola eyed my brother suspiciously, while Francesco stared with concern at my steward, who wore a sword and dagger. When we were alone, Francesco said, "He dresses like a bravo. Are you in trouble?"

"Not at all!" Mocenigo attended me wherever I went, but no one had attacked me and I was in no mood to be cautioned by Francesco, too.

That night Violante said, "You give your brother money for new clothes when you have scarcely enough to pay Campagnola and Mocenigo. And I cannot feel at ease with him in our house. Does he know about us?"

"Everyone does. But that does not matter. I am the master here."

"Is that why you called me your housekeeper?"

"You are." I got out of bed and gave her ten ducats to prove that.

"So that is what my body is worth to you these days."

"It is for your services as a model. Indulge yourself."

"Can you afford it, Tiziano? No one has paid you lately."

"Of course I can. Manutius sold several of my woodcuts recently." I did not add that the fee was disappointing, just a few ducats. When I turned away from her to indicate that money was not the thing that linked us, she came to me with the passion she saved for special occasions.

She used the money to buy a tight-fitting bodice that exhibited her narrow waist and full breasts to the best advantage. There was a joy about her adoration of her person, as if my recent paintings of her had convinced her that my love was genuine. She also found a bronze ring to hold many torches so I could protect my eyes when I painted at night. She got an hourglass, too, to remind me when I worked too late, but most of the time I ignored it. And she gave Francesco our bed and purchased a new one, with a soft, resilient mattress and a flowered canopy.

None of this mattered to me as much as a summons to attend Bembo at his palazzo. It was a cold winter day early in 1513 and I had not seen him for what seemed a long time. I expected him to discuss the *poesia*. Instead, Bembo declared exultantly, "I come from Rome. And as I calculated, Giovanni de Medici is now Pope Leo the Tenth."

"Signore, I gather that is a matter of some consequence."

"It is a matter of great consequence. His Holiness has appointed me Papal secretary. It is a position of great importance and influence."

"Congratulations, my lord."

"I deserve them. No one expected Giovanni de Medici to become Pope but me. He is only thirty-seven. But I had faith in him and I was rewarded."

Bembo was dressed elegantly, although he wore clerical garb. His cross was gold and his long, narrow fingers were adorned with many jewels.

He informed me impatiently, "As the Pope's secretary, whoever I recommend, he accepts." He waited for me to praise his advancement.

His excitement encouraged me to inquire, "Do you like my *poesia?*"

"Leo does. He says it satisfies his spiritual and worldly needs."

"Thank you. It was gracious of you to show it to His Holiness."

"I have a genius for choosing a coming man. Ever since I observed your work in the Bellini bottega, I knew that you had unusual gifts."

"I will be happy to serve you."

He announced portentously, "It is the Pope that you must serve. Leo the Tenth summons you to Rome. On my recommendation."

Overwhelmed, I stammered, "I am not sure that I am worthy."

"Let me decide that. Let your brush speak for you."

"What has His Holiness in mind for me?"

"You are cautious. Anyone else would be too flattered to quibble."

"My lord, I do not care far wall painting. Frescoes rarely endure."

"You will paint the Pope. He has heard about your portraits of Barbarigo and Navagero and he desires that you do his likeness, too."

"What will he bestow on me, my lord?"

"You will be appointed to the bureau where leaden seals are attached to bulls and instruments of state. Others will do that work while your painting will receive five hundred ducats annually. Leo is generous."

"Will it be for life?"

"For his life?" Bembo replied, growing irritable.

Some popes ruled briefly, I thought, and I looked hesitant.

"Michelangelo has immortalized the Sistine Chapel, Raphael is engaged in noble tasks. You will match your gifts against their genius."

I did not wish to measure myself against them or to indulge in rhetoric. I asked, "Will I be assisting Raphael?"

"No. You will paint beside him and, perhaps, even excel him."

Bembo sounded so eager to have me in Rome that I felt he must be very angry at Raphael. I did not like such a situation. I believed I could hold my own with any painter but that was not the reason I painted. Then he had not said whether he cared for my *poesia* and that made me sad.

He asked angrily, "What troubles you now?"

"My lord, did you like my *Three Ages of Man?*"

"Would I be here if I did not! Tiziano, we are entering a golden age. The Pope enjoys the sight of Venus as much as you do. But discreetly. No artist in his right mind would refuse this summons."

"Has Leonardo da Vinci been invited?"

"He is too unreliable. He is off on some wild scheme, as usual, and he is not an artist to depend on. He seldom finishes anything."

He assumed I feared the Florentine, which was not so, but I did not try to correct him. I said, "My lord, I will consider your kind offer."

"You wish to put your affairs in order. That will be allowed."

I realized that whatever I said, he assumed it was just a device to extract better terms and that I meant Yes.

He added, "You have a week to prepare for His Holiness' summons."

He dismissed me as if the matter were settled and turned to greet Navagero, who had come to congratulate him on his good fortune.

Navagero acknowledged my presence but he said nothing else to me. Yet I craved his opinion. He was the only nobleman I knew that I almost trusted. As I strode toward my studio I decided to seek his advice.

The day was so clear that the light reflected from the water and the sky was as bright as any I had seen and it stirred my desire to paint. Even the gray exterior of San Marco glowed and the walls of the Doge's Palace shimmered brilliantly. Wherever I looked the pigments were on my brush: orange and pink and crimson, blue and green and yellow, violet and purple and silver. I longed to rub my fingers into these colors and to transfer their magic to my canvas with my touch.

Despite my eagerness to paint, Violante knew something worried me. While we ate and Francesco sat at our table as befitted my flesh and blood, she asked what troubled me. I told them about Bembo's offer. My brother was surprised that I hesitated; he exhorted me to accept it; he stated that it was madness to refuse the Pope. But Violante said that I should trust my feelings, and that Venice might be better for my brush.

This renewed my need to discuss the situation with Navagero and the next day I consulted him. He knew about Bembo's proposal, yet he was not surprised when I said, "I do not prefer Rome to Venice."

He did say, "Do you realize that this summons means quick recognition? Everything you do will be the center of attention and attract patrons."

"And compared to Michelangelo and Raphael. I do not like that."

"No one will question the Pope's taste. If you please him."

"If I please myself. I do not like to work for just one man."

"Have you ever considered working for the Republic?"

"Of course! Every painter in Venice does. But I am too young."

"And Bellini is too old. Why do you worry about your youth?"

"A nobleman has to be twenty-five to vote in the Council. It is the legal age in Venice. My lack of years is held against me."

"You look twenty-five. That should suffice. How old are you?"

"I am not sure. But to advance myself I have had to be older always than my years. Do you truly believe that Bellini is too old?"

"Many do. He has difficulty finishing anything he tries now. He had a firm grip on state commissions but these days it is weakening."

I did not want to be a fool, but if I understood Navagero correctly he was implying that I should contest Bellini's supremacy in Venice. But how?

He smiled and said, "It will take courage."

I did not wish to antagonize the Pope, and yet, I assured myself, I was a Venetian, my place was here, its colors told me that, but I required encouragement, too. "My lord, I am willing to take risks if there is a chance of success. I do prefer Venice to Rome. What do you suggest?"

"Ask the Council of Ten to be appointed supervisor of the decorations of the Great Council Hall and for a broker's license."

"It is a daring step. If I fail, I could be ruined forever."

"You will never find out where you stand if you do not try."

"No one will support me. You are the only nobleman who has expressed approval of my work. Neither Pesaro nor Aurelio nor even Barbarigo, who praised me earlier, has said a word about the work I painted for them."

"This is a good way to find out. They are members of the Council of Ten. If they approve your petition, they approve of your work."

"My lord, are you sure that they will express themselves?"

"They are my colleagues on the Council."

"I will also be challenging Bellini and the other painters."

"That is why it takes courage. Unless you have been intimidated."

I could not allow him to believe this, although it was in my mind. "What should I tell Bembo if this matter is delayed?"

"It will not be. I will see to it that your petition is considered immediately. And I will help you present it."

The following afternoon I joined him in Manutius' library, where they helped me prepare the petition I was presenting to the Council of Ten. I was filled with trepidation at the dangerous step I was taking. By asking to be appointed the official state painter of Venice, I was challenging every artist in the Republic and I might never be forgiven, and the moment it was known I increased my enemies everywhere.

I did like the tone of the petition when I read what the three of us had written. Most of the ideas came from Navagero and Manutius.

"1513. Last day of May. In Council.

"Most Illustrious Council:

"I, Titian of Cadore, having studied painting from childhood, and desirous of fame rather than profit, wish to serve the Doge and the Signori, rather than the Pope and other lords who in the past, and even now, have urgently asked to employ me. I therefore propose, if it is feasible, to paint in the Hall of Council, beginning, if it please their sublimity, with the canvas of the battle on the side toward the Piazza, which is so difficult that no one has yet had the courage to attempt it. I am willing to accept for my labor any payment that might be thought proper, but being studious only of honor and wishing for a moderate competence, I beg to ask for the first broker's patent for life that shall be vacant in the Fondaco dei Tedeschi, irrespective of all promised reversions of such patent, and on the same conditions and exception as are conceded to Giovanni Bellini, that is, two assistants to be paid by the Salt Office, and all colors and necessaries. In return for which I promise to do the work above named with such speed and excellence as will satisfy the Signori, to whom I beg to be humbly recommended."

Manutius said, "It is persuasive. Enough members should support it."

Navagero added, "I will submit it. So it gets immediate attention."

I did not share their assumption that my petition would be accepted. There were many reasons it could be rejected. Violante was worried, for I was agitated and painted with fury. Francesco was upset because I was keeping the Pope waiting; he feared that would antagonize His Holiness and lead to dire consequences. But even as I felt that my brother might be right and that my petition would offend many in Venice—my fellow artists would be outraged that a young painter like myself dared to challenge men who had painted longer than I had lived—there was no turning back. I pretended indifference and worked more furiously.

A week after Navagero presented my petition it was accepted. He told me triumphantly, "With all the conditions attached to it."

"What shall I tell Bembo?" I was a mixture of jubilation and fear.

"That you are a Venetian, and thus your first duty is to the Republic. He should understand that. And add that you will be happy to paint his portrait to express your appreciation of his kindness."

I did what he suggested but Bembo ignored my gratitude. He resented that I rejected his offer. He predicted angrily, "This is only the start of your struggles. Now you face open warfare. Bellini versus Titian. You cannot win. He has tradition behind him, a half a century of fame. Too much is against you. The other artists will support him. They will see you as a threat against themselves. You are avaricious, selfish. I will devote myself to Raphael. He is appreciative and pliable."

I told no one about Bembo's dire prophecy and I hid my anxieties over the battles I faced as I informed Francesco and Violante that now I was a state painter, that the Council had ordered the Salt Office to give me money for two assistants and materials. Violante said it was what I deserved and she was pleased, but she was unhappy that we were moving into a new studio in the San Samuele quarter. She was devoted to our present rooms, although I pointed out that as a state artist I was entitled to free lodgings in the former palazzo of the duke of Milan, now the property of the Republic. Francesco thought it was a serious, possibly fatal mistake to choose Venice over Rome, but he was willing to assist me and he stated that he would support me as a brother should.

Heartened by the lack of opposition the next few days, I moved quickly. The location was ideal. My new studio was at the bend of the Grand Canal, directly west from the Piazza di San Marco, and an equal distance from the Doge's Palace and the Rialto. Travel to and from it was easy. I was just minutes away by gondola from these two centers of Venetian life and I could even reach the mouth of the Po without difficulty.

I was given an entire floor and while some of the rooms were cold and the roof leaked, I felt these faults could be rectified. The light was good, there was space for my steward and two assistants, and I saw my residence here as evidence that I had succeeded with my petition.

"Still," I say aloud, as I pause in my recollections, "I wonder what would have happened if I had become the Pope's painter."

"You would have altered the course of painting," replies Pomponio.

He has entered my study without my noticing. It is unusual for him to approach me and I feel that he wants something. And I do not trust him. I believe now that he has recovered from what was a convenient illness.

"And it might have brought you even more fame and acknowledgment."

"Or changed my manner so that I became a copy of somebody else."

"You must have had some doubts about your decision. The Pope was the most powerful man in the world. Did you ever regret it?"

I do not answer. I am more interested in his new friendliness.

"Did you like Michelangelo or the Pope when you finally met them?"

"It was many years later and it was a very different pope."

"Did you like Michelangelo?" he persists. "I hear he was strange."

"*Like* is not a word that fits Buonarroti. I remember him saying about my nude *Danaë* that 'the manner and coloring of Titian please me greatly, but it is a pity that the Venetian did not study drawing more.' Yet on another occasion, when he saw my portrait of Duke Alfonso of Ferrara, he commented less grimly, 'I had not thought that art could perform so much, only Titian deserves the name of painter.' He was more somber than I was."

"You have the reputation of being cheerful by comparison."

"I have had many reputations. Son, what is on your mind now?"

Pomponio walks the length of the study, then swings around abruptly so that his dark, full features, which attract many women, are most appealing, and says, "I do not wish to upset you, but Father Algi, the prior of the Frari church, has asked me if he could inspect the *Pietà*."

I ask angrily, "Why has he not approached me?"

"For the reason you exhibit now. He does not wish to offend you."

"His request does. It implies that he does not expect me to finish."

"The prior wants to know when you will finish. But he does not have the courage to address you. That is why he asked me to intervene."

"Is that why he sent a stupid servant to harass me? That priest was so offensive that I do not even remember his name. What do you want?"

"Papa, it is your welfare that is first in my mind."

"Is that why you press me constantly to be examined by a physician?"

"It is because I wish to preserve your life, not shorten it. I want you to finish your *Pietà*. As you finished *The Assumption* for the Frari."

"That was sixty years ago. I had the same trouble with them then."

"Yet even Michelangelo admired that painting. Venetians adored it, and Vasari wrote that it was one of the wonders of the age."

"I did it a long time ago," but I am pleased by his knowing these facts.

"So you, Papa, who have painted many of the treasures of our time, should be given the peace of mind that will allow you to complete your *Pietà*."

"Pomponio, I do not know what you are driving at."

"Prior Algi would like to attend you in the company of a physician."

"Doctor Alberti? No! He is ignorant, superstitious, and a fool."

"Use your own physician. You trust him. And Algi will believe him."

"Believe what?"

"That you will finish their painting."

"My painting."

"What is the difference, Papa, as long as you can finish it?"

Pomponio will never understand, I think sadly, that it has taken me a lifetime to reach my present knowledge: at the beginning I thought of color as adhering to the objects shown, in my middle period I thought of color as something determined by the patterns as they appear on the canvas, but now it is used for the diffusion of space. However, I return to my son, for he is growing impatient, and his present interest in me is so rare that I do not want to lose it. I say, "I expect to finish the *Pietà* shortly, but if it will settle everybody's mind, I will see Algi and my physician."

"Thank you. It is for your own good, Papa."

I interrupt his departure, asking, "Pomponio, were you truly sick?"

He regards me incredulously at the idea that I could doubt him and he exclaims, "Of course! It was your comfort that restored my health."

"Some things still puzzle me. How did you convince Donato to pay a thousand ducats? That is a large sum even for one of my pictures."

Pomponio grins with self-approval and says indulgently, "I told him that it was your last painting. That you would not do any other."

"That I was too feeble? That I could not paint any longer?"

"I left that impression. Papa, I did not mean it but he felt that I did. He was so greedy I could not help but gull him. He deserved it. He did not want the work for himself but he intended to sell it to Philip of Spain at a large profit. I could just imagine his expression when the king turned him down. Donato would have died of humiliation."

"And hated you."

Pomponio shrugs and says, "I have survived worse enemies."

"Yet you said that you were afraid of the blackmailing nobleman."

"That is different. Even if I want to wed his niece, I cannot. Noblewomen are not permitted to marry beneath them. I had to pay him."

I think that for once he may be telling the truth. "I understand."

"I knew you would," he says triumphantly. "When should I arrange for the prior and your doctor to attend you? They are eager to aid you."

"Soon." I wish to do a little more work on my *Pietà* but no one has to know that. "I will inform you when I am ready for this inquisition."

"You jest. You are the leading citizen of Venice. You have sold more pictures than anyone in the world. Every Venetian knows that."

"It does not matter. I cannot remember all the pictures I have painted. Where did you learn the device that fooled Donato?"

"From your best friend, Aretino. He told me that he used this trick to extract money from your patrons. To obtain a larger fee, or when they were slow to pay." Pomponio adds admiringly, "He was quite a rogue!"

"He was a brilliant judge of painting. Even Buonarroti trusted him. But when a genius dies he is either damned or praised beyond reason."

"I liked him. He had so many women and he was such good company."

"The best. When he died a joy and exuberance went out of my life."

"Was it true that he died of an excess of laughter?"

"It would be typical of him. But more likely, it was apoplexy."

"Was he truly the scourge of princes and popes?"

I cannot answer. I still feel his loss as much as anything that has happened to me. I dismiss my son. I am glad that I can talk to him, even if I do not trust him, but my mind is returning to the days when I aroused the envy and hostility of many of my fellow artists.

From the moment I entered the Doge's Palace to start my work for the Republic I was nervous. Foscari escorted me, as the official envoy of the Council of Ten, and I wished it were Navagero. He talked incessantly as we walked through the maze of passages that led to the Hall of the Great Council, while I wondered what kind of reception I would receive from the painters working there. His pockmarked skin was uglier, his body odor was worse, and I decided that the fact Navagero possessed a fine physical presence while Foscari had none was why he had such a need to boast. This nobleman stated, "Because of my skillful representation of the Guild of Painters and my knowledge of art, the Council of Ten, of which I am a premier member, authorized me to assign you where to work and how."

God help me! I thought, if that is true! But I tried to listen to him, although it was difficult; my mind was on my reception.

At the entrance to the Hall, he paused to instruct me further, "Your post is worth one hundred ducats annually."

I was shocked. I expected at least four hundred, which I had heard was Bellini's stipend, and which, also, had been paid to Perugino. However, I had no choice now and I muttered, "Thank you, Signore."

"Plus tax exemption and four ducats monthly for your two assistants."

That was better but it still did not compare with what the Pope had offered me, and I asked, "What about my leaky roof at San Samuele?"

"It will be investigated. Why did you not accept the offer to go to Rome? It is far better than your present position here."

"The air and the excitement there would disagree with me."

"And not here? Do you think your struggles are over? Or intensified?"

Bellini sat in the center of the Hall to conserve his energy while Carpaccio consulted him and Lotto, Bordone, Piombo, and Pordenone stood nearby, and I approached them impulsively, trying to be friendly, but they turned their backs on me. Shaken, I felt a horrible chill. I had not expected to be treated this way despite the warnings. I turned back to Foscari and asked him to show me where I was to paint.

He took me across the vast Hall and pointed to an empty place and my pessimism grew. It had the worst light in the chamber. It was on the south wall between two windows and the brilliant light flowing in from the openings on both sides made the space especially dark. No one would see my work here properly, I thought bitterly. There was nothing here to arouse the exuberance of my imagination.

Foscari stated, "This was a place once given to Perugino."

"I see why he left it empty. It is too dark, awkwardly located."

"This will test your powers. You claim to be first among painters."

I felt he was gloating and I had to reply, "It will be done."

"Your painting must depict a battle that commemorates a victory of the Republic. No other decoration will be allowed."

"I will do the battle of Cadore. It also honors my father and my brother. It was one of the few victories Venice won in the last war."

He assented, but my mind was on the other painters. Perhaps, I thought, when they saw now that I had such a poor place to paint that I could not threaten them, they would be friendly. I approached them again, noting that Bellini looked very old, that Carpaccio was even more shrunken, but the other painters formed a circle around the two older men that shut me out. I walked past them, vowing not to be deterred by their hostility, although I was dismayed by what seemed impossible to fight.

Pordenone sneered, "His frescoes are flat, drab, second-rate."

I asked Foscari, "When can I begin?"

"As soon as possible. Tomorrow. If you are prepared."

"I am prepared," I replied, although I was not certain that I was.

The next day I began work in my place reluctantly, still troubled by the difficulties I faced, but I could not allow the other painters to intimidate me. I brought Francesco and Campagnola to assist me, and Mocenigo to show that I was protected. The painters were present but they remained distant and I made no effort to speak to them. I sketched ideas for the battle of Cadore, with advice from Francesco on the actual details, had Campagnola measure where the canvas was to hang, and I tried not to feel betrayed by the animosity around me. When my imagination dwindled I stared at my surroundings in the hope that they would stimulate me.

The Sala del Maggior Consiglio was one of the largest chambers in the world, able to hold twenty-five hundred noblemen at one time. But my attention was attracted by the walls with their scenes from Venetian history. Splendid painters had done them: Gentile and Giovanni Bellini, Carpaccio, Vivarini, Pisanello, and Perugino. And the more I looked, the more I realized that I had been given the worst space to paint in. It was so unfavorable that I had not the heart to work in it.

I told Francesco and Campagnola to continue my sketches—my brother drew accurately and my assistant could imitate me, and it would be good practice for them—and I stepped onto the balcony that looked out on the lagoon to improve my spirits. The view was lovely and prompted me to move to where I could see the courtyard. Its order was admirable. But before I could absorb this stimulation, I heard my assistants quarreling. I hurried back to halt them, even the other painters were listening.

Francesco said, "As his flesh and blood, I know his intentions."

Campagnola retorted, "But I have more experience with his work."

I was startled; they were painting the panel. I halted them and said, "That is some time away." There was still too much doubt in my mind for me to try anything but tentative sketches. I added, "Both of you have something to contribute." I needed any friend I could find.

When the situation in the Hall did not change, I decided to work at home. After a month of doing cartoons, I still saw no way to make my battle scene imaginative, and I told Foscari, who came to see how I was progressing, that I preferred to paint in my studio, that I could work better there. He smiled as if he did not believe me, but he said, "As you wish. As long as I see a satisfactory panel by the end of this year."

I asked, "What about my other duties?"

"What other duties?" he asked suspiciously.

"I thought I was to paint the Doge. And other state luminaries."

"That has been done by Bellini. No one can surpass him."

By now I felt I had to talk to someone about the difficult and perilous situation I was in, and I wanted it to be a painter, who could comprehend the nature of my problem. So I visited Vecchio to ask his advice.

He had grown completely gray, although he was only in his middle thirties, and I was sad at how he had aged. He was painting for Ferrara again, this time a *Madonna and Child,* and he was giving her a noble form, as if his model were Violante; there was a suggestion of Venus in her, too, celebrating virginal beauty with physical magnificence. I felt he had learned this from me, but I said, "It is admirable. And exquisite."

"Yes, it is. Bellini is not the only one who can paint this subject."

I told him about the hostility of the other painters.

"I am not surprised. You are most impatient with a brush. When are you going to acknowledge Violante publicly?"

"In time, Palma, in time."

"I warned her not to put her trust in men but she would not listen."

"She is happy. She has a good life."

"She bears the imprint of your brush but she does not bear your name. Your color takes every hair of her head into its reckoning but what about her natural role as a daughter, as a mother? Is that being satisfied?"

"You should ask her."

"Violante has not seen me in months. Although I am her closest kin."

"I will bring her next time. I promise."

His sober features lit up, reminding me of the charming and cheerful young man I had met and admired when I had arrived in Venice. He said with a burst of animation, "So you desire my advice?"

I nodded, more hopefully. Once Vecchio had been a good friend.

"I cannot comfort you. Of all the Bellini pupils you have been most persistent in your challenge to him, always pushing forward, and now you clamor to paint with him on equal terms in his most prized commission. No wonder he ignores you. I would, too, under such circumstances."

"Why should I wait when there is so much to paint?"

"I have. Even when I could have excelled him. It is customary."

"And because you expect to inherit his bottega."

"No one will," he said morosely. "Not me or Piombo. If we were his sons, we would, but he sees us only as his assistants."

"That is why I offered the petition. Or I would never advance."

"You could have waited until he died. That cannot be far off now.

But your hasty challenge has shaken and angered him. You try to displace Bellini while he is still alive."

"There should be a place for both of us."

"Not when you desire to be first. Your proposal to work under the same conditions as Bellini and Carpaccio is not tactful. It is like a child telling his father to get out of his way."

I was silent. He would not help me, he had waited longer than I had. But as I turned to go I tried to be gracious. "Thanks for your advice."

"What did you expect to hear? Approval? When you challenge me, too?"

"Palma, I am sorry. I intended to challenge only myself."

"Instead, it is said of you that you are possessed with such ambition that you will not allow anything to stand in your way. If other artists consign you to hell, it is to protect themselves. Tiziano, you will bring Violante to see me? I miss her very much."

I agreed and returned to my studio with a helpless feeling.

A few days later I brought Violante to Vecchio's studio and they embraced so warmly I was sure they were father and daughter, whatever he professed. I said nothing but observed his paintings while she assured him that she was in good health, that our new quarters were comfortable, and that he must come to dinner. She said, "You have always had a great weakness for salads and fruits and I will scour the markets to please you." I added that he would be very welcome. He was about to accept our invitation—only to remember, I thought, that his fellow artists would condemn him if he were in my company —but suddenly he declined, stating that he could not afford to take time away from his work. Violante looked ready to weep and he replied, "Dear, it is for love of you. I can serve you better if my fellow painters trust me."

When Pesaro and Aurelio ordered new pictures from me, I deferred work on my battle picture. I decided that if my failure to complete it was questioned, I would show them my sketches. Pesaro and Aurelio were on the Council of Ten and I felt I could depend on them to support me.

I did not return to the Hall while I worked on what stimulated my imagination. Aurelio desired the same voluptuous women I had painted for him before, while Pesaro ordered a *Madonna and Child*. Neither of them praised what they owned already, as if that would cost them more for their second pictures. They implied that they would pay me what *they* felt my paintings were worth. I accepted; I was not in a position to argue.

I did not resort to detailed drawing or underpainting as was the custom. That disturbed my imagination and interfered with my brush. I designed their paintings for their pictorial effect and stressed the contrasts of light and color, using just a few colors, but vivid ones.

Campagnola said anxiously, "Maestro, you are pushing down the old order. These paintings will make the artists even angrier at you."

I ignored him, fascinated by this manner. I vowed that no one could tell me how to paint in my own studio. I became so absorbed I lost track of the time and 1513 passed without my realizing that it was gone.

Many months after my petition had been accepted Navagero warned me that there was discontent in the Council over my failure to produce anything for the wall of the Great Hall. It was a cold, blustery day in March, and I thanked him for his concern—he had interrupted me as I was finishing one of my nudes for Aurelio—and I turned back to it hurriedly before I lost the conception I intended.

The next morning, remembering the urgency in his voice, although he had not said anything else, but had left me to finish my work, I hurried to the Sala del Maggior Consiglio with Francesco and Campagnola to resume my painting there. My space was draped and it was evident from the smiles of the other painters that no work was being allowed in my place.

Foscari strode in self-importantly and waited for me to approach him. When I did, he informed me portentously, "The Council of Ten has revoked your petition. You will no longer receive the broker's patent for the first vacancy. Now you must wait your turn. You and your assistants are struck off the pay list and your work here is canceled."

This was confirmed in writing. I asked Navagero how it could have happened, I thought I had many friends on the Council of Ten, and he replied, "Last year your petition was carried by a vote of six to four, this year it has been revoked by a vote of six to four."

I asked incredulously, "One man changed the decision?"

"Yes. On March 24th, 1514. The flesh is weak."

"Who was it?"

"I cannot tell you. Our meetings are secret. Be patient. Your day will come again. As long as they do not lay hands on you. I will think of something. But it will take a while to find out what to do."

I declared angrily, "I will not move from San Samuele!"

"A noble attitude. Does your other work progress?"

"Enough. Was it held against me that I put nothing on the wall?"

"It did not help your cause."

"There are many unfinished spaces in the Hall."

"But they say that they know what they can do. You are a newcomer."

"There must be a remedy."

"In time." For a moment I thought Navagero was mocking me, but then I saw that he was upset, too. His fair skin flushed with feeling and his sonorous voice was unusually deep with emotion. "Tiziano, now you must wait until I see in what direction you can move. Do you have enough to support yourself without the broker's patent?"

I was not sure, I was still waiting for my fee for the work I had delivered recently to Pesaro and Aurelio, but I said, "Yes, thank you. I am going to put new furniture into my quarters at San Samuele to express my determination to fight back."

"An excellent idea."

Within a week I bought choice glassware from Murano, a magnificent black velvet dress for Violante that was very good for painting, large wooden closets to store my paintings in, a heavy oak dresser for our clothes. Then I sent a petition to the Council of Ten demanding that the leaks in my studio roof be repaired quickly, otherwise the rain water would cause irreparable damage to my paintings, including the battle of Cadore which was for the Republic. Finally, I told Campagnola, Francesco, and Mocenigo that my license was revoked and said that they could leave my employ if they so desired, I would not hold that against them.

Mocenigo said that was ridiculous, that I was the best painter in Venice whatever those fools in the Council declared. Francesco added that this might be so, only I should have gone to Rome, but I was his brother and Papa would never forgive him if he deserted me. However, Campagnola mumbled that the other painters had hardened their hearts against me and I could not overcome their antagonism, and to stay with me was dangerous, especially for an artist, it could ruin his career.

He packed his belongings and left.

Violante responded to this unhappy moment by saying, "You must beg the Council to take you back."

"I will not beg. I will ask as it pleases me."

She put her arms around me and started to weep.

Mocenigo and Francesco retired to their rooms, embarrassed by such a display of emotion, and I asked Violante what was wrong now.

"You are the best painter in Venice. It is unfair that you should be treated so shabbily. Instead of being given what you deserve."

I was not sure what I deserved but I was determined that this affair of the broker's license must not end this way. I kissed her and when it halted her tears, as I hoped it would, I turned back to my work. I felt, as always, that my painting was the one way to answer my critics. And to be myself. No one could organize my spontaneity. I used her red hair and figure for the voluptuous nude I painted that night. Now I was giving fully of myself. It was a rich experience and it filled me with gratification.

WHAT TRUTHS WE TELL

WHAT TRUTHS WE TELL

to make the lie clear

What lies we tell
to keep the truth pure

Stymean Karlen

EIGHT MONTHS LATER I decided to present a second petition. I was encouraged to do this when there was criticism of the other painters in the Hall, when Pesaro and Aurelio paid me for their pictures and ordered more, and I was allowed to stay in San Samuele, although my leaky roof was not fixed. So I heeded Navagero's advice that it was a good time to reapply. We agreed that my first petition had been revoked because of the intrigues of the other painters and their fear of my brush, and not because I had failed to do a battle picture. Yet that was the official excuse.

Navagero aided me again with my new petition as I argued that my battle picture would have been finished if I had not been interfered with—I implied that I was the victim of a conspiracy of jealous rivals. I added that the cancellation of my work in the Hall had halted a noble contribution to the history of Venice. Then I proposed that since I could not expect to receive the first vacant patent, I should be appointed to the one that would be free upon the death of Giovanni Bellini. Meanwhile, I suggested, the Salt Office should pay me and my two assistants and furnish me with colors as before so I could resume my work in the Hall.

I wondered why Navagero took such interest in my cause. His help appeared to go beyond a desire to vindicate his own judgment. I felt that he wished to outdo someone, or to have the last word, and perhaps, a need to show that he had the taste and power of a Lorenzo de Medici.

He said he would submit this petition at once, but through another member of the Council, so that he would be free to vote impartially, and that he hoped for a quick and favorable response.

A few days later I was visited at my studio by Francesco Valier. He said that he was appointed by the Salt Office to supervise the payments to the artists who worked for the Republic. He was youthful, slender and dark, with fine gray eyes and the firm features I liked to paint.

I introduced him to my brother and Violante, and he replied cordially, which gave me the feeling that he was not a patrician. After he sipped the wine that Violante served him, he thanked her, then begged her pardon, saying he would appreciate it if he could address me privately.

Then he told me formally, "Signore, a resolution has been passed in the Council annulling the previous order that revoked your petition. Instructions have been sent to the Salt Office to give effect to that decree. On the conditions requested in your petition."

"When can I return to the Hall of the Great Council?"

"As soon as it is convenient. I would advise you not to delay. There is much discontent in the Council over the slowness of the work that is being done in the Hall. There appears to be much waste."

"I will resume tomorrow."

"Good. I would erect scaffolding to establish your intention." He stared at a group of nudes that I was painting for my own expression.

I said, "The composition is a bacchanal."

"Signore, I have never seen more attractive and robust nymphs."

I did not tell him that I was demonstrating to myself what I could do with a feast of the gods, as Bellini had painted for the duke of Ferrara. I showed him a Venus which appeared to excite him, too.

He asked, "Is it for Aurelio, the secretary of state?"

I nodded and took him to the Salome with the head of John the Baptist that I was painting for Pesaro, which mixed sacred and profane feeling.

He declared, "You must have remarkable hands to do such vivid work."

I had not thought of that. I knew they were larger, stronger than most, and certainly not ordinary, but the surfaces that mattered to me were on canvas and often I yearned to caress them passionately.

"Your flesh is so warm, so sensuous, so beautiful."

His praise reminded me of what troubled me in my workshop and

I said urgently, to stress my need, "Signore, my roof still leaks."

He took a paper from his doublet and read: "The officials of the Salt Office are requested to take care that the workshop occupied by Tiziano Vecellio should be put in repair because it now lets in the rain, and it might be that the models of the picture intended for the Hall of the Great Council will be spoiled, by which the labors of the painter will be unnecessarily protracted."

Now I was almost certain that I was first in favor in the Republic. I said, "Signore, then the Council supports me overwhelmingly?"

"Not quite. The motion that favored you passed by a majority of one."

The next morning I erected a scaffold at my space in the Hall. I built it high so that it hid what I was painting. I noticed that no one else was working on a scaffold and that Bellini was absent—I learned that he was ill—and that Piombo and Pordenone were not there either. Very little work was being done. Lotto and Bordone left in the middle of the day, and the few who remained looked like apprentices. Francesco heard that Pordenone had left Venice to try his fortune in Florence, and that Piombo had taken the post I had rejected in Rome. I saw this as an admission of defeat, but my brother was dismayed by his appointment. He said it closed the door irrevocably on me in Rome. But it added to my determination to stay in Venice and to gain the same rights as Bellini.

The Salt Office gave me six ducats to repair my leaky roof while Valier warned me that the Council forbid further expenditures. When I questioned this, he replied, "It is a necessary economy. Complaints are increasing in the Council about the wasteful painting in the Hall."

This gave impetus to a scheme developing in my mind. Once again I worked mostly in my studio as I thought out the details. I put a sketch on the wall and I appeared often enough in the Hall, I felt, to satisfy the Council, and I noted that Bellini and Carpaccio were there rarely now and Lotto and Pordenone not at all. So even as I postponed the actual painting of the battle, my private commissions gratified me. Since they were for members of the Council I assumed that I was right to give them preference and so I did them first. This also encouraged me to put my plan into action when I felt that the opportune moment occurred.

Aurelio visited my studio one afternoon to judge how my flesh tones were progressing. When he examined the Venus closely, as if he desired to embrace her physically, and his pleasure was evident, although his forbidding expression did not alter, I said, "My lord, there has been enough money spent on the pictures in the Hall of the Great Council to complete the whole Doge's Palace."

He retorted sharply, "What are you suggesting?"

"Three times as many pictures should have been finished as have been actually produced. At present there is much waste."

He looked annoyed but he was interested also, for he asked, "Do you think that this situation could be improved?"

"Yes, my lord. If one painter was given the final responsibility."

"Yourself, for instance?"

"I do not ask for myself but for the Republic. Choose anyone you please, but be certain that he is young and energetic enough to complete what is begun. Or the waste will grow worse year by year."

He grew reflective, which was my intention, and he said, "It will be investigated. There is much talk in Council about the lavish spending."

Two days later Pesaro came to view Salome and the head of John the Baptist. He liked his picture so quickly I felt he was here on Aurelio's instigation. But he asked, "When will your battle scene be done?"

"Soon. I thought you wanted your painting first. My lord, I do not wish the cost of my battle scene to be excessive as is the custom."

"What do you think such a work should cost?"

"A competent artist could do a worthy canvas for two hundred ducats."

"That is very little."

"I know. Perugino was paid eight hundred ducats a picture. And I hear that almost as much has been paid on paintings that are not yet finished."

"It is being investigated. Many things are."

"Thank you, my lord."

"You seem happy about it and yet you could lose your patent, too."

"I want to see justice done. I want to see the best work rewarded."

Pesaro smiled cynically as he glanced at the numerous pictures I was painting and said, "You may be the man for the broker's patent. There is considerable sentiment in your favor, but resentment, also, at the persistence with which you challenge Bellini. He is revered in Venice."

"My lord, I simply desire to devote my powers to the public service."

"Some say that you are pushing Bellini into his grave."

I was shocked and I exclaimed, "That is not my intention! I admire his brush. I want to paint beside him, not to shorten his life."

"Either way, time is on your side. He is approaching eighty-five."

"I wish I could do something to show I do not want to be his enemy."

"Visit him. It would be a mark of respect if you called on him."

Astonished, I replied, "My lord, what reason could I give him?"

"He is old, ailing, not far from death, and your teacher."

"He will refuse to see me."

"Why not try? No bravo attends him. If any threats have been made against your person, they have not come from him."

"My lord, how do you know these things?"

"Navagero is not the only one who is concerned about art. Whoever follows in Bellini's footsteps, represents a large investment by the Republic. A Bellini has held the broker's patent for half a century."

"I am young, my lord. I could have a long life ahead of me."

"Possibly. But you must remember that while this patent is considered an annuity for life, it is revocable at will."

"I have already learned that."

"Very good." A trace of a smile crossed his narrow lips. "If you could make peace with Giovanni Bellini it could be helpful, too."

"I will do my best. My lord, are you pleased with your picture?"

"Salome is beautiful and John the Baptist is handsome. But you have portrayed them romantically. Even John the Baptist is sensual."

"That was the way Salome felt toward him."

"Vecellio, you are not a man who takes orders comfortably. You could have many difficulties with patrons. Princes and dukes are even more demanding than Venetian Senators. Do see Giovanni if you can. Even if he is angry or critical, he might also be pleased and flattered."

"Suppose he refuses to receive me?"

Pesaro shrugged and said curtly, "You know how old men are."

I called on Bellini a week later and his steward led me into his study. I was surprised; I expected to be turned away. Despite the time I had spent in the Bellini bottega, I had never been in his private quarters.

His study was light and spacious and yet, while the spring warmth enveloped it in a gentle glow and he sat so that the sun fell directly on him, I observed that heavy chunks of wood burned in the fireplace and he wore a fur-lined robe and even then he looked chilled. He was in a high-backed chair with curved, ornamented arms and most of his furnishings were medieval. He was framed by Greek and Roman busts, Gothic antique furniture, and his feet rested on a Turkish rug. What interested me most were his paintings that hung on all the walls and the easel on a raised platform with a picture on it.

He acknowledged me with a nod of his head and when his steward, who was almost as old as he was, hesitated to leave, he dismissed him, saying, "He is a former student." Then he waited for me to address him.

I did not know where to begin. He seemed to expect an apology, but I did not feel that I owed him any. To collect my thoughts I glanced at him in the hope that would tell me how to approach him. He had aged sadly since I had been his apprentice. His round, plump features had become gaunt and wizened and he had shrunk in size. Yet I told myself that this old man was still the best painter of them all in the opinion of the Republic, at least in Venice, and deserved my respect. Then the sunken eyes of age were still full of fire and power as he watched me.

I blurted out, "Maestro, I want to prove that I am not your enemy!"

He growled, "You use strange means to express such sentiments."

I insisted, "I have done nothing against you."

"Is that why you challenge me in the Hall of the Great Council? Where seven of my paintings hang? Is that an act of friendship?"

"Maestro, where else could I paint for the Republic?"

"You could wait," he grumbled. "As I did. First, for my father, and then for my brother. But you cannot wait decently until I am dead."

How could I explain the rush of a young man? I faltered, but I was shaken by his accusation and I had to defend myself. I said, "My petitions were not intended to challenge you or displace you. I just wanted to do the work for which I am fitted while I stay in Venice and support myself."

"So you ask for my broker's patent when it will be free upon my death?"

"Maestro, it is the only one that will be available in the . . ." I could not finish, stuttering to a lame halt.

He was pleased at my discomfiture, as if that was enough to

justify our meeting. "You have your own workshop. Numerous private commissions. You can support yourself in Venice without the work in the Hall."

"I am a Venetian."

"Is that why you addressed the Council as 'Titian of Cadore'?"

I thought angrily, Are there no secrets in Venice? But I stated, "I am painting the battle of Cadore. I wanted to show I was qualified."

Bellini rose from his chair with a painful effort and his hands shook. But he refused the arm I offered him, although he had to take a cane to walk to his easel as he ordered me to view the picture on it. This *Madonna and Child* was a fine composition, I realized, one of his best.

He murmured wistfully as he peered at the painting until his eyes were just a few inches away. "I love light, I love the first clear ray of morning that touches my bed, and the brilliance of the midday sun and the golden light of the ending of the day. And soon it will be gone from my sight forever."

"No, no!" I declared. "You have many years ahead of you!"

"Is that why you apply for my broker's patent?"

"I am sorry. You misunderstand."

"Do I? You are an impatient young man. You no longer want to be influenced, but to influence. Even if it means completing my work."

"What do you mean, Maestro?" I was bewildered.

"You will not allow anything to intimidate you."

"They tried. They threatened me with serious injury."

"They were fools. Piombo feels his gift is equal to yours, although less recognized, while Pordenone cannot endure losing commissions to a younger man. And Lotto and Bordone lack work that will support them."

"Nonetheless, they forced me to arm myself. I do have enemies."

"Then why did you come here? They are my friends."

"As I said, Maestro, I have learned much from you. And you . . . ."

"Introduced you to Giorgione," he interrupted. "I have seen how you completed his work. You retained his manner. To my surprise, honorably."

"He was a dear friend and a remarkable painter."

Bellini nodded and hobbled over to the window and gazed at the Grand Canal that flowed past his bottega and motioned for me to join him. As we looked out on this part of Venice I felt that our love of the city united us. I noticed he had doused whatever he had eaten with garlic and I smelled onions also on his breath, and wondered skeptically, Did he think that would give him strength? I recoiled instinctively from the smell and he must have thought that I was going to leave him, for he put out his hand to halt me. It trembled as it touched me and now I realized how feeble he really was. He said longingly, "I wish I could remember when I saw the sights of *La Serenissima* for the first time."

"I remember," I replied gladly.

"You are fortunate."

"My first view amazed and ravished my senses. Was it so in your youth?"

"They were the happiest years of my life. Sixty years ago Venice was saturated with every manner of fashion. When I strolled about the city I heard all the languages of Christendom, besides those spoken by the barbarians. And Venice was a garden of colors. But now I do not see them."

Perhaps, I thought, because his eyes were failing, but I listened.

"I have outlived my generation, Bellini, my brother-in-law, Mantegna, Verrocchio, Botticelli, and in a way, the painters I have taught, Lotto, Carpaccio, Piombo, Bordone, Giorgione, yourself, many others. When I began to paint in oils it was considered strange, unnatural. I was the most adventurous painter in Venice. Now I am regarded as old-fashioned."

"No!" I denied strongly. "Your work has stimulated all of us!"

He smiled wryly and said, "Is that why you seek to supplant me?" He brushed away my protestations that this was not true and continued, "But I do have something else that I wish to discuss with you."

I realized that he might have wanted to see me as much as I had wanted to see him, for his face became animated and passionate.

"When you were an apprentice in my bottega, Isabella d'Este desired a pagan mythology from my brush. She was an important patron but I did not want to paint such a work, but I also did not want to offend her. So I delayed, and finally, after many arguments, for she set many limitations on my manner, which I disliked, I did this work for the duke of Ferrara."

"Was it *The Feast of the Gods?*"

"Yes. I believe you did some underpainting. As did Vecchio."

And Giorgione, I thought, but I asked, "Maestro, did you finish it?"

"I felt I did. Just before you reapplied for my broker's patent,

I had it delivered to Ferrara and to indicate its completion, I signed it, *Joannes Bellinus Venetus* and received my final fee of eighty-five ducats."

Bellini was so upset I also asked, "Does the duke desire more work on it?"

"Yes. He is dissatisfied. When I sign a work I take full responsibility for it being up to the high standards of my bottega, but this picture is in Ferrara and I cannot journey there. I do not have the strength."

I tried to be consoling, "Maestro, it is not that long a journey."

"It is for me. I will be eighty-five soon." He sighed, then asked what must have been very difficult for him, "Vecellio, will you be faithful to my representation in *The Feast of the Gods?*"

"Why do you approach me? You are closer to other painters."

"The duke will want you to work on my mythology. You have acquired a reputation for retouching as a result of what you did on Giorgione's paintings. Despite your rapaciousness in some matters and your strong hand and individuality, you remained faithful to his manner."

"Painting is my passion. And his painting should be preserved."

"I did not oppose your advancement. Others used my name and reputation to fight you. They were afraid to speak against you openly."

I did not know whether to believe him, but he sounded sincere.

"If you should live as long as I have, you will understand my feelings better. If the duke uses you, be faithful to my brush. Promise?"

Although I still considered the possibility of my repainting his work unlikely, his fervency was so exceptional that I said, "I promise."

"Good. You paint the best breasts and buttocks in the Republic."

"I do more than just that."

"It is what the duke desires, whatever piety he professes."

"I do not intend to confine myself to only one kind of picture."

"Fill your paintings with a festival of light and color and many will crave them. You have the manner for it and it is the entertainment that Venetians thrive on and they will pay for it. You do not need the state sinecures to make yourself secure. They often lessen an artist."

I did not know what to say and so I said nothing.

Then, as if it were an impulsive decision, although I felt there was calculation in it, he pointed to the *Madonna and Child* on his easel and said, "I am giving it to you to show that I am not your enemy."

"Maestro, it is too great a present for what you ask."

He asked suspiciously, "You do not care for it?"

"It is lovely. But I cannot ask that my petition be revoked again."

"That is not my purpose. Just be faithful to my conception and to my brush. As you were with Giorgione, even after his death."

He gave his hand to seal our compact and after a moment of hesitation I took it. His nails were cropped closely and I wondered if he painted with his fingers when his eyes failed him and if that sufficed. I started to leave without the painting, believing his gift was just a gesture, and he told his steward to wrap it while I murmured my thanks.

"It is fitting that you possess it. I have no descendants except those who studied with me and you and Big George were the most worthy."

I felt that Bellini and I had reached a mood of conciliation and now we could work side by side in the Hall. But forces I had set in motion were not to be stopped. The question of waste, always a favorite topic in the Council, dominated their proceedings. Soon after I suggested it to Aurelio and Pesaro, the Senators appointed Valier to report to them on how much the painters working in the Hall were costing the Republic.

After a thorough investigation Valier informed the Council that enough money had been spent on the canvases in the Hall to complete the whole palace. He added that three times as much work had been purchased as had been produced, that two canvases, for which only the sketching was done, already cost more than seven hundred ducats. He pointed out that this was reprehensible, since there were masters in Venice willing to paint such pictures for only two hundred ducats.

Valier's findings caused the Council to order the dismissal of all the artists working in the Hall, and they authorized the Salt Office to select the best painter and to bargain with him for each picture. This time I did not ask anyone's advice. I was sorry that this sweeping dismissal included Bellini, but he still retained his broker's patent and I was glad that he did. I decided to move in a new way.

Valier was chosen by the Salt Office to pick the artist and so I wrote him. I proposed to do each picture for four hundred ducats, payment on delivery, subject to an advance of four ducats a month for one assistant, three ounces of blue, ten ducats of colors, and the reversion of Giovanni Bellini's patent after his death. I pointed out that the Republic would obtain a work which had been given to Perugino for a contract price of eight hundred ducats at half that amount.

Valier transmitted my proposal to the Council, but it was January 1516 before they met to consider my offer. By now I was accustomed to waiting, although I still did not like it, and I hid my impatience, as before, by working harder on my private commissions. In the interval Pesaro, Aurelio, and Barbarigo discussed new work with me, but none of them mentioned my offer to the Council. Francesco learned that Bellini was ill and not in any condition to dispute me. I felt sorry for the old man, for I liked him now, but I felt that he must make room.

I was taking great pains in mixing my tints, as I prepared to paint Violante at her toilette—when Valier requested another private audience with me. After he admired the work on my easel, he said, "Your offer has been accepted in all particulars but one."

"What is that?"

"The Council will pay only three hundred ducats a canvas."

I hid my disappointment over the reduction in my fee, for I was pleased that my offer had been accepted, and I asked, "Is there anything else I should know?"

"The Council has postponed the reversion of the broker's patent to a later date, so as not to offend Bellini. No successor is specified."

I asked myself, Did he see me to outwit me? While the patent did not pay much, it was the final approval of quality in the Republic.

"But you will probably be asked to finish Bellini's paintings in the Hall of the Great Council."

"I am sorry. He should be allowed to finish them."

"He cannot. He is too feeble. That is one of the reasons your offer was accepted. The Council expects your battle scene to be done soon now."

"It would help if I could paint it in a more felicitous location."

"That is impossible. The main reason your proposal was accepted was your statement that you could accomplish whatever was asked."

I thought wryly that the Senators were a shrewd lot. But then that was why they were chosen to rule. I nodded, even as I warned myself that I had much to contend with still, and to accomplish. I thanked Valier for his services and turned back to what I was painting when he entered.

Violante was posing for me with a new abandon.

SINCE I AM BORN EACH MORN

SINCE I AM BORN EACH MORN
I do every day
what I would do if I had my life
to live over
knowing what I know today

Stymean Karlen

"Bring out your dead! Bring out your dead!"

These gruesome plague cries shake me out of my reverie. I rise
from my desk and hurry to the window of my study to see where
they are coming from. My spacious and beautiful gardens separate
me comfortably from my neighbors, but as the shouts of the plague
searchers grow louder I feel I am within the reach of the infection.
As I notice that the smell of the disinfectants comes from the house
closest to mine, fifty paces away, my horror increases. I see the black
gondola of death, with the red skull on its prow—no one who dies
of the plague is allowed to be buried in Venice—and I watch it fear-
fully. Two bodies are carried out of the house next door, a red cross
is drawn over the door as it is padlocked, and a watchman is sta-
tioned outside to prevent anyone else who lives there from leaving,
and I hear him mutter, *"God have mercy on their souls."*

It reminds me that I judge my own age, despite the exaggerations
of time and necessity, as eighty-six, and Bellini died at that age. I
wonder if my moment has come, too. Then I refuse to accept such a
possibility. I have never been ill in my life except for an occasional
chill or fever and I cannot submit to the fears about me. Yet perhaps
I should flee from Venice as so many have. Despite my *Pietà*. And my
memories. I hear my sons arguing in the rear of the house and I
decide to discuss the situation with them, but as I approach Pomponio's rooms I pause. He is whispering as if he does not want to

be overheard. Common sense warns me to walk away, for his tongue has the capacity to hurt me grievously, and yet I feel compelled to listen.

I put my ear to the door and I hear Pomponio say, "As a painter you know even better than I do that Papa should have dropped his brushes years ago. He has painted laboriously ever since our sister and Aretino died. His hand is unsteady and his colors are loose and blurred."

Orazio protests, "That is because he no longer cares what the viewer sees. He is interested only in expressing his own vision."

"Do you know what is happening in his workshop these days?"

"In his personal studio?"

"No. Where Palma Giovane supervises the duplication of pictures. His profitable industry. But he gives me nothing that is earned there."

"You will get it. In time."

"In time! In time! You sound like him. I cannot wait forever."

"He gives you a monthly allowance."

"And denies me freedom. But the moment his back is turned, his pupils copy his best things. Then they give him their copies as if they were his own work and he lives so much in the past now that he accepts them. He touches them up to satisfy himself and they are sold as if by his own hand. Orazio, I did nothing that has not been done already."

"Pomponio, you are malicious. Why are you so critical of Papa?"

Despite my distress, I lean closer to hear his answer clearly.

"He did not marry our mother until he had to."

"That was a long time ago. And you have not behaved any better."

"I am different. You know what I say about the workshop is true."

"It is not done when I am there."

"They do not trust you. You are still too attached to the old man."

"He is still the best painter of them all. When he wants to be."

I wipe the tears from my eyes. I hate myself for crying; by now, I remind myself, I have suffered such shocks that nothing should shake me, but this does; I feel guilty that I am eavesdropping and it does not ease my loneliness. I have put off making my will, feeling that it is like signing my death warrant, but I know that the real reason is my doubts about how to bequeath my paintings. My older son should be my heir, but I fear he will squander them as he has everything I have given him.

"He cannot finish anything. The *Pietà* is a good example."

"He does not want to finish it. As long as he paints it, he is alive."

"You are sentimental. He grows smaller and feebler all the time."

"Pomponio, you have no conception of what his work means to him."

"I know that he is very old. Even if he is not ninety-nine, as he told Philip of Spain, he should stop painting before he disgraces us."

Orazio shouts, "You are impossible!"

"Because I tell the truth."

"You never tell the truth."

"Sssh, he will hear you. He is not deaf yet. If you want proof that I am right, I have a copy of a letter an art dealer wrote Philip. Listen! 'All say that Titian can no longer see what he is doing and that his hand trembles so much that he cannot finish anything, but leaves it to his assistants. They do most of the painting and then they get the old man to add a few strokes and he sells them as if by his own hand.' Orazio, our estimable Papa, the divine, the immortal, the incomparable Titian, as so many have called him, has become a childish old man."

This is more than I can endure. I tiptoe away from my son's door so that my presence will not be detected and retire to my studio. Long ago I have learned that gossip can be malicious and cruel, but I cannot divest myself of the possibility that some of it is true. I have been painting my *Pietà* as if it will bring my life to completion, to please God, and to be my public farewell, but I am troubled that so many are jealous of me. Yet to halt now is to confirm their accusations. I decide to do what I have always done when I feel at my best: to paint a number of pictures at the same time. I prepare four easels, although it is a difficult task and it tires me quickly. On them I put the portion of the *Pietà* I am painting, my new self-portrait, and I plan to do a character study of Pomponio similar to the one I did of Jacopo Strada some years ago, and a shepherd and nymph such as I completed for Philip of Spain recently. Both are works I prefer among the hundreds I have signed.

They may say that I am very old and practically blind but my fingers are still alive. With a few strokes of my brush, which is as large as a broom, I sketch the promise of a beautiful female body. I know that my colors are no longer bright but subdued, yet they are living flesh. When my fingers become tired of holding the brush, they become my brush. To give strength to the nymph I lay a streak of red on the shepherd, as if it were a drop of blood. Lately I paint more with my fingers than with my brush. This brings me closer to my canvas and I see better what I am painting. And it does not exhaust me as quickly.

My passion and determination drive away my despair and I lose track of the time and forget about the plague nearby. But when Orazio enters, the concern on his face reminds me of how he has defended me, and so I pause, wiping my fingers with a rag, and ask, "What is wrong?"

"Papa, the contagion is very close, next door."

"I know. But that is still at least fifty paces away."

"It is still too close for safety. With the warm, wet, windy weather, the plague will grow worse. Fifty paces is not far for the air to convey the contagion. You should flee Venice as so many do and go to Cortina, where you have comfortable quarters."

But I cannot paint there the way I wish to paint now. I look out on my gardens, which are large and fertile. A ten-foot brick wall surrounds them so that no one can intrude on me, but I see that the plague watchman still stands by the house next door although the boat is gone.

"I know that you have enjoyed good health, but even the strong succumb to the infection. It spreads daily. You should leave."

I am grateful that he does not refer to my age. I point to two palm trees in the gardens and say, "They were given to me by two Egyptians in return for two pictures. A Moslem and a Jew. They could not afford my fee, so I took the trees. I love them. They will outlive all of us."

He asks impatiently, "Are you trying to answer me with a parable?"

"I answer you as I feel. I have survived many plagues, other trials, as these trees have. I should be able to survive one more."

"You do not have to consort with the sick to catch the contagion. A mere touching of what they have touched, even a dog or a cat, is fatal."

I do not wish to differ with Orazio. Yet I have necessities within me, which I cannot reveal to anyone else but that I must satisfy. I say, "Whatever happens, it is God's will. Where is Pomponio? Has he left?"

"No. He told me that he will not depart unless you do."

"Why do you not go to Cortina? As you suggested to me?"

"You know that as long as you stay I will. But it is foolish."

"Has Pomponio said anything else?"

He gives me a queer look as he replies, "No. Should he?"

I shrug as if it is a matter of little importance, for I do not want him to become suspicious, and I say, "He worries so much about money."

"Pomponio has difficulty keeping it. As you cannot stop painting."

Despite my distress at what I have overheard I am amused by the way Orazio links our different natures. "In a way you are right. It is true that I prefer to paint to doing anything else."

"As he prefers money. Perhaps he inherited that fondness from you."

I am startled by his candor. He must be upset to speak this freely. "Orazio, I have had to struggle for whatever I have earned. That is why it has made money important. Do you need any?"

"The broker's patent you arranged for me supports me sufficiently."

I notice how delicately he is made in spite of his height. My artist's eye desires to paint him and I ask suddenly, "Will you model for me?"

"For the *Pietà* again?" He sounds reluctant to repeat that situation.

"For a shepherd I have started."

"What about my own painting? Should I discard that once more?"

"Of course not. Is it in the workshop? I would love to see it."

He retorts suspiciously, "You have not visited the workshop in months."

"Then it is time I did. I want to see what you are doing there."

"And to take inventory?"

"I should see if the work that bears my name is being done properly."

"It is not necessary. Unless you do not trust me, Papa."

"Naturally I do. But you are not always there either."

"It is dangerous."

"No one will attack me now. I am too old, too close to death."

"An assistant has caught the contagion and the workshop may be infected, too. That is why I think that you should not visit the bottega."

It is a convenient excuse but I do not argue, deciding to visit the workshop at a more propitious time, when it will not be suspicious, and so I reply as he desires, "Orazio, you are right."

"Why not turn your pictures to the wall, as you prefer to do, then return to them in a few months and reexamine them? This will permit you to spend the summer safely in Cortina and come back to them refreshed."

But I feel that I do not have that much time any more. And these days I am content only when I am engaged in work. My *Pietà* may be my crucifix but it is also my bier and it must be adorned suitably. My son's concern has helped me recover some energy and that gives me a clearer idea of how to color the nymph. I am also still mortified by Pomponio's comments that I am in my decline. I thank Orazio for his interest in my welfare and I assure him that I will be careful to avoid the contagion, but that my new pictures are not ready to be turned to the wall. I beg his indulgence but I must return to my easels. He knows that I am in what he calls my stubborn mood, so he does not argue but leaves me to my labors.

With four brushstrokes, as I have done so often, I create the promise of an excellent figure. Next I examine it rigorously, as if the *poesia* were my worst enemy. I note that the figure and color are not in harmony with my intention. This reminds me that color is the essence of my life and that I never force or torture it into shape but allow it to develop unfettered and free.

Today I desire to entrust my power of expression entirely to color.

Yet as I work feverishly, as if time presses down upon me, the flesh tints of the nymph evade me. I decide it is because I am tired.

While I pause to rest, I think that this may be a good time to visit my workshop to take inventory of my paintings. I have done so much that I have forgotten so much. But when I glance outside I see the watchman still by the house next door and I hear repeated the melancholy cry, *"Bring out your dead!"* It is from a residence just beyond my afflicted neighbor. I think mournfully that death comes frequently these early summer days. I decide to follow Orazio's advice. If the contagion has spread this swiftly, my son is right that it is risky to go to my workshop, for the route passes both houses.

I return to my nymph, but as the conception continues to elude me, my mind turns back to the days when the painting of earthy love goddesses became a consuming passion.

GOD LOOKED DOWN
ON THE WORLD

GOD LOOKED DOWN ON THE WORLD
And He saw His shadow there
He was overwhelmed with a generous feeling
to give life to His shadow
And let it become whatever it wished

God pondered
What would it wish to become
Would it wish to become God
But it was God He realized
Being His shadow

Suddenly God did not trust His generous feeling
He turned away
removing His shadow from the world
And He never cast His shadow on the world again
That is when the fear of rivalry
became a God-given instinct

Stymean Karlen

I SAW criticism in Foscari's eyes as he examined the pictures I was painting, for none of them were for the Hall, and his stern expression indicated that he had no intention of blessing what I was doing if it did not include the battle of Cadore. While he waited for me to explain—he had entered as I was packing to depart for Ferrara—I asked, "Signore, to what do I owe the honor of this visit?"

"The Council is concerned over the way you delay the battle canvas."

I was excited by the summons to attend the duke of Ferrara, for it could lead to commissions of consequence, but I could not ignore

Foscari, much as I wanted to. I replied, "I am surprised by their concern. It is just a few weeks since my offer to paint the Hall was accepted."

"There has been time to do something. Instead, you have not put a single brushstroke on the wall and yet you prepare to leave Venice."

"I have toiled assiduously on the details of the battle but since it does not quite satisfy me, I have delayed placing it on the wall."

"I doubt your excuse will please the Council. They grow impatient."

"Signore, I informed Valier that this work would take some time."

"He has been too lenient." Foscari walked over to the bacchanal in the center of the studio. Even he, whose taste I did not trust, could tell that it was the picture I had been working on. He surveyed it and stated, "You paint so many nudes that it nauseates me. To what purpose? This is not the reason that you are employed by the Republic."

I said passionately, "I am expressing the beauty of the human body."

"So voluptuously? So lustfully? Your colors reek of sensuality! Surely no other connoisseur has requested such a lewd representation?"

"Not yet, Signore." I wished he did not have such an offensive body odor; the more he strode about, the more he perspired and sickened me.

"Suppose you are delayed in Ferrara?"

"I cannot refuse the duke's summons. He is an illustrious patron. His request for my services is a great honor. I must attend him."

"On Venetian time and money," Foscari grumbled. "You fill your studio with private commissions and neglect your work for the Republic."

"Signore, is this view official?"

"It is a warning from the Council. Their patience is not eternal."

I was still not sure whether he spoke for the others or just for himself, but I did not have the time to find out, the duke desired my presence at once. I said, "I promise that as soon as I return from Ferrara, I will put a work on the wall that will please the Council." When he did not seem satisfied, I asked, "Has Valier been displaced?"

"Not so far. But I keep a close watch on all work for the Republic."

Mocenigo appeared in the doorway, bowed formally to Foscari, and said to me, "Maestro, the boat is ready to convey us to Ferrara."

Foscari acknowledged my steward with a curt nod and said, "Vecellio, you will be expected to return to Venice soon to keep your promise to finish the battle scene. Otherwise, there will be grave consequences."

His warning still rang in my ears as I summoned Violante to bid her good-bye. I was surprised that she was so agitated and pale and that she pleaded, "Tiziano, please take me with you!"

"I cannot. We discussed that thoroughly. Your presence in Ferrara would be regarded disapprovingly by the court and the duke."

"The duke's lady lives at the castle even though his wife does, too."

"His position is different. Our situation would be resented."

She turned to the partly painted bacchanal that Foscari had disliked and pointed to the nude I favored in this *poesia* and said, "Yet I am good enough to model for you. To display for the world to see."

"They do not know."

"They know."

I picked up my pouch bag with my brushes. I turned my back on her.

That was too much for her and she cried out, "Yet you take Francesco."

"As my assistant. And Mocenigo. I am paid for two. It is written clearly." I took out the letter I had received from the duke and read: " 'Vecellio will be lodged with two assistants in the *castello* of Ferrara and will be given salad, salt-meat, chestnuts, oranges, cheese, five measures of wine, oil, tallow candles, and five ducats for each week his services are required.' I am taking Francesco and Mocenigo because they are requested. But what is allowed to the duke is not allowed to us."

She sighed and shivered.

I said consolingly, "Violante, there is nothing to worry about."

"You will find someone else to model for you."

"No one as beautiful as you are. When you are not melancholy."

"That will not matter when you need flesh to paint. You cannot stay away from it. It seduces you as you seduced me."

"You came to me willingly."

"After you painted me so beautifully that I could not resist you. It was not fair. And now you desert me, whatever you say."

I was determined not to give in to her, yet I did not want to lose her—she was my best model, her exquisite flesh favored my brush—and so I said, "This commotion is foolish. I go to Ferrara because it offers possibilities for painting *poesias* that I desire. If the duke is pleased, there will be other commissions. I have a chance to obtain a post to which only Bellini hitherto has been exclusively invited."

"Will you take me the next time?"

"If I can. You are the one who I am asking to guard what is most precious to me, the paintings in my studio. I trust you."

"What about your person? Threats are still being uttered against it."

"Mocenigo is a fine swordsman and Francesco has experience with arms. I am sorry that I cannot have your company but now it is impossible."

I embraced her warmly and caressed her lovely red hair. This was an unusual expression of affection from me—she felt that I was too reserved most of the time—and this soothed her. When Mocenigo and my brother came to escort me to the waiting boat, she was composed. She kissed me good-bye and wished us Heaven's protection on our journey.

We took the barge down the coast, then turned up the Po and reached Ferrara comfortably. It was to the south, on a flat, monotonous plain, and at first I saw nothing that excited me, as the sight of Venice did, and I thought that Ferrara was a common-looking town. But I liked the dramatic battlements that surrounded the city and its towering castle.

Mocenigo had been here before and he led us to the castle. We were expected and were admitted into the presence of Jacopo Tebaldi, the duke's agent in Venice, who had arranged for me to come here.

The short, stocky, middle-aged Venetian, whose craggy features were lined from many negotiations, took us to our quarters, in a lower part of the castle, just above the famed and dreaded dungeons. Before I could protest that they were dark and dreary, he left my assistants to fix my rooms while he showed me the chamber where I was to paint.

It was as if I came out of darkness into light. One did not have to live by a candle in this room. The marble sculptures that clothed these walls were of a dazzling whiteness. I marveled at their brightness even as I wondered if their luster would diminish the vividness of my colors.

He said proudly, "This is known as the *camerino alabastro*."

"Signor Tebaldi, it is a beautiful chamber."

"It is the duke's pride and joy. He intends to adorn it with pictures in the classical style. For his private pleasure. He is considering using the brush of Michelangelo, Raphael, and Leonardo."

Why summon me? I thought, but I sensed this was his way of expressing the importance of the work. I asked, "What is the duke's pleasure?"

"He wants one of his *poesias* here brought to perfection."

"Is it *The Feast of the Gods?*" Tebaldi had not specified the nature of my assignment, and now he was directing me back to my quarters before I could ascertain what paintings were in this alabaster chamber.

"My lord will inform you exactly what he wants done."

"When will I meet him?"

"When it pleases him. You will be notified." Tebaldi brought me back to my quarters through a maze of passages that confused me even more.

The next few days we saw no one except the servants who attended us. We were confined to the floor we lived on—we were in the same part of the castle as the servants—and I was cramped and uneasy. At night I heard groans from the dungeons below us; I knew that two of the duke's brothers were imprisoned there because of their attempt to murder him; I felt that I had been located here to be intimidated by his power.

Mocenigo learned that Alfonso was hunting and that he was expected back in about a week, but Tebaldi assured me that if I satisfied the duke I would be rewarded. He gave me five ducats at the end of the week and oils, but I was too depressed to paint. Our windows looked out on the moat and were narrow and barred and we had sun rarely.

After ten days of this isolation I was about to ask that I be released from this situation so I could return to Venice, when I was ordered to attend the duke in his *camerino*. I put on my best doublet and hose and followed an eager but nervous Tebaldi. I was determined not to be cowed by Alfonso, although he was reputed to be irascible and stern.

He stood before a large painting and at first I did not recognize *The Feast of the Gods*, so much work had been done on it since I had seen it. Then I noticed that the nude I had added to the composition as a youngster had been painted over. When I recovered from the shock, I saw that this mythology contained Bellini's sedate style, cautious colors, and a revelry that was austere instead of pagan as the subject suggested.

Alfonso was a heavy-shouldered warrior, of middle stature, shorter than I, whose hand was on his sword as if it belonged there. His skin was dark, his hair and heavy beard were black, and his strong, square face was dominated by a slightly hooked nose. Before Tebaldi could introduce me and I could bow as was the custom, he stated sharply, "Vecellio, I summoned you to Ferrara to complete Bellini's *poesia*."

"Your Excellency," I replied, "I thought it was completed."

"Not to my satisfaction," he growled. "I intend to make my *camerino* the most splendid sight in the world. Raphael is preparing a bacchanal for me and I am commissioning Michelangelo and Leonardo, too."

I had heard that Leonardo was in France and that Michelangelo, after the anguish of the Sistine Chapel, had vowed not to paint again but to devote himself to sculpture. But dissent would enrage Alfonso, so I nodded, although I felt forced to ask, "Why do you want my services?"

"Because you are better at retouching than the others. It was the work you did on Giorgione's pictures that brought you to my attention. Then you studied with Bellini, so you know his manner."

"What does Your Excellency desire me to do first?"

"The landscape. It is insufficient. Strengthen it. In the manner of Bellini, and yet to fit the Dosso Dossi bacchanal that is here now."

I was so involved in Bellini's *poesia* and Alfonso's abrasive tone that I had not noticed the other picture in the *camerino* but now I stared at it with dismay. While Dossi had painted amorous young satyrs their nakedness was without sensuality. If this was a work I had to emulate, I thought mournfully, I was in serious difficulty.

Alfonso stated, "At the moment I just want Bellini's trees changed."

"My lord, I cannot alter a landscape if I cannot see a landscape."

"I do not understand." He looked prepared to swallow me whole.

Tebaldi explained, for the duke glared at him, too. "My lord, I thought it wise to keep Vecellio close to the *camerino*, in the event you desired his presence quickly. Since Bellini refused to come."

"He could not come," Alfonso snarled. "He is too old. He would not dare defy me. My hand reaches into the Venetian Senate and the Vatican."

I said, "My lord, I am honored to serve you. But to paint a landscape worthy of you, I must be able to absorb my surroundings more freely."

"Granted," he said curtly. "Tebaldi, the painter is allowed the freedom of the castle and the countryside." Then he turned back to me and stated, "If your landscape pleases me, there may be more work. If it does not, it will damage your reputation throughout Italy."

The next day I strode through the country about Ferrara in search of stimulation and I did not find any. I desired a landscape as magnificent as the mountains that circled Cadore and this region was marshy and ugly.

Tebaldi showed me through some of the castle, and most of the rooms were filled with arms. The duke's greatest passion was the foundry where his beloved cannons were built and he displayed them as others exhibited works of art.

But Tebaldi stressed that Alfonso's *camerino* was vital to him, too. So I studied how the trees in *The Feast of the Gods* could be strengthened to please the duke. But I was uncertain. I felt bound by my promise to Bellini to follow his manner. And I could not see how I could paint a lively landscape to fit Dossi's static one. A bacchanal should stir with movement, and there was none of this in their work. The more I studied the two paintings in the *camerino*, although I continued to prefer my teacher's, the more I felt that they had painted figures that were decorous and dull. Yet I was not in a position to question their concept.

Two weeks had passed since I had arrived here and I was worried about Foscari's warning—I did not want to leave the Hall in Venice unpainted too long, and I heard that Bellini was very ill and that the broker's patent might be available soon—and so I tried to heed the duke's instructions quickly. The old painter had arranged his bacchanal in the form of a tableau before a glade of trees and while I did not repaint them as lively as a dance, as I desired, for fear of offending Alfonso, I changed the trees into a mass of foliage. While the picture lost some coherence, I liked the added vigor. Next, to give more contrast, I put in a hill and a tower as I had used in my own *Sacred and Profane Love*.

This gratified me so much I lowered the neckline of one of the nymphs to show her breasts. There was a sharpness in the style of the draperies, I thought, that was in the German manner, that Bellini had borrowed from Dürer. I took great pains to make them softer. I was also suggesting more sensuality in Silenus when Alfonso halted me. He was accompanied by his court and he said, "You are not to add anything of your own."

I was provoked rather than persuaded and I replied, "My lord, I wanted everything to fit the new foliage."

"I want no unlettered caprices."

I did not think he knew what he was talking about but I said nothing.

Now that he had established his authority, he ignored me while he showed his court what he had accomplished in his *camerino*. He did not introduce me to anyone, as if he did not deem me worthy, but addressed the lady next to him as if I were not present. "Lucrezia, I am sworn to make my paintings into a great collection that will be worthy of my imperial taste."

His wife replied softly, "You still have three spaces to fill."

"Yes." He added exultantly, "One will be by Michelangelo, one by Leonardo, one by Raphael. It will be their reward and shake our world."

"Alfonso, I have heard that Tiziano Vecellio is also qualified."

He was too busy showing the others what he had done on the Bellini to reply.

Lucrezia addressed me, "Signore, my learned friend, Pietro Bembo, told me that you painted the best nude in *The Feast of the Gods.*"

No wonder he had desired me in Rome, I thought. Then I remembered the rumors that they had been in love. I bowed to acknowledge her person and her praise and replied, "Your Highness, he was most kind."

"Bembo is never kind in matters of taste. But he is usually right."

"Thank you, Duchess."

"The poet also told me that you are the most promising painter in Venice and that your portraits are in demand."

"Your Highness, I would be honored to paint your likeness."

She turned to her husband, who was telling the lady on his right that Dossi's bacchanal was his favorite and that he intended to make Bellini's its equal, since he had taken this prize away from his sister, Isabella.

This gave me the opportunity to observe Lucrezia closely. I expected to see a frightening beauty in the visage of the Borgia daughter and sister; instead she was fair, pale, fragile, with fine yellow hair, and a soft voice. It was the other woman whom Alfonso favored, who was buxom and lusty, whose presence suggested strength. I realized this was Laura Dianti, who was reputed to be his mistress, and I could see why. Her wide shoulders and low-cut gown revealed voluptuous breasts, and her creamy skin was a striking contrast to her black hair and dark eyes.

Finally, as his wife waited patiently, Alfonso deigned to give her some attention. He growled, "Lucrezia, what troubles you now?"

"Alfonso, I would like to be painted by Tiziano Vecellio."

"He has other work to do. I am hiring Raphael to paint you."

"I doubt that the Roman painter will attend you. He answers your requests with promises, but he has not sent any examples of his work."

Alfonso retorted, "He will. In my *camerino* I intend to bring together the masterpieces of the best artists of my time. Do not trouble me with trivial, ordinary matters when I have vital decisions to make." This reminded him that he had some other things to say about *The Feast of the Gods*. "Vecellio, you have overpainted the trees and made the drapery too animated." He paused, for Laura Dianti stood before one of the nymphs and her shadow was far more sensual than Bellini's figure.

I knew now what should be done, but I also knew that any suggestion of mine would be ignored. I waited to be dismissed.

Alfonso said abruptly, as if her shadow spoke to him also, "But since I am a worldly man, lower the neckline on the other nymphs. I want them to be true to Ovid. But do not alter their poses. Do nothing without my permission," he repeated for emphasis, "or you will be dismissed."

He strode off, and as was the custom the others were obligated to follow him, although Lucrezia regarded me regretfully before she left.

The next month I saw little of the court, and then only from a distance, as I sought to satisfy the duke, Bellini, and myself. I knew that I could not please myself until I repainted this *poesia* more thoroughly, and that seemed impossible; I doubted that I could appease Bellini, for his manner, unlike Giorgione's, was too removed from mine; as for Alfonso, I felt that whatever I did, he would prefer Dossi's bacchanal.

When he saw how I had followed his instructions, he said, "I hope no one recognizes your hand in this. Raphael would have been more clever."

"My lord, I did what you requested."

"You have not satisfied my wishes. This picture is still not a suitable companion for Dossi's work, and now whoever does the other paintings for my *camerino* will have an almost impossible labor to perform."

I sensed that his negotiations with Raphael, who was first in his mind now, and with Michelangelo and Leonardo, were not progressing as he desired, but I said, "Your Highness, would you like me to do more?"

"No! As it is, you have incurred my great displeasure!"

"My lord, will you need my services again?"

"Tebaldi will inform you if this will be necessary."

I was glad to be back in Venice. I had been away six weeks, longer than I liked, and only the duke's ducats in my pocket gave me the feeling I had accomplished anything. Whatever anybody else said, and Francesco and Mocenigo stated that I had labored valiantly on *The Feast of the Gods,* I felt that what I had done was insufficient.

As soon as I was settled in San Samuele and Violante was assured that I had missed her deeply, although I had missed my own brush more, I resumed work on the Hall. I sketched a battle scene on the wall. No other painter was there now and sometimes the silence was eerie.

Valier came to see what I was doing and when he appeared to approve, I asked, "Signore, does Foscari have any authority in the Hall?"

He replied, "I am the guardian of this work, but the nobleman has expressed a willingness to observe the interests of the Council, and the Ten, to gratify him, have agreed that he can report to them, too."

This did not tell me whether Foscari was a danger to me.

Valier asked, "Maestro, was Ferrara profitable?"

"I think so. I expect the duke to desire more work from me soon."

While I did not believe this, I repeated it to Foscari, who visited me a few days later to judge whether my battle scene was progressing. I hoped that it would impress him as it had impressed Valier. I was sketching my brother on the panel between the pilasters and he surveyed it skeptically and then he replied, "I am told that the duke solicits Raphael's hand and has obtained the promise of a bacchanal from him." I looked indifferent, although my heart sank— for while I disliked the duke, I desired my bacchanal in his *camerino* and I had most of a new one in my head—and he added, "I have this on the best authority. Raphael has sent an assistant to Venice to purchase his colors. You waste your time pursuing Alfonso. Particularly at the expense of Venice."

"That is for me to decide," I retorted, tired of kneeling.

"Not necessarily," snapped Foscari. "I do not see any progress here."

Sixty years later I still wonder if I should have stood up to Foscari and the duke of Ferrara. My life is full of delayed or ignored payments. I am forever differing with those who seek my paintings over the amount of time I need to satisfy them. It is a constant argument and even now I feel that it will continue with my *Pietà*.

The plague cries ebb with the coming of the dawn and there are no sounds from my sons' quarters. Perhaps today is the right moment to visit my workshop and to see whether Pomponio's charges are correct.

But the past still stirs passionately within me, only the time I approach is about thirty years after this visit to Ferrara.

1545 was a crucial moment for me. I was still struggling to find security for Pomponio—he had squandered the first two benefices I had obtained for him—and now I was seeking a third one from the Pope.

Today, I felt, was the time to make this effort for my son. Aretino had invited me to dine with him and guests he expected from Rome, the goldsmith and sculptor, Benvenuto Cellini, and the occasional painter and gossip, Giorgio Vasari. Both were familiar with affairs in the Holy See and their views could be useful to me.

I dressed carefully; I wanted my appearance to serve me. When I gazed into my mirror I was pleased. At fifty-five I was still strongly constructed with wide shoulders, powerful arms, and firm hands that had gripped the world and made much of it mine. I enclosed myself in a closely buttoned blue doublet which set off my fine frame, and I wore a silk robe with red sleeves trimmed with white lace. My blue skullcap fitted my large head and gave my features the chiseled quality I preferred. My beard and mustache were just starting to be touched with gray and I wore the knight's chain given me by the Emperor Charles.

Servants ferried me by gondola to my friend's splendid palazzo on the Grand Canal. It was located just above the Rialto bridge, where he had a magnificent view and he adored the activity. He felt that the vitality about him matched his own and he considered this the center of the world.

When I docked at his jetty, a servant rang a bell to announce my arrival and Aretino was at my side quickly. He was shorter than I, but he was still very strong. We were almost the same age and he liked to state, "I was born in 1492 to make sure that that year was memorable and I came into the world on Good Friday to have the good will of our Lord."

He embraced me warmly and I responded with the same emotion. I knew no one I liked more or who had been a better or truer friend.

He was wider than I, but there was power in the span of his forehead, in his solid jaw, in his thick shoulders and arms. I enjoyed the fire in his brown eyes and his animated face. His beard was cut like mine but was grayer. He wore a fine black velvet robe over a scarlet gown trimmed with ermine. He also had on the golden collar the emperor had given him as a reward for his services, and a costly chain, wrought from pure gold, that the Pope had sent him to express the pontiff's esteem.

Although I had been in his reception room often, I still marveled at the taste with which he had furnished it. A lavish ebony casket contained letters from princes, popes, artists, kings, great ladies, and merchant bankers. His carved chests, chairs, and tables were of the finest wood. Four of my best paintings hung on his walls and his tapestries were luxurious. His candlesticks were silver and his rugs were Turkish.

Before I could mention what was on my mind a furious quarrel exploded in the next room. He led me into it to see what was happening, and while the screaming was intense he was amused. Two pairs of women were fighting and he parted them with a wave of his hand and asked what was wrong. He thrived on excitement, on the likelihood they were fighting over him.

The first two women, Maria and Gina, who were among the many females living here—usually a dozen or more—were very upset. Both were pregnant, apparently by the same cleric, for each insisted that the shoes sent by a bishop belonged to her. Aretino said with a casual shrug, "No priest is to be trusted. I will buy you whatever your bastards need."

He was more concerned with the second argument. Perina and Angela, his current favorites, were fighting over who should sit by his side when dinner was served. He loved both of them, although they were very different. Perina was a fragile blonde whom he had met when she was just sixteen and he was three times her age. She had deserted him twice for a younger man, yet he had taken her back each time. I felt she was selfish and worthless, and that she used ill health to get what she wanted. I preferred Angela, whose alabaster complexion and dark hair were beautiful, and she was only half his age, quick-witted and entertaining.

He settled the dispute by saying that they would sit on each side of him, and he pushed them out before they could question his decision.

He said to me, "I adore them, but they are jealous. I keep them as a cure for old age but I am not certain that they are the remedy. Now what troubles you, dear friend? You are frowning and that is serious."

"I want the income from the Abbey of St. Peter for Pomponio and it is within the power of the Pope to give it to me, but I do not want to beg."

"One must not beg. Least of all, Titian. I will think of something."

"I could discuss it with Cellini and Vasari. They are Romans now."

"I do not respect their judgment. They are too self-seeking."

"Then why did you invite them?"

"They will know the latest gossip. And since they hate each other, it is intriguing to bring them together. Cellini reeks of ferocity while Vasari is very timid. It will be most amusing."

We were joined by Jacopo Sansovino. We had become so intimate that we were called now "The Triumvirate." I was very fond of this burly, red-haired, red-bearded sculptor and architect. He loved life the same way Aretino did; he was proud that he had never had a sick day, although he was sixty. And while Sansovino had a quick temper, he also had a natural intelligence and sweetness that charmed me. But now he was worried.

He said, "I am not sure I can control myself with Cellini. He thinks he is a better artist than any of us and he is quick to quarrel."

Aretino answered, "If he does, I will humor him out of it."

"That may not be easy," I added. "Cellini has a murderous temper."

He entered a moment later and as he strode around the reception room and praised Aretino's taste, comparing it to his own, he was a mixture of flourish, swagger, and grace. He had aged but his dark eyes were still fiery and his features were finely drawn, as if carved by his perpetual need to assert himself. Slender, of moderate height, his fierce gestures and sonorous voice and arrogant assurance suggested the bravo rather than the artist. Yet I felt that some of his work was admirable.

He regarded me cordially, for I was only a painter and not a sculptor, as he saw himself; he did not know how to treat Aretino, who could bluster as loudly as he could; he was suspicious of Sansovino, who was a sculptor.

We were joined by Vasari, who grew pale at the sight of Cellini. He was small, brown-haired, with soft, round features, and his smile was nervous and apologetic. Yet much as he disliked Cellini, he liked Aretino. They came from the same Tuscan town, Arezzo, that had given Aretino his name, and my literary friend had helped Vasari in many ways.

There was an ominous silence as Cellini glared at Vasari and then Aretino said, "Benvenuto, I hear that you have just come from Rome."

"Yes. I am in the service of the Pope. He favored me greatly until his bastard son, Pier Luigi, accused me falsely and had me imprisoned."

"That is why I never seek the patronage of popes or princely houses. They degrade whoever serves them."

Cellini stated angrily, "I served Clement the Seventh and the present Pope. They did not degrade me. No man does." His hand went to his sword.

Aretino replied, "Yet Paul had you thrown into prison."

"Because of his criminal son, Pier Luigi. But I escaped."

I saw a plan formulating in Aretino's mind and listened carefully.

Vasari shifted uncomfortably as Cellini ignored him and Sansovino took him by the arm to show him the bust he had done of Aretino, but the latter persisted, "Did you find the Pope's son avaricious?"

"Very! And his father, the Pope, will do anything to advance him."

I said, "He wants me to paint him again as the Vicar of Christ."

"He is crafty. He desires my genius, too. I did much work for him."

Aretino asked, "As you say, he always puts his son's interest first?"

"Always!"

I sensed the direction Aretino was going, but suddenly his own feelings overwhelmed him and he declared, "I despise your courts! Look at the poor artist waiting for his master's pleasure, tortured by the cold, consumed by the heat. Where is the fire to warm him, where is the water to refresh him? It degrades an artist to serve a patron. To grow a beard in the service of a mere boy. Spending one's manhood idling around tables for scraps, outside antechambers, inside privies. It is no life for a man."

Cellini interrupted furiously, "No one does that to me!"

Aretino smiled indulgently as if everyone who had served a patron had endured what he hated and he continued, ignoring Cellini's growing rage, "Here, when I am tired, I sit. When I am hungry, I eat. When I feel the inclination, I sleep. All my hours are obedient to my will. Not subject to the whim of a bastard, a panderer, and the hypocrisy of bawds."

Cellini shouted, "You insult me!"

"Insult you?" Even Aretino, who was rarely surprised, was taken aback, while Sansovino and Vasari joined us, startled by Cellini's violent tone.

"You imply that I was gulled by the Pope. I challenge you."

His hand was on his sword but Aretino shrugged and said, "I am not a fool. You know I prefer to fight with my pen. The sword proves nothing."

"It proves I fear no man. No one mocks me."

"And you are willing to die to prove it. I do not find that sensible. I would rather live. Did the Pope approve of the work you did for him?"

"He adored it. He said my sculpture was worthy of Michelangelo."

"Did he pay you?"

"Enough. I am Michelangelo's equal, not his slave."

Cellini glared at Vasari and his implication was clear, but the latter, who idolized the Florentine as an artist and revered him as a man, did not take this challenge but said, "Tiziano, I hope that you will accept the Pope's invitation to visit Rome. We will be the better for it."

"Thank you. I am considering it. Under the right circumstances."

"To be decided later," Aretino said, as if he did not trust anyone else's view, even Vasari's. "Giorgio, what do you think of the bust?"

"It is splendid. Remember, I was the first to praise Sansovino in Rome. His women especially have the utmost grace and delicacy."

Sansovino retorted bluntly, "I cannot say the same for Michelangelo. His women are men in disguise. Bulky, muscular, without sex."

Vasari flushed unhappily but it was Cellini who yelled, "How dare you?"

"Dare what?" I saw that Sansovino's quick temper was rising, too.

"To question our noblest artist?"

"I question whom I please."

"And I take justice into my own hands."

They faced each other like fighting cocks, Cellini fondling his sword and Sansovino making a massive fist, and Aretino stepped between them and said, more casually then I felt, "Friends, so much for your views. You must not spoil the magnificent repast I have prepared for you."

He led us into the dining room before they could reply and as he sat Cellini next to the lovely Angela and she listened attentively to his account of his adventures I sighed with relief. Vasari was put on the other side of the table between Sansovino and myself and he said, "Tiziano, I will speak to Michelangelo on your behalf. I will ask him as a brother artist to say a word for you in the right quarters in Rome."

I repeated this to Aretino after the others were gone and he was about to write to the Pope and to his grandson, Cardinal Alessandro, on my behalf, and he replied, "That will not suffice. Michelangelo is the one man who has not answered my letters. He will not advance anyone who rivals him and even excels him in some paintings. Listen to this!"

He read to me what he had written to Pope Paul III.

" 'Your Holiness, you who love beauty as you love God, must desire to see your noble countenance painted where you have ruled so greatly, in the Vatican, and with your family, who you regard so dearly. Think of how we treasure Raphael's portraits of Julius II and Leo X. Would you offend posterity by denying it the same blessing and glory? Yet I have been reliably informed that the only hand worthy of perpetuating your likeness is considering leaving Italy forever, of accepting the Emperor Charles' proposal to be by his side always . . .' "

"Pietro, that is not true."

"When someone else wants what you want, like grapes, they become more tasty if you can take them away from your rival."

"I hope you do not destroy the Pope's interest."

"I am whetting it. I am not offering him olives on a grapevine but the headiest wine." He continued, " 'Thus, Your Holiness, as you know, Titian is hard to move, and he is deeply attached to the emperor who reveres his brush. I know of only one way to entice him. He may be accessible to the right offer of church preferment for his older son, Pomponio.' "

While I watch in wonder his tone changes abruptly as he reads a second letter to the Pope's grandson, Cardinal Alessandro.

" 'My most Reverend and Illustrious Lordship: I shudder to think that much of what your worthy self and the Holy Father have built so carefully could be ruined by a stroke of my pen. As you know, noble sire, whatever I publish is read more widely than any other writer. Even the French, the Germans, and the English devour my words. I know that you deplore the continuing reports of evil that surround your father, Pier Luigi Farnese, so beloved by the Holy Father. He is rumored to have committed many crimes, and yet he has been endowed with the duchies of Piacenza, Parma, and Castro. Before I spread this unfortunate information, which I would regret, I wonder if Your Grace could consider the award of the income from the Abbey of St. Peter to the son of that most exceptional painter, Tiziano Vecellio. To obtain his services for such a pittance would do honor to you and the Pope. Then I will not have to give support to your enemies while a portrait will be painted of Our Holiness that will surpass all others. The Holy Father will be immortalized for eternity and we will have been vigilant in the pursuit of our duty and of justice.' "

I did not expect Aretino to be heeded, yet a few weeks later Cardinal Alessandro answered him: "My dear friend, Tiziano Vecellio being a most estimable person and painter, I will recommend to His Holiness that he hasten the grant of the benefice of St. Peter to his son. And if the artist could attend the Holy Father in Rome and if his portrait pleases, I believe it will improve the situation and encourage the Pope to act."

I halt in my reflections. I decide to save the memory of Rome for Pomponio, so that he will learn what I have tried to do on his behalf.

I doubt that he knows the sacrifices I have been willing to make for him.

So I summon him to my side, but before I can make my proposal, he blurts out, "Papa, will you please see Father Algi, the prior of the Frari church, before it is too late!"

"Why?" I am distracted and suspicious again.

"No one will come here if the plague gets much closer."

I want more time to relive my memories but I realize now that there will probably not be enough for all of them. And I have experienced some of the most precious. I see Orazio standing behind his brother, waiting anxiously for me to say Yes, and he has not betrayed me, at least, not yet. I walk over to the paintings I have just started to give me time to measure my words and then I say, "Pomponio, if you listen to me, I will listen to you."

"What do you mean?" It is my older son who is suspicious now.

"I would like you to hear what happened to me when I went to Rome."

"When you painted the Pope? And met Michelangelo?" Even Pomponio, who is usually bored with talk of the past, appears interested.

"Yes. If you attend me here tomorrow, I will make an appointment afterward to see Father Algi and my physician. Agreed?"

"Agreed!" Pomponio takes my hand to seal the bargain and then runs out as if this gave him important business to resolve.

There are no plague cries and I say to Orazio, "I think the contagion has abated."

"For the moment. I would not trust it any further than that. I am going to the workshop to see if it is safe for you to enter."

I nod, but my mind already is picking its way back to another one of the vital moments in my existence.

Eight months after I returned from Ferrara and while I was still struggling to put a battle scene on the wall of the Hall that would please me, my brother hurried in and said, "I have just learned this morning that Giovanni Bellini, that most excellent painter, whose fame is known throughout the world, is dead. And he is to be buried with his brother."

My first thought was, Will the Council pass me over for his broker's patent because of my delays on the battle scene? Then I was sad. If I had not loved Giovanni Bellini, I had respected him.

My fears were ended quickly for six days after his passing I entered into all the privileges and immunities previously enjoyed by him.

I was grateful for the recognition but there was still so much more I desired to accomplish. I hoped Bellini had died without pain.

Francesco said triumphantly, "You have become the first painter in Venice. And you are not yet thirty."

I was only twenty-six. But I did not correct him.

THERE WAS ALWAYS A TODAY

THERE WAS ALWAYS A TODAY
Even before time began

Today has the power
to always be itself

And it always will
Even were the world
to end

But it cannot end
Today overpowers it
whenever it tries

Stymean Karlen

NAVAGERO CONGRATULATED me and said that we had conducted our campaign cleverly; Pesaro told me that I had been wise to heed his advice; Aurelio warned me that I must not assume that everything was resolved, that there were still complaints about the cost of the work in the Hall. But as soon as I received what I considered was official confirmation—a hundred ducats at the start of 1517 for that year—I decided to visit Cadore to tell my parents the splendid news. I felt it would make them happy. And now they should be convinced that I had been right in coming to Venice. Francesco accompanied me to verify my good fortune and because he missed them, too. I left my workshop in the care of Mocenigo and Violante, ignoring Violante's wish to go with me, and said I would return soon.

I hired the best coach I could obtain with my new wealth, and as we crossed the frontier between Venice and the province of Cadore and saw the familiar scenery, I felt refreshed. The mountains were beautiful with their white frost and jutting peaks, the sky was startlingly clear, and I loved the strength and clarity of the landscape.

I thought determinedly, They must always be part of my expression.

After our parents recovered from their surprise over our unexpected visit, I assumed they would be joyous. Instead, when I informed them that now I held all the privileges that Bellini had held, Papa asked critically, "How much are they worth?"

"The broker's patent produces a hundred ducats a year and entitles the holder of it to an annual exemption from taxes valued at twenty ducats."

"With your present expenses that is not enough to live on."

"I will also be paid twenty-five ducats to paint the Doge's portrait."

"That is not much to paint the head of the state. And some Doges live a long time. Loredano has been Doge ever since you went to Venice."

"Papa, this is the most important post in the Republic."

"For a painter. Your difficulties are not over. Payments from the Republic are not reliable. They still owe me for services in the war."

But when I gave him twenty ducats to invest for me, he brightened and he assured me that he would find a profitable enterprise.

"Land or grain," he said, "although I prefer to put money in land. It is always there while the soil is not always fertile. Let Mama view you."

She was discussing my living quarters in Venice with Francesco and she told me, "You need someone to take charge of your household."

"Mama, I have someone. What has Francesco been telling you?"

"A model is not a suitable housekeeper. I hear there is disorder."

"Only when I make it. Violante is clean and efficient."

"The unrecognized daughter of a painter? It is not likely."

"Mama, you must meet her."

"What would I say to her? Go in peace, you hinder my little one? If your affairs are to prosper, they should be in the hands of your family. Your sister Orsa is grown now, capable, and could serve you well."

"No! You need her more than I do." Mama had become even more aged and shrunken and it distressed me.

The older of my two sisters, Caternia, had wed a man from Mantua and moved there, but Orsa, a plain, shy young woman, spent most of her time helping Mama with the cooking and the cleaning and I did not think she could be spared. And I had no intention of giving up Violante unless it was my own decision. If Mama met her,

I thought, she would not be so critical of her. I suggested that they visit me in Venice when the weather improved.

Papa said that he would consider it, while Mama stared at my hands and suddenly she stated passionately, "I knew from the moment you were born that you were different. Your hands never stopped moving, even when you were asleep in your cradle. Do they perspire much when you work?"

"Only when I do not like what I have done."

"Little one, even when the other children were playing games you were drawing. Does it drive you hard?"

Papa interrupted impatiently, "Lucia, you worry too much."

"My heart is empty without them. And you are away most of the time."

"I am a town councillor and there is much to do in the province."

"So I am alone. Tiziano, Francesco, you will return often?"

My brother assured her that he would, while I said, "Yes, Mama, if you come to Venice. I want you to see what I have done." No one had mentioned my paintings and that left me with a terrible void.

"I know what you have done," she said proudly. "We receive many reports in Cadore about what has happened to my little one. You do not need my praise to support you. When are you going to marry and settle down?"

I shrugged. I was an artist and most of the painters I respected, Giorgione, Leonardo, Michelangelo, and Raphael, had not married. But when I saw from the entreaty in her eyes how important this was to her, I added, "Mama, I will consider it. When I meet the right one."

"There will never be the right one unless you want there to be."

Happy as I was to be in Cadore, I was happier to be back in Venice. We had been away just two weeks but Mocenigo greeted me anxiously. He said, "Maestro, Jacopo Pesaro requests that you attend him at once!"

I was worried that Foscari had complained about the new delay on the work for the Hall. While I had been in Cadore I had drawn the landscape with the intention of using it in the battle scene. But now I could not go to the Hall. A summons from Pesaro was not to be disregarded.

I arrived at his palazzo apprehensively, afraid that I was about to be removed from the Hall in spite of my broker's patent. I did not trust Foscari or the Council of Ten, they had reversed themselves before.

I was admitted to Pesaro's presence quickly, as if expected, and his commanding presence was that of the warrior who had defeated the Turks.

He ignored my explanation that I had been delayed by my visit to my family in Cadore and asked, "Vecellio, do you have many commissions?"

"Yes. But first comes the Hall. I am working very hard on it."

He said brusquely, "I know about that. Have you any for Ferrara?"

"The duke said he would use my brush again but he did not say when."

"What about your other commissions?"

"A *Madonna and Child,* my lord, several portraits, and . . ."

He interrupted sternly, "You may have to put them aside."

He did not tell me why, but ordered me to accompany him to the Frari church. It was a short walk from his palazzo, on the other side of the Grand Canal. I knew that this Franciscan church was the largest in the city, that it had been consecrated just before my arrival in Venice, in 1492, and he led me to the monastery that was attached to it, and to the head of the order, Father Marco Germano.

Bearded, clad in gray, the thin, elderly, austere prior informed me, "We require an altarpiece to express our devotion to Jesus."

I asked, "Father, what subject have you in mind?"

"A painting of the Assumption of the Virgin."

"It is a noble subject. It is worthy of a great church."

"It must be. We seek an altarpiece such as the one that Bellini painted for St. Peter Martyr on the island of Murano. Do you know this work?"

"Yes." It was gentle and dignified, and appropriate to his manner, but too sedate and undramatic for my taste.

I asked "Where is it to be placed?"

"Come," Pesaro said impatiently. "I will show you."

Since Bellini was their model I assumed they wanted a simple, plain altarpiece. I was startled when they took me to the main chapel of the basilica and Pesaro pointed to the high altar. This was no ordinary setting, this was one of grandeur and immensity. The magnificence of the huge basilica, the vast arch of the roof, the sweep and the long view from the nave suggested a treatment that should soar.

Germano said, "I have ordered a tremendous marble arch to fit the altar. More than twenty-two feet high and eleven feet wide."

Supernaturally large, I thought, and I felt faced with an impossible task. Then the idea of painting such a touching theme in such a dramatic background filled me with passion. I said, "I will treat this subject with the utmost reverence and light."

"In the style of Bellini," Pesaro reminded me. "It is why we use you. You know his manner best and you hold the broker's patent now."

"Signore, a work of this magnitude will cause delays in the battle scene."

"Do not trouble yourself with that. *The Assumption of the Virgin* must come first. I will defend you to the Council if it should be necessary. We desire a painting here that will honor the Republic, too."

"Materials will be costly, my lord. I will need the best colors."

"As it pleases God. The will of Heaven must be accomplished."

"Perugino was given eight hundred ducats for his work in the Hall."

Pesaro was shocked while Germano exclaimed, "That is too much! This is being paid by the church. Four hundred ducats is a suitable sum."

I was in no mood to bargain. The more I thought of what I could paint here, the more I was stimulated by the concept.

So it was settled and I arranged my affairs so I could begin work for the Frari church. With all the other commissions I had in my studio I needed more assistants. I asked Vecchio if he could find me any. My hope was that he would take my bait and offer to assist me; I knew that he needed the money. But his pride was too much for such a situation and he ignored the implication, although he replied that he would recommend anybody he thought was suitable. I desired someone of quality, like himself, not quite as skillful as I was, but skillful.

I was dismayed when he came to my studio with Valerio Zuccato, the youngest son of the family that had bullied me and made me feel unwelcome in Venice. Yet I was also pleased, for this was a kind of approval. Valerio had grown into a moderate-sized, brown-haired young man—about my age, but he seemed much younger—and Vecchio assured me that this Zuccato was a competent craftsman and eager to join the fastest growing bottega in the Republic. After I saw examples of his work, I accepted him as an assistant. His drawing was accurate and his brushwork did him credit. Vecchio was pleased with my decision; he said I was returning the favor he had done for me when he had taken me to the Bellini workshop.

After this transaction was over, he asked me, "What about Violante?"

I gave him a blank stare, as if I did not know what he implied.

"Are you ever going to acknowledge her publicly?" he persisted.

"Palma," I said, "I never interfere in your affairs. I do not expect you to interfere in mine. Thank you for referring Valerio Zuccato to me. I am hopeful that he will become a useful addition to my workshop."

Vecchio left, grumbling that this affair was not ended, but my attention was distracted by the return of Campagnola. He wanted his position back. Francesco and Mocenigo said that I must not forgive his lack of faith, but I said that not everyone could be as strong as they were and that I needed someone who could imitate my manner, and so I took him back.

After what Mama had said, I viewed Violante differently. She was even more beautiful and enticing than when she had entered my bed, and more accommodating. Yet I did not see her as the mother of my children, if I ever had any, a situation I had ignored up to now. I did not doubt her desire to be maternal, but I did not want to lose her as a model, and pregnancy would disfigure her and eventually ruin her sensuous figure.

While my assistants prepared the materials for the start of my work on the altarpiece, I put aside part of each day to paint Violante. I gave orders that I was not to be disturbed as I portrayed her in a variety of poses. In the first I clothed her, but placed her dress and shawl so that they fell below her breasts and allowed me to paint them in a way that had been denied me at Ferrara. I told her that this was a tribute to her, and I gave her buxom breasts a roundness I yearned to caress, as I did with my brush. Then, to prove to myself that this was just a start, I painted her naked. But this time I enveloped her nudity with her long, lovely red hair so that more of her body was hidden than exposed, and so that the contrast illuminated her rosy flesh. Her neck was enchanting and I devoted many hours to it. I felt passionately that her breasts were a work of art and deserved the best from me. Next I modeled her so that her sensual loveliness was revealed in all its glory, freedom, and naturalness. I colored her flesh in a manner that expressed its appeal and exuberant vitality and the desire and pleasure it aroused in me.

Even as Violante whispered to me, "You are exposing me for all the world to see," she added, "yet you have made me beautiful."

"As you are. They will see you as Venus or Aphrodite or Magdalen and put their yearnings into you. As I have. But this is not finished. The sheet you are lying on is not crumpled. And it should be."

She asked wistfully, "Will you use me in *The Assumption of the Virgin?*"

I replied curtly, "If I can." I realized that this mattered more to her than all my nudes, although in them I had glorified her treasures.

"If my face is appropriate for Venus, it is appropriate for the Virgin."

"Violante, they represent two opposite sides of human nature."

"They are both unique. Both women. Each beautiful in her own way."

That was true, I thought, but I did not admit it; I did not want to give her such an advantage over me. Yet I was grateful to her for the way she had posed for me, and for giving me the feeling that I must paint the Assumption joyously, that the miraculous departure of the Virgin from earth and her reception into Heaven were a tribute to the Glory of God. Now it became the only work I desired to paint.

As I pause in my reflections to recall them more clearly, my memory compresses, as if, even so many years later, I am so full of the painting of the Madonna I cannot think of anything else. It is a work I have put so much of myself into, it is a grand theme that requires a grand style.

There is also a fear in me, when the plague cries resume outside, that there will not be enough time for me to fulfill all my memories. So I hurry backward, or is it forward, to the doing of a precious painting.

The rest of 1517 I gave to God. I put aside my *poesias* of Violante and assigned my other work to my assistants so that all of my energy could be at His service. The only thing that mattered to me was my progress on the Assumption. Germano said that the Virgin should be pious and sedate and I saw her as heroic and dramatic. Pesaro wanted her to be formal and restful and my imagination vibrated with animation and color. When I decided to use Violante as my model, there was such an adoration in her—as if I were God for portraying her in a sacred pose—I felt that I was on the right course, that she would express the faith I sought.

I did the preliminary work in my studio but finally I could not put off the inevitable: this altarpiece had to be painted where it was to stand. Much of its composition and color depended on the structure of the church.

I disliked working where I lacked privacy but I had no choice. I transferred my materials to the basilica and began the actual planning of the huge canvas. I was accompanied by Violante, Francesco, Mocenigo, while Campagnola and Zuccato were assigned to take care of my bottega.

The canvas, due to the size and weight of Germano's marble frame, took two men to move, and I shifted it often to determine the best perspective. This was limited however, for wherever I viewed the site, it was confined by the predetermined location.

Where the battle scene suffered from being given space that was too dark, here I had to be aware of the extremes of light. I liked that the Assumption was to be elevated above and behind a double order of steps and the altar—its subject must carry the eye upward. But I was wary of the brightness of the light that poured abundantly through twelve large windows over and beyond the picture and the four mullioned windows on each side of it. Yet most of the time this canvas would be viewed from a distance, for the basilica was very long, and from the far end, very dark. My colors would have to be unusually vivid to be seen clearly.

Germano, who often came to judge how I was progressing, was upset that nothing was started above the altar and asked me why.

"There are problems," I answered. "Serious problems."

"Not if you do an Assumption such as Bellini painted."

I thought that such a composition would be lost in this vast church and express none of my passion, but I said, "This work takes time."

"You delay so much that we are afraid you will never finish."

"I will put up the scaffolding. You will have something soon." When the wood was in place and the canvas was on it, I walked to the end of the basilica, where I studied the perspective. Red became the color to express passion and blue to suggest purity. Then, as I painted the Apostles gathered around the empty tomb from which the Virgin was rising, I made them large and strong, their arms raised upward yearningly.

Germano said, "Your foreground figures are too large."

I replied, "They are appropriate to the Virgin."

Violante was a fine model and the gentleness of her features was what I desired. And her splendid figure was vibrant with feeling.

Germano brought Pesaro on his next inspection and the nobleman stated, "The prior is right. Your Apostoles are too large. They will never do."

I thought that the ignorant are often the most difficult to please, but I said, "The size of these figures is necessary in such a vast church."

Germano replied, "My monks are unhappy with the Apostles. And you have given our Holy Virgin a sensuous tone. The brilliant reds in her garments are more appropriate for a Magdalen than for our most sacred lady."

In the months that had passed since I had met the prior, his features had become more devoid of flesh, as if anything beyond his skin and bones was excessive. He was satisfied, I felt, to be an intimidating presence. And now he wanted to know in advance about the rest of the painting.

I could not tell him; I was seeking spontaneity. I was compelled to dramatize a wondrous event; I was re-creating a passionate experience.

"If we are not pleased, we will have to withhold the final fee."

But I could not tell the prior how I saw God until I saw Him myself. I said, "Father, I am painting every detail with the utmost care."

He grumbled that he doubted such an enlarged, exaggerated view of the Assumption was acceptable; Pesaro feared the scorn of Florence and Rome.

The next few weeks Germano continued his anxious visits and his criticism but I was determined to follow my own vision and not surrender to his narrow taste. I was more troubled by the ignorant brethren from the monastery. They were like gray mice scampering over the stone floor while their heads shook in disapproval and dismay and they complained from under their hoods that this picture was becoming a monstrous thing. I was proud of my ability to shut out distractions, but they made so much noise with their loud whispers, for they meant to be heard, that I was upset and angered by their presence and comments.

So I painted Mary's tunic an even more brilliant red and her mantle a majestic blue in order that she would be the heart of the painting.

I heard the monks say, "His hands profane the blessed Virgin. She is too theatrical. This is not the kind of painting a master does."

I tried to ignore their words and to continue my effort to paint a bridge with God. But when the monks became more vociferous, I asked the prior to evict them and he regarded me with horror and exclaimed, "They are the chosen of God! They desire this altarpiece to instruct the ignorant in the pious story of Mary's miraculous ascent to Heaven. But you make her so passionate and colorful you could inspire wrong thoughts."

I was stressing the heavenly splendor of her deliverance to God and the radiant joy it gave her. I was pushing my imagination to the limit, but I realized that Germano did not understand my conception, no matter what I said or did, and probably never would.

We were interrupted by Mocenigo, who informed me, "Maestro, there is a letter from the duke of Ferrara ordering you to paint him a pagan nude."

"Answer him, in my name, and ask him how he desires that done?" This should take enough time to allow me to finish the Assumption.

Germano frowned and said, "I still think the Apostles are too large. I am beginning to wonder if the picture is acceptable at all."

This was the first direct threat I had heard and I saw only one way to answer it: to work harder. But I said, "Father, will you excuse me? The physical labor of painting such a great object, the constant climbing up and down the steps to view it, are demanding and enervating. I must rest." And consider the final conception that was developing in me.

He retired, mumbling that perhaps my painting should not be accepted.

I was on the final painting, I felt, and that was what mattered. I strode to the end of the basilica to view what I had completed and where I could see the picture to the best advantage, and the worst, and I cried to myself: I am right! The tense, vital, passionate figures of the Apostles, tightly grouped, their outstretched hands and attention fixed with a universal unanimity in the direction of the Virgin, drew the eye to her figure. They made her the center of the painting. And when I looked upward to the top of the Assumption, to God waiting to greet her ascent into heaven, His gaze was fixed on her in such a manner it drew the eye to her again. Everything, the colors, the figures, the lights and shadows, the arrangement of space, of lines and details, led to Mary.

The following month I confirmed that conception with my brush. It was 1518 now and the altarpiece was supposed to be unveiled on the 20th of May, St. Bernardino's Day, when this festival day honored the great preaching saint of the Franciscans and all public offices were closed by order of the Senate. But I heard rumors that the friars did not approve of the picture, that they were not going to accept it, that the ceremony was to be canceled. Yet, I could not quit or alter my intention. I painted an angel at God's side and cherubs about the Madonna, the only nude bodies in the work, and I illuminated the background with colors and a few clouds, although I knew that a landscape was expected.

Then, a week before the scheduled unveiling, Germano insisted on seeing what I had done. I was virtually finished, whatever else I did would be just a matter of detail, and yet I hesitated to show it to him. But he was adamant and when he appeared with Pesaro, Aurelio, and Foscari, and I realized that they felt that the honor of the Republic was at stake, I ordered Francesco to pull off the covering and to expose it.

They viewed the picture at the altar. They were too close, I knew, but when I suggested that they stand back farther, to see better, Germano retorted brusquely, "This is my church. I know where to stand."

As they saw the painting Pesaro groaned, Aurelio was dismayed, while Foscari said gloatingly, "It is as I expected. It is too big, too brightly colored. This picture will disgrace us. Father, you have done a rash thing to engage Vecellio to do this altarpiece."

Germano trembled at the thought of the mistake he had made, looking appalled at the vividness of my vision. Then he said apologetically, "This is not the kind of work that we commissioned."

Pesaro added, "Vecellio, it was agreed that you would be paid only if the Order was satisfied. Now there are grave doubts about its worth."

Aurelio said, "Some of it is beautiful, but not fitting here."

I did not reply. I thought bitterly that the artist had no real property, capital, or security, only energy. Perhaps there was no such thing as security in art. Then I heard a resolute voice behind me.

Adorno, the Emperor Charles' ambassador to the Republic, was speaking. I knew this diplomat slightly; I had met him at Navagero's palazzo, where he had made me feel at ease. A slender, trim, handsome middle-aged man, he said now, "The painting would appear more fitting if we viewed it where it is to rest. Above the altar."

Annoyed by the doubts of the Venetians, I declared, "That is not necessary. No one has to buy it. I will keep the picture for myself."

Germano looked relieved and Pesaro said, "Vecellio, you should concentrate on your *poesias*," but Adorno was not satisfied and he stated, "I still wish to see it in the proper place. For the emperor's sake."

His interest encouraged me and I gave my assent.

It took many men and several hours to place the canvas above the high altar but then, as I drew back to the rear of the basilica to view it, I was relieved. My judgment was right. The figure of the Virgin dominated *The Assumption* as I intended.

The ambassador joined me and exclaimed, "A magnificent woman. Maestro, I am enchanted. You have painted a new world of feeling and perception. If the church withdraws its offer, I will be honored to purchase it."

"For the emperor?" I asked, not sure that I could believe him.

"Yes. It is a marvelous picture. It has a formidable grandeur."

I saw Germano squirm as he said, "But it is so agitated."

"Animated. It transforms a naïve religiosity into a human experience."

Germano consulted with Pesaro, then Aurelio, avoiding Foscari, and said suddenly, "Perhaps we should use the altarpiece. It would disappoint many people if there was an empty space here on St. Bernardino's Day."

Adorno said, "Father, you owe the artist an apology for your doubts."

"It is possible. After all, art is not my profession."

I spoke up. "Prior, I will not bargain again. If you find this work unsuitable, I will be happy to sell it to the emperor or keep it myself."

Pesaro said abruptly, "Let us have no more talk of unsuitability. The church commissioned the altarpiece and the church wants it. It is simply that the monks, being prudent, were hesitant, but they must recognize that the use of the breviary does not convey an understanding of painting. Tiziano Vecellio, we hold you to your bargain."

The Assumption of the Virgin was unveiled on St. Bernardino's Day and I stood in the rear of the basilica and was amazed by the commotion it created. There were many more people in the Frari church than usual because of the rumors that had circulated about the painting. But now it had become a sensation. The Venetians adored the bright colors, the exuberant vitality of the Virgin, and the dramatic intensity of the theme.

Germano stood proudly by the side of the high altar accepting the congratulations for his Order, while Pesaro explained the effects the colors achieved to Barbarigo and Navagero and added, "This is not a work to see in a close examination, but from a distance, as suits the basilica."

I felt empty. Violante was next to me, but no one praised her for the skill and faith which she had exhibited while posing for the

Virgin, and my parents still had not visited Venice and I wished they could see this painting—it should please Mama and encourage Papa.

Adorno joined me in the rear of the basilica where I could observe without being observed—I thought it was fitting that the picture be the center of attention—and he said, "It is a powerful affirmation of faith."

"My lord, I am honored."

"I am the one who is honored. Your Virgin is unique. Today, your brush has put the old art into its grave and you have made our religious experiences come alive."

I introduced him to Violante and said, "She helped me in many ways."

He bowed to her as if she were a great lady and declared, "Signora, you have served us well. As you served his painting. Tiziano, how did you achieve such light and luster?"

"I worked hard, my lord, and had good assistants."

THE BURDEN OF TALENT

THE BURDEN OF TALENT

How many who envy it
could carry the burden it brings

The envious are the first to condemn
anyone who is different from the popular
Yet talent is different

The envious could not tolerate
their own talent if they had it
And be different from the popular

That is why they need to envy
Envy is an easier talent
And has never been different

Stymean Karlen

THE NEXT FEW MONTHS I received many commissions as a result of *The Assumption*. Pesaro asked me to do a large religious work to commemorate his family's piety and power; churches in Brescia, Ancona, and Treviso ordered altarpieces. I accepted a commission from the king of France, with the consent of the Venetian Senate; my *poesias* of Violante were bought by Navagero, Aurelio, and Barbarigo; and there were new patrons. My portraits were in demand, then Alfonso's envoy wanted to see me again.

While I waited for Tebaldi to come to my studio, I asked my brother to find out the latest news about Alfonso's situation, and he learned, as he told me, "The duke's legate in Rome knocked often on Raphael's door to remind him of his promise to paint for the *camerino*. But when the painter heard that the duke also had offered this work to others, he became angry and turned him down. So now Ferrara has given up hope of obtaining Raphael's brush and must search elsewhere."

I asked, "Was my name mentioned in opposition to Raphael?"

"Not directly. But almost everyone thinks Alfonso will approach you now because of *The Assumption*. Now your work is a prize to acquire."

We were interrupted by Tebaldi, who was almost agreeable as he said, "Vecellio, the duke is thinking of considering your brush again."

Francesco remarked, "Signore, I thought the matter was decided."

"Nothing is decided until the duke says it is."

I asked, "On what terms? I am busy and I have no time to spare."

"For the best commission in Italy?" Tebaldi was skeptical.

Despite Alfonso's arrogance the alabaster *camerino* was a stimulating challenge and I was interested, but I still pretended indifference.

When I turned away as if I had other matters to occupy me, Tebaldi said, "Alfonso is considering a worship of Venus for his pleasure."

"What about *The Feast of the Gods?*" I felt better able to support my position since *The Assumption*. "It needs more work, too."

"The duke will decide that."

"I can no longer conform to Bellini or Dossi. It must fit my manner."

"That will be considered."

"Signore, what exactly does the duke desire?"

"As I said, a bacchanal. He will send you a canvas and a stretcher to guide you as to the dimensions of the work. And a sketch with further instructions. He will be explicit about what you must do."

The canvas and stretcher arrived at my studio a week later and I liked their size, it was appropriate for my own conception. But the sketch dismayed me. It was a bacchanal, a subject that appealed to me, but it was by Fra Bartolommeo. This devout Dominican, who had been a close companion of Savonarola and who had died a few months ago, was not the one I would have chosen to paint a paean to the pagan glory of Venus. But by now I realized that Alfonso's mind moved in strange ways.

With the sketch he wrote me, "You will use the incidents in the work by Fra Bartolommeo or you will incur my severe displeasure."

I was pleased with the theme, but the details were too reserved for me.

While I subtly changed the sketch to suit my own taste, I was summoned to the Salt Office and there curtly informed by Foscari, who appeared to have supplanted Valier, for he was absent, "The Council of Ten are greatly displeased with you. Unless you begin at once to work on the canvas in the Hall of the Great Council which you have neglected for so many years, and unless you will proceed to labor on it continuously until its completion, their magnificences will cause it to be painted by someone else and finished at your expense."

But who? I wondered. Bellini was dead, Carpaccio was too ill to paint, Piombo was in Rome, Pordenone was in Florence, and I could not see the Ten considering Lotto or Bordone or even Vecchio, especially since the furor over *The Assumption*. This gave me the courage to reply, "I have not done the battle scene because I have been waiting for the panel on the opposite wall to be completed. I want them to be in harmony."

Foscari snarled, "You know why it is not finished. Bellini is dead."

"That is not my fault, Signore. But I would not want to put a battle scene on the wall that does not fit. Bellini's work is of a military nature, too, and celebrates one of Venice's greatest victories."

Barbarigo entered as I was speaking and I remembered that he was the head of the Salt Office and I turned to him and added, "My lord, Bellini's panel should be completed before any other. Is that not so?"

Pleased that I assumed he was a patrician of taste, he replied, "Foscari, Tiziano should execute Bellini's work first."

"What about his own panel? He does nothing on it."

"I have tried many things," I said, "but until Bellini . . ."

"Until! Until! Until! Is that all you know? My Lord Barbarigo, you were one of those who supported the resolution of the Council."

"Of course. But there is merit in his proposal. Tiziano, how long would it take you to complete Bellini's panel?"

Foscari looked irate enough to lash me but I replied, "That depends, my lord. So many members of the Ten, including your estimable self, desire my work that I cannot give you a precise answer. But if I am constantly harassed by the Salt Office I will accomplish nothing."

"I agree." Barbarigo turned to Foscari, who was purple with rage, and informed him, "Tiziano must be allowed a little more time in the Hall. We do not want to lose him to Rome, or even to Ferrara or Florence."

*　*　*

Those words propel me into the present. Ever since Bembo offered me a post in Rome, it has been a useful weapon to defend me in Venice.

But now Pomponio enters with Orazio and he wants to know why I finally went to Rome. I remind him, "To try to secure a profitable and permanent benefice for you," but I realize that he still does not believe me—he thinks I must have had another, a better reason.

It is a pleasant morning, without any apparent intrusions from the plague, and I am surprised that he has risen so early. I feel that he must be eager to have me see the prior and the doctor to be up by now. Then as Orazio goes to the window to see if there is any new activity at the infected house nearby, and Pomponio stares at the nymph I have started to paint, as if to judge whether I can still hold a brush, my mind goes back to advice that Aretino had given me about my older son.

I do not recall the exact time but it was a few years before I went to Rome. I had acquired the first benefice for Pomponio when he was six, the living from the parish of Medole, and I obtained a second benefice for him when he was fourteen, as canon of the cathedral of Milan. Then, as I asked Cardinal Alessandro for a third benefice that I hoped would make Pomponio independent for life, I was disheartened by a letter I received from a Venetian merchant, Rico Morelli. He wrote me that he had returned from a voyage to Cyprus and found my son in bed with his wife, and unless I paid him four hundred ducats he would make a public scandal of this seduction. This was not the first time such a difficulty had happened and I asked Aretino's advice. He understood this kind of affair, he had been in the same situation. And my friend was the only person Pomponio appeared to respect.

At first Aretino was amused by this entanglement, but when I blurted out, "Pietro, he deprives so many husbands of their wives I doubt he can hold on to any benefice, no matter who defends him!" my friend grew serious and replied, "Perhaps he is not designed to be a priest."

"Others less worthy have been."

"His heart is not in it."

"He might listen to you. He likes you."

"If he does it is because I do not try to change him." Aretino added, "Tiziano, if you stop to think what you did at his age, would you not forgive him and also have a good laugh and pay his expenses with women?"

"I exercised some discretion in my escapades but he shows none."

"Very well. I will intervene if it is that important to you."

Aretino wrote Pomponio:

"I realize the truth that old age is something that young people cannot believe is really possible, just as to old people youth is a fairy tale. That is why youth laughs at old age when it should really weep and why old age weeps over youth when it should really laugh. I tell you this to prevent a young man like yourself from taking a moral lecture lightly merely because it comes from someone like me.

"The other day your father came to my house in such grief it pained me to see him. He said he wished you would change your mode of life. I must myself confess that to me your conduct resembles one of those vulgar farces which actors enjoy more than the audiences. You ought to return to your studies and allow your fine mind to prove it is the equal of any scholar's. It is wrong that the wealth amassed by the brushes, the toil, and the long journeys taken by so great a man as your father should be dissipated by your riotous living. It would be more fitting for you to double the money you get from him than to waste it the way you do."

Yet Pomponio did not change and now, I felt, my journey to Rome was his last chance. If I failed to secure this benefice for him, I saw no future for him.

My reflections are ended by Orazio returning from his observations at the window to announce, "While the plague watchman is still at the door everything is quiet at our neighbor's."

I cannot tell what Pomponio thinks about my nymph, but he listens attentively as his brother begins to discuss our trip to Rome.

"As you remember, Papa took me as his assistant, although I was only in my early twenties, for you were away pursuing women. I knew that he was resolved to obtain for you the benefice of the abbey of San Pietro in Colle, whatever the cost to himself. He was even willing to enter the service of Cardinal Alessandro, the kind of situation that he had resisted all his life, in return for this sinecure.

"He had also written Michelangelo, although Aretino warned him not to, that he might not receive an answer and could be humiliated. But aware of the fact that the Florentine was the Pope's favorite, he asked him as a brother artist to aid his suit in Rome. This was not easy for him, yet he also asked Michelangelo for his drawings, which he said he valued more than all the presents of princes and popes."

Pomponio asks curiously, "Did the Florentine respond?"

I say, "In his own way."

"Then Aretino wrote the Pope and his grandson, Cardinal Alessandro Farnese, and Cardinal Bembo, asking them to obtain a benefice for you."

Pomponio retorts, "I did not ask for it. That was Papa's idea."

"You accepted those he obtained for you."

"When I was six, then fourteen. I did not know any better."

"You did not want them?"

"I said that he should not blame me for what was his idea."

Upset by their quarrel, it serves no purpose, I say, "Pomponio, I simply want you to understand that I have always tried to help you."

I am not sure that he is convinced but Orazio resumes proudly.

"When Papa traveled to Rome, the duke of Urbino gave him an escort of honor that accompanied us all the way from Venice to the Holy City and his entry was triumphant. His mounted escort, his large baggage train, the paintings we carried, his majestic figure all contributed to the splendor of an artist that everyone knew and admired. Papa was treated like a prince and he was given an elegant ducal apartment in the Belvedere, close to the Pope's quarters."

I say, "What encouraged me most was that as soon as we were unpacked, I was visited by Cardinal Alessandro. I had met this brown-haired, thirty-five-year-old Farnese two years ago in Bologna to discuss the benefice and I was pleased with the warmth of his greeting. He said, 'His Holiness will be happy to see you when you are refreshed,' and I replied, 'Your Eminence, nothing would refresh me more than to hear that His Holiness has kept his promise about the benefice. When may I see him?'

"He frowned at my urgency and stated, 'At the right time. The transfer of this benefice is not easy. Many things must be considered.'

"I pointed out, 'I would serve in the house of your Illustrious Lordship if you would acknowledge my talents by the promotion of my son.'

"The Cardinal answered, 'It is a gracious offer, but I have just welcomed into my service the eminent artist, Vasari. He waits outside to attend you. I have assigned him to guide and accompany you.'

"I was not pleased. I did not have a high regard for Vasari's work. But he was full of information and I reconciled myself to his gossip, for he had some comprehension of art, although he favored the Florentines, and we had met recently in Venice, where he had encouraged me to come to Rome.

"While I waited for my audience with the Pope, Vasari showed me the art and the antiquities of Rome. I felt like a pilgrim, for churches dominated the city. Vasari boasted that the marshes were being drained and that the streets were being widened, but I was disappointed by the decay of many of the buildings and that the shallow, muddy, yellow Tiber did not compare in beauty or splendor to the canals of Venice.

"We were joined by Piombo, who served the Pope. We were friends now, and when I noticed that he had grown fat and indolent, he was apologetic, saying, 'Tiziano, you were wise to stay away. I fell under the influence of Raphael and Michelangelo and it was too much for me.' I was annoyed by the implication that it would have happened to me, too, but I listened, for there was much in him that needed to be said. 'So,' he added with a cynical shrug, 'I have given up painting in favor of the convivial life. There are artists here who do more in two months than I do in two years.'

"This did not lessen the anger in me over the decay of one of the most gifted painters I had known. But I was grateful that we were reconciled.

"Pordenone had died a few years before, still hating me, although I had tried to help him. Lotto had done masterly work that I had praised, but he had ignored me and had become a recluse, while Bordone had given up his own style to imitate me, a gesture that I did not respect.

"Vasari and Piombo took me to see the frescoes of Raphael that were damaged during the sack of Rome and I was so shocked by the bad restoration, I turned to Piombo and asked, 'What presumptuous barbarian dared to do this?' and he admitted, shame-faced, 'I did.'

"My scorn made him so unhappy I decided to hold my tongue thereafter.

"Next they escorted me to the Sistine Chapel to view what Michelangelo had painted a few years earlier on the wall behind the altar. He had not responded to any of my direct or indirect efforts to meet him, and I was starting to think that he never would, but I was eager to see *The Last Judgment*. I recalled that he had done these figures in his sixties, after he had vowed not to touch a paint brush again, and Piombo was saying that I was the only artist who could compete with him. I disliked being put in such a position, but

I was interested in seeing what pleased the Pope, for Michelangelo had painted *The Last Judgment* on his orders."

Both my sons are listening intently and it helps me hurry on.

"Vasari and Piombo waited expectantly for my view of the gigantic fresco on the end wall, while I feared that whatever I said would be misunderstood. I was fascinated by the grandeur of the conception, the massive strength of the figures. But then, as I soaked myself in this work, I thought that Michelangelo, even with his brush, is still the sculptor, he is still carving his figures rather than painting them."

I have become so emotional I have to pause to regain energy but Pomponio is disappointed as he says, "Papa, is that all you felt?"

"No. The angels I color become lovely women and handsome men but in his hands they were muscular, twisted, often without beauty or grace. There are arms and legs everywhere and a great abundance of flesh, but it is not the flesh that I know. There is too much for my taste and none of it possesses sex or sensuality, which for me, is the breath of life. The bodies of his males and females are so muscular in contour that there are no genuine differences in their design."

Pomponio asks, quite surprised, "Do you truly think so? *The Last Judgment* is greatly admired. Many call it the finest work of all."

"It may be. But I told my opinion to Orazio when we were alone."

Orazio says, "Then I could understand what Papa meant."

"What did you tell Vasari and Piombo?"

"That the figures were powerful and strongly drawn, which they were."

"Nothing else?" Pomponio is unhappy; he has expected a clash.

"Piombo said, 'If you had come to Rome when I did, you would have studied the works of Michelangelo and Raphael and produced masterpieces.'

"I realized there was still spite in him but I replied quietly, 'I avoided the styles of Michelangelo and Raphael because I wanted to be more than a clever imitator. No artist combines all the excellences of a Michelangelo, Raphael, or a Leonardo. Each has his own excellence.'

Orazio adds, "As does a Titian. To paint like a Titian requires his unique gift, it requires that color become his strength. To draw like the Florentines makes color inferior to design. Papa is right."

I am pleased with his understanding and approval, but Pomponio asks impatiently, "What about the ceiling? You must have seen that, too."

"Very carefully. I examined the ceiling from end to end."

"Yet you never talked about it when you came home. Why, Papa?"

"It was not something to discuss but to see."

"What did you think of it?"

Pomponio sounds so interested I feel that he will not betray my candor. Even now, so many years later, only Aretino has openly criticized *The Last Judgment* and the ceiling is considered even more inviolate.

"Papa, you did not like it?"

"That is not the point. There was so much detail it was difficult to focus on most of the scenes and many of the figures were so powerful and large they burst through their frame and distorted the drama. But *The Creation of Man* and *The Creation of the Sun and Moon* had such a soaring grandeur that I felt the breath of the Holy Spirit. Then it were as if different artists had painted the altarpiece and the ceiling, and the latter, at its best, possessed a genius that I could admire."

"Did you ever consider doing such a work?"

"I was asked to paint ceilings in the Doge's Palace but I refused. It is not the way I want to view a painting. The perspective is wrong."

"Then you did not approve of *The Creation* either."

"Pomponio, I did not say that."

"What about the Pope? What happened with him?"

"Soon after my visit to the Sistine Chapel, he granted me an audience. I hoped it would be private and I was dismayed when I saw that he was attended by his grandsons, Alessandro and Ottavio. I did not trust Ottavio and I was not sure that I trusted the cardinal. The Pope had aged since I had painted him several years before and he looked seventy-eight as he sat by his table, but I was attracted by his taut, querulous face and the tension in his body as he listened to Ottavio whispering in his ear. Alessandro stood behind him, dignified and contained, but Ottavio bowed obsequiously while the Pope regarded him suspiciously.

"The younger brother wore the elegant costume of a courtier, yet his thick features, bent nose, and narrow eyes remained subservient while he continued to converse with his grandfather, but it was evident that the Pope was still suspicious. Paul turned his head with a quick and irritable motion in the direction of Ottavio and regarded him sharply, as if to chide him, and this situation excited me. The Farnese family were so dramatic and colorful I decided to paint them in this manner.

"It also reminded me that Aretino had warned me to be careful of any promise made by this powerful family, that the Pope would do everything he could to further their fortunes even as they conspired against each other. There were rumors that the unscrupulous, greedy Ottavio plotted to depose his equally unscrupulous father, and I felt that this was the reason for the Pope's anger. But when he told me that he was pleased that I was going to paint him again, I replied, 'Your Holiness, if my son is given the benefice of St. Peter's, it will be a great aid to my brush.'

"He said, 'I authorized Alessandro to investigate the situation.'

"The cardinal added, 'We are trying. But there are difficulties.'

"Ottavio suggested, 'Why not give him the seal of the Papal Bulls?'

"I was shocked. This office was held by Piombo. I exclaimed, 'My lord, I would be depriving an artist friend of his livelihood!'

"Ottavio said, 'Piombo does no work. And he will be dead soon.'

"The Pope was listening indulgently to his grandson, as if he approved of this bribe, and I said, 'Your Holiness, it is the benefice that concerns me. As I told the cardinal, if it is given to my son I would be happy to serve in his illustrious house or in your own.'

" 'We would be honored, but we are served already by Michelangelo.'

"Aretino had warned me not to offer much, that it would be abused by the Farnese, but I had been put off so much I suggested, 'Holy Father, my work will show the measure of my devotion and my son's worthiness.'

"Ottavio responded eagerly. 'Fine! I desire a *poesia* illustrating the fable of Danaë.' I wondered if this was appropriate—the Pope had just summoned the Council of Trent to put down corruption, sensuality, simony, and Protestantism—but Paul said, 'Whatever pleases Ottavio, pleases me. As long as you paint me with my devoted family.'

" 'Whenever it suits Your Holiness. I would be honored to paint you as you are assembled now. To honor the Farnese name.'

"Alessandro said, 'It is a fine idea,' and Ottavio, not to be outdone, added, 'and clever,' and Paul ordered me to make the proper arrangements."

"My ducal apartments in the Belvedere Palace contained many rooms and I converted the largest and choicest one into a studio. I had been installed here because this placed me near the Pope's quarters and it was easy for him to reach. I was excited by the opportunity to paint the heart, mind, and soul of the most influential family in Italy.

"I arranged them as they appeared at my audience and they seemed pleased that it was to be a painting of the Farnese as a family.

"But as the Pope sat for me in his armchair, he looked even more bent with age and worn with care. Paul also had become very thin and I studied the tautness of his skin, the bony structure of his features, the shadows on his face. He had put an hourglass on the table upon which his right hand rested as if to suggest the shortness of even a pope's life, but as he turned to look at Ottavio, who bowed obsequiously again, as Ottavio believed was fitting, I felt that it was not the end of his life that troubled Paul but other matters. The Vatican was full of rumors that he was upset about the spread of Protestantism and the emperor's refusal to give the duchy of Milan to Ottavio, although Charles' daughter was wed to his grandson. There was also gossip that Ottavio planned to seize his father's lands and that this duplicity would lead him to oppose Paul.

"Yet I could not ignore what I saw. As my brush responded to my eyes, the family portrait revealed a sober cardinal, but the Pope became more bent with age as he peered suspiciously up at Ottavio, whose unctuous and hypocritical smile was a cynical mixture of servility and flattery.

"While I was engaged with the faces, the Pope praised my modeling and the coloring of the red drapes and robes, but he said the expressions were too personal, too dramatic. But I felt this was one of my best portraits and I was not in a mood to be halted. This work had the possibility to be as fine a portrait as I had painted. But now the sittings slackened."

Pomponio asks, "Do you think that the Pope was offended?"

"I could not tell. No one scolded me but gradually Paul sat for me less, and finally, not at all. His excuse was that he was too occupied with theological matters, but I felt that he had become too old, too ill, and too peevish. I was able to finish the heads of Alessandro and Ottavio, as if they thought that it was important that my brush depict them in the presence of the Pope, but I was forced to leave him incomplete."

Orazio says, "I think it was the Farnese way of stopping you. They were afraid of the disclosures your brush implied, and yet to halt you for that reason would have caused a scandal and attracted even more attention to the painting. So they made the best of it, for even incomplete, it is one of your most penetrating portraits."

Pomponio asks, "Is that why they refused to give me the benefice?"

"No. I found out later it had nothing to do with it. The cardinal had lured me to Rome with a benefice it was not in his power to give. The Pope had bestowed it already on the archbishop of Severina in return for that prelate's support against the emperor. But I knew none of that. Then, I was still hopeful. The Farnese were enthusiastic about the *Danaë* I was painting for them, and I was composing one of my most sensual pictures to please their taste."

Yet I am even less certain that Pomponio believes that I have done all that is in my power to help him, for he says, "Why did you not appeal to Michelangelo since he had considerable influence with Pope Paul?"

"I did, when I finally met him. But that was not easy. Pietro Bembo, who had given up poetry to advance in the church, asked me to paint him in his cardinal's robes. Now he was gracious to me —he claimed to have discovered me—and I did not differ with him since it gave him pleasure.

"It also increased my importance in his eyes and when he said, 'Tiziano, I can still recall how the painting you did while you were still an apprentice caused me to realize how satisfying is the loveliness of the female figure,' I replied, 'Your Eminence, not everyone thinks so.'

"He was surprised and he exclaimed, 'That is not possible! You are the most widely praised painter of the human body that I know!' and now I said, 'I doubt that Michelangelo shares your opinion.' "

Pomponio declares admiringly, "That was clever."

Orazio says, "And true. And it did provoke Cardinal Bembo."

"Yes," I resume, "he examined my *Danaë*, which I had just finished, and responded as I hoped.

"He said, 'Tiziano, she is an alluring *poesia*. I must have Michelangelo view her. I am sure that he will be impressed.'

"I was not so sure, but a week later Vasari asked me if I would mind if Michelangelo visited my studio. 'As a brother artist, of course.'

"I replied, 'I would be honored. I have long looked forward to it,' and Vasari beamed as if he had arranged a meeting between two great powers."

Orazio adds, "Which it was, Papa."

"I would not attach such significance to it. Michelangelo might consider himself many things, but I considered myself, simply, just a painter. But while I doubted that he would approve of my work, he was so moral and such a different personality, I hoped that he would intercede with the Pope on Pomponio's behalf. He had a reputation for being harsh with other artists' work, but the benefice was not a challenge to him. And I wanted him to consider me as a friend and not as a rival."

Orazio says, "When he arrived, I was disappointed. I expected him to be better looking, his fame was so great. I thought all great men were impressive in appearance like Papa and Aretino. But he was small and worn."

I remind him, "He was seventy and he had toiled prodigiously."

"Nonetheless, I did not expect his beard to be so gray, his features so sunken, his nose so flat and wide, his expression so dour and grim."

"But his eyes were penetrating and his hands were still strong. As they took mine his grip had the firmness of the stone he adored. I was glad he had no sign of any physical infirmity. I bowed to him, as befitted the respect owed to an older and esteemed artist and he returned my courtesy with unexpected civility. I had heard that he preferred to dress rudely but today he wore fine leather boots, a black damask jacket and a closely fitted doublet and hose, all quite neat. Vasari proudly accompanied him and we exchanged pleasantries. Neither of us mentioned the other's work as if that were a dangerous subject but I said, 'Signore, I would appreciate some advice.' He glowered until I added, 'It concerns His Holiness. I have been informed that you are close to him.'

"He shrugged as if that were a matter of little consequence but I saw that he was pleased while Vasari declared, 'Pope Paul regards the master as one of his most trusted friends and treats him as an equal.'

"Michelangelo said, 'Vasari exaggerates, but I can wear my old felt hat in his presence and he does not chide me when I talk frankly.'

"While I wondered why he had not answered my letters or seen me sooner, I decided to approach him, for he was in a good humor. I told him about the Pope's promise to bestow a benefice on my son and he stated brusquely, 'I am an artist, not a cleric.'

" 'This is a special situation,' I urged. 'I have given the Pope my best service and I believe that it merits a just reward.'

" 'No doubt you will receive that at the appropriate time.'

"His geniality had vanished and he had become grim again. But I had taken too many long and difficult journeys and suffered too many vicissitudes of fortune, often without reward or profit, to accept his indifference quickly or easily. I retorted, 'Certainly an esteemed master such as yourself would be heeded by His Holiness?'

" 'I have some influence in matters of art. None in anything else.'

"He was so curt and Vasari looked so distressed I felt like a fool in my pursuit of the benefice. I had worked harder for this office than anything else I had done and I wondered if it made any sense."

"No," Pomponio says abruptly, "it did not make any sense. Even if you had obtained it for me, I would not have held it. As I hold nothing."

I am startled by his admission. Is it an act of contrition? Or a confession of guilt? Or a gesture in my direction? Or self-pity?

Pomponio asks, "Did Michelangelo look at your work?"

"Vasari said, as if he were purchasing peace between two warring powers, 'Maestro Tiziano, my great friend relinquished an important appointment to pay his respects to you. He would be honored to have the privilege of viewing what you have painted while you have been in Rome.'

"Michelangelo nodded somberly, still regarding me suspiciously, but he did not make a move to depart, as he was reputed to do when he was displeased, and I said, 'I will be happy to show what I have done.'

"I had painted another likeness of the Pope in the company of his son Pier Luigi—from memory; and in the same fashion, Margaret of Austria; a Venus, a Magdalen, but the canvases that attracted his attention were the unfinished portrait of Paul with his two grandsons and the *Danaë*.

"Now he was not in a hurry. Then he spoke brusquely—and I realized that was his natural manner—'You make Paul so old, so bent.'

" 'He is.'

" 'Perhaps. But so am I when I am assailed with many cares. I wonder if it is fitting. The Pope is also capable of great piety and he has a genuine regard for the arts. They have flourished under his Papacy.'

" 'That is one of the reasons I am here. To commemorate that.'

"For a moment I expected Michelangelo to be critical of the incomplete group portrait, but then, as if he had come resolved to be on his best behavior, he said, 'I think these figures are executed firmly, as far as you have gone. But it is the *Danaë* I am most interested in viewing.'

"I led him to the canvas where she lay nakedly on a couch, her hips scantily covered with a delicate veil. I felt that she was one of my finest creations, superbly proportioned, pulsating with life, a striking and voluptuous Venus that was my Venetian answer to Rome. Everything else—the cushions, drapes, couch, landscape, clouds—was secondary."

Pomponio asks with sudden interest, "What did Michelangelo say?"

"He praised it to my face, but when he said, 'It is interesting,' I sensed he was uttering the usual polite words that people use when the artist was present and that he was hiding his true feelings."

"How can you be sure?" Pomponio asks, prepared to be belligerent.

"When Vasari published his *Lives of the Most Eminent Italian Artists* their views became clear. I have their words before me."

I read: " 'After they left they started to discuss Titian's method and Buonarroti commended it highly, saying that his coloring and style pleased him very much but that it was a shame in Venice that they did not learn how to draw well from the beginning and that those painters did not pursue their studies with more method. For the truth was, he went on, that if Titian had been assisted by art and design as much as he was by nature, and especially in reproducing living subjects, then no one could achieve more or better, for he has a fine spirit and a lively style that could have produced works that none would have surpassed.' "

Pomponio asks, "Papa, were you surprised?"

"No. It is almost impossible to accept another artist's style if it differs strongly from your own. And we are very different artists."

Orazio says, "Yet Michelangelo was impressed. This was praise for him."

Pomponio continues curiously, "What happened to the *Danaë?*"

"The Farnese took what I painted in Rome. But no benefice was forthcoming." Suddenly these memories threaten to overwhelm me with the emotion they evoke and I am exhausted. "Many other things happened in Rome but they are not worth remembering."

Orazio becomes reflective as if this journey into the past reminds him of things he has forgotten, while Pomponio says at the door, "I kept my word. I listened. When can I bring the prior and the physician?"

I am too tired to dispute this or to delay any further. "Whenever you like." It is a relief to return to the Venice of my maturing manhood when no matter what confronted me, I believed that I could surmount it.

Soon after my visit to the Salt Office I started work on Bellini's unfinished battle canvas in the Hall. Then I was interrupted by a summons from Alfonso to appear in Ferrara to discuss his *camerino* and word that my parents were coming to Venice to visit me and to see *The Assumption of the Virgin.* I wrote the duke that I would come as soon as I could but at the moment I was delayed by work for the Republic, and I decided to give my parents all the time they needed. I expected their visit to Venice to be a happy and festive occasion and I waited for them with anticipation.

TELL THE PROPER LIE

TELL THE PROPER LIE

And it will be accepted
As pure truth

Tell the less proper truth
And it will be rejected
As a clear lie

Stymean Karlen

VIOLANTE WAS FLUSTERED by the news that my parents were visiting me. She feared that they would not approve of our situation and tell me so, yet she felt that she had contributed to my career and that they should know this. I was surprised by her anxiety. I agreed that she was an essential part of my household and that my parents should realize this. But before I could reassure her and remind her that it was my opinion of her that mattered, and that they should like her as everyone did in my bottega, she cried out, "Do you think they will be very critical of me?"

We were standing in my studio where I was using my painting skill on her glorious hair, so that every strand might be counted, and I replied, "They will be enchanted with your beauty and charm."

"I doubt that. You are a man of the world but they are village folk. What do you think I should wear? Something as modest as possible?"

"You should dress as becomes you and as I paint you. In your best brocade and velvet and the blue that suits your complexion and your hair."

Yet when I introduced her to Papa and Mama a week later, I was not sure that my advice had been right. Violante wore a blue velvet gown that was as smooth as her skin and her presence was pervaded with charm. But while her costume gave her splendid figure the beauty my brush adored, it was a sensual outfit and accentuated the voluptuous curves of her figure. And the contrast with my parents' plain country clothes suggested an even wider gulf between them. Papa still possessed his sturdy figure and his dark hair was just tinged with gray, but Mama was old, white-haired, gaunt, and her scrawny, scarecrow body was compressed all in black.

I said, "I would like you to meet Violante, who models for me." I saw admiration in Papa's eyes and I was glad he was not too aged to be pleased by a lovely woman, but I sensed that Mama disapproved of her.

I added, "She was the model for *The Assumption* and for many of my *poesias*."

Papa wanted to see one of them and I showed him the bacchanal I was painting in which Violante was the central figure, a ripe womanly Venus watching over a field of frolicking cupids. He was startled to see so many naked bodies, even if they were mostly cupids, and yet his eyes lingered on the Venus a long time.

Mama exclaimed, "Little one, I came to see the ascent of the Virgin!"

"You will. But this could be a vital commission, too."

"It is offensive," she declared. "Lewd and sacrilegious."

"Mama, it is a Greek myth. It is taken from the poet, Ovid."

"It does not matter. Women should not be painted unclothed."

"This expresses my spirit and my senses."

"No decent girl would pose for this."

My brother was uncomfortable as Violante blushed and he said, "Mama, this work is the fashion and Tiziano does it better than anybody else."

She asked Papa, "Gregorio, is this why you sent him here?"

"Lucia, it was his wish and you supported him, not me."

"I thought his brush would be devoted to the glory of our Lord."

My brother cut in, "Mama, he is the leading artist in Venice."

"I want to be proud of my little one, not ashamed."

Violante ventured, "Signora Vecellio, he was asked to paint the Pope."

"Then why did he not do so?"

I intervened, "Mama, I must also paint what pleases me."

"And that which pleases God."

Violante said, "That is why you must see your son's *The Assump-*

tion of the Virgin. It is the finest devotional painting in the world."

"I hope that it is more pious than what I see here."

Papa said, "Lucia, it is talked about even in Cadore. They say that everyone who visits Venice goes to see it. Did Francesco help you much?"

"Very much. He did most of the underpainting."

"He is a good son." Papa put his arm around Francesco to express his affection. "I miss him in Cadore. How does his fortune progress?"

Francesco answered, "You know that the family always comes first with Tiziano. He pays me well. I have whatever I need. And now I am helping him finish the Bellini in the Hall of the Great Council."

"What about your own brush? When will you set out on your own?"

There was an embarrassed silence and then Francesco muttered, "There is no demand for my work. But there is for Tiziano's."

"You are a Vecellio." Papa was indignant and upset. "You have talent."

"And I am pliable. I can imitate Tiziano's manner accurately now."

"Then why are you not like the Bellinis, two brothers in art?"

I could not tell Papa that Francesco lacked the gift of making a canvas come alive, that color was my primal matter but that in his hands it was flat and motionless. I said, "I am better known because I have been here longer. But in time they will want his manner, too. You will see."

"I would not give too many years to such a wait."

Violante said, "Signor Vecellio, he uses perspective excellently."

Papa glared at her as if to say, What does she know about painting? and I said hurriedly, "She was brought up in the house of a painter."

Mama stared at the altarpiece I was painting for the Pesaro family, which I had just begun, although it had been commissioned months ago. Most of my painting was on the Madonna and Child that was to be the theme of the work. I liked her animation and I had used the same red I had in *The Assumption*.

She asked, "Who is this work for?"

"It is the *Pesaro Madonna*. It is to go into the Frari church, too."

Papa said, "Lucia, they are an illustrious family. Tiziano is honored to paint them. They have contributed much to the glory of Venice."

"It is pious. Gregorio, this is what I expected from my little one."

"Each picture has its place. Francesco, is that not so?"

My brother nodded and led him around the studio, pointing to one partly finished painting after another and saying, "This is for Aurelio. This is for Barbarigo. This is for Navagero. And this is for the Doge."

Papa replied proudly, "You see, Lucia, our son is appreciated by the lords of Venice. You should be happy over what he has accomplished."

I felt that Mama was still troubled, for she did not smile approvingly, as Papa did, but regarded Violante critically. Violante shrank from her, conscious of her disapproval, while my brother joined her to indicate that he supported her and stated, "Mama, Tiziano has achieved much. The patricians of Venice are difficult to please. I do not have the talent for it, but he knows how to be adroit, to satisfy their demands, it is as vital as a gifted brush. Come, now we must show you Venice."

We took our parents to the Piazza San Marco by gondola where they could see the city in its most beautiful and captivating mood. Papa sat in the front like the soldier he was, but Mama squirmed uncomfortably by my side and complained about the rocking motion. I thought that they would be excited by the dazzling pageant of courtiers and merchants, the silks and the velvets of the ladies, but Mama was appalled by the crowd before the Basilica of San Marco, she said that she had never seen so many people in one place in her life, while Papa stated that it reminded him of a battlefield, there was so much commotion and pushing. The Doge's Palace that I adored struck her as ostentatious and too large, and the inside of the basilica disturbed her; she felt it was too pagan to be truly pious. Papa enjoyed the richness of the decorations but he thought that the frescoes were foreign and frightening. Neither Francesco nor I tried to change their minds. We sensed that our parents felt out of place in Venice and were homesick for Cadore.

That night they slept on the landing below my private quarters. Violante had not objected to my brother, Mocenigo, Campagnola, and Zuccato living there, but my parents' presence disturbed her. She refused to allow me to touch her as long as they were in the same house. As their visit lengthened into a week, for Papa was determined to get his fill, I grew restless and irritable. I began to wish that the visit I had looked forward to eagerly would end. I was also angry at Violante; I felt that her sudden modesty was unnecessary.

But she was adamant. She pointed out that she was not my courtesan, but my model and housekeeper. There were moments when I became so angry with her that I felt I should be rid of her, but I had no better model, so I accepted the situation, resentfully.

The day before my parents were to return to Cadore I took them to see *The Assumption of the Virgin.* I invited my uncle and aunt and my cousin, who was grown-up now, to accompany us, for I felt they would help Papa and Mama feel more at home. I had not seen them for years and as they met us at the Frari church I wondered if they ever changed. Except for aging, they were much the same as when I had come to Venice almost twenty years ago.

I hoped that when Mama saw the madonna in *The Assumption of the Virgin* she would realize that Violante possessed character, that it took taste and intelligence to pose skillfully and piously. But when we entered the basilica my aunt spoke so loudly it was difficult to concentrate on the altarpiece. Only when a priest showing the painting to a group of pilgrims hushed her did Daria desist. Most of the people in the Frari church were staring at *The Assumption of the Virgin* as if it were the thing to see, but I wondered what else they saw. I felt no one else shared my feelings.

Mama knelt in prayer before the altar, then we joined her, but I could not tell what was in her heart. She had hardly looked at the painting, once she had determined that it dominated the basilica.

I heard Papa whisper, "The blessed Mary is so alive."

"Not everybody approves," my aunt grumbled. "Some say she is more like a Magdalen than a madonna. The red is almost scarlet."

My cousin said, "Tiziano, could I work for you? Everyone says that you are flourishing and need hands. And I have some skill with a brush."

My uncle added, "Toma Tito draws excellently. Remember, I was the one who introduced you to Zuccato and Bellini."

That was not how I remembered it, but I nodded—I did not want to argue and Mama looked pleased at the idea—and I said, "I will consider it."

Then Mama compared Violante—who was dressed modestly in a plain brown dress—with the figure of the Virgin and she stated suddenly, "I wish the madonna had more humility. She is too worldly for me."

I was glad that she was finished with the senseless kneeling; I felt there was no mercy in her heart for Violante. Half weary and half disdainful of what had become a mean and common crowd in front of my work, I had an instinctive need to separate from them. In this moment there was no love in me for anyone, only hurt that whatever I painted there was someone who found fault with it. Yet there was nothing to say. If the work did not speak for itself, I could not.

One other memory remains of the visit. I have carried it with me all my life. Michelangelo and Mama, each in their own way, certain that they were right.

An hour before my parents were to depart Mama contrived to see me alone in my studio while everyone else was helping Papa to pack, even Violante.

Then she questioned me passionately. "Tiziano, where does she come from?"

"Bergamo."

"It is not our kind of town. Who is her father?"

"I do not know."

"She must have a father."

"It is thought he is the artist, Palma Vecchio, but no one is sure."

"Without a family a woman is nothing."

"She is a fine model and an excellent housekeeper."

"That is not enough."

"Violante suffices for my needs."

"Little one, she will betray you."

"It is more likely that I will betray her."

"Tiziano, she is nothing without your brush."

"Did you like *The Assumption of the Virgin?*"

"It is a noble subject and you are my son. She should not have modeled for it. That was not fitting. At the best, she is only your mistress."

"Magdalen modeled for our Lord. If He had mercy, so can we."

"He was our Lord. That was His mission. But how do you know what you need in a wife when you know only one woman? And a model at that!"

"Mama, would you pose for my next madonna?"

"I would not know how. But I do know what you need in a wife."

Deeply irritated, I had no intention of pursuing this matter any further. I realized, too, that despite what I had suggested, I could not paint her now, she had aged so. I said, "I hope that you have an easy journey home. I have provided the best accommodations for you."

"Little one, you will employ Toma Tito? He is a Vecellio, too."

"If I can. But he will have to do as much work as anyone else."

Papa entered. He was escorted by my brother and he said, "Francesco is right. The painting in the Frari does you much honor, it is in the most conspicuous part of the greatest church in the Republic. But do not squander your money. Patricians and princes are untrustworthy."

"I will send whatever I can spare to Cadore for you to invest."

"Good. I do not trust this city of lagoons. There is much dissipation here. But I am satisfied with your situation. Your work is held in high esteem. I trust that Francesco's fortune will grow the same way."

I nodded, although I doubted that my brother, more placid than I, possessed the passion and imagination to fulfill Papa's wish.

My parents prayed for our continued well-being and left.

After my cousin became another assistant in my bottega and I put him in the care of my brother, as I had put Zuccato's son, I arranged to meet Alfonso in Ferrara, accompanied this time only by Mocenigo.

The duke greeted me impatiently, demanded to know why I had kept him waiting, and before I could blame that on the demands of the Republic, he declared, "The sketch I sent you by Fra Bartolommeo illustrates what I want. Vecellio, have you studied it thoroughly?"

"Yes, my lord, I . . ."

He cut me short. "I will show you where it is to go." He led me to his *camerino*, striding vigorously as if he were going into battle, and Tebaldi and I had to run to keep up with him. He pointed to an empty space on the end wall, asked, "Do you know the writings of Philostratus?"

"Some of them, my lord, but not all. What do you have in mind?"

"The *Imagines* the Greek scholar wrote in the third century."

I realized that he wanted to impress me with his learning and so I nodded admiringly, although I was not sure I agreed with his choice of a subject.

"In it he describes sixty-four antique paintings he saw in Naples. I am determined to have classical pictures to rival any in the world."

"My lord, what about Raphael?"

"He may still do one. We are still in negotiation. But your *Assumption* has brought you to my attention again. I am not totally pleased with it, but it has attracted interest in your pictures and I will try one of them."

Tebaldi said, "That is why my lord sent you a stretcher and a canvas."

"Yes," stated Alfonso. "Have you followed Fra Bartolommeo's sketch?"

"Essentially, my lord. But some of his details are vague."

"My instructions are precise. The work I desire reproduced is a painting of a shrine to Aphrodite in a garden full of cupids."

So I had assumed from the sketch and my worship of Venus was going in the right direction, but I bowed and said, "My lord, it will be as you wish."

"Tebaldi will give you a copy of Philostratus to read so you do not make any errors. If this *poesia* is satisfactory, there may be others."

"On a similar theme, my lord?"

"I will decide that when I see how you follow antiquity. I am resolved to re-create three vanished masterpieces of classical art."

I wondered what had happened to his wish to obtain the work of Leonardo and Michelangelo but I realized that such a question might offend him. I said, "My lord, I am convinced that the greatness of art among the ancients was due to the assistance they received from great princes."

"Of course. Remember, I desire a poetical invention. A poem."

I repeated, to avoid misunderstanding, "A *poesia*."

"Naturally. I do not expect to be outdone by anyone."

Tebaldi said, "Vecellio, there is no better way a painter can serve our famed poets of antiquity than by becoming himself a poet in paint."

Alfonso added, "My agent will settle all the conditions."

I had one of my own, I thought, and I retorted, "My lord, I am grateful for your interest in my brush, but I cannot echo Bellini or Dossi's work."

"Who said that you should?" the duke snapped angrily.

"My lord, you suggested that before."

"When you were touching up *The Feast of the Gods*. This is different."

"My *poesia* will be by their side."

"That will be considered. Now do not irritate me any further or I will bestow my mercy elsewhere. Do not change Philostratus' story."

"My lord, I will follow it carefully."

* * *

Then, instead of dismissing me as I expected, Alfonso commanded me to paint a likeness of the duchess. He had made all the arrangements already and I felt this was another way of testing me. And although I was not sure I could please him, I was eager to paint her portrait. Many Venetians saw Lucrezia as a poisoner but she was also the mother of six children and poets like Bembo, Strozzi, and Ariosto had praised her in verse. Yet she was the pale, frail beauty who at thirteen had been wed to a man twice her age only to have the marriage annulled on the grounds of impotence. Soon afterward, her second husband, the duke of Bisceglia, just a year younger and whom she had loved, had been murdered on her brother's orders in front of her. She had not blamed Cesare Borgia, but had dutifully married the duke of Ferrara as her father, the Pope, had arranged for the third time.

I thought of all these things as I arranged the sittings. She had grown thick in the waist—she was pregnant again, I learned, although that was not evident except that she wore a loose-fitting black velvet gown and many veils. With her increase in weight she had aged shockingly since I had seen her several years ago, but she dressed elegantly, to show her pride in being a duchess and the daughter of a pope. Her famous hair was still fine, yellow, and long, but I suspected it had been dyed. Her voice was still soft and resigned, which I found mysterious for one who had led such a questionable life. Perhaps, as Mocenigo suggested, while he arranged my materials, "She is more sinned against than sinning."

I recalled, too, that she had supported me against Alfonso, that she had asked that I paint her, and when the duke had said that would be done by Raphael, she had been skeptical and had disagreed that the Roman would.

So I resolved to give her likeness the discernment and grace I felt resided within her. I sensed, too, that she desired me to make her vital and beautiful, but she sat so passively that it was very difficult. She wore such an air of resignation, and with her heaviness, her once magical profile had lost its distinction. And the black velvet did not suit her complexion, it made her look too pale. But her hands were supple and I gave them a nobility of gesture, and I colored her accessories so they had splendor, and suggested the woman whose beauty had been great.

Finally, to use contrast to heighten the drama of the portrait, I painted a marble cupid on the table next to her and a blue, sunny sky behind her. The light animated her features, and as she had been a classical beauty, I wanted my colors and design to tell a cheerful story.

When she saw that I was depicting her with grace, wit, and elegance, she grew more animated. She said, "Pietro Bembo was right. He praised you often to me. He thought your portraits would become much coveted."

"Your Highness, I wish he had encouraged me in this fashion."

"He did when he asked you to come to Rome."

"Duchess, I appreciated that, but my first obligation was to Venice which taught me whatever I know. But I wonder if I had gone. . ."

Suddenly there was a glimpse of the famed Borgia temperament as she cried, "Rome is a pestilent place, it corrupts all it touches. Even in Ferrara. But here at least, they appreciate fertility, if nothing else."

"Duchess, poets have praised your beauty, as I hope my brush will."

She opened the book she had been reading and asked, "Have you read Bembo's *Asolani?* His poetry talks about the need of painters to be poets."

"Not yet, my lady. But I will. I am painting a *poesia* for the duke."

"I was one of those who recommended you. He still thinks that Raphael will accede to his demands, but I doubt it. The Roman is too busy as it is, overworked, harassed by the demands of the Pope, worn out . . ."

"Too old perhaps, Your Highness, for what he is asked to do?"

She smiled wryly. "I am three years older than Raphael."

"Duchess, I meant that Raphael may have experienced too much."

"I trust that you use yourself more carefully. How old are you?"

"I am not quite sure, Your Highness."

"Some say that you are only thirty, but your portraits are mature."

Not quite thirty, I thought, as far as I could tell, but this was not a subject I liked discussing; too often my youth was held against me.

When she tired at the next sitting she ordered one of the gentlewomen who attended her, and who was her constant companion, to take up the lute and to sing softly to her. I was glad, for while her comments were useful, I was finishing her portrait and I did not want to be distracted.

After it was done Lucrezia showed it to Alfonso and said, "His work has a remarkable freshness and insight. I am masterfully delineated."

"Do not exaggerate," he replied curtly, but later Tebaldi gave me thirty ducats for the portrait, which for me, confirmed her judgment.

Yet when I packed to return to Venice to complete *The Worship of Venus,* the duke still had his overwhelming need to intimidate me so that he could maintain his superiority. I felt that he had given me enough instructions, but he had more, and he repeated others. "It must fit the end opposite the entrance to the *camerino,* that is why I sent you the canvas. It must catch the eye of whoever enters, even the most jaded."

"My lord, if you gave me more liberty, you would be served better."

"I cannot leave the subject to you. It is my *castello.* The bacchanal must fit the alabaster marble sculptures of Lombardo and ancient Rome."

"Very well, Your Highness, as we agreed."

"As I agreed. This poem must follow my instructions. I have found the passages in Philostratus I wish illustrated." Tebaldi handed me the two passages that were to be the subject of the *poesia,* while Alfonso added, "And follow the sketch by Fra Bartolommeo I sent you. Line by line."

"My lord, I have followed your instructions already."

"Naturally. If there are too many figures in the sketch for your purpose, you may leave some of them out, but you must not alter the idea. Venus must be depicted as she is in the sketch. Be sure to put in the landscape, the rocks and hills and trees, as described by Philostratus. You are not to add anything of your own. Or there will be no more work."

At my studio in Venice I studied the words of the philosopher-poet and compared them to the sketch by Fra Bartolommeo. When I had received it, I had viewed it casually, for it was not to my taste, but now I had to regard it seriously, however I differed with it. Even so, I liked it less. It was in the Florentine manner, yet primitive in design. The Venus on the pedestal was in the center, which I found old-fashioned; the fervor of the figures worshiping her was pious rather than pagan. I returned to the sketch I had made and strengthened the structure by placing my Venus on the side where she dramatically dominated the scene at her feet. I kept the nymph that the monk had drawn—she was offering the goddess a mirror, the historic view of Venus—but most of my figures differed from his.

The next few weeks I put aside the *Pesaro Madonna,* the altarpieces, the commissions for Barbarigo, Aurelio, and Navagero, the Bellini battle scene in the Hall. No one was allowed in my personal studio while I painted Violante as Venus. I had to avoid distractions and I did not want her to become self-conscious.

Francesco and Mocenigo arranged for my assistants to do what could be done without me and as I began to accomplish what I imagined, my hours lengthened. Finally Violante complained to my brother that she could not pose for me and continue to keep house and she asked him to intercede.

I was startled by this interruption and by her complaint. It was approaching midnight and we had been laboring since early afternoon, and to avoid distractions, without anything to eat except a little veal, fruit, and wine, and she was exhausted, but I was not done. I shouted at my brother, "If she does not want to model, she should speak to me!"

Violante said, "I have. But ever since your parents were here, you listen only to your family. Like Francesco."

He said, "Pesaro, Barbarigo, even Navagero, who has always supported you, are complaining that you are neglecting their commissions."

"They are jealous of the attention I am giving this *poesia.*"

"That may be. But their wishes should be considered."

"And mine."

Violante cried out, "I try, Tiziano, I do. But I cannot stand here forever." When Francesco had entered the studio she had draped herself with a sheet, but she still shivered from the cold and I could see the bulges of her body which were accentuated by the tightness of her covering.

I dismissed my brother and asked her, "What is truly troubling you?"

"Your mother does not approve of me. I can tell. Your brother looks embarrassed whenever he is with me, as if he has been told that is wrong."

"He is not that weak-minded."

"He is influenced by your parents."

"I am not." I was angry at her for what she was implying, but I was too close to what I desired in this *poesia* to allow that to halt me. "I am sorry you are cold. I could have lit the fireplace but I expected to be done by now. But I am almost finished with today's work."

She said morosely, "You will never be finished with this picture. It means too much to you. You do not want to give it up to anyone else."

I wondered how she knew. I had not mentioned that, only painted more passionately. And I knew no model who pleased me better; I must contrive to keep her content. I asked her to remove the sheet from her figure.

She was still shivering but she did as I requested. She was perfectly formed, I thought, her figure as lovely as her face. I felt I was right to persist; she possessed the ideal model's body: a long, graceful torso, a tapering waist, wide, splendid hips, beautifully developed legs, firm and fully formed buttocks, and her greatest treasure of all, her round, swelling breasts. Violante was a subject worthy of my best and I felt, If I were to paint her as Aphrodite, she must feel like Aphrodite. I was intensely involved. I lost my painter's detachment. I desired her as I had never desired anything in my life. Too much time and energy had been spent in painting the bacchanal, I realized, and not enough in living in it. Revitalized, I had to feel her body to capture its flow. My hands stroked her breasts to capture their exact contour, their passionate thrust, and her flesh seemed to throb under my touch and she embraced me instinctively and clung to me as if shaken by a convulsion. Now nothing mattered but our pairing.

She responded with a passion I had not experienced since she had met my parents. Then, as she lay beside me afterward, she kissed my hands, fondled them proudly, and held them against her breasts.

Suddenly I got out of bed, lit a candle, threw on a velvet robe to keep warm, and hurried back to the *poesia.* She followed me and asked tearfully, "What is wrong?" and I answered, "I was a fool. I was painting a myth instead of reality. The viewer must fall in love with Venus."

"As you have with me?"

"Do not distract me."

"And now that you obtained what you desire you no longer need me."

"No. I may have to do the work over. Too much of it dissatisfies me."

"What about the duke? He is grumbling already about the delay."

"He can wait. I never should paint a figure all at once. He who improvises his poetry can form neither learned nor well-turned verses."

The next day I repainted *The Worship of Venus* in a more lively manner. Now I moved the figures with passionate gestures, especially the many cupids. Even the hills, trees, and clouds—which I drew from my memory of Cadore—became animated. I made other alterations as I used my colors to suggest ripeness, the blossoming of the flesh. My landscape, too, grew emotional. I gave nature a force of expression I had missed in Bellini and others, and seen, although not as much as I had desired, only in Giorgione. I was determined that my landscape must have a soul. I felt a special energy in my colors and feeling. To give this *poesia* the greatest luminosity, I put into it what I had learned in Venice about the brilliance and richness of light.

Violante posed for me without question, as if my love had restored her to cheerfulness. These days she radiated the joyfulness I sought for Venus. There was a new splendor about her and I was finding a harmonious whole for the composition. I used very little of my favorite red, but when I did it heightened the other colors. I was searching for light, light that would glow from this canvas, and give the flesh the vibrancy and tone of life. This stimulated me and as I painted lyrically so that the colors acquired a beauty in themselves, I felt that I might be able to live with this *poesia* a long time. I was striving to express the glory of the human body in the person of a Venus that would be so pleasing the viewer would desire to give all that he possessed to win her.

At the end of long days and nights of painting that went on for several more months, Tebaldi insisted on seeing the picture. He said, "It is done."

But I was not satisfied. I replied, "I need a few more weeks to finish it. I want to do some little things."

"What are they? I see nothing unfinished."

No one else would note them, I thought, but I would. I stated, "The Venus needs more work." I refused to explain any further.

Tebaldi said angrily, "You will incur the duke's displeasure. If you do not deliver the work soon, he will commission someone else."

I had heard that Alfonso still awaited a canvas by Raphael, but by now I did not care. I said, "He will have it by the end of this year."

When another month passed without delivery of the work to the duke, he wrote me by way of Tebaldi: "We thought that Titian, the painter, would some day finish my picture, but he seems to take no account of us whatever. Thus we instruct you to tell him instantly that we are surprised that he has not finished my picture, that he must finish it under all circumstances or incur our great displeasure, and advise him of this."

But I was valuing myself more, for my other patrons were waiting, too, and while they complained about the delays, they did not cancel their commissions. And this was the one way I could express my independence.

It was many weeks after Alfonso's heated letter that I arrived in Ferrara with the finished work. I was saddened to hear that Lucrezia Borgia had died bearing the duke's seventh child, but he did not mention her or her portrait, but seemed relieved, almost buoyant, as if a burden had been lifted from his brawny shoulders. I was accompanied by Mocenigo and Francesco and I took the journey in a leisurely fashion.

Alfonso reproached me about the delays and I replied, as we stood in the *camerino* where I had delivered *The Worship of Venus,* "I did not want to spoil the work, my lord. I trust that it suits your needs."

"It is too large," he growled. "It is too bold, too energetic."

"My lord, I painted it according to the canvas and stretcher you sent me."

"It does not fit where it is to go. I will have to cut it down."

I feared he was going to butcher my *poesia,* but finally, after I reduced the width by a few inches without violating my intention, I was able to place the canvas in the space for which it had been painted.

Alfonso hovered over the picture, saying, "You altered my intentions."

"Your Highness, it is *The Worship of Venus.* As you requested."

"Not as I designed it. Your interpretation is too free."

"My lord, if it is unsatisfactory, I will withdraw it. I have had several offers for it."

"From Venetian noblemen?" he asked suspiciously.

I nodded, although no one else had seen it and I did not know how it would be received. But I could no longer be craven in his presence.

Alfonso wavered, as if he was not sure he believed me. Then he said abruptly, "Navagero and Barbarigo are admirers of your work."

"Signor Aurelio, too, and His Excellency, Jacopo Pesaro," I reminded him. "And Pietro Bembo. He asked me to serve the Pope, my lord."

"I know. The duchess told me. That reminds me. I have created a pattern for this chamber that is the same as the three phases of love in Bembo's poetic dialogue, *Asolani*. You will be given it to read."

"Why, my lord?" I was puzzled.

"To paint, you fool. I need two more poems for my chamber."

"My lord, then you do approve of what I have painted?"

"That is not the question. Your manner conflicts with Bellini and Dossi and something will have to be done about that. But I cannot endure a fourth manner. At least your next *poesia* should be consistent with the one you have just delivered."

"Thank you, Your Highness. I am grateful that you are pleased."

Alfonso turned to Tebaldi, who stood behind him like a shadow. The duke wore a striped silver doublet and a splendid gold-trimmed cape worthy of a portrait, but before I could suggest that he would make a fine painting, he grumbled, "Your nudes should have more variety. I have seen several of them in your other pictures and while they are amply fleshed, as is this Venus, they are too much alike. That is a grave mistake. It is as if they are drawn from the same model. If you wish to please many tastes, you must give us many different nudes."

For once, I thought, he might be talking sense.

"Remember, I expect your second *poesia* to express exactly the second theme of love in Bembo's *Asolani*. As this *poesia* does after a fashion. Tebaldi, you can pay the painter, Tiziano Vecellio."

I departed in high spirits, for I was going back to my work.

THE POEM IS LIKE A PAINTING

THE POEM IS LIKE A PAINTING

A poem without the poet's name
is like a painting
without the picture frame
The poem is not alive
The painting will never rise

A poem without the poet's name
is like a painting
without the signature
The poem will never breathe
The painting will never appear

The poem is like a painting
in a gallery
Under each the name of one
who gave them air to breathe
so they could live

Stymean Karlen

TWENTY-FOUR HOURS HAVE PASSED since I have seen my sons and I am surprised that Pomponio has not come with the prior and the physician, there had been so much urgency in him. I decide that perhaps the prior has fled from Venice because of the plague and I return to my memories, to the doing of the *poesias* that are as vital to me as any I have done.

The moment I reached my studio I read Bembo's *Asolani* as the duke had ordered. It was a poetic dialogue about platonic love but I felt that Alfonso preferred pagan love. I doubted that my brush could fit the three aspects of emotion that the poet evoked. They were: "Chaotic love—Harmonious love—Divine love." I did not believe that *The Worship of Venus* was chaotic love but evidently Alfonso did. Then, while the second subject that he had chosen for me, "The Bacchanal of the Andrians," which was also from *The Imagines* of Philostratus, was appropriate to the first mythology I had painted for him, it did not fit Bembo's themes.

A week later Tebaldi came to find out how I was progressing and when he saw that nothing was done, he said sharply, "The duke will be angry."

Alfonso was always angry, I thought, but I said, "There is confusion. Bembo's poem does not suit Philostratus and I do not know whom to choose."

"His Highness wants reproduced the passage from the Greek philosopher where he describes a celebration honoring Bacchus on the island of Andros."

"Does he wish me to represent a feast or an orgy?"

"According to Philostratus, Dionysus puts a spring on Andros that flows with pure wine. The natives, drinking these unpolluted waters, are in a state of joyful, perpetual intoxication. It is a tribute to Bacchus."

"That is clear. But Bembo writes of 'Harmonious love.' "

"Which is the duke's intention. He is ingenious."

I did not think Alfonso was clever for applying Bembo's poetry to two passages of Philostratus. But the subject, as before, appealed to me and to show that I understood what was desired, I quoted, *"He who drinks and does not drink again, does not know what drinking is."*

"Exactly. It is a sumptuous subject. My lord desires it quickly."

"Signore, I will do my best, but I have many other commissions." I pointed to the altarpieces and portraits that filled my bottega.

"They can wait. The duke will send you another canvas and stretcher and further instructions. And expect the *poesia* soon after."

I had more instructions already than I could assimilate but I nodded and added, " 'The Bacchanal of the Andrians' is a fine and ingenious idea."

Apparently that satisfied Tebaldi that I was sincere, for he smiled in agreement and left me, as I desired, to my own devices.

While I waited to receive my materials from Alfonso so I would know the dimensions of his second poem, I returned to the *Pesaro Madonna*. My brother had done some underpainting on it, but not to my satisfaction. This altarpiece was to be erected in the Frari church and I wanted it to equal *The Assumption.* I enlivened Francesco's flatness and I painted secondary figures that gratified me, but the concept I was searching for continued to evade me. So, as was my custom when I was dissatisfied, I turned this picture to the wall and decided to return to it later.

I felt the same way about the finishing of the Bellini battle piece in the Hall and my own work there, and I did not touch them, hoping that they would germinate in my mind during the interval. No one had said anything recently about these delays and I hoped that it would remain that way.

I finished my altarpiece for Ancona, an *Adoration of the Virgin,* and it pleased me, for I executed it with a joyfulness and a judicious contrast of tints and tones that I felt were just right for this work.

The altarpiece for Brescia, *The Resurrection,* was a larger and more difficult picture. The five panels needed variety in addition to depth and intensity and I painted it intermittently, then put it aside.

At the same time new, important patricians wanted me to paint their portraits. The first one I did was of the aged Antonio Grimani, for he was the most dramatic. He had been Captain-General of the fleet, only to have been put in jail for having lost to the Turks. Then he had regained power and had become Procurator of San Marco. He had lived through more than even Lucrezia Borgia; he was in his eighties, yet he retained his vigor. I painted him as he was, erect and tough, his piercing gaze both cunning and strong.

Andrea Gritti was also elderly. He was in his sixties, but his ascetic features were still handsome and commanding. His wide-apart eyes, his broad forehead, his finely cut nose, his resolute jaw became a favorite likeness and when it was finished this Senator wanted more work from me.

Francesco Donato was much younger and yet there was distinction in his presence, too. His long features became strong under my brush, with his black goatee, flashing dark eyes, and his spirited expression.

Age was often more moving than youth, I thought, until Aurelio asked for another Venus and then I was not sure. At this moment, whatever I painted, and my studio teemed with activity, I preferred my *poesias.*

My brother supervised the allocation of the work for my assistants, while Mocenigo took care of my living arrangements and the protection of myself. Since I had acquired the broker's patent there had not been any threats against me, but I still felt I should move warily. Most of my fellow painters were elsewhere now: Pordenone in Florence, Piombo in Rome, Lotto in Pisa, Bordone in Milan, and I had not seen Vecchio in a year. But it was rumored that I lived loosely, with a lust for wine and women, and there was other malice. I doubted this was a grave danger to me, but Mocenigo felt that it was best to accompany me most of the time.

This became remote as I used Violante for Aurelio's Venus. She had been my model for his *Sacred and Profane Love,* too, and that was a favorite among Venetians like *The Assumption,* as if these pictures reflected the opposite sides of their nature, the reverent and the light-hearted.

Aurelio was pleased with the erotic beauty of his Venus lying on her couch, naked and asleep, waiting for her lover to arrive and join her.

She enchanted Barbarigo, and so I did another Venus for him, rising from the sea—newborn but truly grown—with lovely, lustrous hair.

Navagero saw this as such a felicitous view that I painted a third *poesia* for him: Venus standing in the sea and combing her radiant hair. The grace of her motion was innocent, yet exuberant. The bright sheen of her red tresses was precisely the contrast I wanted against the light of the water and the sky and should arouse ardent desire.

All three were happy with their *poesias,* but while I liked what I had done and Violante had posed perfectly, I craved new models. I had a need to explore, to feel free of dependence on any one person or model, to have my imagination stirred afresh, and I remembered the duke's criticism.

When the canvas and the stretcher for *The Bacchanal of the Andrians* arrived from Ferrara, I summoned Francesco and Mocenigo to my private quarters and informed them, "I require other models. There will be an abundance of nudes in my new poems and I must have more choice."

Mocenigo regarded me dubiously and said, "I do not think I will find anyone as appealing as Violante," but my brother was glad and he stated, "I know a few women who should please you. When will you view them?"

"As soon as possible. Tomorrow, if it can be arranged."

Violante was stunned when a dozen young, pretty women arrived at my bottega the next day to be examined as possible models. She drew me aside and asked, white-faced and trembling, "What is wrong with me?"

"Nothing," I replied. "But since you prefer to be my housekeeper, I must have other models that I can call on when you are busy."

"Tiziano, I have never been too busy to model for you."

"You were not very helpful when Mama was here."

"You are punishing me because she does not approve of me and I said so."

"Please, Violante, let us not be stupid. I have much to paint."

"You are a master craftsman. Your imagination creates your nudes."

"Will you please stop delaying me?"

"I do not understand. What did I do wrong?"

I was furious but she looked in such a state of shock that I gave her ten ducats and said, "You can buy the draperies you wanted."

"You are sending me away."

"I am not. You have your place in my home. As you have on my model stand when the occasion requires. But the duke desires more variety."

Now that the truth was out I was relieved and yet irritated that she had forced this admission from me. I resolved not to give her any more advantages. I returned to the waiting females and ordered them to undress. Violante retired in dismay while I waited for the prospective models to reveal their figures. Two refused, then I saw that most of the others were not what I wanted, gross or coarse, or too awkward for my brush. I was left with four who appeared suitable: Bella and Mona, who had been brought by Mocenigo; and Clara and Cecilia, who were here at the invitation of my brother. Then, while the first three women were willing to undress and pose before me, Cecilia blushed and refused.

Mocenigo, who was in charge, said bluntly, "Maestro, she is of no use. She will not disrobe in front of anyone else, even the other females."

Yet she possessed an exquisite body, possibly the best in the group, It looked perfect to my gaze, although less ample than Violante's, but she was younger, and her slender figure, rosy complexion, and fair hair stimulated me. I told myself that it was just my imagination that was stirred but I was curious about her youthful nakedness. I asked softly, "Would the young lady pose for me in private, undraped?"

She met my inquiring eyes and smiled shyly, and smiling seemed to reveal the sun shining through the clouds. Then she nodded delicately.

I told her to wait and I turned to Bella, who moved nakedly with such assurance I felt she was a courtesan. She had a heart-shaped face, an inviting mouth, glowing eyes, a captivating figure, and she said, "Many men tell me that I have the features of a madonna." Or for a Magdalen, I felt, but I replied, "I will decide what you will portray."

I indicated that she was satisfactory, and surveyed Mona. But once she was naked it was evident that she was a common whore, she swaggered so obscenely, yet her fleshy body was voluptuous and worth considering.

Clara was too much the lady, posing stiffly and awkwardly. Yet there was nothing wrong with her figure, I thought, except that she did not know how to express it. I told her and Mona that I might use them later.

I dismissed everyone but Cecilia, who waited apprehensively and yet, I sensed, eagerly. When I asked her to disrobe, she did so slowly, but enticingly. Deliberate or not, I thought, her blushes and shy behavior added to her charm. As I had judged, Cecilia was perfectly formed, slighter than Violante, but with a youthful nakedness that strongly stirred my emotions.

I told her to return tomorrow with Bella and after she left, I asked about their background. Francesco said that Cecilia came from Cadore—and I wondered if he was trying to please Mama—but that she and her father had lived in Venice for several years and that he repaired galleys in the Arsenal. Mocenigo said that Bella was a courtesan who felt that a portrayal of herself in a *poesia* by Tiziano Vecellio would make her celebrated and increase her value to the patricians who were her patrons.

I was amused instead of flattered.

Mocenigo asked, "Maestro, what about Violante?"

I scowled and said, "I do not know what you mean."

"She is a superb model."

"But growing heavier," said Francesco. "Cecilia is younger, slender."

I asked, "Is that why you brought her here?" My brother was pleased with himself, which was unusual, and quite familial.

"She will give you an innocence that will be a dramatic contrast to Bella's worldliness. It is just what your new bacchanal needs."

I was not interested in his advice and I withdrew to my studio. But when I began work on *The Bacchanal of the Andrians*, I saw sense to his suggestion. So, as I sought to express the glory and joy of this theme as poetically as I could, I modeled Bella as the nude who lay in an ecstatic state of intoxication while Cecilia became a spirited nymph engaged in a graceful dance. But I intended this as a love song to Bacchus, also, and I painted a sheet of music in the foreground and wrote on it what I had said to Tebaldi: *"He who drinks and does not drink again, does not know what drinking is."* But I was far from satisfied.

I stopped several times that year to turn this *poesia* to the wall when I felt I was improvising instead of expressing a genuine joy of life. I wondered if this was because I was troubled within myself. My new models came to my studio whenever I needed them but I was impersonal with them.

Violante devoted herself to the household and was responsive to my amorous needs and I was relieved that she was by my side when I wanted her. She had bought gold and black silk draperies for our bed and an alabaster table for me to use when I had a sudden, impulsive idea in the night.

Yet I had odd dreams of a young girl with a slender body like Cecilia's. I felt divided and that made me sad, almost desperate.

I returned to my altarpiece for Brescia and my sorrow seemed to help the painting of this commission. I painted the anguish of the martyred St. Sebastian with a muscular power I had used rarely. I had a need to show that I could paint as vigorously as Michelangelo, and I came to believe that the figure of the saint was one of the best things I had done.

I had just finished this work when Tebaldi strode into my studio. He said angrily, "You keep us waiting and yet you are not even working on the *poesia!* You will force the duke to take his commissions elsewhere."

Raphael had just died and while the news grieved me, it eased my fear of losing this *poesia.* The only painter who could equal mine was gone, yet I answered, "It is almost done. Another few weeks should suffice."

Tebaldi declared, "I must see it and decide for myself."

I took it off the wall where it had hung for months and now I felt like painting it again; rested—I knew what had to be done.

Tebaldi said, "So far it fits the duke's instructions. You must finish it in Ferrara. Where you can make it appropriate to the *camerino.*"

"What about my models?"

"Bring them."

"They will be costly."

Tebaldi hesitated, but he had gone too far to halt and he blurted out, "It will be arranged. Who are you painting the St. Sebastian for?"

"It is an altarpiece for Brescia. The Papal legate commissioned it."

"A worthy picture. I must call it to the duke's attention."

Bella said she would be honored to visit Ferrara as my model, if she were properly paid, but Cecilia wavered, did not discuss money, and only when I assured her that I would be accompanied by my brother and Mocenigo did she agree to go. I told Violante of the expedition and said it was solely to complete the *poesia* in the best possible manner. To my surprise, she did not ask to join me but assumed an air of indifference. Now I was the one who was concerned and I asked, "Will you be here when I return?"

"Is there any reason I should not be?"

"No! No!" I said hurriedly. "None at all! I will be back soon."

"Who will take care of the business of the studio?"

"My cousin. Toma Tito is a poor painter but he has a gift for commerce. I have appointed him to buy all my materials for me."

"From his father, no doubt?"

"It is in the family." I kissed her, to show that I still cared for her and expected to miss her, but I could not tell whether she agreed.

Standing in Alfonso's *camerino* and seeing what I had achieved with *The Worship of Venus,* I realized what the second bacchanal still needed and I regained my confidence. Neither model expressed the zest for life that Violante did, but my colors could compensate for that. I used my oils richly and vibrantly to dramatize the joyous abandon of the nymphs and the satyrs. I painted my vision of nature vividly so that everything grew intensely alive. The clouds, the trees, the clusters of grapes, the flowing rivers of wine became a bacchanal in which some were dancing, some drinking, some laughing and some sleeping, but in everything there was a sensuality that sang of the Venice I loved.

I became so emotional that I craved amorous sustenance from the flesh that I adored. Each member of my party had a separate room in the castle, as if the duke did not want to allow anything to hinder the completion of his *poesia,* and I sensed he would do anything to encourage that. I had easy access to Cecilia's; I felt this had been arranged by Alfonso. I had not known any woman but Violante for years and now I desired Cecilia.

One night my party was invited to a dance at court and as I watched the duke's entourage enjoying themselves while I sat, I saw Cecilia standing nearby. I was in no mood to dance, for the floor was crowded with fashionable figures and I preferred to express my love of movement on my canvases where everything was graceful and lovely. I eased up to her and touched her with my fingers. Cecilia turned with a frightened gasp, but when she saw who it was, she clutched my fingers as if she could not let them go. Then she apologized hurriedly. Yet her eyes shone, her face was flushed, and her flesh was warm.

I led her to a secluded garden where we were away from everyone and I kissed her passionately and she responded with a fervent embrace. She gave me the feeling that she desired me as much as I desired her. So I guided her to her bedchamber. Cecilia did not protest, walking by my side with a kind of dazed wonder. Her room was plainly but neatly furnished with a crucifix behind her bed, flowers on the windowsill, and a mirror and combs to arrange herself for the numerous posings.

Her slender but full body was even more amorous against mine than it had been in my imagination. Her breasts and buttocks were so firm I felt they were untouched and she seemed to react to my touch by instinct and impulse rather than by experience and knowledge.

I must be the first, I thought, and then I was not sure. In my haste and excitement I forgot to take my usual precautions, but when she saw my concern she assured me that there was nothing to fear. And later, when we became accustomed to each other, our pleasure grew.

The duke seemed distracted when I told him that *The Bacchanal of the Andrians* was done. He stood in his *camerino* to make sure for himself and he said critically, "I told you to bring your models with you."

"I did, Your Highness. You have seen them about."

"I have not seen the one who modeled for *The Worship of Venus.*"

"My lord, you requested variety."

"To improve my *poesias*. None of these women favor us as she did."

I thought wryly, Inconsistency is the consistency of Alfonso, but

I said, "My lord, I will use her in the third. As the main figure, Ariadne."

"Do not keep me waiting or you will incur my great displeasure."

"I will do it as quickly as I can, my lord." But I felt that since Alfonso did not keep his threats, I did not have to keep my promises.

Orazio interrupts my reverie to ask, "Papa, have you seen Pomponio?"

"Not since I agreed to meet the prior and the doctor. I thought that would please him." Many hours have passed since I began to relive the memories of my bacchanals and it is the middle of the afternoon now.

"It is difficult to know what will please him."

"Do you think my account of my struggles brought him any closer?"

"I will try to find out. Have you stopped painting?"

His soft, delicate features, which remind me so much of his mother's, are taut and lined and I realize that he is not a young man any more; he is past fifty. I look up from the mass of papers in front of me and I ask, "Would that trouble you, Son?"

"It would trouble all of us who are favored by your brush."

I am moved and I reply, "That is a gallant thing to say."

"It is true, Papa. You must not doubt so much. If Pomponio behaves strangely sometimes, he is that way with everyone. Have you eaten?"

"I only need a glass of wine and a mouthful of bread." I have a vast need to push on with my memories, as if in the recalling of how Cecilia became the mother of my children, I might understand them better. "I will be here if you want me. Is there any news of the plague?"

"Not much. The watchman is still outside our neighbor's house but I have not seen the death boats today. I will bring you an admirable wine and other delicacies. You must not neglect yourself."

He goes to feed me while I return to the circumstances of his birth.

As soon as I saw Violante I embraced her affectionately, as if she were the most companionable woman I knew, and told her that the duke approved of the second *poesia* and that he wanted her to pose for the final one. This pleased her and she said that she would be honored to do so.

Since I planned to use Cecilia in this *poesia*, too, I decided to keep them apart. I rented quarters within walking distance of San Samuele and lodged Cecilia there. The rooms overlooked a small canal and they were next to the Campo San Maria Formosa and near San Marco and the Rialto.

Cecilia had a bedroom, kitchen, and living room in addition to my studio, which had excellent light, and she liked looking out on a small courtyard with a garden and two trees; it reminded her of Cadore.

I gave her thirty ducats to furnish it as she wished, which she regarded as a fortune—she told me that she had never seen so much money before—and she bought a small wooden chest for her clothes, gray brocade draperies for the square wooden bed, and heavy woolen blankets.

There was no opposition from her as I expected and when I mentioned her father, she said, "He went back to Cadore while I was in Ferrara."

"And left you alone?" This surprised me and made me suspicious.

"My mother is ill. He knows that I can take care of myself. He says that it is a great honor to model for the first painter in Venice."

"Did you know Francesco in Cadore?"

"My father did. I was too young."

I wondered if my brother and her father were contriving to put me in her marriage bed. Now I felt Cecilia was younger than she admitted, perhaps only seventeen, and yet she had never resisted my advances in spite of her modesty in my studio. She had succumbed so swiftly that when I thought of that my suspicions increased. Yet possibly, I told myself, she was truly in love with me. When she was with me, she gave of herself wholly and was as ardent as any Venus that I had painted.

I began *Bacchus and Ariadne* with great care. The first step was to sketch the three main female figures, for I wanted them to dominate the painting, and I decided to do this in separate studios. So I drew Violante as Ariadne in my principal one; I did Cecilia as the most prominent nymph in her lodgings; and I used Bella for the second nymph in an auxiliary studio that was attached to my bottega. There was another canvas and stretcher from Alfonso to tell me what dimensions he desired but it lay on my easel untouched. He also sent me the usual instructions but I disregarded them. I knew what I wanted to paint: the moment the youthful Bacchus saw Ariadne and fell in love with her. This was a poignant time; it was the moment she was bidding a melancholy farewell to her love, Theseus, as he sailed away from the island of Dia.

As I composed my concepts in my mind I knew I was a long way from what truly mattered. There must be a grace, motion, and color in this poem that equaled the first two bacchanals and yet was unique in itself. I wanted the spirit of the antique to permeate beyond the frame.

I also worked with Violante and Cecilia on different days, for when my new infatuation posed for me, it was only the first part of our meeting; after the sitting we made love. And I did not want to be engaged in such energetic activity with two women in the same day.

But one evening, several hours after I had spent an ardent afternoon with Cecilia and I had come to bed quite tired, Violante invited me to enjoy her amorous charms. At first I felt that she was testing me, but as she caressed my manhood I realized that she was seizing the initiative to express her love for me. She was plump by contrast with Cecilia's slenderness but she was also more skillful and gradually my fatigue vanished as she evoked many pleasures within me. However, while I was gratified, I was worried, too. My intense expressions of manhood with Cecilia—as if I had to prove to her that I was not too old for her—had drained me and I had to force myself to have enough energy for Violante. And now she expected me to repeat our act of copulation, as we usually did. Instead, I fell asleep and she awoke me with an angry jolt in the ribs and I murmured apologetically, "I am working too hard."

She sat up in bed and asked, "How many pictures are you painting?"

"Presently?" She nodded and I said, "I do not remember all of them, but there are several new altarpieces, another portrait of Grimani, now that he is the Doge, the *Pesaro Madonna*—sometimes I think I will never finish it, it is so difficult—two other madonnas, a study of a bravo, for which I am using Mocenigo, *The Entombment of Christ,* a Magdalen, and now Alfonso desires a portrait of himself and his new wife, Laura Dianti, although he never mentions the one I did of his first wife, Lucrezia Borgia, and commissions I am too tired to recall."

"Too many for even one with your tremendous energy."

"And I have not even mentioned the paintings for the Great Hall."

"Suppose the patrons grow impatient and turn elsewhere?"

I shrugged and stated, "I will do what I can. What I prefer."

"Give some of them to Francesco or Campagnola. They know your style."

"I am shocked by your suggestion. They will not be my pictures."

"Do not be righteous. Other painters have done this. Even Raphael."

I got out of bed abruptly, using my disgust with what she was saying as an excuse to avoid any further intercourse that evening.

"Why am I being punished now? For being your housekeeper?"

"Violante, as the daughter of a painter you should know better."

"Palma Vecchio has never admitted that he is my father and you should not bring that up. I hear that your new models are pretty and young."

"They are suitable. But you are my Ariadne."

She gave me a strange look, as if she was not certain what she was, and she sank back in our large double bed, apart from me.

The next week I touched neither Violante nor Cecilia. I knew that Violante was right, that I had accepted more commissions than I could paint myself and deliver on time, and yet I could not give up any of them. So I decided to put off what I could and paint what I preferred. I stopped my sketching and turned to the canvas that Alfonso had sent me for the third *poesia,* hoping that would end my discontent, but after I painted only two figures and a leopard-drawn chariot my mind became blank.

To stir my imagination, I resolved to paint Cecilia as a Venus. I thought that she would be enchanted with the idea. Instead, although she disrobed and lay on the couch in all her naked glory as I ordered and her flesh pleased my brush, she seemed ill at ease. I told her to put her left hand over her pubic region, as was the fashion and to add enticement, while her right hand fingered red roses to heighten the contrast to her pink skin and fair hair, but her left hand continued to stray to her stomach. There was no reason for her to hide it, I thought irately, and I ordered her to lie motionless. She did briefly and just as I felt I had the proper curve of her body she shivered.

She whimpered, "Maestro, I am cold."

I shook my head in disgust. Whatever she was, she was not Violante.

"And I am so tired," she groaned.

"You should have braided your hair. It is disorderly."

Cecilia combed it obediently and I rearranged her in a reclining pose, like a Venus that Giorgione had painted and which I had admired. She seemed settled and I threw more logs on the fire to take away the chill of the marble floors, and just as I was about to resume painting she covered her stomach with both her hands. In my exasperation I pulled them away and she cried out in pain, "I cannot help it, Tiziano!"

"Help what?" I pushed my easel into a corner with disgust, wishing that I had used Violante, who was dependable and resourceful.

She sobbed, "I could not stop it. I tried. I did. I tried."

I felt her stomach—I trusted my sense of touch as I trusted little else—and suddenly I knew. But it could not be true, I told myself, I had taken the proper precautions, except . . . and I remembered the first time in Ferrara and I exclaimed, "It is a lie!"

"No," she wept piteously, "it is true."

"Am I the father?"

"Tiziano, I have not known anyone else. Ever."

I was tempted to throw her out—she had assured me there was no danger of pregnancy—and I was not prepared to have any children. I did not want anything that could take me away from my work, and I was not certain that I loved her, at least that much; I preferred Violante in many ways. Yet she looked so helpless and it probably was my child. I was almost sure that I was the only man that she had known and so I hesitated.

She pleaded, "You do want the child?"

Even there, I was not sure.

"And we should be married. For the child's sake."

"Is that why you are pregnant?"

"I told you, Tiziano, it must have been an accident."

I doubted that and I wondered if my brother had a hand in this, or even Mama—Cecilia came from Cadore and Francesco had brought her to my studio—and she began to shake as if she expected me to beat her and I sat beside her to soothe her. I was still furious at her but I did not desire a hysterical girl in my studio. As I stared at her, trying to decide what to do next—I did not want to marry her and yet I did not see how I could desert her—Violante rushed in.

She seemed to expect what she saw now, a beautiful young naked woman lying near me, and she grew white-faced and agitated.

I said hurriedly, "Violante, I was modeling her."

"While you are sitting close to her? You never model that way!"

Cecilia shrank from Violante's withering and accusing gaze, looking ashamed and guilty, and this added to the latter's rage.

She screamed, "Next you will tell me that she lives here with her widowed mother and that they are both devoted to the holy life!"

"I am using her for a *poesia* of a Venus I propose to do."

This offended Violante even more and she shouted, "She will never pose for you as amorously as I did. She has not the body for it. She is thin."

For an instant I thought she was going to strike Cecilia, who was cringing and crying, and I shouted back, "Who told you about this studio?"

"It does not matter. You will never have another Venus like me."

"Is that why you spied on me?"

"Tiziano, you said you loved me."

"We are not married. I can paint whom I choose."

"And cuckold me?"

I had not thought of it that way. Even in the *Decameron,* which I had read several times, it was always the man who was cuckolded. But in a way she was right, only I could not admit that to her.

She said, "You promised Vecchio that you would marry me."

"If I could."

"You gave Palma your word. It is why he consented to let me go."

Cecilia stood up with a burst of energy, stared at Violante as if to measure herself against my Ariadne, then said, "He should marry me."

"A strumpet like yourself? He is too selfish for that."

"My only sin is that I love him."

"It is a common one. I have committed it, too. It is not enough."

I stepped between them to prevent them from coming to blows, but Violante turned away from Cecilia with a disdainful air. She was heavy next to the younger woman, and yet she possessed more presence and in this moment I preferred her. But I could not bend to either of them. Yet when Violante started out I followed her and I was annoyed when Cecilia halted me and cried out, "What about me, Tiziano?"

By the time I turned to answer Violante was gone and I said impatiently, "I will be back. As soon as I settle several things."

"Do not heed her. Believe me, the love of a good woman like myself, a country girl who understands you, is a precious thing."

"I refuse to discuss this any further." I could not risk losing Violante now, I told myself, not while she was such a perfect Ariadne.

When I reached my bottega she was packing. I said, "You must not act hastily," and she retorted, "Will you leave her?"

"I cannot," I answered. "Not yet." I could not explain, for if I told her why it would only make her more hostile.

Mocenigo, hearing the commotion, joined us. This was very unusual and I thought that he must like her very much to risk my displeasure.

He said, "Maestro, our signora has served you well."

"I esteem her many services. But no one can dictate how I live."

"Except his paint," Violante said mockingly. "He does not sleep, he paints. He does not eat, he paints. He does not think, he paints. He does not breathe, he paints. He does not live, he paints. He . . ."

I interrupted harshly, "To paint is to live."

"Your colors are your blood and breath and bone and everything else, when it truly matters, is nothing, less than nothing. I will not come back."

"Where will you go?" I had never seen Violante so determined.

"Where I will not be a servant!" She resumed her packing, frantically now, as if it took all her courage and energy. "Where I will not share."

"Violante, you know that I love you."

"But I am not your wife."

Mocenigo retired so I could speak more freely, but I did not want to marry, even her. It could hinder my brush, narrow my view, blunt my perspective. And I could not beg. Yet I blocked her way.

"Will you let me pass?"

I wavered, and then I did, although I felt grief-stricken.

Violante walked out looking as pale as death.

I waited a week for her to return and when she did not, I moved Cecilia into my own quarters. I still missed Violante desperately, but it was more evident that Cecilia was pregnant. She was willing to model for me again, but I decided that it would be bad for the child. I used Bella for my new Venus and she posed so naturally it was a relief not to be involved emotionally. Perhaps she was the ideal model, I reflected, she knew what her body was worth but she did not overvalue it. Even so, as I painted this Venus I put some of Violante into her. I did not touch the third bacchanal, for I could not paint Ariadne, that hurt too much.

I am grateful for the admirable wine and the roasted fowl and the luscious grapes that Orazio brings me, for these memories have exhausted me. As he sets them on the table before me, and I see Cecilia in his graceful movements, he has news. "I met Pomponio below. On the dock. He has arranged with the prior and his physician to attend you tomorrow morning. He said that you agreed to whatever time he set."

That is not precisely as I remember it, but I nod: I will have more energy in the morning.

Orazio must have sensed my concern with this medical examination, for he adds, "I will also have your personal physician in attendance. Papa, you are not a mean or vulgar work to be viewed by a quack."

"Thank you, Son. Does the plague grow worse?"

"No one seems to know. When do you expect to finish your *Pietà*?"

"When God wills. Some of my paintings took many years. I spent over six on the *Pesaro Madonna,* almost four on *Bacchus and Ariadne,* and the battle of Cadore was not put into the Great Hall for more than twenty years."

Neither of us says what is on our minds: I no longer possess the luxury of time. I ask Orazio to excuse me, I would like to nap. But after he departs, I rush through my memories as if I may not have another opportunity to relive some of the most precious days of my life.

I CAN ONLY DO

I CAN ONLY DO

what I have done

Will I do the next one
I cannot tell

I only know
I trust myself

And that is most
of doing

Stymean Karlen

POMPONIO WAS BORN just as I was warned by the Council to finish the battle scene for the Great Hall. Their tone was threatening, but many of my commissions were unfinished, and so, while I was upset by their tone, I was too pleased with the birth of my son to allow anything else to capture my attention. I had resented Cecilia's pregnancy, feeling trapped by this situation and blaming her for Violante's departure, but with the arrival of a boy I felt better. I decided he would be a painter, as the Bellinis had become the artistic heirs to their father.

Cecilia assured me that he resembled me closely. I felt this was her effort to prove that he was mine, but whatever doubts I had about that were almost gone. I had no evidence that there had been anybody else.

Mocenigo was depressed by Violante's flight, but my brother seemed relieved, as if an obstacle to his plans had been removed.

One thing did sadden me more than the loss of Violante. Mama died soon after she returned to Cadore and did not know of my son. But Papa was proud of him, and after a proper period of mourning for Mama, he told me that I should wed Cecilia, that it was important for the child's sake.

I put that off. Although I continued to enjoy her amorously, I still suspected that she had contrived to create her pregnancy. Once she was installed in my quarters she became a natural housekeeper. She no longer wanted to pose for me, saying that it was unseemly for the mother of my son, and she devoted herself to her household duties with industry and passion while Bella became my main model. Cecilia cooked cleverly, she was fanatical about cleanliness, and meticulous about her own person. If anything, she was too attached to me; I felt that she ate with my mouth; slept with my eyes; and moved with my desires; while I wished that she displayed some of the independence that Violante had expressed.

I was playing with Pomponio in his crib, caressing his tiny fingers and hoping they would become a painter's, when I was called to my door. A messenger was there from the Council with orders to deliver into my hands a copy of a resolution passed by them. I read: "This remonstrance has been passed on the 11th of August 1522, calling on the painter, Tiziano Vecellio, to finish the canvas fourth from the door in the Hall of the Great Council before the 30th of next June, under pain of losing the broker's patent and all the advances made by the Salt Office."

Shocked and alarmed, for with the Council's resolution in my own hands I was bound under the circumstances to obey, I decided to ask Navagero to help me in this awkward situation. *The Pesaro Madonna* and the *Bacchus and Ariadne* were still unfinished and I was having trouble delaying Jacopo Pesaro and Alfonso d'Este, and I wanted to avoid any further difficulties. But the patrician, who had been abroad as an ambassador for the Republic, was not sympathetic as he used to be and as I expected.

He paced up and down the drawing room of his palazzo where two of my pictures hung and he stated, "You enjoy an excellent appointment under the Signoria of Venice, but many have come to feel that you abuse it."

"My lord, I paint what I can. But I do want to serve the state."

"Some doubt that. After you finished your portrait of our new Doge, Grimani, members of the Council discovered that you have not done any work on the Doge's palace in years despite your many promises."

"I offered to finish Bellini's painting of Pope Alexander III and the Emperor Frederick Barbarossa. It should be done before I paint the battle scene. My lord, it is on the opposite wall and they should not clash."

"Do so. No one will oppose you."

"Then, my lord, the Bellini painting will be the work required of me?"

Navagero said sternly, "Yes. But what about your own battle scene?"

"Bellini's is much greater in scope, my lord. It should be done first."

"That is not the way you have worked for the duke of Ferrara."

"My lord, the old man's work has the most felicitous location in the Hall."

I could not tell whether Navagero truly accepted my reasons but a few days later the Council ordered me to finish immediately the recognition of Pope Alexander or they would withdraw my petition. I felt I had won a victory and I applied myself to Bellini's grand canvas. The theme of this picture was supposed to be the sight of the Emperor Frederick Barbarossa kissing the Pope's toe in San Marco but while I painted this dutifully, I put my passion into the portraits of the Venetian Senators supporting Alexander III. Although this event had happened over three hundred years ago, I painted the Senators in the likeness of Aurelio, Bembo, Navagero, Donato, Grimani, Pesaro, Gritti, and Barbarigo. I also made other changes in Bellini's design as I put my other commissions aside, for I sensed that these portraits would arouse the most interest and praise.

I was trying to appease the duke of Ferrara about the continuing delays on his *Bacchus and Ariadne* when Orazio was born a year later. Cecilia had a harder pregnancy, although we had deliberately had this child, and the doctor warned her that another pregnancy might be risky. I was delighted with this son. He looked like his mother, fair and delicate, and he was more cheerful than Pomponio, who cried constantly.

This reminded me of Alsonso's frequent complaints. The Council was pleased with the assurance and style I had added to Bellini's battle canvas, and the members who were in the work were flattered, as if I had glorified them, and now they accepted my word that I would do my own work soon, but Alfonso did not trust anything that I said about his *poesia*.

He wrote me irately, "I am much displeased with your lack of effort on my behalf. Years have passed without delivery of my

Bacchus and Ariadne. If you do not finish it soon, you will suffer severely."

I was not a subject of the duke's and I did not think he would dare to touch me now, too many important patrons desired my work. Thus, I was indignant when Tebaldi came to my bottega without notifying me to examine what I had done on Alfonso's *poesia.* When he saw that most of the space on the canvas was blank, that only the chariot drawn by the leopards and two figures were completed, and the rest, including the landscape, was not even begun, he was astonished and outraged.

I could not tell the agent that since Violante had left me the nature of Ariadne had evaded me; no one else satisfied me as the model for the wistful goddess. And that I was distracted by the birth of my two sons and had taken time away from my work to be with them. With my brother and my cousin in my studio, my family feeling had grown. Since neither of them displayed sufficient ability to succeed me, I visualized Pomponio and Orazio becoming another Gentile and Giovanni Bellini.

Tebaldi's exasperation grew as he stared at the nearly empty canvas and he exclaimed, "If you offend my lord, you offend many others. He is tied by blood and sword to Mantua and Gonzaga and Rome. One of these days he will lose patience with you and translate his anger into action. You will lose many of your princely patrons and suffer in Venice, too."

I knew this was not an idle threat, and so to hide my own irritation, I replied, "It was the work for the Republic that has delayed me."

"Then come to Ferrara and finish it there."

"Signore, I cannot undertake that journey now."

"Why not?" Tebaldi looked furious enough to attack me.

"I have better models in Venice. There are no good models in Ferrara. And it is too difficult to bring them with me." Tebaldi scowled and his hand went menacingly to the sword at his side and I added, "Besides, since, as you say, some ill feeling has risen, the duke will have to give me an assurance of safe-conduct before I visit Ferrara."

"It will be given. How long will it take to finish this *poesia?*"

"A few weeks. Once I get down to it."

He muttered, "The ingratitude of painters. My lord would have been better served by Leonardo or Michelangelo, if they only had had the sense to work for him," and he departed still disgusted with my continual delays.

* * *

Now, however, I felt I had no more time. I put everything else aside to concentrate on the completion of this bacchanal. The main problem remained Ariadne, although Bacchus was in the center of my design, and I painted Violante as I remembered her. I could always depend on my imagination when I needed it and I dressed her in a vivid blue robe, a Titian blue, I thought joyfully, with one shoulder exposed, only a red scarf over it, a Violante red, I told myself. Her flesh grew ample and full as I preferred her and I felt splendid and when it came time to paint the landscape I knew what I wanted. It was as if my fingers exhaled the perfume of love and the most beautiful object in the world was the human body. This *poesia* became one of my most romantic paintings.

I was giving the satyrs and nymphs my sense of impetuous motion to express the spirit of the *poesia* when Tebaldi charged into my studio with a new message from Alfonso. "My Lord must see the work before it is finished. Or he will not accept it. He wants to be certain that it fits the other bacchanals in the *camerino* as he instructed you."

I found excuse after excuse, but Tebaldi would not accept any of them.

Finally I said, "I will need a few more months."

"You already have had three years. He desires the picture, not your promises. Deliver the *poesia* now or do not deliver it at all."

I said reluctantly, "I will do my best to bring it early next year."

"That is too late." But when he saw my dismay, he added, "However, as a gesture of friendship the duke invites you to spend Christmas in Ferrara. Bring the work with you so that you can finish it on the spot."

I was resolved to spend Christmas with my children but I said, "I am honored, but I am overwhelmed with orders and cannot finish them unless I use this time."

"If you deliver the work by January, you will be asked to repaint *The Feast of the Gods.* Otherwise, it will be given to another artist."

That was bait I could not refuse and I said, "Signore, January is fine."

"Leave it unfinished, so the duke can complete it to suit himself."

So it was agreed.

When January came, while I was given a safe-conduct in Ferrara as I had requested, for Alfonso was notorious for his hot, hasty temper, as a token of my good faith I sent the unfinished canvas in advance of my person. It left Venice by water for Francolino, the port of Ferrara, and then a porter carried it on his back to the city. But I decided not to go directly. I felt that my chief weapon was to delay and to show how other patrons desired my brush. So I traveled to Ferrara by way of Mantua.

Isabella d'Este, the dowager duchess of Mantua, and the sister of Alfonso, had a famed art collection and the duke was jealous of it and was using me in his effort to excel it. Then her son and his nephew, now the marquis of Mantua, wanted my work, too. I told him that I would be happy to paint for him, but that first I must honor my promises to his uncle.

So he wrote the following to Alfonso and asked me to deliver it. I knew the contents, for he asked me to read them before he sealed them.

"Most Illustrious Uncle: When I asked Titian to execute certain works for me, he declared himself unable to serve me at present because of his promise to do certain things for Your Excellency. For this reason I send him to attend you. But I beg he may be sent back to expedite the work I have on hand for him. In this you will have done me a singular pleasure."

I felt this was the best safe-conduct of all and when I arrived in Ferrara, after a leisurely journey from Mantua, the marquis' letter aroused Alfonso as I had hoped. He told me that *Bacchus and Ariadne* was already in place, that only a little had to be done to complete it, and he led me to it impatiently. I thought it was sensible to keep these fine lords waiting, the longer they waited the more eager they became for my work, and I followed him slowly. This added to his impatience and at the *camerino,* where all my *poesias* were in place, he snapped, "Why do you dally?"

"Your Excellency, I am enchanted with your costume. The black velvet trimmed with rose will make a stunning portrait."

He was pleased, but he retorted gruffly, "Later! Now I must show you what must still be done on the third mythology."

His alterations were minor, simply a need to assert his authority.

After I agreed to them, most of them could be done simply with my thumb, he stated, "You were wise to follow my advice and return to the model you used in *The Worship of Venus.* She is the most beautiful and memorable part of the *poesia.* Raphael could not have done any better."

"My lord, what about *The Feast of the Gods?* It is even less appropriate now."

"We will make adjustments. Especially with the infant Bacchus."

When I began to repaint Bellini's *poesia* so that it would harmonize with my taste and Alfonso's, which had become mine, I remembered my promise to my first master. So while I sought to give it the animation and vitality of my bacchanals, I also struggled to be faithful to his contours and conception. It became one of the most difficult assignments I had ever attempted. I did not want to betray the old man, but I did not want to betray myself either. Yet it was also one of the loveliest works that Bellini had painted, and I told myself that I was merely bringing it to completion. I took great pains to execute it in my best manner.

My biggest problem became the question of style. In the years that had passed since Bellini had done this *poesia* many changes had occurred in me.

I tried to make his figures less static, to give them the tempo of a dance, although I preserved as much as possible the shape of his figures. I also strengthened his landscape and made it more dramatic, to fit my three bacchanals. Other details engrossed me, too, the lowering of a neckline to reveal a lovely breast, adding drapery to a nymph to give her more allure, altering some legs and arms, particularly to imply more motion and abandon. But Bellini's view was essentially pastoral while mine was pagan and I could not add what I felt it needed most to fit my bacchanals: exuberance and joy and a great passion for life.

I finished my work on *The Feast of the Gods,* feeling that I could not do enough to satisfy myself, that whatever I did, at the best it was a compromise. While his *poesia* could be admired for itself, it was still not appropriate to my poems. The differences were insoluble. He had given birth to his mythology in the manner of the fifteenth century and I was painting in the sixteenth. And my vision was poetic and his was not.

Alfonso did not thank me. He could not give me that satisfaction, I thought, but he ordered me to paint a portrait of him and his new wife.

I felt I knew him accurately now and I labored to give his likeness the power it possessed. He was approaching forty, his hair and beard were turning gray, but the severity of his features still dominated his presence. He wore a dark-red costume with gold trimmed sleeves and a darker cloak lined with sable. His left hand rested regally on his sword, while his right hand fondled his beloved cannon. So I was able to stress his energy.

His former mistress and present wife, Laura Dianti, was less exciting for me, but he was far more interested in her portrait than the one I had done of Lucrezia. She was resplendent in brilliant colors as he clothed her in light yellow, ultramarine, white, lavender, blue, and striped green. It was more of a challenge to my technique than to my nature, but I completed a harmonious likeness that I felt he should desire to fondle.

I was curious about what had happened to my portrait of Lucrezia, but when I mentioned that to Tebaldi, who had come to pay me, he changed the subject. He said, "The duke is interested in your St. Sebastian."

"Thank you, Signore. I will be happy to consider the offer."

"Good. Meanwhile, my lord is willing to employ you as his artist."

It was an offer most artists would accept eagerly but I was determined not to become a court painter, or to depend on one patron, even Venice. I said, "I am honored, but you must excuse me at the moment. I have so many commissions to finish I could not attend him for several years."

Since I knew Alfonso hated to wait, I felt I had refused him wisely. Tebaldi replied, "You do procrastinate. It is a difficulty."

He gave me Florentine florins instead of the Venetian ducats that I preferred, to show me that Ferrara was independent of the Republic now, but the gold bags were perfumed as a mark of the duke's royal favor.

As I returned to the *Pesaro Madonna,* I was still speculating why my portrait of Lucrezia had vanished—for I felt it was one of the best I had done—when Jacopo Pesaro ordered me to paint the Borgia coat-of-arms on his triumphant battle flag. I accepted his instructions willingly and thanked the bishop, whose features had become lined, leathery, and old while waiting for me to finish his family's altarpiece, for his patience.

I was determined that this votive picture be a fitting companion to *The Assumption,* for it was to be placed in the Frari church, too. And only now had I found the approach I desired. Instead of the design suggesting serenity, as was the custom, I was stressing movement; this was a dramatic scene and should be seen as such. I also painted the many characters as they really were and my colors as vividly as I had in my bacchanals.

I was starting a new conception of a nude, a Diana bathing with her nymphs, with Bella as the model, when Cecilia rushed into my studio. I had put the *Pesaro Madonna* aside so that I could return to it in a few weeks refreshed and I was shocked by her intrusion.

My orders were strict that I must not be interrupted when working and my anger grew. I was searching for a beauty that would surpass anything I had done so far, and if she would not pose for me, she must not interfere with someone who did.

"What is wrong?" I asked, pausing irritably and impatiently.

"Am I so ugly?" she demanded of me.

"You are young, graceful, and still very pretty."

"In spite of the children I have given you?"

At this moment I wished I had chosen Bella as my companion. She lay on her couch uneasily, but until Cecilia had entered she had been the perfect model. Bella had become first among the courtesans in Venice because of my paintings of her, and I was tempted to try her charms, too, but I did not like to share and I was afraid that it would ruin her as a model.

Cecilia moved closer, added abruptly, "The children need a father."

I replied curtly, "They have a father."

"Not a true one."

She was starting to sound like Violante in her worst moments and she was distracting me from a vital commission for the marquis of Mantua. He praised me effusively to everyone and he wanted a *poesia* of splendid nudes, for which he had promised me a benefice for my first born.

"Tiziano, your first duty is to your family and sometimes you observe that, you give your brother and your cousin every chance to advance themselves, although their gifts are small, but not your own children."

I dismissed Bella, not wanting to be embarrassed any further by Cecilia's hysteria, and then, turning away from my easel, which I hated doing, I asked her when we were alone, "What is truly troubling you?"

"The position of your sons! Now they are just two small bastards!"

There were tears in her eyes and I saw that it had taken great courage for her to confront me. I replied, "That is complicated."

"To give them your name? It is the simplest thing in the world."

"Cecilia, I have tried to please you. I bought you a comfortable new bed, a costly carpet for your feet, an abundance of linen, a large toilet table. You refused to use any of the things my previous house-keeper used."

"She was extravagant," Cecilia said contemptuously. "Perhaps she was a good model, but that was all. Now we have better plates and crockery. I have ended waste in your household. Your account books show a profit. I would wash your feet if you asked me. I buy whatever vegetables and fruit you want, strong herbs for your omelettes, and spices I make myself."

"You are an excellent cook. As good as my mother was."

"We are from Cadore. But you do not appreciate that."

I thought that the shy, reserved girl I had loved was no more, and yet in some ways she had not altered much. She still took very good care of her person, as if she knew that was the bond that held us together. Most Venetian women dyed their hair yellow, or wore false hair, but Cecilia's was a natural yellow and as soft as silk. Her complexion was still fair and despite the two births, her figure was slender and enticing. She did please me in bed, although occasionally I missed Violante's passion.

"If you do not marry me, I do not know what will become of our children."

"They will become artists, as I am, and inherit my bottega."

"Without your name. And suppose I have a daughter next?"

I said sharply, "You are not supposed to have any more children."

She sobbed, "But I am still young. When you love me, it fertilizes me. We should have as many offspring as God wills. But a daughter, without your name, will never find a proper husband. Even in a city as large as Venice, our situation cannot be concealed. And you are a public figure."

But Cecilia was not in my paintbrush as Violante had been and I grew irascible and shouted, "I will marry whom and when I please! Do not interrupt me again or I will . . ." I halted, not sure what to threaten.

". . . throw me out. The mother of your children."

I knew that was not likely and so did she. I did possess a strong sense of family and she was part of it now, whether we were married or not. I said, "We will talk about it later. When I am not working."

I turned back to my *poesia* of Diana, but now I could not work, for while she retired from the studio as I ordered, she looked so distraught I was troubled. Yet nothing more was said the next few months.

The following year, 1525, I finished the *Pesaro Madonna* as I wanted, which gratified me. Finally, I felt, this altarpiece was worthy of being placed by the side of *The Assumption of the Virgin*. Despite the subject's solemnity, this votive work had become my rhapsodic expression of devotion to the Madonna. I also completed my *Diana* in a new manner. She sat at the edge of her bath, and her beautiful bare breasts and fine long legs were those of Bella, and I wondered if she was as desirable as she looked.

But one night, when it came time to go to bed and I caressed Cecilia in the hope of arousing her, she recoiled from me unexpectedly.

Once again I found myself asking, "What is wrong?"

"I cannot, Tiziano," she said abruptly. "I am pregnant."

I exclaimed, "But the doctor warned you that was risky."

"What do they know?" she said disdainfully. "I am not your madonna."

I was furious; I felt that she had become pregnant again in the hope of convincing me to marry her. Then, instead of discarding her nightgown as I requested, she put on a heavy robe. Perversely, I was certain, as she withdrew from me to the opposite side of our large bed.

She said soberly, "I must protect the child. I must not catch cold."

I laughed incredulously and retorted, "You are many months away."

"Not that many."

But as I touched her as passionately as I did my oils, she discarded her robe and nightgown and pulled me close with a physical response that became rapture. Toward midnight, when we fell asleep, lying naked, we held on to each other as if we would never let go. Yet near sunrise she awoke and began to shiver uncontrollably. I threw two woolen blankets over her but she did not stop. She whimpered that she had a chill, but the room was warm and I thought that she was shivering from fear.

I reached out to console her and tears of self-pity wet her cheeks. She pulled away from me and sobbed, "It would damage our child. I am cold and the moon has changed and I can feel it moving within me."

I did not agree with her, but while I waited for this child to be born I did not touch her. She lay apart from me in bed and I was too proud to pursue her. Often I felt her shivering but I attributed it to fear and I absorbed myself in my commissions and I had many. With the placing of the *Pesaro Madonna* in the Frari church and my new *Diana* at the court of Mantua, I needed to toil twenty-four hours each day to satisfy the requests for my brush. I was busier than I had ever been.

My mind was not on Cecilia the morning Mocenigo stood in the doorway of my studio and said agitatedly, "Master, the signora has fallen ill."

"Is it her pregnancy? She was told that another one would be difficult."

"I do not think so. The symptoms are different. Could you attend her? I think it is serious and I have called a physician."

By the time I reached her side the doctor had arrived. Cecilia was paler than I had ever seen her and her belly was swollen and yet I felt that her time had not come, for she was shivering constantly.

Doctor Carlo Braccio was a short, stout middle-aged graduate of the University of Bologna, whose round features were fat from excessive eating. His first examination was for the plague and when he saw that there were no buboes or other plague spots or sudden fever, he sighed with relief and said, "It is not the pestilence. God be praised."

I asked anxiously, "Is she about to give birth?"

He felt her stomach and replied, "No. There is not any movement yet."

Cecilia mumbled, "Doctor, will you pray for me? Only Jesus can save."

He did but her shivering only grew worse and he declared, "You have a tertian fever and it has inflamed your blood. I must bleed you."

After he bled her copiously, he also purged her.

I thought that he was weakening her and said, "Doctor, what about her pregnancy? We do not want to lose the child."

"It will come when it will come," he concluded with medical solemnity. "The moon is in the wrong phase. We must pick three sage leaves before sunrise and say three Paternosters and three Hail Marys in honor of God and the Holy Trinity. Our patient is handsomely formed."

But her shivering resumed and she began to tremble, too.

He said, "If milk exudes from the right nipple, it will be a boy."

That seemed to help her, as if he was assuring her that she would not lose her child, and when I took her hand and sat by her side she stopped trembling and fell asleep. She was a little better the next day. Her shivering was gone, too, her pallor was less, and she was more composed.

I visited her daily and as the pangs of labor began, I hired the same midwife I had used for Pomponio and Orazio. Signora Serlio had delivered my sons skillfully, as she had many other children, including those of patricians, and she had been recommended to me by Navagero and Barbarigo.

When the moment of anticipated birth arrived, she pared her

nails, anointed her bare arms and hands with oil, crossed herself, lifted the modesty cloth, and poured more oil into the birth passage to make it easy of movement. She inserted her fingers while Cecilia writhed and cried out in pain and I turned away, unable to look, to endure her anguish, and gradually—it seemed an infinity to me, but it must have been just a few moments—she slipped the infant out of the womb and exclaimed, "It is a girl! Now the master will have someone worthy of his brush!"

I felt that our difficulties were over, for I trusted Signora Serlio.

Cecilia seemed pleased, too, that we had a girl and that she was alert and healthy. She whispered that we must call her after her mother, Lavinia. I agreed and that appeared to make her happy.

But she did not get out of bed in a few days as she had with our sons. Instead, when I said nothing about marriage, her chill returned. Within a week her speech was almost inaudible, her hands and feet were cold and clammy, and her pulse was dangerously erratic and weak.

I called Doctor Braccio and Signora Serlio and he stated that Cecilia's illness was caused by a too-abrupt delivery of the infant; she retorted that he should not have bled and purged the patient while she was pregnant, that this had weakened her and given her a chill. Neither of them was able to cure her and so I dismissed them and tried to comfort her. I felt that her worse affliction was her melancholy. I did not trust any of the doctors I knew—Braccio was the best of a bad lot—and I believed that her recovery depended on me. When she saw me bending over her, she sobbed, "Tiziano, I would leave this world willingly if not for my children. Or enter a convent as penance for my sins."

"You have not sinned," I denied strongly.

"I am being punished for having three illegitimate children."

"Many people have done so. Especially popes and princes."

"We are humbler folk. Our children will suffer for it."

Her pain and terror grew and I said, "I will call another doctor."

"No, he cannot help me. Please, call our priest."

"Why?" I still felt her complaint was melancholy but she looked worse.

"I am dying. Would you deny me the consolation of the church, too?"

I told Mocenigo to summon Father Novato, our priest, who lived nearby. He came promptly and at the sight of the tall, thin, elderly priest, she said faintly, "Father, I am expiring. I have sinned. I love my children dearly but their father will not acknowledge them."

He asked me sternly, "Tiziano Vecellio, is that true?"

"She is overwrought. Father, is she dying?"

"I cannot tell. But her soul is in sore straits. I cannot deny her the last sacraments. Her condition may be more serious than we realize."

As he prepared to administer them, Cecilia moaned, "He does not love me. Or his children. And that is the most terrible sin of all."

"That is not true!" I shouted loudly. Her accusation about my children was more than I could bear. "Father, I will marry her! Please, will you marry us?" Now that this was out I did not feel as bad as I thought I would. "If our situation has been irregular, it can be remedied now."

She said weakly, "I do not have the strength. I am at death's door."

I believed her. I could barely detect her pulse and she was very cold and the priest was praying for her soul and I felt guilty.

She murmured, "I listened to the devil's voice, I exposed myself in a moment of passion when I should have given allegiance to God."

Perhaps she was right, I thought, I had brought her to this state. I implored, "Cecilia, you must find the strength. For our children's sake."

I took her limp hand, wishing it were not so clammy, kissing it as I did, and although I was not certain that Cecilia would live to hear the words she treasured so much, Father Novati made us man and wife.

The next day she began to improve. She refused to take any medicine or to be bled or purged but asked for wine, fruit, and broth from a fat capon. I satisfied her requests promptly and my concern appeared to help her, too.

After a week she was able to eat veal and I told myself that in spite of her imperfections I would settle for one full year with her. She stopped shivering from her chill and said I must return to my painting.

The morning she rose out of bed I took her into my studio to show her what I was working on. It was a Madonna and Child in the style that I had used for *The Assumption of the Virgin* and she recognized herself in it and smiled for the first time in months and was pleased that I had used her. She whispered, "Our children will be proud of that some day."

"Are you, Cecilia?"

"You have made me happy. I am sorry that I upset you, but I was afraid that I was going to die and I had to call the priest."

"It was the natural thing to do."

"I called him for the children's sake."

I was not sure what to believe, but she had become so pleasant and pretty and passionate again since I had married her that I decided it was foolish to doubt her any more Then the birth of my daughter was so precious to me—I loved Lavinia from the instant I saw her—that if she was the price I had paid for my marriage she was worth it. And I was glad that I had sons to carry on my name and my work.

This put new strength into my hands and I was prepared to paint the world. I was just thirty-five and there was still so much to achieve.

With the responsibilities of a growing family, I was resolved to collect all the money owed me, and not to deliver any more *poesias* to the marquis of Mantua until he obtained the benefice for Pomponio that he had promised me. My older son was going on four and the sooner I provided for him the better. Cecilia was modeling for me again, but not for my nudes. She said that as the wife of Tiziano Vecellio it was not fitting, that it was appropriate that she pose only for my madonnas.

And so it was. And I felt like a triumphant eye.

What do I remember?

What does one remember?

I wonder whether I can tell Pomponio the truth and can he bear it.

I pick up what I had written just for myself shortly after I had married Cecilia. *May God grant my sons grace so that they will grow up good men.* But Pomponio sold all the paintbrushes that I gave him.

THE MOMENT CAME TO YOU

THE MOMENT CAME TO YOU

And you felt so unloved
And you felt so untouched
That you could not feel yourself

Or feel why you were
And the moment would not pass

You opened the window full
And you shouted to the full moon
I love you   I love you
And the echo came back full
I love you   I love you

Then you put on your clothes
And it made a person of you

Stymean Karlen

I FEEL there is no turning back. A delegation waits to examine me in my studio. I have been up much of the night reliving my memories before it is too late and I am tired and sleepy but I am determined not to show any sign of weakness. This is essential and I dress for the occasion in a black velvet robe trimmed with gray fur, and put on a red skullcap. I also wear the gold chain that signifies that Charles V made me Count Palatine and a Knight of the Golden Spur, titles that give my sons the rank of nobility. I hope this will please Pomponio, who yearns to be a Venetian patrician, an aristocratic position so far denied him by the Republic.

The group is led by the forty-year-old prior, Dino Algi, who is robust, ruddy faced, and well fed. He is the Franciscan brother in charge of the commission for the *Pietà* and he introduces his doctor, Leo Certaldo.

I know this physician, having met him in the palazzos of patricians who fancy his physic. He is an authority on old age, an elderly, scrawny, crow-faced believer in astrology, rhetoric, alchemy, and devout prayer.

Pomponio stands behind him, eager for the examination to begin, and I am relieved to see Orazio and that he is accompanied by Doctor Bruno Gusti.

My personal physician is in his fifties, tall and lean, with fine features. He is a graduate of the University of Padua; he studied medicine under Vesalius; now he lectures in his place. He has a calm manner and I respect his intuition and common sense and that he depends largely on nature and the patient's state of mind.

But all of them look so serious I feel I am brought before the Inquisition for examination. Even Gusti is grave, Pomponio is uneasy, Orazio is uncomfortable, Certaldo is officious, while the prior is grim.

He says, "You have failed to deliver the *Pietà* as you promised."

I do not ask any of them to sit down, but stand apart from all of them, as if they were enemies, and I reply, "The picture will be finished."

"When? It is two years since you began. And you delay and delay."

I retort defiantly, "There are no delays. It takes time to perfect it."

Pomponio intrudes. "Begging your pardon, Father Algi, but first you informed me that you wished to ascertain my father's health."

"Yes." Algi says to me, "I trust you do not mind my concern."

"Why should I? Years ago your predecessor worried about the delivery of *The Assumption* and *The Pesaro Madonna* and that was unnecessary."

"But time is a factor now."

"And age," I said.

Pomponio says, "Papa, do not be sensitive. It is a necessary precaution."

I feel as if I am to be disemboweled but I try to stand as straight as I can. I shiver—not from cold or fear, I tell myself—but from rage that I should have allowed this to happen. And yet, my mind runs on, if it will bridge the gulf between me and Pomponio it will be worth it.

Certaldo examines me first, as a courtesy to the prior. He does not touch me, his learning forbids that, and he says respectfully to me, "I am honored to serve such an excellent artist," viewing me from a distance.

In middle age I acquired an ample paunch but my large stature gave me presence and assurance, but now I am shrunken, I have no excess weight, and I am unhappy that the robe I filled once with dignity and grandeur is loose on me and my favorite skullcap covers increasing baldness.

Certaldo says pompously, "I see no sign of the plague."

"Good," says the prior. "That is one thing we do not have to fear."

"But as Aristole says, 'Old age is the pathway to death.' "

Orazio interrupts sharply, "Doctor Certaldo, that is not why you were brought here. Michelangelo lived as long as my father."

"I am not examining him."

The Florentine would not have allowed it, I think irately, but I say, "Should I disrobe?" I do not want to do so, but I prefer accuracy.

"It is not necessary." Certaldo adjusts his scarlet robe so that it fits him better and shambles about me with an awkward gait and informs the anxious prior, while Pomponio regards him cynically, "The patient is much troubled with age. No one lives this long who could not die at midnight. He cannot bring back youth. Maestro, do you pray?"

"Often. When I am on my knees, my blood seems to be in my head."

"Fine. Say a Paternoster and a Hail Mary and eat a sage leaf and you will keep the devil away. What other complaints have you?"

Pomponio says severely, "Doctor, that is for you to find out."

He looks to Gusti for assurance, but the latter's face is impassive, while Algi nods impatiently for him to continue. He announces, "God is everywhere. Coitus in advanced age damages the body and this patient has reached a great old age and so his future is filled with uncertainty."

Pomponio says irritably, "We know that. Is anything else wrong?"

"It is difficult to know. His stars are unfavorable. He is fortunate to have lived so long. This is most rare."

Algi asks, "Do you think he will be able to finish my altarpiece?"

"I will give him powdered stones, potable gold. That will sustain him. I am skilled in alchemy and I have studied Aristole and Galen thoroughly."

"But can he see? There are rumors that his vision is impaired."

"Prior, I am not wearing my spectacles. I cannot tell."

I state, "Father Algi, I can detect the smallest objects."

"Your colors are not distinct as they used to be. They are too dark."

"Because the tomb is. That is a somber situation, as dark as death."

Certaldo asks, "Maestro, which eye pains you? If it is the right, take the right eye of a frog, lay it in a piece of cloth and hang it about your neck, it will cure the right eye if it is inflamed or bleared. If the left eye is grieved, do the same with the left eye of this frog."

I know now that I have to be rid of this doctor or he will destroy me with his delusions. I say abruptly, "This examination is finished!"

Pomponio says passionately, "You promised to be examined thoroughly."

"Certaldo has made his verdict clear. All I suffer from is old age. It is a common affliction. But advanced age has not dulled my pigments."

Pomponio turns to Gusti, asks him, "What do you think? You know my father's health better than anyone else. Can he finish the *Pietà?*"

"It is for him to decide. Only he will know when it is done."

"Papa, you trust Doctor Gusti. May he examine you now?"

"If it will make you happy."

Gusti feels my pulse, examines my chest, asks me to read at a short and a long distance, whispers to see if I can hear him, and when I satisfy him that I can do all these things, although I have to strain to hear him and I am grateful that he puts the book in the strong sunlight where I can see it best, he inquires if I sleep soundly or toss and dream much.

Orazio says, "Papa sleeps very little these nights. He is so busy with his memories he even sacrifices his rest to them. Doctor, it worries me."

I reply, "I am a little tired today but I will rest tonight."

Pomponio asks, "Doctor, how do you find him?"

Gusti is so grave that I am anxious, too. He says, "No one in his nineties can expect to be in perfect health or to do what they once did."

"I am closer to eighty-six," I remind him. "As far as I remember."

"Even at that extremity of age you are remarkable. But your sons are right to be concerned about the way you labor. Indomitable old men are still more vulnerable to afflictions than young ones. You must be more moderate in what you do. You can no longer work all night without sleep or paint until your hands are numb. And you must not take any matter to heart and grieve about it. All that my physic and my master, Vesalius, taught me is that worry can harm you more than anything else."

Algi has become restless and I feel that Pomponio is disappointed but Orazio seems relieved while Certaldo mutters that Gusti's views are heretical, but the prior ignores him, asking, "When will you finish it?"

"In a week, a month. As long as is necessary. It is impossible to say."

"Suppose you become ill? Die? No, we cannot give you any more time."

I say with a sudden fury, "I am not going to fail. I cannot fail."

"Everyone can fail. Even a Titian. We will not accept this picture if it is by someone else's hand. It looks finished to me."

Orazio has put the *Pietà* on three easels because of its size and he is offended. "Prior, as Doctor Gusti said, only Titian can decide that. As he did with *The Assumption* and the *Pesaro Madonna*."

"That was a long time ago and he was a young man. I will submit the painting to the inspection of judicious men. Or I will not accept it."

"What about our compact?" I ask with alarm. "You agreed . . ."

". . . To bury you in the Frari if you delivered it completed by your own hand. But our patience is not eternal and the plague spreads daily."

I question Doctor Gusti. "Do you think the pestilence is a danger?"

"Yes. It has slain a quarter of the population since last summer, and it is always worse now, in August. You would be wise to retire to your villa in the mountains of Cortina and finish your painting later."

Algi's dour expression indicates that he cannot wait that long and in this I agree. And there are other reasons for staying in Venice. I reply, "I will leave after I finish the *Pietà* and complete several other duties."

Gusti warns, "Then it may be too late. Many have fled already."

But I must visit my bottega to investigate Pomponio's charges. So while I trust Gusti, I think that he may exaggerate out of his concern for me, and I say, "Doctor, you walk the streets."

"Not willingly. I came only at the behest of Orazio."

"I will go to Cortina after I visit my workshop."

Prior Algi asks, "What about my altarpiece? May I take it now?"

"No. This is not the final painting."

He turns to Certaldo and Pomponio, feeling they will listen, and speaks angrily. "When the artist offered to paint a Pietà for the Franciscan brothers of the Frari church in return for burial in our chapel, I had to persuade them to accept his proposal. They knew his reputation for delay, for slowness, and they doubted he would keep his word and they were right."

I ask, "Father, will I be buried there whatever happens?"

"How can I promise? You do not keep yours. That offends many." He strides out, followed by Certaldo, without having looked at the *Pietà*.

Gusti declares, "Maestro, it is a noble work. So true to the spirit of Venice today. I never forgot the drawings your assistant did for the *Fabrica* of Vesalius and the help you gave him. The anatomist was very pleased with your interest. Your anatomical illustrations were marvelous."

Orazio says, "I thought the anatomical drawings were done by Calcar."

"Most of them were. But the best, including many of the human body, were drawn by your father. And he supervised Calcar's work."

When I see Orazio's surprise, I say, "I had to know more about anatomy."

"But you were already in your fifties and long acclaimed."

"I am still learning. And Vesalius' work fascinated me. He had one of the best minds I ever met. Doctor, would you like to accompany me to my workshop? You may see a picture you like."

"Later. I am needed elsewhere. More urgently than you needed me."

After a glass of wine and some fruit—I am living almost entirely on fruit this summer—I have the strength to start for my workshop. My sons accompany me. Pomponio is quiet, as if he is reflecting on what has happened, while Orazio takes the least populated alleys, stating that they will be less dangerous. I feel I am taking a last look at my beloved Venice and it becomes a grim one. Black crepe is on many doors and the dreaded red cross marking the presence of the plague, and no one is about. I recall that just a few years ago jubilation swept over the city when the fleet returned with news of its great victory over the Turks at Lepanto.

I was awakened at dusk by the sound of powder exploding. It was October 1572 and at first I thought Venice was being invaded. I had been napping, dreaming of a Diana I desired to paint, as if in the doing I would possess her, and I saw fireworks curving in brilliant colors across the sky. Citizens were parading through the city in an ecstasy of joy. By the time my gondola reached San Marco, the

Venetian captain, Giustiniani, was being borne in triumph to San Marco, while the Doge and Council marched there to hear a Te Deum. All the shops were closed and on many of them was chalked: "Closed for the death of Turks." Even the debtors' prison was broken open and the inmates were released to share in the general joy.

Now, at the Rialto, shops are shut again but the mood is somber. The stricken city is desolate and I ask Orazio, "Is it the same at San Marco?"

"Worse. Only mourners attend the services these days."

Pomponio declares, "You must have vital business at the workshop to disregard Gusti's warnings. He is one of the few people you heed."

"Is that why you have come with me?"

"I am here because it is a son's duty to be at the side of his father."

It does not sound like him and I do not believe him. Yet possibly, I tell myself, my efforts on his behalf may be reaching him after all.

"Papa, have you painted many Doges?"

"All that have lived during my lifetime. Gritti, Donato, Grimani, Lando, Venier, Grimani, some I have forgotten. This is no ordinary city. No matter where I have gone, I have always longed to return here. It is as if Venice rose miraculously from the bosom of the sea and the squares and the canals were arranged by a great artist to ravish the senses."

"Yet you have never painted it. Like Bellini and Carpaccio did."

"I do not have to be literal. Venice's lively spirit, vivid, abundant colors, luxuriant light and space are in most of my paintings."

Orazio adds warmly, "I see this in them often."

It is evident he prefers that I do not enter the workshop at San Canciano, but he follows me obediently, while Pomponio's curiosity is obvious. It is empty except for Palma Giovane, who supervises the work.

My small, dark, middle-aged assistant is a quiet, scholarly craftsman. He is amazed to see me; I have not been here for a long time.

Then the workshop is not what I expect. Without the bustle of the dozen assistants and apprentices I employ, it is like a tomb.

Giovane says somberly, "Maestro, it is the plague. One of the apprentices caught it and so I thought it best to keep everyone out for the time being."

I ask, "How is he?"

"He died in twenty-four hours. What brings you here, Maestro?"

"I hear that pictures are sold with my signature that I have not done."

"None that I know of. When you paint on ground previously covered, it is called yours, but any forgeries have been perpetrated behind my back."

I see Pomponio staring suspiciously at Orazio, who shakes his head No, to indicate he has said nothing to me, while Giovane looks bewildered, and I state, "I want to see what hangs in my name."

Giovane mutters, "This insults me," but he takes me about the workshop.

I find it difficult to discern some of the copies from my originals, my assistants have imitated my manner obsequiously and meticulously. But those I believe to be mine possess more force, life, enchantment. Then I am not certain. I stand before a *Venus and Cupid* that I do not remember. I do recall my *St. John the Baptist*; it is one of my most heroic figures, with a life-sized vitality I treasure. I am also pleased to see my *Allegory of Prudence*, one of my favorites. It is a painting of three heads over three wild animals: a portrait of myself in youth, in middle age, and in old age. No one can mistake who has done this painting. Then suddenly, I must sit down, overwhelmed with emotion and fatigue.

I am afraid I will never know whether Pomponio's charges are correct. Yet I feel I must take an inventory before it is too late. I think that Pomponio has exaggerated the situation in my bottega, that he must always attack me. But even if this is so, the why still evades me.

Orazio asks, "Papa, why did your brother leave your workshop?"

"When my father died in 1527, Francesco went back to run his lumber and grain business, and then painted mostly for his own amusement."

"Was it also because he knew he he could never equal your reputation?"

"It is possible. He was gifted but when he tried to imitate me his work lacked distinction. He would have been better with his own manner."

"I liked him. When he died in 1559, I missed him."

"I have lost many I cared for. It is one of the trials of old age."

Pomponio asks, "Is it not true it was Vecchio's kin, Violante, who was your favorite model? And you had the affection of a lover for her?"

So many years later I am still reluctant to discuss her, yet my sons know I had several mistresses after their mother died, although my sister, Orsa, took care of my household and raised the children, and also an illegitimate daughter who died at birth. I have not been a celibate and yet it is not easy to reply. I wonder if it is always this way between fathers and children as I answer, "Violante was a fine model. And dear to me. Before I met your mother. She was gone by the time you were born."

"Did you ever see her after she left? Francesco told me about her."

"Vecchio died the year after my brother left my studio and I attended his funeral. I heard that she had returned to him and I sat in the rear of the church and saw her in a front pew. But I could not approach her; I was deeply attached to your mother. I never saw Violante again."

"Then Mocenigo was murdered the next year," Pomponio remembers.

"That was another blow. I am still not sure why he was slain. But the worst blow of all was when you mother died the next year, in 1530."

"I was about eight. She seemed fine one day, and suddenly she was gone."

"She had a fever and a chill, then she was better—she had recovered from such attacks before and she was not yet thirty—and just as I was certain she was cured she died. None of the doctors knew what was wrong, but I felt it could have been the plague, although she had no spots. It was in Venice, as it has been so often in my life, and it was August."

Pomponio continues intensely, "Was she as pretty as I recall her?"

"Cecilia was one of the most attractive women I ever saw. Dainty, slender, with a heart-shaped face and a lovely fair complexion."

"I remember her yellow hair. Did she model for you?"

"For some of my madonnas."

"What about your Venuses?"

"I started one with her posing for it, but when she became pregnant I did not want to risk hurting her or the baby and so I stopped."

"Was that when she was carrying me?"

"Yes."

Pomponio is silent and Orazio is tearful, while Giovane is glum and preoccupied, still troubled about the possibility my work had been forged.

"After her death, my sister Orsa came to care for you and we moved to Biri Grande. I could not stand the sight of where your mother had lived. It was one of the worst times in my life. Her passing was so unexpected."

Pomponio asks, "Could it have been averted?"

"I thought so, but no doctor would admit that. I could not paint, although I had many vital commissions, and one of them, the altarpiece, *The Martyrdom of St. Peter Martyr*, was very dear to me."

Orazio says proudly, "Vasari wrote that it was your best work."

"There is no best work."

"It is permeated with anguish and sorrow."

"I thought that your mother had died unjustly, in a way a sacrifice."

Pomponio exclaims, "You thought that, too?"

So that is one of the things he holds against me, I think, but I nod and I want to reach out and embrace him, to cry out, I love you, I love you. But will he understand? I stand motionless, silent, waiting for something in him to indicate that I will not be repulsed.

He says, "I heard that you loved Violante more than my mother."

I did but that is not his business, I tell myself angrily. I say, "Pomponio, I have loved many things. My children, too."

"Then may I see your private account books?" His face breaks into a crooked, cynical grin, as if to say, Now you can prove your love. As I hesitate, he states, "Is that not the reason you brought us here?"

"I brought you here . . ." I pause. I cannot accuse him to his face of trying to cheat me or slander me. I have no proof. "I wanted your company."

"But not my trust."

"Pomponio, whatever I leave will be shared equally by you and Orazio. It is already decided. I beseech you, for the love I bear you, do not worry so. There will be enough for both of you. Be content with that."

He mutters, "No wonder there is so much talk about your love of money."

"It is not as you think. Giovane, fetch my private account books."

My assistant unlocks them and as he opens the large ledgers for Pomponio to examine a puzzled expression spreads over my son's face. The account books are not a record of what I have earned, as he expects, but a detailed chronicle of expenditures and experiences, recording the births and deaths of those dear to me, what I spent on the salary of my servants, for a prayer book for Cecilia, a shipment of oils, on clothes, my organ, other musical instruments, and gifts. The most numerous items are a list of what I have spent on him, several times to free him from prison.

His rage grows with his confusion and he explodes, "All you care about is what you gave me and what you think I owe you!"

"I did not intend to show this to you until you insisted."

"I wanted to see what I am entitled to as your legitimate son."

"My earnings are in my head."

"But not where I can know what I should inherit."

He is seized with such resentment, I realize I have made no impression on him. I think sadly, Perhaps Leonardo and Michelangelo were right not to have any children. Now I am too disheartened to examine my work for possible forgeries. Whatever I do, Pomponio is against me, and I feel that Orazio may be, also, for he has not uttered a word in my defense. I do not even have any grandchildren and there is little prospect that I will ever have any. My sons are past fifty, unmarried. My reason tells me that my name will endure only as long as my work does. It is the only consolation I possess and it drives me to view the pictures I feel have the most chance of permanence: my altarpieces.

As a gesture of reconciliation I ask Pomponio and Orazio to join me—a number of the altarpieces are within a short walk of the workshop—but Pomponio shouts, "You have betrayed me!" And he rushes out in a temper.

Giovane is embarrassed while Orazio tries to apologize for Pomponio, but I am weary of excuses that I do not trust and I silence him.

It is a relief to be in the quiet of San Salvatore, where two of my altarpieces are. Orazio waits outside so that I can view my work without distraction, but I am still seething over Giovane's offer to finish my *Pietà*. I am offended, although I know that he intends it in a spirit of charity, perhaps that is what offends me the most. But when I see the friendly interior of the basilica that is forgotten. I have invested much of myself here. There is a *Last Supper* by Bellini on the left and a historical epic by Bordone on the right, but it is the sight of my two altarpieces that lifts my spirits.

The examination by Certaldo, the pettiness of the prior, the fears about the plague, even the selfishness of my son become distant and less important as I gaze at my work. I think of something Violante said.

"You do not think, you paint. You do not feel, you paint. You do not breathe, you paint. You do not live, you paint."

But as I view what I have done and contemplate what I must continue to do, I say to myself, If I paint, I think. If I paint, I feel. If I paint, I breathe. If I paint, I live. If I paint, I am. All the Titians that are and were and ever will be. I like these totals and I feel better.

I can love *The Transfiguration*. It is a passionate work. The figures of the Apostles stirred by the vision of Jesus have a power that pleases and excites me. I feel that it belongs on the high altar, for it has much of the majesty of *The Assumption*, although I painted it only ten years ago. The colors are softer, less finished, but it has the same motion, intensity, and drama that the earlier work possesses.

My *Annunciation* on a side altar is not as emotional but the figures are animated and there is a brilliance and boldness in them that excites me, and the cupids at the top of the painting are as lovely as any I have done.

Greatly heartened, I summon Orazio and inform him that I wish to visit the Doge's Palace to see more of my work.

"Papa, it is too far to walk. And the plague . . ."

"I am tired of hearing about it," I interrupt. "I have lived through a dozen, I should be able to live through one more. Hire a gondola."

"There are none about."

"For ducats, a Venetian will do anything." I reach under my robe for my money bag, which I have taken without telling anyone, and give him three. "That will obtain transport. I will wait here until you find it."

My tone is so authoritative he does not dare to disobey me, and moreover, he is pleased that I am feeling better.

He returns soon with the news he has found a gondola. I do not like the look of the gondolier, he is scabby and pockmarked, but the passion in me to see my work, the simple necessity to shout to the world and especially to Pomponio and the stupid prior that I am still Titian, overcomes my apprehension, and we set out for the Doge's Palace and arrive quickly.

There are only a few boats on the Grand Canal and some of them are death craft, but with my new emotion and energy I try to ignore them. I do not know how long it will last and I want to use it while I have it.

Orazio doubts that I can ascend the many steps at the Doge's Palace, but I am determined not to allow anything to halt me—I have needed such a feeling for much of my work—and so I climb despite the extreme effort it takes and I pretend my shortness of breath is due to the August heat.

I am responsible for much of the work in the Great Council Hall now and I know I should view the large panels first, but inevitably I stand before the Battle of Cadore, for no picture has given me more problems.

Orazio has finished some of the decorations I began and while he examines them to make sure their surfaces have not darkened or become dirty or deteriorated in any way, which has happened to older panels, I recollect how bitter the struggle grew over this fresco.

I was toiling at home, rarely visiting the Doge's Palace, when Valier came to see me. It was 1537 and I had not seen him for years. I had many commissions to do, mostly portraits, and I was in no mood to be interrupted, but he was insistent. I had given him a *poesia* in return for past favors and I realized that he must have something of import to tell me. But I was not sure what to make of his news, when he said, "Pordenone is being employed by the Council to paint in the Great Hall."

I tried to be disdainful. I knew this painter hated me and he had threatened my life when I had been given the commission to paint the altarpiece which had become my precious and much-praised *St. Peter Martyr*. The church had invited a number of artists to seek this work which had intensified his hostility. Yet he was noted for his speed. Some said he was the best fresco painter in Italy. And he had killed another man in a street brawl. Yet from Valier's tone I felt that the Council might be my worst enemy, since they had put Pordenone next to my empty panel.

Valier added, "If you do not take the hint and finally finish the battle scene, I fear they will take your broker's patent from you."

"After all these years?" I replied, sounding shocked.

"After they have waited twenty years. Make an effort at least."

I promised, but when other commissions I preferred became urgent, I ignored his warning. A month later I received a decree from the Council of Ten: "Since December 1516, Titian has been in possession of a broker's patent and drawn his salary without fulfilling his promise. Thus it is proper that this state of things should cease, and Titian is called upon to refund all that he has been given for the time he has done no work."

Pordenone painted next to my panel, wearing a sword and swaggering about the Hall as if he owned it. I did not wish to duel with him as his behavior suggested, yet I could not ignore the Council. I had received several thousand ducats from them and now they were demanding that I refund the money.

The present Doge, Andrea Gritti, who had held the office since 1523, strongly supported my brush and had awarded me much patronage. So I arranged an audience with this commanding, handsome figure—I had painted his elderly likeness a number of times, and he was a friend of many of my patrons. Yet when I told him what had happened, he replied, "One grows old and weary of defending you. You were warned to proceed in 1518, then in 1522, but you have not completed one object in the Great Council Hall."

"My lord, that was not my intention."

"Thousands of ducats have been spent on the Hall without anything to show for it. But you go to Ferrara, Mantua, Augsburg to do much work."

"My lord, I am still a Venetian."

"Why not act like one and paint for us as you have for foreign lords? You have nothing to fear from any other artist. No one excels you in skill or taste, but your dilatory ways could ruin your reputation."

I heard a threat in his voice I had not heard before. If a friend felt this way, I could comprehend the vindictiveness of my enemies and rivals. Yet I must not show any fear, I must behave with courtesy and affability. I bowed before the elegantly dressed Doge and said, "My lord, I will be happy to devote myself to the battle picture until it is finished."

"Until it is finished!" Gritti scowled to stress the issue.

"My lord, if the decree against me is revoked I will start at once."

"Foscari told me that you made this promise before and did not keep it."

"I will keep it this time, my lord. If I am not molested by Pordenone."

"You will be kept apart. He will paint elsewhere until you finish."

Pordenone was *being used*, I thought, not employed, but I said, "Unless you do not trust my ability to satisfy the taste of the Republic, my lord."

"We want your taste here, not in a hundred other places."

"What about the money, my lord? To refund it would delay my hand."

"I will speak to the Council about that. But do not expect any new payments until we are satisfied that you will keep your word this time."

The battle of Cadore became one of the most descriptive scenes

I did. I depicted a great mass of Venetian horsemen driving the enemy before them. It was natural to paint the landscape in a grand manner, the mountains were my native Cadore and they became the strongest part of the picture. But the details of the fighting were difficult. I was not a painter of lances and shattered bodies and blood, except that of Jesus and the saints. But when it was done the Council said it was satisfactory, I had drawn it from life, and expressed Venetian valor without giving offense to the emperor. The broker's patent was returned to me and only once again was it suspended, in 1551, for being away from Venice too long. And it was reinstated when I assigned Orazio to work in the Hall while I was absent.

This foray into the past is a fond moment. Some of my greatest victories, I smile to myself, were in diplomacy even when painting came first.

Orazio notices my improved humor and it gives him the courage to ask, "Papa, do you think that I am another Francesco?"

"No!" I say positively. "He did not persevere. But you have."

That seems to satisfy him, at least for this moment, and he replies, "I hope that you do not allow Pomponio's behavior to make you ill."

"With or without his love I have painted and I will continue to do so."

"Then you do expect to finish the *Pietà?*"

"After I paint several other things first. I have been working on it too much. I have been painting *poesias* all my life, there is no reason to stop now. Come, we must return to the studio. There is much work to do."

He takes my hand and as he helps me descend the giant staircase his touch revives me, while he asks, "Was Violante the most beautiful person you knew?"

"She was my most beautiful model."

I pause to impress on my memory the scene outside the Doge's Palace: the great piazza, the mole, the four bronze horses, and the clock tower.

"I recall best what Giorgione said to me, *'Never apologize, never explain.'* I am sorry that you never knew him. He was the most beautiful person I knew."

My eyes fill with tears as I think of him. But this journey into the past must not be wasted, and so I try to stand erect so that I can paint properly. That has been the greatest necessity. I never wanted to be a Leonardo or a Michelangelo. I just wanted to be a painter.

NO MATTER WHAT

NO MATTER WHAT

I have used all my doubt
as energy
and created with it

I have used all my pain
as energy
and created with it

I have used all my anxieties
as energy
and created with it

I plan to use my death
as energy
and create with it

No matter what
Death's plans
are for me

Stymean Karlen

THE NEXT FEW DAYS I spend every moment I have in my studio. Orazio moves a bed into it so that I can be close to my easels and he puts up those I was painting before my memories interrupted me: a *poesia* of a nymph, a self-portrait, a study of Pomponio, and the *Pietà*. But now, without hesitation, as if my visits to my work taught me what I must paint, I thrust aside my devotional picture, as if I have to find my redemption elsewhere, and focus on the *poesia* with passionate intensity.

The *Pietà* is too somber for my present mood, too afflicted with doubt and anguish; I have a need to believe in my energy and purpose. I cannot worry now whether the Frari will accept me after I can no longer paint for them; I must obey God's will.

The nymph becomes a young woman with a soft skin and round features and an ample body and shining red tresses. Today's fashion in Venice favors yellow hair but I am painting this *poesia* for myself, which is rare. I am so grateful that I can sketch and paint that I work feverishly.

One thing troubles me. I see imperfections in my brush. The older I become, the more critical I become. If I can only have a few more years, I can do much with this *poesia*. There is still much to learn.

Nobody visits me except Orazio, who brings me wine and fruit, and once in a while a portion of fowl. My steward and servants have fled because of the plague but it does not appear to be any closer, the watchmen have left the houses near us, and I am hopeful that it is subsiding. I have not seen Pomponio, and Orazio does not bring him into our conversations. All he says, aside from asking how I am feeling and commenting on the excellence of what I am doing, is that he is painting in the workshop with Giovane, who is considering reopening it, for the health of the city seems to be improving. I am pleased with his news and I express the hope that his work is flourishing.

He shrugs, as if to say that it is not a matter of consequence, and I have too much to do to take the time to encourage him or to console him.

Then, a week after my journey on the alleys and canals of Venice, I fall ill. It is a strange feeling—I have been sick seldom and I have spent only a few days in bed my entire life—and yet I know that something is wrong with me, for I cannot paint. I grow dizzy, my eyes blur, for an instant I fear that I am going to lose consciousness. But when I lie down my senses revive a little and I can see where I am, yet I have no vigor, although there is no pain and I do not feel feverish. It is activity that distresses me. I try to sit before an easel and the dizzy spells return, objects spin in my vision, my hand trembles and I cannot hold a brush. The possibility that I may not be able to paint again is the most terrible feeling of all. There is sensation in my fingers—they are not numb—and that is some relief, but I am so tired I cannot return to my *poesia*, which is almost done. Every time I try to rise out of bed I become faint.

When Orazio brings my dinner later and finds me in bed, he looks stricken—it is not like me to halt when I am so close to completing a picture—and he exclaims, "Papa, you must be sick!"

"No. I have no pain. I am just very tired."

He examines me carefully and while he does not say it, I know that he is looking to see if any of the dreaded plague spots have appeared. He is relieved when he finishes but he says, "I will call Gusti."

"It is not necessary. I will be fine tomorrow. I just need rest."

But the next day, when I still do not possess the strength to get out of bed, he calls our doctor. Orazio has sat by my side all night, although I have begged him not to. If I have the contagion despite my lack of symptoms, it could be dangerous, but he does not heed me.

I expect Gusti to chide me for having disregarded his warnings, and he does say, "You showed more valor than discretion."

"What is wrong, Bruno? I have no pain and there are no buboes or spots."

"You must rest. It is the best cure."

"Do I need brimstone to clear the air?"

"That is a barbaric custom. Eat and drink moderately, perspire if you can, even if it means covering yourself with many blankets, and keep the windows open so that the air will be fresh, and try not to worry."

While Gusti is calm, his tone is serious, and I can see from Orazio's expression that I am very sick, for he is on the verge of tears.

I ask, "Is it the plague? Am I infected with the corruption?"

Gusti hesitates before he replies and then he speaks with deliberation. "Tiziano, it is impossible to be certain. You have such a strong body that even now it fights valiantly to overcome whatever has attacked you. And the symptoms are confusing. But you cannot work."

I want to cry out: Then I cannot live! But they will not heed me.

Orazio says, "I will nurse you."

I ask, "What about those who practice that trade? Are none about?"

Gusti declares, "Not for love or money."

Now I am almost certain that I have the plague.

"I will come back later to see how you are and I have advised your son to take all the necessary precautions, although I doubt that he will."

Orazio covers me with many blankets but while I perspire freely, I only feel worse, and so I throw them off. He continues to sit by my side, although I beg him not to, my clothes could communicate my illness, but he ignores me. I have no appetite for the fruit and wine he brings me. I am dozing and thinking of *The Assumption* and the

Bacchus and Ariadne and a *Christ Crowned with Thorns,* where I paint spears significantly and give Him a poignancy and resignation that is fitting—when I am jolted out of my reverie by the sound of Pomponio's voice. He must think that I am sleeping, for he is making little effort to conceal what he is saying.

I hear him ask, "Orazio, is the old man dying?"

"Ssssh. I do not know."

"Is it the plague?"

"It is possible. But there are no buboes or purple spots."

I cry out, "Orazio, has Doctor Gusti returned?"

"It is me, Papa."

Pomponio enters the studio and I am shocked by his appearance. He looks as if he has dissipated for days. His long black hair, which is usually carefully combed, hangs in a disorderly tangle to his shoulders. I see that it is turning gray at the temples; his face is pallid, his eyes are sunken, there are dark puffy circles under them and his lips twitch.

"Papa, how are you?"

"I expect to be out of bed soon."

He does not believe me, for he keeps away from me, saying, "You lied."

"I do expect to resume painting soon."

"That is not what I am referring to. It is your account books. You do have others that include your earnings. But I am not good enough to see them." He adds bitterly, "I am probably not even in your will."

"Pomponio!" Orazio pleads. "Some other time!"

"There will be no other time! He will never get out of bed again!"

Orazio's tone changes and he says with a savagery I had not thought in him, "You cannot even apologize for your haste!"

"I do not want him to die. But one must be aware of the truth."

"You have not told the truth one day in your life."

"Sons, please . . ." I try to get out of bed to stop them but I cannot.

Pomponio shouts, "I have as much right to see his will as you have."

Orazio retorts angrily, "I have never seen it. I doubt there is one."

I have drawn a will recently but it is to avoid such quarrels that I have hidden this fact. But they are so hostile to each other that now I say as loud as I can, "Pomponio, the house in Cortina and the land and lumber mill in Cadore will go to you, the workshop and the house in Venice to Orazio."

"What about the paintings? They are what truly matters."

"You will both get some. I have tried to divide them evenly."

This effort to reconcile them is too much for me and all I can do is lie inert, while Pomponio snarls, "If he has your house and workshop, he will have the best, the most valuable pictures. And you wonder why I seek my friends elsewhere. You treat me as you treated my mother. You give me only what you have to give, as you wed her only when you had to."

I murmur, "Who told you this?"

"Your brother. But this gossip was in the workshop while we were growing up."

Rarely have I felt so lonely. Orazio is stunned by Pomponio's charges and speechless, while my older son surveys me contemptuously and states, "You never wanted to be my father. It was an accident you could not avoid. You made a virtue out of necessity. You made the best of what you felt was a mistake on your part. But I will live to claim what is rightfully mine." He rushes out in a fury, as if he has annihilated his enemies.

For a horrible moment I am afraid that Orazio is going to join him. Then, as my younger son sees that I am terribly shaken, he runs to my side and shouts, "Papa, he lies! It has to be a lie!"

"As with so many things, what he says is half true and half false. I was manipulated in a way into marrying your mother, but not into having you. You were a result of our love, deliberately, fondly. I wanted you."

He says bitterly, "I do not like him. Sometimes, I think, I never have. I could excuse his disappointment when you did not show him your other account books. I know that you have them. But as to the rest, he is shallow, vain, selfish, always searching for excuses to justify what he does. He can only take and never give. But you have always felt that you could improve him, as you improved your paintings. That is impossible. I will have nothing more to do with him and neither should you."

I do not know what to say and so I am silent. But I caress Orazio's hand as he sits beside me, and then I lapse into unconsciousness.

When I recover my senses it is Gusti I see and he tells me that several days have passed while I lay inert. I ask, "Where is Orazio?"

"He is busy," Gusti replies self-consciously, which surprises me.

"And my other son?"

The doctor wavers, then says decisively, "He has fled from Venice."

"But not Orazio?"

"No."

"Doctor, when will I see him again?"

"That depends on your recovery."

"Then I do have the plague?"

"You must not worry yourself over the nature of your illness. You must devote all of your energy and thought to recovering."

"Do you think that I can? I feel so weak."

"Yes. Your body continues to fight against whatever has attacked it. I will attend you as much as I can."

Perhaps I do not have the pestilence after all, I think, for most doctors avoid patients who have it to preserve themselves from infection. But I remember that Gusti is different; he is the kind of physician who would risk his life whatever the danger to himself. I try to sit up but my head spins again and suddenly I blurt out with what little strength I possess, "Gusti, I suffer from dizzy spells. If I should die, will you take the precaution of seeing that before I am presumed dead, my body is left for twenty-four hours upon earth to avoid the possibility of being buried alive?"

He nods, too upset by that thought to talk.

"And you will call the priest if that should become necessary?"

"If that becomes necessary," he repeats.

"I must find someone who will finish the *Pietà*."

"Tiziano, you are exhausting yourself with all these questions."

But my hearing is still good, for I hear the cry, *"Bring out your dead!"* The strong wind brings the smell of brimstone and now I feel that I do not have much time left. I say, "I want it finished in my manner."

"Tintoretto lives nearby but they say that you do not like each other."

"We have had our quarrels and he left my studio when he was still young because he could not follow my style, but then I did the same with Bellini. Yet when he saw my *Christ Crowned with Thorns*, he begged me, as his master, to give it to him as a present, and when I did, he hung it in his own studio. '*As*,' he said, '*a model of what a modern picture should be.*'"

"He is out of Venice and he may not be back for months."

"Paul Veronese was here recently and he is closer to my manner. Where Tintoretto is prickly, he is pleasant." I reflect, "Too pleasant for this subject. And the only other pupil worthy of this work, although many studied with me, is in Spain and his manner is very different from mine."

"The Greek?" Gusti asks, wanting to be sure he understands me.

"Yes. Domenikos Theotokopoulos. He came to me from Crete about ten years ago, and called himself El Greco, to express his nationality, although he began by copying me. But now he has his own individual manner."

"What about your son?"

My head rises and I exclaim, "Then he has not deserted me?"

"Tiziano, did you truly think that he would?"

"After Pomponio, it is hard to trust anyone." I come to a decision. "Bruno, tell Orazio that he must apply the last finishing strokes to the *Pietà* with pious care. It will help his reputation."

"First, I must find someone to attend you. Is there anything else you desire?"

I feel that my consciousness is ebbing and I whisper hurriedly, "I recall that when Perugino died of the plague he was thrown into a common grave, and the same thing was done when Ghirlandaio died of the pestilence."

"It will not happen to you."

"I do not trust the Franciscan brothers of the Frari. And I do not like being obligated to them. Or being put in the pesthouse and the morgue. Bury me in Cadore, beside my parents and my daughter, it is more fitting."

Gusti says, "I will do my best." He covers me warmly with blankets, he opens the windows looking out on the lagoon so that the air will be fresh, he gives me wine to drink that will help me perspire and sleep, and then he departs with the assurance that he will return as soon as he can.

I think about the many who have studied with me and that even the grim, dour Michelangelo had said, despite the differences in our style, "Only Titian was worthy of the name of a painter." It brings a smile to my lips. I have treasured this comment, even if it is an exaggeration. Maybe it is better that the *Pietà* remain unfinished. And thus, more suggestive. Then I am not certain where I am. I feel that I am slipping into a haze where I am half awake, half asleep, and yet in neither world.

When the familiar objects of my studio take shape and I know where I am again, I have no idea how much time has passed. Gusti left me as it was growing dark, and now it is light. The sun is bright and it reminds me that there are things I must do before it is too late.

I manage to struggle out of bed and to shuffle to a window, although it takes what little strength I possess, and when I look out it is as I fear. A plague watchman guards my door and he is saying to the man who has come to relieve him, "God have mercy on their souls."

The new watchman asks, "Is their condition that serious?"

"I hear that they are very sick."

"The old master or the young master?"

"Both."

"Orazio!" It is more than I can endure. He must have caught it from me. I must squeeze every second that remains to me. My body feels cold and clammy but I am grateful that I can still use it and that there is life in my hands, and that they help me find a letter in my desk. I have kept a copy of what I have written to Philip, the King of Spain, where it can be found easily, for it is precious to me. I read it while I can still see:

"Your Most Gracious Majesty, I enclose this list of paintings which have been delivered to you from my hand at your command, for which, for reasons best known to yourself, payment is still forthcoming. I pray that out of Your Majesty's royal and exalted liberality, you will put this money to my son Orazio's balance, for he has assisted me devotedly:

> *Venus and Adonis*—1556.
> *Calisto pregnant of Jove*—1561.
> *Acteon entering the Bath*—1561.
> *Europa carried off by the Bull*—1562.
> *Andromeda bound to the rock*—1566.
> *Christ in prayer in the Garden*—1562.
> *Allegory of Lepanto*—1574.
> *Christ in the Sepulchre*—1562.
> *St. Mary Magdalen*—1564.
> *Venus, to whom Love holds a mirror*—1575.
> *The Nude, with the Landscape and the Satyr*—1567.
> *The Last Supper*—1564.
> *The Marytrdom of St. Lawrence*—1567.
> *The Fall of Man*—1574.
> *Adam and Eve*—1575.

"With many other pieces, Your Gracious Majesty, which I do not remember."

I put this letter and list on top of my desk where it can be found by anyone who enters this studio, particularly Gusti, who is observant.

This effort is too much for me and I grow dizzy again. I am afraid

I am losing consciousness and I sit down, for the bed is too far away. Gradually the air from the lagoon clears my head and I feel a little better. I decide that if I remain active I will remain conscious. I examine my hands and arms where the buboes and purple spots are most common, but there are none. This encourages me and I find enough strength to place an empty canvas on the easel before my chair. It no longer matters to me whether I finish the *Pietà*; God has willed me to paint and that is enough. I feel now that whatever redemption I will find in His Mercy, it will be because of all that I have done.

My lovely Lavinia is my fondest memory. If anyone has cared for me truthfully, it has been my daughter, dead in childbirth these many years. I feel that she loved me for myself and not for my reputation.

So I start to sketch her likeness as I recall her. At the time I painted my favorite portrait of my pride and joy. But now this is not a memory of the past; she is part of the living present. She stands before me in my old age, but as I remember her most fondly.

Lavinia is just twenty, in the full bloom of her youth and beauty. Her soft, round features, her full cheeks and wide brow, and her fair, delicate skin and complexion are as attractive as any I have painted. Her yellow hair is braided and adorned with a jeweled diadem I gave her for her birthday, and I portray her from the side where her splendid, ample figure curves most enchantingly. I paint her dress with rich colors, but she has a modest appearance, for only her neck is bare.

She holds a silver dish piled high with fruit and flowers but now I want to paint just her. There is feeling in my fingers and I portray her in white. This time I want her light to prevail over form and color.

She says, "Papa, you make me more beautiful than I am. Always."

I reply, "Lavinia dear, I paint you as you are to me."

Now there is another sound in my head. At first I cannot recognize it, and then I am sure it is Giorgione singing, so sweetly and softly, and for a moment I do not see Lavinia but Violante walking with Vecchio.

"But all I ever wanted to do was to paint," I hear myself saying. I want to shout to my paintings, I love you! I love you! But if I do, I will squander what little energy I have left and I must paint Lavinia.

Once again she seems to emerge from the mist that surrounds me and she says, "Papa, do I resemble my mother?"

"Very much. Except that you are prettier."

"But I was told that she was very pretty."

I am losing my concentration and I reply, "You must be quiet if I am to paint you accurately." Then, as I hear the plague watchman crying out, *"Bring out your dead!"* I am melancholy and I cannot see her.

I feel the chair to make sure that I am sitting on it and I can see the canvas and Lavinia is on it. In my old age I have learned to paint with many fewer brushstrokes, to conserve my energy, and it seems that with just four I have achieved her likeness.

Next I sketch a crucifix on her portrait. I feel that Christ is gazing at me, as I have gazed at Him so often. Then I see other faces, Lavinia, Big George, Violante, Aretino, Vecchio, Orazio. I cry out in relief but the noise seems to frighten them and they vanish.

I try to stand up but I cannot. I realize that I am tied to my chair and easel. I sit there thinking of the world I have portrayed. I have painted such a multitude of pictures that I have forgotten many of them. But I am glad that I have not wasted my time. I have tried to paint honestly, to observe, to express nature. A Venus, a Magdalen, a madonna all formed with the same devotion by my brush. So many paintings that I do remember and treasure.

I feel the warmth of the sun on my face and hands and yet it is growing dark. Now I sense that I am going toward Lavinia and the others that I have loved. I turn to face the shadows approaching me and I am grateful that I have a brush in my hand. For those who find me, this is the way I desire it to be. The air about me is no longer bright but gray and is becoming black. But I can still see. In my mind's eye and imagination. I must continue to paint for painting's sake. Even after death. Even after . . .

TITANUS F.

AFTERMATH

THE PLAGUE had entered Titian's house as he had suspected and he died of it on August 27, 1576. Laws had been passed by the Republic that forbade the burial of a victim of the contagion in any of the churches of the city. But the canons of San Marco set aside the law for Venice's first citizen and on August 28 he was buried in the Frari church.

Two days later Orazio died of the plague that he had caught while attending his father. He was taken to the charnel house of Lazzaretto Vecchio, the old pesthouse near the Lido, and thrown into a common grave.

Before Pomponio could return to Venice to claim his father's property as the sole heir, thieves broke into the house on the Biri Grande and looted it of most of Titian's possessions and as many of his pictures as they could carry. Pomponio lived eighteen years after his father and squandered whatever was left him, selling off Titian's pictures and possessions to support himself, and died in obscurity and poverty.

In 1577 a great fire burned what Titian had painted in the Great Hall of the Doge's Palace with such effort, including the Battle of Cadore.

Other disasters, especially wars, destroyed or damaged more paintings.

Yet many survived to find homes all over the world and influenced Rubens and Rembrandt, Velásquez and Van Dyck, Delacroix and Rodin, and a galaxy of other artists. Probably no other painter exercised so much influence for so long over so many great artists. And gave so wide a variety of pleasure to his viewers. That would have gratified him.

Palma Giovane finished the *Pietà*.

February 1976, in the 400th year of his death